THE DHAWAN BROTHERS

A NOVEL BY

LUCIE ATAYA

What Readers Are Saying

"This novel feels raw and deep and it's evident it's been written with heart and intention. Highly recommend it to anyone who enjoys books with road trips, real human struggles and a focus on relationships with family, friends and the self. Another book from Author Lucie Ataya that I am gushing over!"

"The Dhawan Brothers quickly grips and pulls you into their intense and emotional family journey. I found myself resonating with the brothers distinct characteristics at different stages of their journey. The story is sophisticatedly sewn together as you hop from person to person, gaining an insight to their own perspective. The struggles and triumphs of childhood, love, loss and family relationships had me crying at moments and beaming in heart warming joy in other moments."

"This is one of those books that is so well written you feel a little sad when it's over. Lucie uses multiple POVs, and there isn't a moment where they feel unnecessary or make the story drag. Some of the parts of the story were predictable, but how she got there threw me for a loop. The plot and execution was so much deeper than I could've ever predicted. She handled the sensitive subjects with so much care, and the emotions were perfectly done. The way grief was shown was so realistic and relatable as someone who has been through loss. This is a great read, and I highly recommend picking it up, especially if you're someone who likes a more emotional read."

"A unique and heartbreaking story of family struggles and the fight to overcome. Was quickly drawn into the Dhawan brothers' shared, but at the same time wildly different, experiences in coping with such tragedy. You are continually rooting for them to come out the other side okay. Truly enjoyed their journey, even though it was hard at times to get through the deeply sad stuff. A few twists felt like really?! Come on, these poor boys have had enough! Overall great read, characters and storytelling from Ataya!"

"The Dhawan Brothers by Lucie Ataya is a beautifully written novel that masterfully blends suspense and deep emotional insights. The story follows the Dhawan siblings and their unbreakable bond, showcasing themes of family, resilience, and sacrifice. Ataya's engaging and thought-provoking writing makes this book a compelling read, filled with richly developed characters and profound moments."

"This novel is a must-read for anyone who appreciates powerful storytelling about the strength of family ties and the human spirit. Highly recommended!"

"A very emotional rollercoaster and fast-paced read that sucked me right in. I loved the different POVs and their clearly distinguished voices. I think the idea of family trauma and secrets that haunt you until you face them is an important topic and lingers after reading. Rolled into the road trip plot, it gives it the sense of

adventure and excitement that is needed to be an enjoyable and exciting story rather than gloomy and depressing."

"The story of the Dhawan brothers grips you from the first page and does not let you settle down until the last one. This fast-paced, intelligent and relevant novel touches on many themes we struggle with today - mental health, belonging, opening our hearts to others - and makes it for both an entertaining and a reflective read. I believe that each one of us will find ourselves reflected in the thoughts and feelings of the four brothers, and will take something away for our own lives."

"This book is soo compelling! I loved seeing the bond and relationships between the brothers. This book touches on some deep fragile topics and Lucie Ataya handles them with such grace, very well written. I thoroughly enjoyed this book and would highly recommend this book."

"Readers will become emotionally invested quickly in the lives of these siblings, whose trials only strengthen their bonds. Told in alternating POV, The Dhawan Brothers is filled with raw emotion that Lucie Ataya does a phenomenal job of depicting. Highly recommend."

Printed in Great Britain

First Edition
First Printing 2024 | First Edition 2024
ISBN: 9798333105967
Cover Design by Lucie Ataya
Independently Published through Amazon KDP by Lucie Ataya

Second Edition
Printed 2024 | Second Edition 2024
ISBN: 978-1-83654-401-2
Cover Design by Lucie Ataya
Independently Published through Ingram Sparks by Lucie Ataya

Extract from *No Pain, No Game* by Lucie Ataya, Copyright © 2020

For more information about the author, visit
https://www.lucieataya.com | Instagram: @lucieataya

ALSO AVAILABLE BY LUCIE ATAYA

Dystopian Fiction

No Pain, No Game

Non Fiction

Passing It Forward: Lessons on Self-Publishing & Book Promotion for Indie Authors

Children's Books

Tiny Little Simon

Lovely Lenie

Mar's Journey Home

THE DHAWAN BROTHERS

Trigger warnings:
sexual assault, depression, suicide ideation, alcohol addiction

To all the stranded souls.
Whatever you've been told,
You're not truly broken.
You never were.
May you have the strength to let go of anyone
who made you feel you could never be mended.

Prologue

The child was born in the early hours of the morning. He came without a fuss, which was as much as I could have handled. Anand wasn't there. In truth, I didn't even know where he was. I hadn't seen him for days. Though we had tried to pretend nothing was the matter, we both knew our relationship was on its last legs. I simply could not have looked into his eyes as I pushed the baby into the world. I never could have managed it.

Amit—gentle, sweet, devoted Amit—was home with the boys at my request, coming to our family's aid once more, as he had so many times before.

The nurse placed the baby into my arms, a beautiful, pale-skinned, light-haired little thing with wide-open bright blue eyes. As I gazed at his tiny face, I thought he looked rather surprised, as if he had never expected to find himself here. It wasn't his fault after all. None of it was.

Anand and I hadn't done our usual naming ritual. We never discussed it, and I didn't bring it up. I think we'd been trying hard not to think of the moment it would all become real. So when the nurse asked me the baby's name, I asked her whether she had a dictionary at hand. She looked at me quizzically, probably wondering if the labour hormones had rendered me temporarily mad, but she found one somehow. I was left alone with the book and the baby. By then he had curled up in my arms and fallen fast asleep. I flicked through the pages, but it wasn't the same without Anand there. Nothing was the same. Nothing had been the same for a while.

In frustration, I opened the dictionary at random and read the first word at the top of the page: Pharaoh. I grunted, because the irony of it was simply too much to bear. I looked down at the baby in my arms. Not just any baby. My baby boy. My son. I was crying, hot, heavy tears that fell onto his little hands, and he wriggled in his sleep. I looked at the page again, the word staring back at me.

When the nurse came back, I wrote down my son's name on a piece of paper and handed it to her. She looked at it for a moment, frowned, then glanced back at me. She asked me if I wanted to think about it some more and told me there was no rush, but I just shook my head. She shrugged and left, leaving me with little Farao snuggled contentedly in my arms.

Chapter 1
Terran

As he approached the steps to the Peace Pagoda, Terran slowed down, coming to a stop by a park bench. He glanced at his watch. He'd been slower today, and the extra time spent on his run meant he would have to rush the rest of his morning routine. He jogged past the white-stone monument and along the river, accelerating as he caught sight of the Albert Bridge. He kept going, exiting Battersea Park without a backwards glance at the views he knew by heart. He jogged all the way down Anhalt Road until he reached his front door.

As he stepped into the hall, the smell of fresh coffee and burnt toast told him at least one of his brothers was up. He peeked through the kitchen door and, sure enough, Kendrik was setting four plates down on the dining table. He was already dressed in one of his staple navy suits, his light blue tie flung across one shoulder to prevent it dipping down onto the toast he was buttering.

'Hey,' Kendrik said, looking up. 'Good run?'

Terran shrugged. 'Are the others up already?'

Kendrik did not respond; he simply made a face that might have meant he either did not know or did not care. Terran shook his head and hurried up the stairs, climbing them two steps at a time. He banged on the bathroom door and Orson's voice came shouting back at him that he would be down in a minute. Terran snorted. As if it ever took Orson a minute to do anything, especially when it came to his appearance. He ran up the second flight of stairs and opened the door on his right. The air inside the room was stuffy and oozed an odd smell Terran did not care for one bit. His youngest brother, Farao, was sprawled on his bed, in his underwear, fast asleep.

'Farao!' Terran called out. 'Farao, get up. You're going to be late for school. Again.'

Farao groaned and turned on his side, facing away, pulling the covers over his head.

'Oy!' Terran shouted, picking up a notebook lying on the nearby desk and throwing it at Farao's sleeping figure.

Farao sat up with a start, massaging the back of his head.

'For fuck's sake, Ter, what d'you do that for!' he moaned, throwing the notebook back towards the door. Terran dodged it lazily.

'Breakfast,' Terran commanded. 'Downstairs. *Now.*'

Terran ran back down the stairs, ignoring Farao's swearing. On his way down, he banged on the bathroom door again, and Orson called out, yet again, that he would only be a minute.

'Coffee?' Kendrik asked when Terran finally sat down at the breakfast table, already feeling exhausted.

Terran nodded and watched his brother fill a large cup for him. Orson came prancing into the kitchen, all smiles as usual, and took a seat next to Terran.

'Good morning, family! What a wonderful day it is to be alive, isn't it?' he exclaimed. 'Ah, coffee! Ken, be a dear and pour me a cup, will you?'

Terran shook his head and rolled his eyes, glancing at Kendrik and noticing that, like him, he struggled to suppress a smile. When Orson walked into a room, his jovial and carefree nature attracted attention and drew people to him in a way that neither of his older brothers could ever manage. He carefully curated his style, an unlikely but effective mix somewhere between boho-chic and luxury Victorian. Today he was wearing old-fashioned black trousers and a cream shirt, rolled up below the elbows and made of such light fabric it was almost sheer, his heavily tattooed arms and torso showing through. Several leather bands and heavy metal rings adorned his wrists and fingers, and his thick, shoulder-length black hair was tied in a rough ponytail.

'Is Farao up?' Terran asked.

'Affirmative, my good sir!' Orson nodded at him. 'I believe he's getting ready as we speak.'

'Good,' Terran sighed. 'I'm sick of getting calls from the headmistress complaining he's always late…'

'Terran, honestly,' Orson laughed, 'the only reason the head summons you in all the time is because she's clearly got a thing for you. Surely even you can see that?'

'What?' Terran frowned, causing Orson to burst out laughing. Kendrik chuckled as he took a seat at the table with them.

'My dear brother.' Orson smiled sympathetically. 'Never in my life have I met anyone as clueless as you. It's rather endearing… most of the time, at least.'

Terran was about to protest when Farao came galloping down the stairs, his school backpack flung over one shoulder. He headed straight towards the front door, but Terran called after him.

'Farao. Breakfast.'

'Not hungry.' Farao stopped with one hand hovering over the door handle, giving his brother a shifty, annoyed glance.

'That's not the point,' Terran said in as calm a voice as he could muster, since they had a repeat of this same conversation almost every day. 'Come on, just sit with us for a moment.'

'What about being late for school?' Farao sneered, his voice sarcastic.

'I'll drop you,' Terran sighed. 'Come on. Everything's ready.'

Farao grunted in response, and backtracked into the kitchen.

'There he is, our little ray of sunshine!' Orson exclaimed, clapping Farao on the back as he slumped into a chair. 'How are we feeling today, little brother?'

'Don't call me that,' Farao mumbled.

'What?' Orson said, opening his eyes wide, feigning surprise. 'Little brother? Would you prefer *baby* brother, perhaps?'

'Fuck off,' Farao mumbled under his breath, reaching out across the table and taking ownership of Terran's coffee.

'Language…' Kendrik warned, looking sideways at Farao.

'Ah, Farao… Charming, as always.' Orson's smile widened.

'So, Ken,' Terran interjected, trying his best to defuse the tension he could sense mounting in the room. 'Today's the big day, right?'

'Yeah.' Kendrik nodded. 'Interview's at four.'

As they spoke about the promotion Kendrik was going for, which he had been eyeing for months now, and the questions he expected the managing director of the advertising company he worked for was likely to ask him, Terran noticed that Farao had fallen silent, munching broodily on a piece of toast. Terran glanced at his watch.

'Come on, let's go.' He looked at Farao. 'I'll drive you.'

Farao stood up without a word and followed Terran out onto the driveway. They climbed into their parents' old SUV and drove the fifteen-minute journey to St Thomas' Academy in silence. Terran was used to his youngest brother's mood swings, but still, habit had not made it pleasant to endure. He watched Farao jump out of the car, slamming his door and striding through the school gates without a backwards glance.

On the drive home, Terran met with traffic and his thoughts drifted back to Farao. He knew that, as the youngest of four brothers, Farao did not always have it easy, but he wished he could find a better way of dealing with his emotions than by rebelling against the semblance of routine Terran tried hard to instil in their lives.

Terran wondered if, in a parallel universe, Farao might have turned out more grounded and level-headed, but he brushed the thought off immediately. Farao had been six months old when their father died, and had just turned ten when their mother's turn came, after months of battling the cancer that took her life. Though Farao had always been a quiet child, overshadowed by his brothers' achievements and personalities, he had never been mischievous or unhappy before. By the time Terran had to settle as the head of the family and Farao's legal guardian, however, his younger brother had turned into a resentful and angry teenager, one he struggled to keep in check. He supposed he could not blame Farao. All of them had dealt with their grief in their own way, but he wished there was something he could have done to prevent Farao from closing down entirely and shutting his brothers out in the process.

When Terran walked back into the house, Kendrik and Orson had already left for work. The kitchen was eerily quiet, and the remnants of their breakfast had been cleared away, as though their shared morning meal had never happened. A quick shower later, Terran made himself another cup of coffee before heading into the living room and switching on his laptop.

Terran had been just twenty-three when their mother passed away, and he had dropped out of the architecture degree he was doing, signing up instead for a fast-tracked coding course. The money from his mother's life insurance had been just enough to cover the mortgage on the house and his brothers' school fees. As the eldest of the four,

Terran had needed an income, sooner rather than later, and something that gave him the flexibility to be home and look after everyone. That had been seven years ago now, and the existence he had once known, where he was free to care only for himself, felt like a lifetime away. He hadn't wanted any of his brothers to make that sacrifice, but Kendrik and Orson had taken it upon themselves to contribute in any way they could.

Kendrik, two years younger than Terran, had been twenty-one at the time of their mother's passing, and about to finish his marketing degree. His very first pay check had been spent replacing the house's old boiler when it broke down that winter. Orson had been seventeen and still in high school, but Terran always wondered if his brother's decision not to pursue further education and instead find himself a job as quickly as he could, however menial, had been his way of trying to help his elder brothers carry the burden of their finances. Farao had been so young—just ten years old—and the older three had come to a tacit agreement that, at least, they could try to safeguard his innocence by not letting him see how much went into maintaining the bare necessities of their day-to-day life. Terran often thought that in trying their best to contain their precarious financial situation, they'd missed out on the things that truly mattered—being there for Farao, not just in terms of the logistics of daily life, but as brothers, friends and confidants, too. They were paying the price for it now.

As he opened up his inbox, his eyes fell on the pile of post on the mantelpiece, and his shoulders sagged a little. At some point he would have to face the paperwork and bills that needed his attention. He chose to ignore them for now, but at the back of his mind he could hear his father's voice reminding him that delaying the pain of dealing with something never made it any easier to handle later on. The thought made Terran think of Farao again, and he wondered what his father's advice would have been on that front.

He forced himself to push the topic away from his mind, because there was no point in pondering such matters. No one could rewrite the past, and Terran knew better than to let himself wallow in sadness. He simply could not afford to crumble. He had to be the strong one for all of them.

With a great, heaving sigh, he refocused his attention on his email inbox and started work.

Chapter 2
Farao

The ringing of the bell dragged Farao out of his snooze. He lifted his head, which had been buried in his arms throughout class, and straightened up from his chair.

'Farao,' Mrs Gerald called out from behind her desk. 'A word, please.'

Farao groaned and picked up his bag. As he walked from the back of the class, his gaze fell on Serena in the second row. She was gathering her books into her bag, talking to one of her friends. Farao could see the outline of her profile as she spoke, her smile lighting up her eyes, her long brown hair cascading around her face like a waterfall. He felt himself stiffen as his gaze traced the outline of her jaw and travelled down the side of her neck. When she stood up her eyes met his for a brief moment, and she flashed him a shy smile. He looked away instantly, his stomach doing a sudden backflip. He cursed under his breath, wishing he had not turned away. He wanted to have smiled back, maybe to have spoken to her for a moment, even if just a casual 'hey, Serena', but somehow whenever he was around her all he could do was act like an absolute moron.

'Farao.' Mrs Gerald's voice brought him back to reality, and he went to stand by the teacher's desk.

Mrs Gerald waited a moment, ensuring all other students had left the classroom before continuing. 'I have said this before,' she said sternly, and Farao knew what was coming, 'but I will give you one final warning. If you use my class as a substitute bedroom again, I *will* have to report this to the headmistress. I mean it.'

Farao looked down, rolling his eyes at the floor.

'This is an important year,' Mrs Gerald continued, her tone softening a little. 'And I'm sure you don't want to repeat the year a second time. You *have* to pay attention, or the school will be obligated to consider other options for you.'

Farao snorted. *Other options.* He was well aware of his unfortunate position and the school's repeated threats of his expulsion. He knew that Terran had pleaded with the head for another chance. As if he cared what they thought. As if he needed this shit in his life.

Mrs Gerald gave him a concerned look. 'Listen, I know your situation is a tough one—'

'You. Know. Nothing,' Farao seethed, his head jerking up. 'You don't know a *fucking* thing about my situation. So why don't you shut the *fuck* up and stop trying to pretend like you understand *anything!*'

Mrs Gerald seemed lost for words, shock spread over her face, her mouth hanging comically open as she looked at him. But Farao did not wait for her response, and he stormed out of the classroom, his hands shaking with anger and his jaw tense. He rushed into the nearest boys' bathroom and locked himself up in a cubicle. He dropped his bag on the floor and rested his forehead on the dirty partition. The waves of fury rushed through him, and he clenched his fists, punching the wall, again and again, until the skin on his knuckles scraped and tore.

The door to the bathroom flung open, and someone called out from outside the cubicle.

'Farao?'

Farao did not respond. A second later, his friend Nick's face popped over the partition, looking down at him, his mop of dark hair falling over his eyes.

'Hey, mate, are you alright?'

Farao breathed in deeply. 'Yeah,' he said. 'Yeah, I'm fine.'

'You sure?' Nick threw a concerned glance at Farao's hands.

'Yeah,' Farao breathed. 'Just Mrs Gerald giving me another fucking pep talk...'

'Ah...' Nick nodded knowingly. It hadn't been the first time their maths teacher had pulled Farao aside. 'You coming to second period?' he asked, climbing down from the toilet he was perched on as Farao opened his cubicle door.

'No.' Farao shook his head. 'Can't be arsed. Plus, I bet Gerald's already blabbed about what I said. I'll probably be sent home anytime anyways.'

'She might not.' Nick shrugged. 'She didn't last time...'

'Yeah.' Farao made a face, because though he wasn't keen to get in trouble—the fights that always ensued with Terran were never fun—his teacher's persistence at trying to mollycoddle him, like he needed her protection, pissed him off. 'Still. I think I'll lay low for a bit, see if it blows over.'

Nick looked at him for a second, as though considering whether he should argue the point or not, but seemed to decide against it.

'Okay,' Nick said. 'Maybe see you in French, then?'

Farao caught sight of Nick's knowing smirk and couldn't help smiling. Miss Morgan, their French teacher, was the fittest member of staff at St Thomas'. His time spent in French, far from teaching him much about the language, had fuelled more than one of Farao's fantasies, and as poor as his overall attendance record was, he always made a point of showing up to her class.

'Yeah,' Farao grinned back. 'See you in French.'

They parted in the corridor and Farao made his way out into the school grounds, past the basketball court, all the way to the furthest corner, where he slumped down onto the tarmac behind the janitor's shed. Here, he knew he was unlikely to be disturbed, or found, until he was ready to go back. He took his phone out of his pocket and switched on his earphones, pressing the shuffle button on his favourite playlist. The music came bursting into his skull, and he leant his head back against the wall, closing his eyes.

The anger he had felt at Mrs Gerald's bullshit comment dissipated, leaving in its wake an odd sense of emptiness. He felt tired, not so much physically but mentally. He wished he did not have to deal with school, with his teachers throwing him sympathetic looks as if they knew what it felt like to be him, or talking to him like he was a bomb about to explode. He knew what they thought. They *pitied* him. The poor weird kid with a weird name and no parents. They thought they *got* it. But they didn't. No one did. Even at seventeen years old, years after his parents' death, everyone still treated him like a delicate child.

He wished he could drop out of school altogether, but Terran would never allow it, and Farao could do nothing about it as long as he was underage. The thought of his elder brother sent a fresh wave of annoyance through him and he increased the volume on his phone. Perfect, *fucking* Terran. Of course, *he* would never have insulted a teacher. *He* would never have bunked class. *He* never had to repeat his final year of high school. And all that gave him a hell of a high horse to sit on. Farao groaned and banged his head against the wall behind him, wanting to physically knock the thoughts of his brother from his mind. He was ready to bet the school would have called him again, to complain about his outburst at Mrs Gerald and the fact that he had not showed up for second period. There'd be new threats of expulsion, for sure, and Farao wondered if he'd done it this time. Surely there were only so many screw-ups the school would allow before they kicked him out. Farao grunted, clenching his fists, and immediately wincing from the pain in his bloodied knuckles. Most of his interactions with Terran revolved around everything Farao did wrong, all the ways in which he made Terran's life difficult, and the lack of consideration Farao showed for his family, or for the memory of their parents.

Their *parents*. Farao shuddered despite himself. How much consideration can you show to a man you never knew and a woman you can barely remember? Their father was gone shortly after Farao was born, and though he had no recollection of him whatsoever, he had heard his brothers talk about him so much he felt like a constant presence amongst them.

Their father. The family's hero. The one all three of his brothers looked up to, even now he had been gone for so many years. The man his mother had loved with such intensity that it had consumed her, and she had not had it in her to fight the illness that killed her. The long-gone Anand Dhawan was an invisible force in Farao's life that he had never been able to shake, a shadow looming over every step he took.

It had never helped that Farao looked nothing like his father. Whilst Terran, Kendrik and Orson took after Anand, with their light-brown skin, dark eyes, black hair and athletic statures, Farao alone took after their mother. He had her tall and skinny frame, her light skin, her blue eyes and light chestnut hair. It was as if he had come out of a completely different mould altogether. As a child it had made him feel closer to his mother, like they shared something unique, something she didn't share with the other three. These days, all it did was distance Farao ever more from the idea of the man whose last name he bore, like a mystery he could never solve.

He felt a nudge against his shoulder and jumped. A girl with short blond hair was towering over him. Her name was Melissandre, though he knew she hated the name and would throw abuse at anyone who refused to call her Mel. They had first met in this exact spot, used as they both were to skipping classes regularly. This was the same spot where she sometimes allowed him to kiss her—for practice, she had said, because she could not believe how little experience he had. Once or twice she had even let him cup her breast, and Farao had struggled to make his way back to class after that, he was so hard. He took off his headphones.

'Hey,' he said.

'Hey,' she responded, taking a seat beside him.

They sat in silence for a while, as they often did. Neither of them was a fan of small talk.

'Heard Mrs Gerald gave you a hard time earlier,' Mel eventually said, not looking at him.

'Mmm,' Farao said, not sure he wanted to get onto the topic.

Mel hesitated a moment before speaking again.

'Heard Nick tell New Girl on their way to biology.'

Farao could not help but look up at her. 'New Girl' was what Mel called Serena, and though they had never discussed it, she seemed to have noticed Farao's interest in her and never failed to bring her up.

'Yeah?' he said, in a voice he tried to keep casual, as though he did not really care.

'Yeah,' Mel said, her fingers playing with the hem of her skirt. 'Apparently she asked where you'd gone…'

Farao said nothing. The idea that Serena had been looking for him sent a jolt up his body and he felt he could jump to his feet and punch the air. He had to try really hard to pretend the information was irrelevant.

'Mmm,' he repeated, feeling Mel's side glance on him. 'You going to French after this?' he asked, keen to change the subject.

Mel shrugged. 'I dunno… It's not like I get much out of it.' She grinned. 'She doesn't really do it for me as far as wanking material goes. I think I might just get out of here altogether.'

Farao nodded. Mel was the only person he knew whose attendance and overall attitude to the school system was worse than his.

'Cool,' he said.

'Do you wanna snog for a bit?' Mel turned to him abruptly. 'Wouldn't want you to lose your touch for lack of practice,' she teased.

'Yeah, okay,' Farao said, popping his headphones in his bag and angling his torso towards her.

Mel leant forward and wrapped her arms around his neck, her lips confidently finding his, her fingers playing with the hair at the back of his head. Farao kissed her back, his hands avidly travelling over her waist and up to her chest. As his fingers travelled down again, they lingered on the soft flesh of her thighs under her skirt. All he could think of was Serena's pretty, smiling face. He pictured the gentle curves of her figure under her uniform, imagining how firm she would be to the touch, and he felt himself intensify the kiss, his breathing growing more impatient, his trousers growing tighter by the second, wishing that the girl wrapped around him was a different one.

Chapter 3
Orson

Orson pushed open the staff room door in the small music shop, his arms loaded with a stack of vinyls. As he moved around the room, sliding the discs into their rightful places, he looked over at the open door, towards the busy Camden street beyond. Despite it being a weekday, the area was already crawling with tourists and passers-by. He loved the area's vibrant energy. He breathed it in with a sigh. Behind the till, Sandy was handing a customer their purchase with a smile. Orson winked at her when their eyes met and she gave him the middle finger, returning his grin with a chuckle. When he finished restocking the vinyls, he walked back towards the staff room, passing a young woman who was staring at their noticeboard with interest. Feeling Sandy's eyes on him, but refusing to turn back to look at her, Orson stopped by the young woman.

'Hi,' he said with a smile he knew to be charming, making her jump a little. 'Can I help you?'

'Oh.' She turned to face him, momentarily startled as she took in his good looks, her mouth slightly open as her eyes rested on his for a second too long. 'Erm…' She shook her head. 'Yes. Yes, you can. I'm, erm…' She paused again.

'Are you looking for something specific?' he said softly and grinned, leaning against the wall, cocking his head towards her.

'Yes,' she repeated, slightly flushed. 'I'm actually looking for guitar lessons?' She said it uncertainly, and it sounded more like a question. 'I heard you have instructors here.'

'You heard right!' Orson's smile broadened. 'Have you ever had lessons before?'

'No.' She shook her head. 'But I've wanted to learn forever. Do you have anyone who teaches complete beginners?'

'You're looking at him! At your service, my lady.' Orson gave her an exaggerated bow, and she giggled. 'I teach all levels, including absolute… complete… beginners,' he purred.

She blushed and averted her gaze, but he noticed her body leaning in towards him ever so slightly.

'Why don't you give me your number,' he said, foraging in his pockets and handing her a piece of paper and a pen, 'and I'll be in touch. I would love to teach you a few things…'

The young woman went bright red in the face, momentarily seeming to consider his suggestion, before shaking her head again.

'I'm sorry, I just… I have a boyfriend,' she said apologetically.

'That's no problem sweetheart,' he purred again. 'Bring him over too. I'm sure I can also teach him a thing or two…'

He winked at her and, after a moment's hesitation, as he knew she would, she wrote down her name and number and handed it to him.

'Thank you'—Orson glanced down at the paper—'Jenny. I look forward to our lessons.' He smiled at her again. 'But until then, you'll need some material.'

He led her through the store, piling items into her basket until, before she realised it, she had bought more things than he knew she had planned to when she first entered the shop. She looked back at him and waved as she stepped out onto the busy street.

Sandy elbowed Orson in the ribs, rolling her eyes. 'You never stop, do you?' She shook her head.

'I can't!' He raised his hands in mock apology. 'Not when there's fun to be had and life to be lived! Seize the day!' he exclaimed, throwing his arms in the air.

'Seriously, Orson, I don't know what galaxy you come from, but it's got to be far, far, *far* away,' Sandy laughed, walking around the counter to go help another customer.

The morning passed quickly as the flow of customers intensified, and before Orson knew it, it was lunchtime. He gestured to Sandy that he was popping out, and she nodded at him from behind the counter. He walked down the street, his hands in his pockets, wondering what to have for lunch. He passed a pop-up food stall which offered wood-fired pizzas.

'Excellent!' He rubbed his hands.

He took his place in the queue, noticing the appraising side-looks from the group of girls standing in front of him. Glancing over the menu, he ordered a margarita and took a seat at one of the wooden tables. The young man who brought him his food gave him a long, lingering look and a knowing smile, which Orson returned. When he opened the lid of his pizza box, he noticed a name and number scribbled inside it, with the words 'call me' and a smiley face. Orson looked up, amused, and caught the young man's gaze, raising an eyebrow at him.

He ate slowly, enjoying every mouthful, taking his time. He hated to rush. He would rather not do something than have to whizz through it without being able to embrace it entirely. He threw himself into everything he did, experiences and social encounters alike, living every minute to its fullest, regardless of what anyone else thought. He lived only for himself, and for the pleasures life had to offer. *And* for his brothers, he thought, for his family.

He pulled his phone from his pocket and texted Kendrik.

'Go get 'em, tiger! Perfect timing for a promotion. Bring in the cash, I've been wanting to put my feet up and lead a life of leisure!'

He pressed send, and the reply came almost instantly:

'You twat, if we add any more leisure into your life you'll self-combust!'

And, then, a second later: *'Thanks, bro.'*

Orson smiled. He checked his watch and, opening his chat history with Farao, he typed another text:

'No more bunking classes today.'

Farao's response was also immediate: *'piss off'*.

Then, a few seconds later: *'it was only second period'*.

Followed by: *'that teacher's a right arse anyways'*.

And then: *'don't tell Terran'*.

And finally: *'Please'*.

Orson heaved a big sigh and typed back:

'My lips are sealed. No more skipping classes. Or I'll have to come down to your school and kick your skinny arse.'

He pressed send. Farao texted back a couple of eye-rolling emojis and Orson grinned to himself. He sent a final text, to Terran this time:

'Finishing early today, want me to pick up anything on my way?'

Then he added:

'…a hot date maybe? You looked like you could use one this morning. Just say the word!'

He slipped his phone back into his pocket, knowing Terran rarely answered messages right away. Checking his watch again, he stood up, tearing off the piece of cardboard bearing the waiter's phone number and popping it in his back pocket, with a final grin at the young man eyeing him from behind the counter.

He walked the long way back to the music shop, choosing to stroll along the canal for a bit, his hands in his pockets, a faint smile on his lips. He wondered if the school had already called Terran about Farao skipping classes today or if his teacher had covered for him again, and he could only imagine the argument that awaited them all when they got home if she hadn't. Orson shook his head slowly. He knew Terran and Farao were both doing their best, but they were just on such different planes of reality there was little chance they could understand each other. Terran, the responsible one. The one who'd had to keep their lives from falling apart when their father passed away, and then their mother. The one who'd had to put a tight lid on his grief because there was so much to be done and no one else to do it. Terran, Orson knew, had trained himself to plough on, to put aside his own desires and dreams so that they could all keep going. Farao, on the other hand…

Orson frowned at the thought of his younger brother. Farao had no clue. When their mother had passed away, and they had all sunk, Farao had spent much, much longer than the other three under the surface. By the time they had realised what had happened, the damage was done. Orson felt a familiar tinge in his chest, one that crept up on him whenever he thought of it all.

And then there was Kendrik. Sweet, lovely, dependable Kendrik, who was not quite as in charge as Terran or as carefree as Orson, and who hovered somewhere in the middle, seeming to find it hard to find his rightful place. Orson had found his own way of dealing with it all, with everything that had happened, by refusing to give in to life's minor bumps in the road. He had insisted on living his existence on his terms, so that should he, too, have to make a hasty exit, he could do so without any regrets.

Terran's reply came as Orson stepped into the music shop:
'Thanks. We're out of milk and kitchen roll.'

Orson watched the speech bubble as Terran typed a second message.

'And I'll pass on the hot date. I have enough on my hands with you three idiots to bring a Yoko into the mix!'

Orson chuckled, but even to his own ears his laughter sounded sad and hollow. He wished Terran did not feel like he had to sacrifice himself for their sakes. He typed a response:

'Fine, but don't you come complaining to me when your balls fall off for lack of use.'

'Why don't you make sure yours don't shrink from overuse instead of worrying about mine?' came Terran's response, followed by an eye-rolling emoji and a winky face.

Orson typed and pressed send. *'Fine, just milk and kitchen roll it is, then. You're no fun!'*

'Fun?? What's that? Never heard of it!' Terran replied, and Orson's smile faded.

He thought for a moment before responding. *'Are you saying keeping your three unruly younger brothers in check ain't fun? I'm shocked!'*

Terran sent three dots and a smirking emoji back. Orson let out a long breath, a familiar pang of guilt tugging at his heartstrings, and slipped his phone back into his pocket.

Chapter 4
Kendrik

Kendrik adjusted his tie and surveyed his reflection in the mirror. He took in a sharp breath and sighed. He looked so much like his father when he'd been young—in appearance at least. He had the same warm, chocolate brown eyes, the same smooth olive skin, and the same dark wavy hair arranged in a clean, short haircut. He straightened the collar of his shirt and suit jacket, and wondered, as he often did on big occasions, what his parents would say if they saw him now. If they knew how he'd turned out, would they be proud? *Not now*, he told himself. *This isn't the time.* He took a deep breath in before nodding at himself and walking out of the men's bathroom.

The corridor was pretty quiet at this time of day, with people either in meeting rooms or head down at their desks trying to finish things off before end of day. He walked past the open-plan desks and a woman's voice called out to him. He turned to see Claudia, one of his colleagues, walking towards him.

'Hey,' she said with a beaming smile when she reached him, her Australian accent perceptible even in her greeting. 'Are you going in?' She cocked her head to the large corner office behind them.

'Yes.' Kendrik nodded, not sure what else to say.

'Well, good luck! If you get it we'll have to celebrate.' Claudia blushed.

'Sure,' Kendrik said with a grin. 'If I get promoted, I'm definitely buying everyone in the office a drink!'

'Oh.' Claudia's face fell a little, but she recovered quickly. 'Sure… Well, good luck,' she repeated, giving him an awkward smile, and walked back to her desk.

'Yeah. Thanks,' Kendrik replied, feeling like he'd missed something.

He watched her body slump onto her chair, her cheeks a little pink. He went to knock on the corner office's stained glass door. His manager, Scott, was at his desk inside.

'Come in!' Scott's voice called out, and he looked up from his computer when Kendrik came to sit on the other side of the desk. 'So, Ken,' Scott announced, diving right into things. 'As you know, following the recent restructure, we have an opening for a Customer Success Team Lead in EMEA. This meeting today is to discuss your suitability for the role and your vision for the team, should you be successful, alright?'

'Absolutely.' Kendrik nodded.

The rest of the meeting went smoothly, Kendrik knowing that his five years in the company and sterling performance played in his favour. By the time he left the corner office an hour later, Scott had offered him the role and they had shaken on it, with details of his transition to be discussed later on.

Kendrik walked back to his desk with a spring in his step, feeling suddenly much lighter than he had in a long time. He had been busting his arse for this promotion forever and, Orson's jokes aside, their household desperately needed the extra cash, especially with Farao finishing school at the end of the year and his higher education just around the corner. If *Farao finishes school this year,* Kendrik thought with a frown. His brother had already failed the previous year, and ended up being the only student in his grade to repeat a year. The news had come as a bigger shock to Kendrik and Terran than it had to their younger siblings. Farao had simply shrugged, saying he could not care less and would rather drop out altogether, and Orson had stayed unusually quiet. But Terran had refused to entertain any ideas of Farao's education coming to an end so soon. They owed it to their parents to help Farao succeed, so Kendrik, Terran and Orson had worked extra hard to gather the cash to pay for an additional year at the private high school Farao attended, and the matter was closed. Or so they thought. Soon St Thomas' was calling almost every week to report Farao's behaviour. Incomplete homework, skipping classes, arguing back with teachers and fighting with students… Their little brother seemed to take the repeat of his last year of school as an opportunity to test his limits—and his brothers'.

As Farao's legal guardian, Terran dealt with most of it, and was summoned to the school on a regular basis. Already that year, barely a week into the new term, he'd had to beg the headmistress not to expel Farao altogether. But more than Terran's colossal achievement of saving Farao's spot in the school, it had been Orson's magic which had kept their youngest brother in check. The day Terran had come home from the headmistress' office, frustrated and exhausted from pleading Farao's case, Orson had dragged Farao out of the house without a word and they had returned several hours later, in the dead of night, refusing to give either Terran or Kendrik any details of what they'd been up to. But after that, Farao's behaviour had marginally improved, or at least phone calls from the school had become a little less of a regular occurrence. Whatever Orson had said to Farao, it had been enough to get him to tune down his irresponsible behaviour.

Kendrik didn't get it. He did not understand Farao's persistent lack of consideration, and he wondered what Orson could possibly have said to get through to Farao to get him to cooperate. Sometimes it felt like their brotherhood was split in two, with Kendrik and Terran on one side, and Orson and Farao on the other… Orson in fact often seemed to be the bridge between the two eldest and the youngest in their clan, managing apparently effortlessly to translate situations into words they could all understand.

'How did it go?' Claudia's voice dragged Kendrik out of his train of thoughts.

Kendrik looked at her beaming face. She came to lean against his desk.

'It went well,' he said, his voice level. 'I got the job.'

Claudia's eyes widened, and after a short pause she burst out laughing.

'What?' Kendrik asked, baffled.

'Kendrik, you're the only person I know who can be so blasé even when great things happen to them! Anyone else would be jumping up and down with glee right now.' She shook her head, smiling.

'Ah…' was all Kendrik could find to say.

There was an odd pause. Claudia opened her mouth to speak, but Kendrik was distracted by his phone vibrating in his pocket. He gave her an apologetic smile and pulled the device out to glance at the screen, where Terran's name was flashing.

'Sorry,' he said awkwardly, 'I have to take this.' And he turned around to take the call, catching a glimpse of her disappointed expression. 'Hey,' he said in the receiver.

'Hey, Ken,' Terran's voice sounded at the other end. 'Sorry to bother you at work.'

'No, no, it's ok,' Kendrik said with a furtive look in Claudia's direction, noticing she was sitting at her desk again, her back to him. 'What's up?'

'Farao's school,' Terran started, and Kendrik found himself tensing, holding his breath, 'is asking for his passport details. Apparently there's a trip to Spain coming up at the end of the year... I had completely forgotten about it, they've just called to chase, it's due today. I can't find it—any idea where it's gone?'

'It's not in the metal cabinet in the hallway?' Kendrik frowned.

'No, I've checked... Come to think of it, I can't remember the last time I even *saw* his passport... I'm not even sure it's still valid.'

'I guess the last time we saw it was...'

There was a heavy pause on the line, and Kendrik regretted his words instantly. He knew what they'd both be thinking. The last time they'd needed Farao's documents would have been when they'd needed to finalise the custody paperwork. Right after their mother had died.

'Yeah...' Terran breathed, his voice strained.

'Have you checked in the attic?' Kendrik said quickly, in an attempt to move on from the moment. 'I think there's some stuff there.'

'Mmm... I was hoping I wouldn't have to go in there...' Terran groaned, and Kendrik could not blame him. The attic was full of their parents' belongings, and they all avoided it as much as they could. 'But I'll have a look, thanks. By the way, how did your meeting go?'

'Great,' Kendrik replied. 'I got the job. And a pay rise.'

'Amazing! Congrats, Ken! Think that calls for a shot tonight, right?'

'Sure,' Kendrik smiled. 'I'll see you tonight.'

Kendrik hung up the phone, sat back at his desk and switched his laptop on, a grin still spread wide over his face. Those *shots*... It had been their parents' ritual, but it had carried on long after they had both passed away. It was a way for the brothers to celebrate even the smallest of things.

Their parents had started the tradition back when their mother had fallen pregnant with their first child and, as the third trimester drew to an end, they still hadn't agreed on a name. One evening, Anand and

Gabrielle Dhawan had sat on the wooden floor of the small apartment they then occupied in Nice, and decided that night would be the night their baby would be named. There was a power cut in the building that day, so they had lit candles all over the tiny living room. As the night grew darker outside the small windows, their mother had fetched a French dictionary, opening it randomly for inspiration, and read the word at the top of the page: *terrain*. Amongst much laughter and bantering, they had taken the word and made it into a name that was as unique as they felt their son would be. And so Terran's name had been chosen. To celebrate the achievement, their parents had opened a ridiculously huge vintage tequila bottle someone had gifted them at their wedding and they had poured themselves a single shot each, downing it swiftly. It was back when pregnancy restrictions weren't as well-defined as they later were, their mother always explained. Kendrik still remembered their parents laughing about it as they told their sons the story of how they picked each of their names.

As a child, Kendrik had disliked his own name, tired of having to spell it out constantly. He had longed for a first and last name that everyone would take in from the first time he said it, not one he had to repeat and explain every time he introduced himself. He had always wanted to blend in. As he grew older, he had made his peace with it, because it was one of the last reminders he had that his parents had not just lived, but had shared the sort of bond that had made them cheekily make up their unborn sons' names over an open dictionary and a bottle of tequila. It felt like a link to the people Kendrik knew they had been, and the kind of love they had felt for one another.

The shot tradition had stayed, and even now the brothers lit some candles and took a single shot each on every important milestone in their lives. It was one of the rare occasions when there seemed to be no tension between them. For these short moments they were a clan, beyond their differences, beyond their disagreements, and they were reminded of the power of the blood that united them.

Chapter 5
Terran

Terran pressed his laptop shut, rubbing his eyes as he sat back into the couch. He knew there was more work to be done but he needed a break. He also knew he could not postpone a trip to the attic any longer. When Farao's school had called to ask about the passport details, they had also pointed out the previous two reminders they had given him, and had insisted that unless they received the relevant information by the end of the day, Farao would simply not be permitted to take part in the trip. *Another expense to plan for,* he thought wearily. Standing up, he made his way to the top floor and pulled open the latch, unfolding the ladder leading to the one room he tried to avoid at all costs. The last time he had gone in there had been after his mother had died, to bring in boxes full of her possessions, settling them alongside his father's old things.

He climbed the ladder and hoisted himself through the hole in the floor, landing amongst a thick layer of dust. He switched on the light and glanced around. The attic looked exactly as he remembered, with boxes roughly lined up against the wall, amongst a variety of useless items they had discarded there over a lifetime spent in this house. Taking a few steps forward he squinted, the stale air making his eyes water a little. He rummaged through the boxes, checking labels, looking for one that indicated it might contain important documents. He found a metal box tucked at the back of the room labelled 'papers' and bent over to pick it up, but as he did so, he lost his footing and stumbled to the side, knocking over a pile of boxes. He swore loudly as he fell to the floor with a loud thud. Sitting up in the midst of the mess, he swore again, and made to stand. He was just about to get to his feet when his eyes caught a glimpse of something. He leant aside to look at it more closely. One of the fallen boxes had burst open, its contents spilling amongst the dirt on the floor.

One item, a framed photograph, its glass shattered, grabbed his attention. He picked it up and brought it closer to his face, examining the picture. It was an aged, black and white shot, showing a group of young men in uniform, neatly arranged in rows, standing tall and staring at the camera. In the front row, Terran spotted his father's unmistakable face, looking back at him impassively. He was standing in a place of honour, right next to the highest-ranking officer, distinguishable by the row of medals pinned to the front of his jacket. Terran guessed it must have been taken during his father's posting in the south of France, where he met the woman who would later become his wife, and the mother of their four sons.

Terran smiled, a sad, painful smile that only cropped up when he came face to face with memories of his parents. He missed them. Every moment of every day. He'd been stumbling around in the dark ever since they passed away, trying his best to make them proud even though they could no longer witness his efforts.

Terran stood there for some time, staring at the picture but no longer seeing it, incapable of moving a muscle, completely out of breath. *That* day—the day it had happened, the day his mother had died —he hadn't been there. There had been some issue with Farao at school and, since his mother had been in no state to go anywhere, Terran had needed to go in her place. He could not for the life of him even remember what the problem had been; all he remembered was his mother's weak smile as she thanked him for going in her stead just before he left the house, and the cold, excruciating sensation that his heart was being ripped out of his chest when he heard Orson's shaking voice on the phone, telling him to come home immediately. Terran had grabbed Farao by the arm and started running. Everything in between was a blur. He remembered sprinting up the stairs to their mother's room to find Orson kneeling by the side of her bed, his hands over hers, sobbing uncontrollably. He remembered Farao's face as he stepped into the room behind him and took in the scene. But more than anything that day, Terran remembered the scream. The piercing, agonising scream that came out of ten-year-old Farao's mouth as he collapsed against the chest of drawers. The sound had filled the air until it resonated under Terran's skin. It had felt like an eternity before he was able to move. He had watched the room around him as though through frosted glass.

Eventually, with one last long glance at his mother's still, ashen face, something inside him had shut tight, forcing him to spring into action. He had to take charge. He had to take care of things, of everything. And so, as if on autopilot, Terran had lifted Orson off the floor and picked up Farao. He had led them out of the room, closing the door behind them. He had called an ambulance, though he knew little could be done for their mother now. He had settled Farao and Orson on the couch in the living room with cups of hot chocolate that would be left untouched and grow cold. He had called Kendrik, getting his voicemail, and left several messages telling him to come home. Then he had called Amit Shandhar, their parents' oldest friend. He had explained to the stone-faced paramedic what had happened and said that there was no one else to be called, that it was just them. It was just them. *Just them.* That was it. The reality had only just begun to register in his mind, his shocked brain refusing to compute it fully.

He had made sure his brothers were out of the way when his mother's body was carried down the stairs, made sure they didn't catch sight of the black body bag. He had signed forms and answered questions. He had broken the news to Kendrik when he had finally come home. And from then on he had been the one in charge, for no other reason than, as the eldest, he felt it to be his duty to be the strong one.

Terran snapped back to attention, his eyes refocusing on the picture in front of him. *Enough,* he told himself, *there's no point in wallowing.* He inhaled sharply, and a cloud of dust filled his nostrils, making him cough. Then, without thinking, he lodged the frame under his arm, turned around, and carefully made his way down the ladder.

Chapter 6
Gabrielle

I've been wanting to come clean for a while. I've wanted to tell the story of what happened, and now feels as good an occasion as any.

It feels a bit cliché to think about your life's biggest regrets when you're on the verge of dying, I know, but I suppose that such realisations often trigger a need for confessing your sins and secrets.

I need to get it out. I need my story to be revealed, if only so that it doesn't weigh me down in whatever afterlife awaits me.

There's so much to tell, and so little time. The pen in my hand hovers over the blank page in front of me as I wonder where to start. My wrist is aching. In fact, everything's been aching for a while. The meds are barely making a difference anymore. There's nothing I can do about it. I look at the sheet of paper in front of me, propped on one of the hardcover books Orson's been reading to me. The Great Gatsby. *I suppose that's fitting enough.*

I think hard for a moment, and the memories start flooding my tired brain.

I guess it all began on the day I turned twenty-one, not just because it was my birthday, but because that was also the day I finished my nursing training. We had been awarded our diplomas that very morning, but all the girls in my batch could talk about was the reception organised for us by the local RAF base near Nice. The party took place every year, partly as a recruitment tactic for the RAF, but also to give the male officers and female nurses a well-deserved opportunity to let their hair down after long months of toiling in their chosen path without interacting with the opposite sex. The event was like a rite of passage for us nurses, something we talked about long before we probably should have.

To me, it was a somewhat frightening prospect. I wasn't as outgoing as some of the other girls, nor was I desperate to fool around with a man like many of my friends were planning to.

We got ready on the day in an atmosphere of excited fervour we'd never shown for our nursing classes. I hadn't been able to afford a new dress, my weekly allowance already spent on a new set of books I wanted to take with me on the month's worth of travels I'd planned around the south of France before I took on my first assignment.

Nurse Magda gave us a look-over before we left the building, insisting that although we were officially no longer her responsibility, she expected sterling behaviour from each and every one of us, in the name of the institution that had just given us our professional qualification.

As far as I was concerned, I thought at the time, she might as well have saved her energy, because none of my plans for the future involved getting cosy with an officer or joining the army. I wasn't about to risk ruining my life like that.

But the girls were giddy and the idea of the event was still a welcome change from the rigid routine of our three-year-long training.

I look back down at the page in front of me, wondering how to explain it best. How much to say, how far back to go so that my boys understand when they finally read what I have to share.

I suppose I'll have to start the next part of this story by admitting how wrong I was. I never knew it was possible to be so mistaken about anything before that night at the RAF base.

I had gone in with a clear vision of how it would pan out. God, how unprepared I was! Never in my wildest dreams would I have thought it would turn out the way it did…

But I shouldn't get ahead of myself…

We all reached the compound a little before 6pm, and to our surprise and delight, a group of young uniform-clad officers were lined up in two rows, on each side of a red carpet. They welcomed us with such gentlemanly manners and respect that, despite myself, I felt warm and fuzzy inside. I tried to keep my cool, but even I'll confess that the sight of so many handsome faces and uniforms made me a little weak in the knees. They saluted us as we walked off our bus and they escorted us to the reception room, each officer offering his arm to one of us. There was a speech from the head of the compound and the RAF recruitment officer, inviting us to consider a career as army nurses, and a champagne reception with delicious canapés.

I mainly let the others make conversation. I felt like an idiot standing at the back, barely able to say a word. I grew even more nervous when the music started and several pairs made their way to the dance floor. I stayed back, watching them all swirl around the space, wishing I had the other girls' confidence and grace.

That was when I saw him, standing on the other side of the room.

Anand.

He was looking straight at me, and I had to look away for a moment when I met his eyes.

When I glanced back at him his gaze was still fixed on me, and he was walking across the dance floor towards me.

My heart skipped a beat when he came to stand in front of me. He was the most handsome man I had ever seen. When he smiled at me I could no longer think. My newfound resolve to make a life for myself as an independent woman evaporated.

He said nothing, and just gave me his hand. I took it with shaking fingers.

We danced all night and the whole time he was looking only at me, and I only at him. Then he led me out into the night and we walked around the base, talking of everything and anything. At midnight, he escorted me back to the bus and placed a light kiss on the top of my hand. He was on duty the following day but promised to meet me the day after that.

By the time he was due to pick me up for our first date, I had been ready for hours.

I hadn't been able to think straight since we'd met.

I'd never believed in true love before. I'd always been too focused and pragmatic for that. But as I watched his car pull up in front of my building, and my eyes found his face when he stepped out from behind the wheel, a wild electric current coursed through my veins. I knew then I'd met my soulmate and that my life was about to change forever.

Chapter 7
Farao

Farao let the door slam behind him as he walked into the hallway. He stomped up the stairs to his room, noticing as he reached the last step that the ladder to the attic was pulled down. He stilled, looking at the gaping hole above him with a lump in his chest. He knew too well what the attic held. Had Terran gone up there today? What could he possibly be after that required a trip to the attic, when they all tried their hardest to pretend it was not even there? Farao stepped forward and glanced up the ladder. His foot was just hovering over the first step when Terran's voice came from the stairway.

'Farao, is that you?'

'Yeah.' Farao's gaze snapped away from the ceiling and he stepped back.

Terran appeared at the bottom of the stairs, looking a little flustered, his eyes on Farao and the unfolded ladder.

'What were you doing up there?' Farao asked, and he could not keep the accusation out of his voice.

'Oh,' Terran said, seeming taken aback by the question for a moment, before regaining his composure. 'I was looking for your passport.' He banged a hand on his forehead. 'For your school trip. Kendrik thought we might have some papers up there,' he added quickly.

Farao frowned.

'I have my passport,' he grunted. 'It's in here.' He pointed to his room and stepped inside, marching to his desk.

He rummaged through a couple of his drawers until he found it. One of the covers was badly bent. He handed it to Terran, who had followed him.

'Thanks.' Terran flicked through it and studied the main page. 'Good, it's still valid.' Then, with a suspicious look at Farao, he added, 'Why do you have this here?'

Farao only shrugged, looking away quickly to avoid meeting Terran's searching eyes. He was not ready to admit he had kept his passport at hand, along with a few valuable possessions, ever since a few months ago, when he had thought he'd had enough and considered running away for good. He still remembered the night he had sort of made up his mind about it all: Orson had waltzed into his room in his usual eccentric manner and dragged him out for a drink—an actual, proper drink, despite Farao being underage—and they had stayed out all night, talking about nothing much, Orson taking care of most of the conversation. By the time they had stumbled back home and Farao had crashed into bed, he had somehow discarded all thoughts of escaping his life. Terran had been pissed off the next day at the state of them when they rolled up at the breakfast table with major hangovers, but for some reason he had not given them too hard a time.

'Anyways,' Terran said, apparently choosing not to push the topic further, 'I'll go call the school to give them the details. Homework before dinner, please.' He gave Farao a pointed look and disappeared out of the room.

Farao sat on his bed, pulling his school books out of his backpack. He glanced at the list of assignments he had for the next day, but could not gather the will to get started on any of them. Instead he grabbed his guitar, a present Orson had given him when he had turned twelve, and let his hands rest on the familiar instrument. He closed his eyes and allowed his fingers to make their way over the strings, playing his favourite tunes. Learning the guitar had been Orson's idea, and he had taught Farao himself. To Farao it had come as a revelation, a means to let his emotions surface in a way he couldn't manage otherwise. It had also been a chance to bond with the only one of his brothers who hadn't become completely obsessed with order and discipline after his mother died. Terran and Kendrik had proclaimed themselves in charge, intent upon keeping Farao on 'the right track', though neither of them had ever really bothered asking Farao how he felt about it all. Orson had been the only one to see Farao for who he was, and to think not only of what he needed but of what he wanted, too.

Farao admired the way Orson lived life on his own terms, never compromising for anyone or anything, choosing not to pursue higher education but instead work in a trendy shop and teach music. To Farao, Orson had it all figured out. He knew where he was going, and he didn't care what anyone else thought. Farao wished he could do the same, but he knew that as long as he was still a minor, Terran's status as his legal guardian meant he never had a say in the matter. Farao hated that he had no control over any of it, that his life didn't seem to belong to him anymore. He hated that he kept being treated like a child, as though he hadn't gone through enough shit to prove he wasn't one anymore. He just felt so angry all the time, so ready to lash out. He hugged the guitar tighter against his chest and kept playing, focusing on the songs he knew always calmed him down.

When Farao eventually went down for dinner, he hadn't started to look at his homework, but he felt marginally calmer than he had a few hours before. Terran and Kendrik were in the kitchen, setting the table and talking animatedly. From the conversation, Farao gathered Kendrik had got the promotion he was going for. He mumbled half-hearted words of congratulations and Kendrik gave him a beaming smile. Farao still wasn't too sure what Kendrik did for a living, all he knew was that he wore boring-ass suits and clocked in from nine to five, toiling away to make someone else money. Orson joined them just as Terran glanced at his watch.

'Good evening, brothers!' Orson exclaimed, and Farao smiled despite himself.

'Thought you were finishing early today?' Terran frowned, taking the bag of groceries Orson was handing him.

'As a matter of fact, I did, but I got slightly sidetracked on my way home…' Orson gave Farao a wink.

'*Sidetracked*…' Kendrik rolled his eyes. 'What was her name this time?' And then he added. 'Or was it a he today?'

'Wouldn't you like to know…' Orson laughed. 'I'm afraid you'll have to find your own encounters to fuel your nighttime fantasies, Ken. Someday you'll have to stop living your romantic life vicariously through me…'

Kendrik spat the water he was drinking back into his glass, coughing loudly.

'Romantic?!' he barked, a disbelieving look on his face. 'You call your sleeping around *romantic*?'

'My dear Ken, that's where you're wrong. It's not sleeping around. I'm merely embracing every opportunity life sends my way.'

'Sounds a lot like sleeping around to me,' Kendrik mumbled.

'Maybe if you gave it a try you wouldn't be so grumpy all the time!' Orson chuckled as he caught Farao's eye.

'Ok, ok, enough with the both of you.' Terran intervened before Kendrik could respond.

'Absolutely.' Orson nodded with a flourish of the hand. 'Let us not quarrel!'

Kendrik rolled his eyes but didn't respond. Dinner went without any other incident, and Farao soon phased out his brothers' dull domestic conversation, his thoughts drifting back to the time he had spent skipping second period with Mel. She was his first everything; the first girl to persevere with him long enough to actually get through to him, the first girl to let him touch her, and his very first kiss. She had practically *made* him kiss her the day he had reluctantly told her he had never kissed anyone before. She was not his girlfriend—they had both made that clear from the start—but he was glad she let him practice with her so that… His mind finished the sentence before he could stop it: so that when he grew the balls to ask Serena out he would not look like an inexperienced moron. He felt his cheeks redden at the thought of Serena's lips on his.

He jumped as he felt someone kick his leg under the table, the sting of it making him look up. He let out a muffled 'ouch' under his breath, rubbing his shin, and caught Orson's amused smile from the corner of his eye, as if somehow he could tell what had been going through his head. Farao knew without needing to see it that his face had gone crimson. Terran and Kendrik were both staring at him expectantly.

'What?' he blurted out, as Orson cleared his throat next to him.

'What happened to your hands?' Terran asked, frowning at the slim crust of dried blood on Farao's knuckles.

Shit.

He'd forgotten to wash his hands.

'Nothing,' Farao lied, looking down into his plate. 'I fell.'

There was a pause, one moment where Farao knew things could go either way, depending on how much Terran fancied probing him on the topic.

'Did you finish your homework?' Terran finally sighed, shaking his head.

'Yeah.'

'Good,' Terran said, though Farao had a feeling he wasn't fooled. 'Because we have an occasion to celebrate today!' He turned to slap Kendrik on the back.

Kendrik went on to explain what his new role would be, not that Farao paid too much attention, but he still nodded and half-smiled at regular intervals. It had been a while since they'd had what they called a 'shot-worthy occasion'. Up until recently, Farao hadn't been allowed the tequila the others used during their ritual, but Orson had campaigned on his behalf that he was now old enough to be allowed to partake, which Farao was grateful for.

They cleared away their dinner plates and Terran went into the living room, setting the huge tequila bottle and four shot glasses on the hardwood floor. He grabbed some candles and lit them around the room, their light glittering in the now darkened space. Outside, beyond the French windows in the conservatory, night had fallen. They all sat on the floor, around the bottle, and Terran poured four glasses, keeping Farao's glass only a quarter of the way full. Farao didn't protest, because he knew too well where that argument was headed, and he didn't have the energy for it. They all raised their glasses.

'To Kendrik's new job!' Terran said.

'And to more cash in the bank!' Orson added, making Farao chuckle.

'Hear, hear.' Kendrik grinned, shaking his head.

They all downed the contents of their glass at the same time. The harsh liquor warmed Farao's throat.

'Here,' Orson said, handing Kendrik a piece of paper. 'Since none of us got you a present…'

Kendrik took the paper from him and frowned as he unfolded it and read the words scribbled on it.

'Who's Jenny?' he asked, baffled.

'Someone who'll gladly meet up with you for some fun!' Orson gave him a cheeky smile. 'If you ask nicely, she'll bring her boyfriend along and you can have your very first threesome.'

'You're such a prick!' Kendrik laughed, throwing the piece of paper back at him. Orson didn't bother dodging.

'And yet, you still love me dearly,' Orson smiled, as though Kendrik had just paid him a compliment.

A comfortable silence fell between them, the mood made considerably lighter by Orson's never-ending cheek. Farao closed his eyes. He had often tried to pretend he didn't care for their little ritual, but in truth, he loved it. It was the only time when he felt like he truly belonged among his brothers. On those odd moments, there was no problem between them, no fight to be won, no argument to be endured. When they sat in the candlelight around the tequila bottle, they were no longer orphans, divided by the burdens and responsibilities they each carried. They were united, bonded by blood and the cherished memories of the parents they no longer had. For those rare moments, they were simply brothers, and Farao found himself wishing for the feeling never to end.

Chapter 8
Orson

Orson lay back, propping himself up on his elbows. He took in Farao's relaxed expression—his eyes were closed and his jaw free from its usual tension. Kendrik was humming a tune that Orson did not recognise. Terran was uncharacteristically quiet, seeming lost in thought, and Orson wondered what was on his mind. They sat together quietly, as they often did on these occasions, allowing themselves to simply be with each other. The ritual always brought Orson back to his mother, and to the gleeful expression on her face as she retold the stories of how each of them was named.

'When we opened the dictionary for *you*...' She would smile a cheeky smile at Orson every time he asked to hear the tale again. '...we ended up on the letter B.'

'The letter *B*!' young Orson would always exclaim, excited for her to continue.

'Yes.' She would grin at him, her hand tucking a strand of his hair behind his ear. 'And we found the word "bear".' She always paused for suspense at that point. 'But at the time, you see'—she would lean forward and whisper—'your father was learning French, and he pointed out that the French word for "bear" was "ours". I already felt that you would be just like an adorable little bear... *un petit ourson*. And so your father and I decided on your name: Orson!'

The story moved Orson every time he thought about it. Maybe because he had been the youngest for a long time, he had been closest to his mother, back when Terran and Kendrik were growing into teenagers and looking for independence. Orson and his mother had spent countless hours talking, exploring, sharing experiences and memories that would mould him into the man he now was. Maybe this was why she had felt like she could confide in him above the others. Maybe that was why... Orson's eyes involuntarily found Farao's face again and he sighed. He supposed he would never truly know *why*, all he knew for certain was that, in her final moments, she had entrusted him with secrets she could have easily taken to the grave, and that was enough.

It was some time before any of them moved, but Terran finally put the bottle away, blew out the candles, and they made their way to their respective rooms. As Farao moved past him to enter his own bedroom, Orson placed a hand on his shoulder to stop him. Farao turned around silently and Orson gave him a smile and a quick nod, which Farao returned, in silent understanding that they were here for each other.

Chapter 9
Gabrielle

We got married a year later, on the first Saturday of June. The sun was out, the smell of spring was in the air. I stood by Anand's side in front of the civil servant officiating that day, and I knew that this was it. For the rest of our lives we would stand together. We would face everything life had to throw at us and never crumble.

Anand was looking more handsome than ever in his wedding suit, the navy blue uniform he wore to every formal occasion. To this day the image of him in that suit still gives me the shivers. More than the man I loved, he was the air I breathed. I wish more than anything that, one day, each of my boys gets to experience a love as intense and all-consuming as their father and I shared.

We settled in a small flat near Nice.

We were happy. Happier than I ever believed I could be, happier than anyone should be allowed to be, really.

Maybe we were too happy.

Perhaps no one is ever allowed a lifetime of happiness, and one day or the other we had to pay the price for so much bliss.

Chapter 10
Kendrik

'Farao, hurry up, I'm already late!' Kendrik banged on the bathroom door.

Farao's muffled voice came from the other side of the door, but Kendrik didn't have any time to waste. Of all days, *today* had to be the morning he slept through his alarm. He could count the number of times he'd been late in his life on the fingers of one hand, but he'd had such a busy few weeks. The promotion had, as he'd thought, come with a generous side of overtime at the office, and he'd been running around so much he'd barely been able to switch off. But today was even more hectic, because it was his first on-site meeting with their biggest customer in his new role. It was a great chance to cement his position, to prove he was indeed the right man for the job, and he couldn't bear the thought of ruining it for himself.

He rushed to the kitchen, grumbling under his breath.

'Well, aren't you a lovely little ray of sunshine this morning!' Orson greeted him from the breakfast table.

'Oh, shut up,' Kendrik growled, but Orson just grinned back at him.

'You'll do great. Just *breathe*,' Orson said soothingly.

'I'll breathe when I'm showered and ready to head out the fucking door.'

'That's the spirit!' Orson said, but Kendrik was too irritated to respond.

He poured himself a coffee, brought the mug to his lips and burnt his tongue. He swore again, bringing the mug down on the counter so fast that the coffee spilt over his pyjama bottoms.

'Oh, for crying out loud!' he exclaimed.

Within a moment, Orson was by his side, gently pulling him away from the mess.

'Sounds like Farao's done with the shower,' he said calmly. 'Why don't you go, and I'll tidy up here.'

Kendrik opened his mouth to say something, but Orson was already pushing him firmly out of the kitchen. He showered and got dressed in a jiffy, then double checked the contents of his bag as he rushed down the stairs and to the front door.

'You'll smash it!' He heard Orson call out to him as he stepped through the door, and he allowed himself a wry smile.

You can count on Orson to lift you up when even you seem to have given up on yourself, he thought.

As it turned out, he was only a few minutes late to the meeting, and he was so pumped on adrenaline by the time he took his seat at the large conference room table that the build-up of nerves that had been accumulating for the past few days simply flew out of the window. When he left the client's office block two hours later, Claudia diligently by his side, he felt better than he had in a long time. He *had* smashed it, getting the client not only to renew their contract, but removing the previously added break clause, and increasing their minimum fee. All in all, a great morning.

Kendrik pulled out his phone from his pocket and checked his messages. There was a text from Orson containing a single thumbs-up emoji. Kendrik smiled, and typed a response:

'Thanks. *Sorry about this morning*'

Orson's reply came almost instantly:

'*Don't worry your pretty little head about it. Just tell me you nailed it this morning.*'

Before Kendrik had a chance to start typing a response, Orson followed up:

'*And please tell me you finally grew a pair and asked Claudia out already!*'

Kendrik breathed out sharply, closing his eyes. *What a twat*, he thought, but all he could do was smile.

'Everything alright?' Claudia asked from behind him.

'Erm, yes.' Kendrik quickly slid his phone into his pocket. 'Yes, just my brother… Never mind. Shall we?'

They made their way back to the office, where they were greeted like heroes when they shared the news from the morning's meeting. *Honestly*, Kendrik thought to himself, grinning widely as he sat at his desk and opened his laptop, *there is absolutely* nothing *that can screw up this day now.*

Chapter 11
Farao

'Farao?'

Farao glanced up from his plate of food to see Nick looking at him with concern. He hadn't been listening to a word he'd been saying.

'Mmm?'

Nick considered him in silence for a moment. 'Are you ok?' he finally asked, frowning. 'You're looking a bit pale.'

'Huh?' Farao shrugged. 'Yeah, yeah, I'm fine. Just not hungry.' He put down his fork and pushed his tray away from him, his lunch plate untouched. 'I'll see you in maths, ok?'

Before Nick could respond, Farao stood up, propped his bag over one shoulder and carried his tray to the pile of dirty dishes in the corner of the cafeteria. He made his way to the boys' lavatory, which he was glad to find empty. He dropped his bag to the floor and leant forward over one of the sinks. The truth was, he wasn't feeling too good. His stomach had been in knots since he'd woken up, and he hadn't been able to eat anything all day. He felt queasy and lightheaded. He closed his eyes and tried to slow down his breathing, but it was like the air around him was too thick to be inhaled.

A sudden, sharp pain in the pit of his stomach made him double over, and he cried out. It felt like someone was stabbing him over and over again with a hot blade. The pain was excruciating. He cried out again, because it was all that he could do not to implode. He fell to his knees. His vision blurred, but from the corner of his eye he could see the shape of the door opening and feet rushing in towards him. He vaguely felt the cold tiles of the bathroom floor against his cheek. Before anything else could register, he had fainted.

Chapter 12
Terran

Terran paced the corridor, back and forth, back and forth, hugging his mobile phone tightly in one hand, glancing at its screen every other second. He had called Orson and Kendrik on his way to the hospital, but it would be some time before they would get there. With a ball of nerves lodged deep into his chest, Terran had then rung the only other person there was to call, Amit Shandhar, an old friend of his parents' and a respected surgeon. Amit would know what to do.

In his mind's eye, Terran relived the moment, *that* moment when he had seen the number of Farao's school flash up on his phone. He had sworn out loud. He hadn't been able to help himself. He had let a second or two pass before he'd answered, wondering what on earth Farao had done *now* and how soon he'd be summoned to the headmistress' office. Terran had been annoyed, instantly jumping to the conclusion that his youngest brother had found yet another way of ruining a morning's worth of work for him. As he'd picked up the phone and answered the call, he'd braced himself, readying his voice for what might have been the hundredth apology to the school about Farao's behaviour.

But the words he had heard on the other end of the line had knocked the wind out of him, and he'd been instantly filled with a sense of guilt so immense it had frozen him in place. The voice had not been that of the head, but of the school nurse, informing him Farao had taken ill and been driven to the nearest hospital. He had noted down the details she was giving him with shaking fingers. He had allowed himself a full thirty seconds of immobilising terror before he forced himself into action.

When he reached the hospital, he was told that Farao's state had stabilised and that he was sleeping. There were more tests to be run, consent to be granted and more time to pass before they could know what was wrong.

Now, as he paced around the sterile hospital corridor, waiting for Amit and his brothers, and for news of Farao's tests, Terran found himself praying. For the first time since he had laid eyes on his mother's lifeless body, he felt truly powerless. He couldn't muster up the strength to deal with this. If anything happened to Farao... But he couldn't think like that. He mustn't. And he had to snap himself out of the state of guilt that threatened to overcome him, for the thoughts that had popped into his head when he'd received the call from the school.

Orson was first to arrive, shortly followed by Kendrik, and Terran filled them in on the little that he knew.

'I've called Amit,' he said after he finished explaining what had happened. 'He's on his way.'

'Good,' Orson said tensely, rubbing his temples.

Kendrik only nodded. They waited in silence for another half hour before Amit's familiar silhouette appeared at the end of the corridor. He was a tall man with light brown skin and jet black hair, kind eyes and a gentle demeanour. In the many years since Amit had entered their lives, helping out their parents in any way he could and slowly becoming a semi-permanent fixture in their day-to-day, Terran couldn't remember him once getting angry. He was soft-spoken, understanding and fair, and a calming presence in any situation he came into.

'How is he?' Amit asked Terran.

'He's stable, but they're running some tests to find out what the problem is.'

'Ok.' Amit nodded. 'Who's the doctor assigned to his case? Ah, yes,' he added, approvingly, checking the name on the paperwork Terran handed out to him. 'I know him. He's good. Let me go and find out where they're at.'

Terran watched Amit walk away, feeling like the weight in his chest had eased ever so slightly. *Amit will know what to do*, he told himself again, sitting down, his head in his hands.

'He'll be fine,' Orson said gently, placing a hand on Terran's shoulder. 'He's a fighter, our little brat of a brother.'

Terran couldn't help a small, broken chuckle.

'Yeah,' he said, looking up. 'That he is.'

'What?' Kendrik asked, his voice coarse. 'A fighter? Or a brat?'

They exchanged half-smiles, and fell back into silence. Terran swallowed hard. He needed the lightness, the banter, because the alternative, the idea that Farao might be in more trouble than they suspected, sent his head spinning uncontrollably. *He'll be fine*, he kept repeating to himself, willing himself to believe it, forbidding his mind to launch into the downward spiral that threatened to overtake him.

Amit eventually reappeared, a sombre expression on his face. Terran stood up. Kendrik and Orson were instantly at his side.

'What's wrong?' Terran asked, cold terror starting to rise in the pit of his stomach.

'I…' Amit started. 'Listen,' he added slowly, in a conciliatory sort of way. 'Farao's still asleep, and he'll be passed out for a while. I've spoken to Mark, the doctor on the case, he'll be over in half an hour to discuss the details. Why don't we head outside for a bit and grab ourselves a coffee? There's no point waiting here.'

'Amit.' Orson's voice was shaking. 'What happened?'

'Coffee,' Amit repeated, in a gentle but firm tone. 'Come on.'

They followed him. Terran could no longer feel the ground beneath his feet. He realised he had started sweating. He rubbed his palms on his jeans, apprehension growing with every step they took. Amit led them to the hospital cafeteria, expertly navigating through the maze of corridors. He ordered four coffees, and they sat down at a table in the far corner of the small courtyard. It was a few seconds before Amit spoke.

'Mark said Farao's blood sugar was extremely low when he came in today. It looks like it triggered a chain reaction in his body. They needed to do further tests because the symptoms he was showing were all over the place, so they had to proceed by elimination.'

Terran held his breath, his heart pounding against his ribcage. 'And?' he pressed him.

'Why don't we wait for Mark. I've told him to meet us here,' Amit said gently. 'He was going over the latest results, and he'll be able to answer questions much better than I can at this stage.'

Terran sighed and slumped back in his chair. Kendrik groaned.

'I know this is frustrating,' Amit said with a nod, his face tense, 'but we'll get to the bottom of this, I promise.'

They sat in silence waiting for Mark. To Terran, the wait felt unbearable. He had a feeling that Amit knew more than he was letting on, and the fact that he wasn't willing to tell them any more didn't seem like a good sign.

'There he is,' Amit finally said, standing up from his seat and waving someone over to their table.

Terran jumped to his feet. Kendrik and Orson both stood and turned around, and they shook Mark's hand in turn before sitting down again. The grave expression on Mark's face made Terran shiver.

'Before we start,' Mark said, leaning forward, resting his elbows on the table and interlacing his fingers, 'Farao's doing fine. We've sedated him, so he'll be sleeping for a few hours. His results just came in. I've been over them with the team.' Mark's voice was neutral, that mechanical tone doctors often adopt when breaking bad news. 'There's no easy way to say this, I'm afraid... Farao has a condition called aplastic immunodeficient anaemia.'

A stunned silence followed Mark's words, and he gave them a moment before he continued speaking.

'Farao's bone marrow is struggling to create the right blood cells to help the rest of his body function. This means his immune system is so weak that small infections or bacteria, which a healthy human being could easily fight off, can send his body into shut-down and trigger a wide range of other conditions. In his case today, it looks like the abnormally low blood sugar levels kicked off the disease, which in turn triggered the kidney failure and loaded his system with toxins that healthy kidneys would normally cleanse automatically...' Mark took a breath. 'He's stable now. With the right medication, and some lifestyle and dietary changes, we can get his kidneys back on track... For now, at least.'

'What do you mean *for now*?' Orson cut in sharply.

'Even with the right treatment, and thankfully we caught it before it got too serious, kidney failure can only ever be fully addressed with a kidney transplant.'

Terran felt the words hang around them in the noisy cafeteria, their meaning refusing to sink into his mind.

Infection.

Chain reaction.

Kidney transplant.

'Can any of us be a donor?' He looked from Mark to Amit, his mind already in problem-solving mode.

Mark nodded. 'We'll need to take some blood from each of you and see if that's an option.'

'An option?' Orson shook his head, leaning forward, his voice rising almost in indignation. 'But we're brothers! Isn't that enough?'

'Even with blood relatives there's no guarantee any of you will be a match,' Amit said in a low, calming voice that Terran only found infuriating. 'We'll do the tests, and take it from there.'

There was a pause, and Terran saw Mark and Amit exchange the briefest of glances. He wanted to shake them, to force a solution out of them, something better than 'we'll take it from there.' It simply wasn't good enough.

'What if...' Kendrik's voice was low and feeble, and he suddenly sounded much younger than he was. 'What happens if we don't... If the transplant... If there's no donor...'

'For the time being,' Amit cut in softly, placing his hand on top of Kendrik's trembling fingers, 'Farao's stable. In normal circumstances, with the adequate treatment and a controlled diet he could be fine for another five, even ten years. Normally, we would have more time. But in Farao's case, the underlying condition is complicating things. It means regular treatment may not buy us as much time as it should.'

Terran shuddered. 'So, the other stuff... The immuno... something.'

'Aplastic immunodeficient anaemia,' Mark said. 'A.I.D.A. That's more concerning. It's a really rare genetic disorder...'

Mark paused again, and exchanged another look with Amit.

'What?' Terran pressed.

'When I say rare,' Mark said slowly, 'I mean really, *really* rare. But what we know for sure is that it always gets transmitted from the parent who carries it. For Farao to have tested positive for the disease, it means one of your parents had it, too, so you might be carriers as well.'

Terran stared at Mark, then at Amit. Next to him, he could see Kendrik frown.

'One of our parents…' Kendrik repeated, his voice numb.

Terran felt himself freeze.

'But…' Orson was shaking his head. 'We're fine. *We…*' He gestured to Terran, Kendrik and himself. 'We're alright, aren't we?'

'Sometimes it's more latent, and sometimes it's very acute. We see patients for whom it's dormant for most of their lives. The research is fairly new and unfortunately limited. It's unclear exactly what causes the condition to worsen,' Mark explained.

'I knew your parents for a long time,' Amit added. 'And I wasn't aware that either of them had it. When your mother was ill it never came up.' He took a long breath. 'For now, Farao is stable. In the meantime, let's get you three tested and take it from there.'

'Wait,' Orson said abruptly. 'Farao… How do we cure him?'

Mark's jaw tensed almost imperceptibly. 'The A.I.D.A. will require treatment for the rest of his life. Medication, regular check-ups and a controlled diet. There are really promising clinical trials going on at the moment which give me hope he can go on living a relatively normal life…'

Terran's stomach clenched.

Relatively.

'But…?' Terran frowned, sensing there was more.

'But…' Mark winced a little. 'The kidney failure is obviously a concern. We can keep him stable for a while,' he added quickly, seeing their worried expressions, 'but it can't just be reverted. We'll need a kidney transplant. Ideally, sooner rather than later so that Farao's body doesn't have to be under prolonged stress. We'll have to find as close a match as possible. We'll check if any of you is a suitable donor. That's the closest probability. Otherwise, we'll have to check the open donor waiting list.'

Terran felt Kendrik tense on his seat, and Orson's gaze trying to find his, but he couldn't look at either of them.

He'll be fine. He'll be fine. *We'll all be* fine, he repeated to himself over and over again, and it was all he could do to keep himself from breaking down.

Chapter 13
Orson

They sat in the waiting area for what seemed like an eternity, waiting to be called for the blood tests that would reveal whether or not one of them was a suitable donor, and whether they all carried the disease. It all felt too unreal, too insane. *It just can't be true*, was all Orson could think.

His gaze brushed over the dull-coloured linoleum floor, his heart racing with a lingering panic he couldn't seem to quash. He fidgeted in his chair, the most uncomfortable seat he'd ever sat on, his back and lower body protesting against the plastic. He checked his watch without really noticing the time, because all he could say with absolute certainty was that time seemed to be moving at its own excruciatingly slow pace. Every moment he spent in the overly sanitised room was a moment not spent making Farao better, and the lack of action was hurting more than he'd ever have thought possible.

He closed his eyes for a moment and breathed in deeply. There was a lump at the base of his throat that he couldn't swallow. The overwhelming presence of a truth he'd wanted so badly never to have to reveal. A secret he'd wished he could bury forever. But in this instant, Orson knew it was all about to come undone. There was a fifty-fifty chance he would need to say those words he didn't want to say, tell that horrible story he didn't want to tell, and watch the reality of it sink in on his brothers' faces. If Farao was the only carrier of the disease, he'd have to do what he knew he should have done long ago.

But again... He might not have to. If it turned out they were all sick, he wouldn't need to say anything at all. Orson exhaled sharply and shook his head, the words in his mind sounding as crazy as he knew they were. Was he really hoping that they were *all* infected with a rare genetic disease so that he wouldn't have to come clean to his brothers about everything he knew? Was he really that big of a coward? The word stung beyond anything, and he felt himself wince.

He shut his eyes a little tighter, rubbing his fingers against his temples. He couldn't think like that. He didn't want to be a coward—he winced again at the word—any longer. He'd avoided telling them anything for as long as he could. He had wanted to spare them the hurt. He had carried that secret for years on his own, teetering on the edge of madness for it, so that they wouldn't have to endure it. The secret had threatened to engulf him, but he would have done it a hundred times over if it meant none of his brothers ever had to face it. He wasn't scared of hardship, and he wasn't scared of death. He could take it. And he would, in an instant, if it meant they didn't have to suffer, without the shadow of a doubt.

Orson opened his eyes and he glanced around the room, to the disparate set of posters on the pastel-coloured walls, some of them so faded they looked like they'd been pinned there since the dawn of time. On one wall, a large advertising board made of brown cork held flyers listing everything that could possibly go wrong with the human body and mind. As Orson's gaze ran over each of the bold headlines, it occurred to him how breakable people were, how fragile. After what had happened to his parents, it amazed him that the fact still seemed to surprise him.

Minutes ticked away as though in slow motion, each of them feeling like hours. He observed the flurry of staff walking by at irregular intervals, having long since stopped looking up hopefully at every scrubs-clad person that waltzed by, wishing they would come to announce it was finally their turn.

Amit came to check on them after what turned out to only have been an hour and a half, but had felt like days, informing them they were next in the queue, and that someone would be coming to get them soon. Soon, as it happened, ended up being another forty-five minutes.

They were called in for someone to take their blood samples, and then they were waiting again, a cotton ball roughly taped into the crook of their elbow. At one point, Terran stopped a nurse to enquire about Farao, only to be told he was still asleep but they would be informed as soon as he woke up.

To Orson, this was the most maddening part of all. The interminable waiting to be spoken to. To be given an update. To be reassured. The waiting that never seemed to end, whilst around them the hospital kept buzzing with activity. It frustrated Orson that people could still be going about their business when his entire life felt like it was crumbling to dust between his fingers.

Amit joined them a while later, bringing them each a takeaway cup of coffee. He told them he'd just checked on the lab and they were doing their blood work as they spoke, so they should hear something soon. But by then the word 'soon' had lost most of its meaning, and Orson simply shrugged the update away.

He could feel the beginnings of a headache worm its way into his skull, fed by the unnaturally harsh lights emanating from the large bright squares in the ceiling and the constant buzzing of one thing or other around the room. The ventilation system was a constant purr in the background. One of the light bulbs seemed defective, and emitted a regular clicking sound above their heads. There were beeping noises in the distance, from unidentified machines and monitors. He caught fragments of murmured conversations between passing medical staff, from which he only picked up a word or two each time. *Critical. Ultrasound. Blood work. Surgery.* All the things he tried hard not to think about, but he couldn't help but wonder if they referred to Farao.

Eventually, a nurse came to inform them that Farao was awake and that they could go in to see him, but warned them he had been heavily sedated, and that he might still be groggy for a few hours.

Orson felt like he walked into the small, sparkly clean room in slow motion, each beat of his heart resonating inside his head as he approached Farao's bed. Farao was sitting propped up against some pillows. There was a tube poking out of the top of his hand, and he had been dressed in one of these revolting-looking hospital gowns. He looked exhausted, Orson thought, as he swallowed hard.

'So,' Orson said shakily, 'here is our drama queen! You know, there are more efficient ways of getting our attention.'

'Piss off,' Farao grumbled. His voice sounded tired, but he managed a small smile.

'How are you feeling?' Terran asked, taking a seat on the chair by Farao's bed.

'Grand…' Farao managed, with a slow grimace. 'Never better.'

'That's our boy.' Orson forced a smile, though the paleness of Farao's skin sent a chill down his spine.

'What happened?' Farao asked feebly.

'You fainted,' Terran said carefully, catching Orson's eye. 'They're doing some tests to make sure it wasn't anything serious.'

Farao said nothing for a moment. A small cough made him suddenly wince and close his eyes. Terran, Kendrik and Orson all rushed to his side, but Farao lifted a hand slowly and dismissed them.

'I'm fine, jeez…' he croaked, but Orson could see that he was still in pain.

A young nurse walked in, all smiles, making light conversation with Farao as he checked the monitors and the intravenous bag. He gave Farao some pills to swallow, made some notes on his file and announced, with yet another smile, that the doctor would be in shortly. It was a testament to how worried Orson was that he completely failed to notice what the nurse looked like.

By the time Amit joined them a little while later, Farao had fallen back asleep. Amit gestured to them to follow him out of the door, his face an unreadable mask. They stood together in the corridor, and Orson waited for the blow to fall. For some horrendous and imminent piece of news that they were all going to die. He could deal with his own demise, but the thought of his brothers having to face any sort of hardship broke his heart into a million pieces.

'I've just spoken to Mark,' Amit started, a pained expression on his face. 'Your test results came back. I've just… I wanted to be the one to talk to you.'

Orson felt himself rooted to the spot, incapable of the smallest of movements.

'And…' Amit continued, shaking his head in disbelief. 'I… I don't know how to say this… You're fine. All three of you. Completely *fine*. They re-ran Farao's tests to be sure, but it's definitely aplastic immunodeficient anaemia. But none of you is a carrier.' Then he added, almost as an afterthought, 'Or a suitable match for a donation.'

'Wait. What?' Kendrik's head jerked up suddenly. 'We're not carriers… What does that mean?'

Terran and Kendrik looked at each other, dumbfounded, and took in Amit's tense expression. Orson knew what was coming before he heard the words. Just as Amit opened his mouth, Terran spoke first:

'If the disease always gets transmitted from parent to child… And Farao is definitely positive for it…'

Orson's chest tightened.

'It means…' Terran whispered. 'Tarao's not our father's son. Is that it, Amit?'

Amit nodded slowly, and Orson could see that he wished it weren't true.

'What?' repeated Kendrik, louder this time. 'That can't be right. That's nuts! Amit, you need to tell them to check again, clearly they made a mistake.'

But Amit said nothing, he simply stood in front of them, his gaze slightly lowered.

Orson looked down at his shoes. Finally, it had come to this. Way too late, and still much sooner than he had hoped. Of all the scenarios he had played in his mind, this was not one he had imagined. He'd thought he'd have time. So much more time.

Somewhere in the background, Kendrik was still protesting, but none of the words reached Orson. He closed his eyes. When he felt a hand take a firm hold of his shoulder, he looked up, finally meeting Terran's stare. He gazed at his older brother, and he knew his expression and his silence said it all. He could see surprise, then recognition and hurt spread over Terran's face.

'You already knew,' Terran said.

There was no emotion in his brother's voice. It was a simple statement of fact, not even a question. Slowly, agonisingly, Orson nodded, and he finally gathered the courage to confess to them the biggest secret he'd ever had to keep.

Chapter 14
Gabrielle

We were happy for a long time. We celebrated the smallest of things and appreciated every little life victory. We lived in such a bubble of bliss we were at risk of never, ever touching solid ground again.

We rented the top floor flat in a gorgeous white-stone building. We made room for Terran, then Kendrik, then Orson.

We made up our very own ritual for naming our boys, and for no reason at all it made us feel like we were on top of the world. We were sharing so much love and happiness that it was manifesting into new life.

When he wasn't at the base, Anand would take the boys out for long drives to the beach, when the tide was low, and teach them to play cricket on the wide stretches of wet sand.

By the time they came back, dirty and wet but ecstatic, I would have dinner on the stove and the bath ready.

I wouldn't have wanted it any other way. It was the most wonderful time of my life. Even thinking about it now, it fills my heart with joy.

These were the happiest moments of our lives.

And then.

And then…

This is the part of the story where I feel myself faltering. I glance at the letter I've painstakingly started, and I find myself struggling for air. After so long carrying this secret, I don't know where to begin.

It was Anand's work Christmas party, a celebration held at the base every year, where the regiment and their partners came together for the occasion. I knew most of the officers and their wives by sight, though since the boys had been born we hadn't made time to socialise with them much. The party was held in one of the larger reception rooms, very much like the one where I had first met Anand, so many years before.

Anand was soon taken aside by one of his superiors to talk shop, as often happened given his status as squadron leader, and I excused myself. I set off to look for the restroom. I'd had a couple of glasses of champagne already, and the corridors were dark. Before I knew it I was lost. There was no one around to ask for directions. I kept walking for what felt like ages, my toes hurting from the high-heeled pumps I was wearing.

That was when I saw a light at the end of a hallway.

To this very day I can still remember with vivid accuracy the feeling of relief I had at seeing that light. It makes me sick to my stomach to think about it now.

I walked towards the light, intent on asking for directions back to the reception, and when I reached the open door, I saw a man standing there, bent over a filling cabinet. I knocked on the doorframe to signal my presence, and as he turned towards me I recognised the base's air commodore. He was a tall, portly man with an impeccably trimmed moustache. I'd only met him once or twice before, but I'd have recognised that man's narrow gaze anywhere. It had unsettled me before and it unsettled me then.

I can recall that, for a second or two, something in my tipsy brain told me to backtrack and run in the other direction.

How I wish I'd turned on my heels and run. Right there and then.

But, either because I was tipsy or out of consideration for manners and protocol, I didn't.

I look up at the ceiling, tears rolling off my cheeks and onto the letter in front of me.

Forgive me, Anand, I just didn't.

Chapter 15
Kendrik

Kendrik stared at Orson. He wanted to say something, to shout, to shake more answers out of his brother, but he found himself rooted to the spot.

'How?' Terran asked, his voice empty.

Orson suppressed a sob, and Kendrik thought how fragile he suddenly looked, devoid of his usual grandeur and banter.

'Since she... Since after she...' Orson whispered.

They waited, their eyes fixed on Orson. Kendrik couldn't move, waiting for the blow to fall.

'Before she died...' Orson started again, but he seemed unable to complete the sentence.

The silence thickened around them, suffocating and heavy. Orson took a deep breath.

'Before Mum died,' he repeated, seeming to steady himself, 'she left a letter. She gave it to me a few days before she… She said not to open it until she'd…' Orson winced. 'Until she was…'

He fell quiet again, and Kendrik couldn't bear to wait any longer. He opened his mouth to speak but, maybe sensing an outburst, Orson continued.

'She asked me to read it, and share it with you guys when the time was right… I didn't open it for a really long time. I just… I couldn't.'

'Orson.' Terran's voice was grave. 'What was in the letter?'

'That Farao… That she…' Orson shook his head, his eyes now tightly shut.

'Orson!' Kendrik was growing impatient, the unknown eating at him like a parasite.

'It's all true. Dad wasn't Farao's father,' Orson croaked.

'But what happened?' Terran pressed.

'She was…' Orson choked out, his voice merely a whisper now. He took in a deep breath and looked down. 'She was raped.'

Kendrik felt like he'd just been punched. The word rang in his ears, refusing to sink in. It couldn't be… It just couldn't. He couldn't accept it. He saw Terran mouth the word, as though trying to make sense of it. Next to him, Amit's jaw had fallen open, his face white as a sheet.

'What…' Terran shook his head, but he didn't seem able to finish his sentence.

They stood frozen in time. Kendrik thought they might never move again. The silence stretched, painful and claustrophobic, wrapping around them like a deadly snake.

'Did you know?' Terran asked, his voice sounding distant, a note of accusation in his tone.

Kendrik looked up, and saw Terran was looking at Amit.

Amit winced. 'Of course not.' He sounded hurt. 'I never... I didn't...' He was shaking his head, then seemed to recollect something. 'When you were doing the custody papers, do you remember whether your dad's name was on Farao's birth certificate?'

Terran looked to be considering Amit's words, but it was Orson who jumped in.

'The birth certificate's lying.' His voice was quiet. 'Dad knew, but they pretended like Farao was his.'

Terran gave Orson a long, searching look, then closed his eyes for a moment, seeming to still himself. 'Where's the letter?'

'At home.'

Terran's face was blank. He nodded quietly.

'Does Farao know?' Terran asked.

Orson shook his head. Tears were rolling down his cheeks, and Kendrik couldn't remember the last time he'd seen his brother cry. Terran looked at Orson sharply, still nodding. Kendrik felt Amit shift next to him. It couldn't be happening, was all Kendrik could think. It just couldn't be true. There was a sense of dread building up inside him, crawling up from the pit of this stomach, drowning him from inside. The sensation was enough to paralyse him. *This can't be happening*, he told himself again, over and over, willing for it to be true.

'Amit.' Terran suddenly changed gears, his tone back to an almost business-like manner. 'What do we do now? About Farao's condition?'

For a second, Amit looked taken aback by the change of topic, but he regained his composure.

'I'll check the donor directory, and we'll get him on the waiting list but...'

'But you don't think that's enough?' Terran interrupted him.

'No.' Amit shook his head sadly. 'Because of the aplastic immunodeficient anaemia, the likelihood that his body will reject a foreign organ is higher, so we need a near exact match, and the odds of

finding that out of a pool of random strangers are very low. Maybe…'
Amit paused and took a deep breath before continuing, adding, almost
as an afterthought. 'But, no… I mean, even if we knew who Farao's
biological father was, there'd only be a slim chance he'd be a viable
donor option… Who knows…'

They all turned to Orson, who shook his head.

'There's no name in the letter, but she talks about his rank…
I'm sure there's a way of finding out…'

'You never looked into it?' Terran asked, his tone almost
defiant.

Orson simply shook his head. There was a heavy pause and
Kendrik shuddered. The whole thing made him sick.

'Fine,' Terran said again, taking charge of the situation. 'Amit,
how long do we have?'

'It's hard to tell exactly. The A.I.D.A. can be unpredictable but
with adequate medication we can keep it under control. It's the kidney
failure we need to worry about…'

'*How long?*' Terran insisted.

'Without a transplant… Eight months, a year at the most…'

'Eight months…' Terran repeated, his voice shaking.

Kendrik watched Orson's face drain of its colour. Kendrik had
to lean against the wall to prevent himself from collapsing to the floor,
feeling suddenly dizzy. He looked around frantically, his hand over his
mouth, and spotting a cleaning trolley at the other end of the corridor,
he sprinted towards it, leant over the open bin bag hanging from it and
vomited heavily into it. The rush of bile burnt the back of his throat,
the acidic fluids spreading on his tongue. Suppressing a second gag
reflex, he spat as much saliva as he could into the bin. He straightened
up, wiping his mouth with the back of his sleeve, but he couldn't wipe
away the rancid aftertaste.

He walked feebly back to the others. Orson was crouched
against the wall, his eyes closed.

'Why don't you head home,' Amit was saying, addressing Terran directly. 'You guys need to talk this through, and this isn't the place for it.'

'We're not leaving Farao,' Terran snapped.

'He won't wake up for some time,' Amit insisted, then he added, seeing Terran ready to argue, 'Listen, I'll stay with him, ok? And I'll call you as soon as he wakes up. But you three have to take some time to talk about this.'

Terran still looked unsure but said nothing. Amit took out his phone and focused on the screen for a moment before looking at them again.

'I've ordered you a cab. Go home. I'll call you when Farao's awake.'

Terran hesitated for a moment longer. Then he shook his head and, reluctantly, led the way out of the hospital.

Chapter 16
Amit

Amit stepped onto the pavement outside the hospital doors and watched the cab turn around the corner of the street, taking Terran, Kendrik and Orson home. He waited until he was sure the car was well out of sight. Only then did he allow himself to crumble. He headed to the nearest bench and collapsed onto it, his head and heart heavy. He'd needed to be a pillar of strength for the boys, but he wasn't sure he could have kept his own grief under the surface much longer. He buried his face in his hands and sobbed, letting himself be swallowed by the pain of that new fragment of truth, that bombshell of everything that he'd just learnt.

'Gabrielle…' he whispered, and the feel of her name on his lips sent him sobbing harder.

He wished he'd known. He wished he could've done something —though what, he wasn't sure. He just wanted, more than anything, to have been able to help her bear the weight of her secret. And knowing that he hadn't, that she'd had to carry that terrible truth with her until she died, felt like a knife to Amit's heart.

He wiped his face with the edge of his sleeve, sniffing loudly. He passed his hands through his hair, his fingers closing around it in fistfuls, gripping with such force he thought he might just tear it out of his head. How had it come to this, he thought, and how on earth could he live with this revelation? He didn't know if he could do it. He wasn't sure he could take any more.

But he must, one way or the other. There was no other option. In his mind's eye, he tried to picture another life, another Amit, somewhere in a parallel universe, going about his day, living his life without any knowledge of the Dhawans. A version of himself who knew nothing of the family's hardships. He couldn't even imagine it properly. It felt wrong. The image seemed empty and colourless. The path he'd been on had taken so much from him. But it had also given him everything. He knew he wouldn't have had it any other way.

Amit's father, Ramesh, had been personal secretary to Anand's family in the forties back in New Delhi, managing the Dhawans' affairs. When partition had struck and Anand's father had lost everything, Ramesh had followed his employers to England, and together they had built a new life there. But despite starting over in the gutters in a new country, the bond of one-sided servitude that had existed between Ramesh and the Dhawans in India had persisted. A few years later, Anand was born. A few years after that, Amit came into the world and the relationship of deference between the fathers was inherited by the sons, growing exponentially when Amit's parents suddenly passed away and he was taken in by the Dhawans.

It was only after Anand's parents had both died, and Anand had been posted to a base in the south of France, that Amit had allowed himself to live a little. The sense of freedom he'd felt from being temporarily released from his service had been intoxicating. For many years he'd revelled in it, enjoying every minute of his independence, flourishing in his medical studies, planning a life for himself that no longer catered for Anand's every need.

But as with all good things, that wasn't to last. One fine day, years after Anand's move to France, Amit received a call from him. The voice that spoke on the other end of the receiver was unmistakably Anand's, but it was emptier than usual, hollow and dull. He was bringing his family back to England, he said, and preparations needed to be made. Amit had found a house, a car, arranged for their travel, and he'd been right there at the airport to pick them up when Anand finally landed, with three grown boys in tow... and her. Halfway through her pregnancy, and looking excruciatingly sad.

Her.

Gabrielle.

Amit had known right there on the spot that whatever he would do from then on would no longer be out of his obligation to the Dhawans. It would be for *her.* The moment he'd laid eyes on her, he'd wanted to take away her sadness, to wrap his arms around her and never let her go. He'd wanted to make everything alright for her, and fix whatever unspoken problem seemed to be lingering between her and Anand.

Amit had never known the extent of the story that had brought the family back to London, and he hadn't asked. He'd had his suspicions, of course, but he'd never been let in on the secret. As Anand veered further and further away from his family, so Amit took a more prominent role, picking up the slack, taking care of the boys, supporting Gabrielle as well as he could. She didn't talk much, but he could see in her eyes how grateful she felt for his presence, and that was all the encouragement he needed to persevere in his efforts. He'd never deluded himself into thinking she could ever be his. Regardless of what had happened between her and Anand, he could see she would forever love him. But that didn't matter much. Amit could be there for her. He could be her rock. And at times, when he was serving her and the boys dinner, when Anand was nowhere to be found and there was laughter around the table, then Amit could almost pretend, just for a moment, that this was all his. And for that one moment he felt complete. Utterly content with the world.

The months following Anand's passing had been tough on them all, and Amit had had to be stronger than ever to keep everything on track. For some time he'd slept on the couch in the Battersea house, getting up every few hours to feed baby Farao whilst Gabrielle got some rest. He'd taken care of paperwork, school logistics, life insurance, everything. The boys were too young, and Gabrielle was sinking further and further away from them all with each passing day, buried in grief. At the back of his mind, if Amit was honest with himself, he'd nurtured the hope that, in time, Gabrielle might come to regard him as something other than just a friend. That one day, maybe, she might find something like love in her heart for him. But that hadn't happened, of course. Even from the grave, Anand's ghost continued to haunt her, and it left no room for Amit to become anything other than he was—a good friend, someone to pick up the slack to keep them all afloat. He'd never overstepped.

When Gabrielle had passed away ten years later was the only time Amit had felt himself waver. His entire world had threatened to collapse around him. Once more, however, it hadn't been about him. There was no time for his own grief, because the boys, Gabrielle's sons, her everything, needed him more than ever. So he'd parked his sorrow and stepped up again, though at that time Terran was old enough to take up some of the load too. Amit had tried to convince Terran to let him apply for Farao's custody, to take care of them all, assuring him that he could carry the responsibility for them, but Terran had categorically refused. Amit had never managed to get him to budge on the matter, so he'd settled back into his supporting role, part of the family in some ways, but never quite a fully fledged member of it. It'd stung more than he'd cared to admit it, but as always, he'd swallowed his hurt. This wasn't about him. He knew it had never been, and never would be. But he had to be there. He had to help them.

And so life had gone on, with its twists and turns, with its difficulties, and Amit had stuck around. For her. For the memory of her. Because he knew that her sons had been her biggest pride and joy, and that he couldn't let her down.

Amit jumped out of his reminiscence when he felt a hand rest on his shoulder. He looked up to see Mark standing over him.

'Are you ok?'

'I'm fine,' Amit sighed, his voice still raw, standing up and straightening his jacket.

'Are you close to the family?'

Amit nodded. 'They're all I've got.'

Marked nodded slowly. 'I'm sorry it couldn't be better news.' His expression softened a little.

'It's alright.' Amit shook his head, because he knew better than anyone that this part of the job was never an easy one. 'Thank you for letting me break it to them.'

'Sure, that's no problem.'

They walked back to the hospital, stepping through the entrance doors and crossing the hall.

'I've already checked the donor list and put Farao's name down. It might take a while, but that's our best shot.'

Amit nodded again. 'Thanks, Mark. Keep me posted, will you?'

'Of course,' Mark said. 'I will.'

'And I'd like you to test me, too. See if I'm a match.'

Mark considered Amit from the corner of his eye for a moment.

'Of course,' he said again. 'Do you want to come by the lab now? I just need to get the paperwork ready.'

'Thanks, Mark.'

They walked through the corridors quickly, Mark leading the way, Amit trying his hardest to shake himself back into action.

A little while later, Amit stood, paperwork in hand, by the lab's waiting room.

'Amit,' Mark said, his tone sombre now, 'I know I don't need to tell you this, but you need to be prepared for the high likelihood that you'll just have to wait for a match on the donor's list. Just...' He frowned. 'Manage your expectations, that's all.'

Amit simply nodded. He'd given a similar speech of warning to countless people before, and he knew why he was at the receiving end of it now. He knew he needed to be rational, to think about the situation logically. To accept that the law of probability wasn't in his favour. But there was nothing rational or logical about the maddening sense of hope he felt at that moment, about the idea that he might be a suitable donor, that he could be the one to save Farao's life. He wanted more than anything for the universe to let him be the only one who could rescue him, not just for the boys' sake, but for *her*.

When the results came back negative a long while later, all Amit could think was that, once again, he was being reminded of his place. And it wasn't as her saviour. All he was good for was to be on the sidelines, a sub perpetually relegated to the bench, desperately waiting for a chance to prove himself worthy of her.

Chapter 17
Terran

The cab turned onto their street. They'd gone the entire ride in complete silence. To Terran, every passing second since they'd left the hospital had been torture. The sense of confusion and emptiness that had hit him after Orson's revelations had slowly been replaced with a desperate, frantic craze to get out. To step out of the car and run as fast and as far as his legs would take him. He couldn't stay still. He couldn't be here.

The moment the cab stopped by their house, Terran got out and ran up the steps to their front door. He fumbled with his keys, his hands trembling. He ran into the corridor and up the stairs to his bedroom, Orson on his heels.

'Terran,' Orson called out behind him.

'Not now, Orson,' Terran growled without looking at him, rummaging through his drawers, fishing out his running gear.

'Terran, we need to talk about this,' Orson pleaded.

'*Not. Now.*' Terran's voice trembled, his manic energy slowly morphing into cold fury.

He threw his clothes onto his bed and slipped into a tee-shirt and shorts. He had to get out of here, and fast. He couldn't do this. He couldn't talk. And he couldn't look at Orson. Not yet.

'Terran, please.' Orson's voice broke.

'I said *not now!*' Terran shouted, making Orson flinch.

He regretted his outburst the moment he finally looked at Orson and took in his pained expression. Terran bent over to lace his trainers, forcing his voice to settle.

'Orson,' he breathed, focusing on his laces, and it was all he could do not to lash out again. 'I can't do this right now. You had years to digest this. All this... You've had time to take it in. Right now I... I just can't. Just... Give me some time. We'll talk later, ok?'

Orson nodded quietly as Terran strode past him, grabbed hold of his keys and his phone and ran down the stairs. A glance through the living room told him Kendrik had gone straight into the garden, and was sitting on the stone steps leading onto the lawn. Somewhere at the back of his mind, Terran knew he should stay. He knew he should be there for them, but the overwhelming sense of chaos in his heart overrode whatever reasonable argument his mind was trying to make.

He headed out onto the street and began to run, setting out faster and harder than he normally would. He sprinted down the road to the nearest entrance to Battersea Park. There he picked up his pace even more, pushing himself harder, because the more intense the burning sensation in his legs and his lungs, the easier it became to ignore the burning of the horrible truth he could never unknow.

Before long, he was drenched in sweat and completely out of breath. The rush of frantic energy he'd felt just a moment before was evaporating, leaving in its place a growing sense of panic. He came to a halt by the Peace Pagoda, the tall white-and-gold structure towering over him like a godly presence. Then, suddenly, he leant forward, hands on his knees, and burst into tears. Orson's words swirled around in his head, mingled with Mark and Amit's medical spiel. None of it felt real. None of it felt like it belonged in their life. He wanted more than anything to wake up and realise it had all been just a bad dream. He wanted to go back to the time when the hardest part of his day was getting Farao out of bed, or fending off calls from the school, or paying their bills. The reality he had to deal with now was something he didn't think he could bear.

Terran sat on the steps, facing the Thames and its murky, swirling waters. He didn't know what to do. He felt lost, and confused, and hurt, and powerless. But above all, he felt angry. Angry that his mother hadn't told him any of this. Angry that Farao was sick. Angry that Orson had kept the truth from him. Angry at the man who had brought his dark shadow over their lives. And the more he thought about it the more his fury grew, until he was certain that had he been face-to-face with that bastard, he could have killed him with his bare hands.

His mother's face flashed into his mind and he felt himself tremble. She'd been sadder after they moved to London. Although he'd been young at the time, he remembered noticing that much. She'd looked preoccupied and distant, but he'd never really stopped to think about it. And then when their father had died, there hadn't been time or space to think about anything else. They were all grieving and struggling. But now he knew what else she'd been through, Terran could no longer think straight.

He wanted justice. He wanted to drag the monster who had hurt her through the dirt. He wanted revenge. He wanted to find that arsehole and expose him and ruin his life like he had ruined theirs. He wanted to look him in the eyes and hear him admit what he'd done. He wanted to destroy him and everything he held dear. He wanted to make him suffer, and in that moment it felt like that was the only thing that would ever make it even remotely ok.

By the time Terran made his way back to the house, his mind was made up. It wasn't in his power to undo what had happened, or to fix Farao's health, and the idea that there was nothing he could do to make it all better killed him from inside. But one thing he *could* do was avenge his family. He wouldn't let that bastard get away with it, even if it was the last thing he ever did.

***

When Terran walked back through the front door, he found Orson and Kendrik sitting at the dinner table. Orson had his head in his hands, and Kendrik was wearing the same stunned sort of look he had since they'd heard the news at the hospital. They both looked up when Terran came in.

'Terran,' Orson started, but Terran raised a hand to stop him and took a seat opposite him.

Orson looked pale, and more scared than Terran had ever seen him.

'Show us the letter,' Terran said firmly, and he saw Kendrik squirm in the chair next to him.

Orson said nothing. He simply stood up and made his way out of the room, disappearing up the stairs for a few minutes before coming back into the kitchen, taking his seat again. He placed an envelope at the centre of the table. Kendrik shuffled in his seat but made no attempt to take it. After a moment, Terran leant forward and picked up the letter, sliding it from the envelope and unfolding it carefully. There was a second envelope in there, addressed to Farao, and he raised a questioning eyebrow at Orson.

'That one's for Farao,' Orson said quietly, stating the obvious. 'I haven't opened it.'

Terran nodded and glanced at Kendrik, asking him silently whether he wanted to join in, but Kendrik closed his eyes and shook his head.

Terran refocused on the letter, grimacing at the familiar handwriting, wishing he didn't have to read what he knew his mother's words would say. The letter was five pages long, addressed to the four of them, and he read every bit of it carefully. He took in his mother's story, her secret, the reality of what had happened, why they had moved to London. He swallowed as he read her apology, and her failure to find the will to fight her illness, her guilty relief at knowing her end was near. By the time he reached the end, Terran felt sick. It had been one thing to hear the truth from Orson. It was quite another to read the confirmation of it from his own mother. He rubbed his face with one hand. He wanted to stand up, to do something, *anything*, but he wasn't sure his legs would support his weight right now.

Next to him, Kendrik had gathered his courage and picked up the letter, taking his time to read it too. A long, impenetrable silence settled around them. Eventually, Kendrik folded the letter again, and slid it back into the envelope along with Farao's sealed letter, his face grave.

'I can't believe you kept this from us,' Terran said, finally looking up at Orson.

Orson looked back at him, his eyes glistening with tears.

'I didn't know how to bring this up…' he murmured. 'I was waiting for the right time.'

'The right time!' Terran banged his fist on the table, making them all jump. 'The right time was seven years ago, Orson!'

'You think it was easy?' Orson shook his head, his expression pained. 'You think I *liked* carrying this around?' He gestured at the letter. 'That I liked having that kind of responsibility? I didn't know what to do with it! How could I?!'

'You should have told us.' Terran clenched his fists on his lap, trying to control himself.

'I'm sorry, ok?' Orson's breathing had grown erratic. 'I didn't tell you, and I'm sorry! Everyone was all over the place after she died, you were doing so much. I didn't know what to do. I didn't want this. I didn't want that stupid letter. I wish she'd given it to *you*. I never wanted to know, alright? I never wanted her secret, I never... I...'

Orson burst into tears and buried his face in his hands again, and the sight of his brother crumbling made Terran's anger waver, and then vanish. A long moment passed.

'No, Orson...' Terran leant forward and rested his hand on Orson's arm. '*I'm* sorry. I guess... I guess it's not your fault. I can't imagine what it was like going through this on your own.'

Orson glanced up, his face stricken with grief.

'I still wish you'd told us,' Terran said softly. 'But I suppose I get why you didn't.'

They fell quiet again.

'What do we do now?' Kendrik asked quietly, after a while.

'I don't know...' Orson breathed, shaking his head.

Terran stilled himself for what he was about to say.

'I want to find this guy.' His voice was cold, and he felt his brothers' gaze instantly on him.

Both Orson and Kendrik looked at him wide-eyed.

'*What?*' Orson frowned.

'I want to find this arsehole, and I want to make him pay for what he did.'

Kendrik stared at him, dumbfounded. 'Are you *serious?*'

Terran glared back at them, daring them to contradict him.

'Ter, what are you saying?' Orson shook his head. 'We can't go after this guy. What about Farao?'

'What about him?' Terran snapped.

'He needs us,' Orson insisted. 'He needs us *here*, with him. We can't get distracted now.'

'Distracted?' Terran felt the anger rise again at the pit of his stomach. '*Distracted*! This guy *raped* our mother, Orson! *Raped* her! And you want to let him get away with it?' he exploded, jumping to his feet.

'Of course not, but what can we do?' Orson's voice was rising too. 'Do you think that would fix anything? It won't! It happened so long ago, Ter! It's *done*. I hate it as much as you do, but there's nothing we can do about it now. And besides, we have no proof. We don't even know who this guy is!'

'Then we'll find out!'

'Terran, come on! Be reasonable!'

'No!' Terran shouted, slamming his hands on the table, the loud bang resonating in the kitchen around them. 'Our mother went through *hell*! Farao is *dying*! For fuck's sake, Orson, I won't stand by doing nothing whilst this guy is out there roaming the streets!'

'We don't even know that,' Orson groaned in frustration. 'We don't know who he is, or where he is. Damn it, we don't even know if he's still alive!'

'Then. We. Will. *Find. Out,*' Terran growled.

'Terran…' Orson pleaded.

'No! This isn't a discussion.' Terran cut him short, his temper threatening to take over again. 'If you don't want to help, *fine*, but I'm finding this bastard and I *will* make him pay.'

Terran strode out of the kitchen, leaving Orson and Kendrik in shock behind him, and stomped up the stairs. He went straight to the attic and pulled down the ladder, climbing up to the darkened room. He switched on the ceiling light and looked around him. He wasn't sure what he was looking for exactly. Orson was right, they had very little to go on. All they had was the man's rank at the time and the year it happened. They did know he'd been assigned to the same RAF base as their father, and that was a start. Terran rummaged through some of the boxes, looking for anything that might contain a clue.

Orson appeared at the top of the ladder and hoisted himself up into the attic, followed by Kendrik.

'I'm not discussing it,' Terran warned in a low voice.

'We're not here to discuss it,' Orson sighed. 'If you're going down this crazy rabbit hole then we won't let you do it alone.'

Terran glanced at Orson, then at Kendrik, who was still very quiet, and simply nodded.

'Good,' Terran said.

'What are we looking for?' Orson took a step forward, surveying the attic.

'I don't know...' Terran shrugged. 'Anything from Dad's RAF days, I guess.'

They found several boxes of interest, and they carried them downstairs, lining them all up down in the living room, ready to be inspected. They were about to get started on opening everything when Terran's phone rang.

'Amit?' Terran immediately picked up, dread bubbling at the back of his mind. 'Everything ok?'

'Yes.' Amit sounded tired on the other end of the phone. 'Farao woke up for a bit earlier, I went in to speak to him. He's a little groggy, but otherwise he's well. They've given him something to help him sleep again. It's unlikely that he'll wake up before tomorrow morning.'

Terran breathed a sigh of relief. 'Ok, thanks, Amit. I'll be down there in a bit. I can spend the night there.'

'You can't,' Amit said. 'They don't allow overnight visitors unless it's an emergency. Farao's fine, he'll be awake tomorrow, you can see him then.'

'Amit, I can't leave him alone there, I—'

'Terran,' Amit interrupted, sounding even more exhausted now. 'There's nothing you can do here. Farao's in good hands, they'll call you if they need anything.' Amit lowered his voice. 'Right now, it's Orson and Kendrik who need you. Focus on them, ok?'

Terran glanced at his brothers, who were both quietly looking at him.

'Ok.' He nodded. 'Just, call me if there's anything. I'll be at the hospital first thing tomorrow morning.'

'I'll see you there.'

Terran hung up and slid the phone back into his pocket.

'Is everything ok?' Kendrik asked.

'Yeah.' Terran knelt down on the hardwood floor, opening one of the boxes. 'Farao woke up for a bit earlier, but they've given him more pills and he'll sleep through the night. We can go back tomorrow.'

'Erm, Ter?' Orson said tentatively.

'Mmm?'

'We'll get started on these.' Orson gestured at the boxes. 'How about you start with a shower? No offence, but... you stink.'

Terran stared at him, only then realising he'd been wearing his running gear since he'd gone out earlier. Kendrik chuckled lightly behind them, though the sound of it felt shallower than usual.

'Fine.' Terran rolled his eyes, dragging his feet out of the living room. 'But no slacking in my absence!'

As he climbed up the stairs and stepped into the bathroom, he felt a little lighter. They were hashing out a plan, and the idea that there was something they could do, however mad it sounded, gave him more comfort than he could say.

Chapter 18
Orson

'Orson, are we seriously doing this?' Kendrik asked in a low voice, once they heard the shower start on the first floor.

Orson shook his head and sighed, his gaze on the ceiling.

'I don't know… I think Terran just needs something to focus on right now.'

'But this is *crazy*,' Kendrik insisted in hushed tones, coming closer. 'We can't track this guy down! And even if we can, what are we going to do? Show up at his house and beat him up?'

'I don't know…' Orson repeated, his heart heavy. 'I've never seen Terran like this before. Let's just…' He inhaled deeply. 'Let's just indulge him on this one. Maybe he'll realise how mad this is on his own, and we can all move on from it.'

'Mmm.' Kendrik frowned.

'Maybe knowing who that guy is, regardless of what we do about it, will give him some closure...' Orson shrugged. 'Maybe it'll give us all some closure.'

Kendrik gave him an uneasy look, but he didn't argue any further.

By the time Terran joined them a while later, they were sitting on the floor surrounded by paperwork, old records and photographs from their parents' life in the south of France.

'Any luck?' Terran asked as he took a seat next to them.

'Not yet.' Orson pointed at a small pile on one side of the floor. 'These are Dad's army records. We found the name of the base, but nothing about who was there with him.'

'Well, let's keep digging then.' Terran rubbed his hands together and grabbed hold of a box, rummaging through its contents.

Kendrik threw Orson a side glance, but said nothing. Orson sighed; he wanted to help Terran through this, and he knew better than anyone that learning something so traumatic could mess with someone's brains, even someone as rational as his older brother. He'd had to face the music when he learnt his mother's truth so many years before, and he knew he hadn't handled it well at all. He wished that, at the time, someone had allowed him to go a little crazy without judging him. *One brother at a time,* Orson thought, feeling drained. *Let us deal with Terran tonight, so we can get back to Farao tomorrow.*

But try as he might, Orson struggled to get Farao out of his mind. He couldn't help but remember what he had felt when he had finally plucked up the courage to read his mother's letter. He'd been seventeen then, the age Farao was now. A few days before she died, just as he was taking a seat to start reading to her, his mother had handed the envelope to him with shaking hands.

'For later,' she'd said in a feeble voice. 'After... After I'm gone.'

Orson had frowned then, staring at the letter like it was poisonous.

'Share it with your brothers,' his mother had said, pushing the envelope into his arms. 'Read it, and share it with them when they're ready. Please'

Orson could still feel the sense of dread that had submerged him at the time.

'Promise me.' His mother had closed his fingers around the envelope, her eyes pleading. 'Orson, promise me.'

'I promise,' he'd whispered, nodding slowly.

After she'd passed away, he had left the envelope unopened for weeks, carrying it around with him everywhere he went like a dangerous artefact. He hadn't dared to read it; he had not wanted to know what it contained, for fear that it would bury him in a pit of sorrow and grief even deeper than the one he had carved out for himself.

But eventually he hadn't been able to avoid it. He had needed to face it. He had bought a bottle of Smirnoff at a corner shop, fake ID in hand, and he had gone to sit on a bench in a quiet corner of Battersea Park.

It was strange that one of the things he remembered most vividly about that night was that he'd looked over at a couple sat on a picnic blanket on the grass a little way away. The guy had taken his shoes off and was wearing mismatching socks. One of them was navy blue with white stripes, and the other was red with some sort of polka dot pattern. Orson remembered watching the guy's socks, shaking his head, and becoming steadily angrier and angrier. It'd been irrational and silly—who cared about people's socks?—and he knew it had never really been about socks, but he could still picture it as clear as day, and he could still feel the uncontrollable anger that it had triggered.

He'd sat on his bench for a long time. There, eventually, he'd taken a strong gulp of the cheap liquor, then a second, then a third and finally, warmed by some Dutch courage, he had pulled the envelope from his jacket pocket, torn it open and read its contents.

He had read his mother's story, all five pages of it, with mounting horror and dread. He had reached the end of the letter and found himself frozen into place, his body and mind catapulted into an alternate universe where he no longer knew up from down and right from wrong.

It had taken a long, long time for the words to sink in. Those moments of numbness, sensing the truth grow and expand like toxic gas inside his mind, had been the closest Orson had ever got to an out-of-body experience.

But soon enough, emotions had come rushing in like a storm. It had started with shock, panic and incredulity, though that hadn't lasted. No. No, that had washed off pretty swiftly, to be replaced by only one thing. Anger. Fury of a magnitude he'd never experienced before in his life. His blood had felt like it was boiling under his skin, and all he had been able to think of at that time was the unfairness of it all. Why would his mother have done this to him? Why would she have burdened him with a secret so heavy and so painful? At his age! And why *him*? Had she not thought it would destroy him, as much as it had destroyed her? How was he supposed to live with that knowledge?

He'd stood up suddenly, letter in hand, looking around for something to kick, or punch, or both. The rush of adrenaline coursing through him needed an outlet, so he'd stomped to the nearest bin and kicked it, over and over again, until the pain in his legs commanded him to stop. He'd almost ripped the letter to shreds right there and then. He'd wanted nothing more to do with it. He'd wanted it gone. He'd almost, *almost* done it. His hands had been clasped around the paper, ready to tear the pages into bits.

But he hadn't done it. He'd tried. He'd tried so hard to, but he couldn't. And his inability to follow through had made him sit down again and read the letter a second time. Orson paid closer attention to the postscript the second time around, where his mother referred to a letter for Farao, which she trusted Orson would give him when he deemed his brother ready to hear the truth. And, in fact, upon closer inspection, there was a second letter in the envelope, a much thinner one, sealed and addressed to Farao.

The weight of so much responsibility had made Orson feel sick. It had crushed his insides and he had carried his anger around with him for a couple of years before it abated. He'd used his fury to fuel a lifestyle of extravagant partying and experimentation.

But even his anger had eventually run its course. It had vanished when, one day, in the dead of night, he had stumbled home from another drunken escapade to find young Farao sat in his pyjamas on Orson's bed, in the dark, crying.

Seeing his younger brother so powerless, so lonely and distressed had been a wake-up call for Orson. He'd felt an instant wave of shame wash over him. As he went to sit next to Farao and hugged him tight, Orson had finally known why his mother had chosen him. She had known his strength better than he had. She had known he would be the one Farao would need the most. And he knew that he had let her down.

Since that night, Orson had turned himself around. He had quit drinking in excess. He had started looking out for Farao. He had made sure he was there for him. He had wanted to do everything in his power to make amends, though he knew some damage had been done. He'd been a coward. A *coward*. A *fucking coward*. And he had a lot of making up to do.

Day after day, he had lived with the knowledge that his mother's confession and the envelope addressed to Farao lay neatly hidden in the lining of his guitar case, following him around like a ghost wherever he went. He told himself that when the time was right, he would know what to do. He'd thought that for years now, and he'd been waiting for that moment to manifest itself. After seeing how Terran and Kendrik had reacted, he was losing hope that there was such a thing as the 'right' time. Deep down, he dreaded the day he would hand over that second envelope to Farao and have to watch his brother's entire world crumble to dust around him.

Chapter 19
Terran

They kept at it for a couple of hours, mostly in companionable silence, sorting through everything they found, keeping a pile of anything that looked like it could be a lead. They came across some of their parents' wedding photos and passed them around, smiling at the radiant faces in the black-and-white shots. Terran studied one of the photographs. The bride and groom had their arms around each other, grinning broadly at the camera. The perfect picture of happiness.

'I can't believe Dad knew…' he mused.

'Mmm…' Orson stretched his legs, massaging the side of his neck. 'Things did feel tense between them after we moved…'

'I don't know… I guess I didn't see it at the time. Now I wonder if I just wasn't really looking properly.' Terran frowned at the photograph.

He wished he'd known better, and that he'd asked his parents the right questions when they were alive. But everything had felt a little

upside down back then—a new country, a new house, a new school…
There'd been so much going on, he hadn't read too much into the
weirdness at home.

Terran sighed. On the other side of the room, Kendrik was
quiet.

'You alright, Ken?'

'Mmm?' Kendrik looked up. 'Yeah, I just…' He glanced around
the room, and back at one of the wedding pictures he was still holding.
'This… It's just a lot, you know…'

'We'll get through it.' Terran nodded. 'We've got some leads. We
can look into the RAF base tomorrow, see if we can get more
information on that and…'

Terran paused, because the ceremonial dress uniform his father
wore in the wedding picture suddenly reminded of something. He
jumped to his feet and ran up the stairs, ignoring Orson's enquiring look
as he passed him. He rushed to his bedroom and picked up the framed
photograph from a shelf, the one he'd taken down from the attic not so
long ago. He checked the photograph and spotted his father again, in
the centre of the front row, right next to… Terran squinted. He
couldn't make out all of the medals on the man's uniform but he looked
decorated enough, possibly the highest rank in the base at the time.
Holding his breath, he removed the picture from the frame and turned
the photograph around. On the back of it were printed the names of
the entire squadron.

Terran let out a sharp breath. He went through the list. He
spotted the air commodore, marked by the abbreviation 'Air Cdre' in
front of one of the names: Aurelius Johnson-Bowles. *Wow*, Terran
thought. He even *sounded* like an arsehole. He checked the inscriptions
for the photograph's date—2004, a year before Farao was born—and
shivered when he realised it could match.

Could it be… Could this be their answer?

Orson and Kendrik walked into the room.

'Terran, what the—' Orson started.

'Look!' Terran exclaimed, pushing the photograph in front of their eyes. 'Here, see!'

Orson and Kendrik frowned at the picture.

'What...' Kendrik shook his head.

'Now, see here. That's the air commodore.' Terran turned the photo over, pointing excitedly to the date. 'The highest ranking officer. And here. The date. It fits! This could be our man! We've found him!'

Terran felt himself buzz with anticipation. They had done it! He was sure of it. They had the answer; all they needed to do was find out where this man lived, and they could... they could... He frowned. Could *what?* He shook his head, his gaze finding the round, stocky figure of the air commodore next to his father in the front row. He swallowed with difficulty. He had to know. He simply *had to*. He just had to find that man and look him in the face, and see him take responsibility for what he'd done. He didn't know if he could live with himself otherwise, knowing he'd never tried to right that wrong.

He looked up to share his thoughts with his brothers, and caught Orson and Kendrik exchanging a meaningful glance.

'What?' Terran frowned.

Kendrik looked awkwardly to one side. Orson seemed to brace himself to speak.

'*What?*' Terran repeated, his annoyance spiking up again.

'Ter...' Orson said carefully, and he took the photograph from Terran, putting it back on the shelf. 'Just... Think this through.'

'I *have*. We've already spoken about this,' Terran groaned.

'I mean *really* think this through,' Orson said calmly. 'Say this is our man. Say we can find him. *Then* what?'

'Then...' Terran started, unsure how to phrase his earlier train of thoughts. 'Then... We go.'

'Ok.' Orson raised his hands, speaking in a measured sort of way that was getting on Terran's nerves. 'We find him. We go. Then what?'

'Then…' Terran hesitated. 'I don't know, ok!' He stormed past them out of the room, grabbing the photograph on his way, and stomped down the stairs.

Orson and Kendrik followed him.

'Terran,' Orson called after him. '*What* is this? Why is it so important to meet this guy? Can't we just put it behind us?'

Terran spun on his heels, fuming again beyond reason.

'*Put it behind us*, Orson? Are you serious? You read what this guy did! Farao's in the fucking hospital because of him! We have to find him!'

'It's not going to solve anything!' Orson said loudly back. 'It just isn't. It's *done*, ok? You can't change that!'

'So what?!' Terran shouted. 'We're going to know what's in this letter, and accept it, and do nothing? What are we? Fucking cowards?! Because that's what we are if we sit there and do *nothing!*'

Shock spread across Orson's face, soon replaced by resolution. He walked slowly past Terran into the living room, pausing in front of the mantelpiece, his eyes flickering to the family pictures lined up there. When he turned back towards Terran, his face was unreadable.

'Is that what you think?' Orson said gravely. 'That I'm a coward for knowing about this all this time and doing nothing?'

They stood facing each other. Once again, Terran's fury flickered away, until it was no longer there, as realisation struck.

'Orson, that's not…' He took a step forward. 'That's not what I meant.'

'Yes.' Orson nodded. 'That's exactly what you meant.' He glowered at him from the other side of the room, his voice so low it was merely a rumble. 'You think this didn't kill me, too? You think I didn't hate myself every single day for knowing the truth and not being able to do anything about it? What? You think I felt *special* being the one to bear this burden? And you think *I* never wanted to find that guy and kill him?'

Terran shook his head, regretting his outburst but not knowing what to say.

Kendrik stepped in beside him. 'Guys, let's not…'

'No,' Orson said sternly, slamming his hand on the mantelpiece. '*Let's*. Let's put it all out in the open.' He walked towards Terran and stopped right in front of him. 'You think I don't want closure, too? I do. You want to go meet this guy? *Fine*, let's go. But don't you call me a coward, Terran. You've known about this all of ten hours and you think you know what it's like? Try living with this for seven *fucking* years. Try growing up with that knowledge as a teenager and having to act like everything's fine and life's a walk in the park. And then… *then*, we'll talk about who's a bigger coward.'

'Orson…' Terran choked.

He reached out for Orson's shoulder but Orson shook him off.

'I knew what it felt like,' Orson murmured. 'Living with that secret. And with the certainty that nothing could ever be done to change it. So, no. I didn't tell you. I *couldn't* tell you. I couldn't give you that curse, too. If I could have, I would have taken it to my grave.'

Terran leant forward and enveloped Orson in a tight hug. This time Orson didn't resist.

'I'm sorry,' Terran whispered. 'Orson, I'm so sorry.'

'It's ok,' Orson said quietly.

But Terran knew it wasn't ok. Nothing was. And nothing would be until they all had closure. Now that they all knew, they had to do *something* about it. And maybe finding the air commodore wouldn't fix anything, but right now it felt like their best shot of ever being able to move past this.

Chapter 20
Kendrik

They sat in the darkened living room for a long time, empty takeaway containers dotted around the room, their only source of light a candle Terran had lit. Orson had poured them each a shot, and their empty glasses lay on the hardwood floor beside them. Kendrik's forehead was resting on his knees, his fingers knotting and unknotting around his shins. He was feeling queasy again, unsure whether or not he might throw up. Terran and Orson's earlier confrontation replayed in his mind, making him feel more light-headed than ever.

'Farao cannot know.' Terran's low voice resonated in the quiet room.

Kendrik looked up and stared at him.

'About any of this. He *cannot* know. He's so volatile already, this will destroy him.'

'Ter...' Orson started, his voice cautious.

'No.' Terran's tone was firm. 'We can fix this. We can find this guy. We can get a donor on the donor list. And Farao doesn't have to know until we've arranged for a solution.'

Both Orson and Kendrik were silent for a moment. Kendrik stared at Terran in disbelief. The last thing they needed, he thought bitterly, was more secrets.

'He has a right to know the truth,' Orson said quietly.

'He won't be able to take it,' Terran insisted. 'We're *not* telling him.'

'So what,' Orson snorted. 'We'll keep all of this from him? That's not fair.'

'It doesn't have to be fair,' Terran snapped. 'It wasn't fair on us either, but here is it. It is what it is. We can *fix* this,' he repeated. 'So that he doesn't have to worry about it.'

'We can't hide this from him.' Kendrik shook his head. 'This is too big.'

'We can,' Terran said, louder this time. 'And we *will*. Until we have a donor.'

'And the guy?' Orson probed.

They seemed to have reached a tacit agreement to never speak the man's name.

'Once we've found him,' Terran said carefully, 'we'll tell Farao everything. So he has a choice. He can come with us to see him if he wants to.'

'I'm not sure about this, Ter…' Orson frowned. 'See how you reacted when you found out *I* hid the truth from you? It'll be a million times worse when Farao finds out about this.'

'He'll see that we were trying to protect him,' Terran persisted. 'Like we did, with you. Eventually.'

'Even if we find this guy—and that's a big *if*,' Orson said, 'why would he even speak to us? What if he doesn't even hear us out? And what would you even say?'

'I…' Terran looked dumbfounded for a moment. 'I don't know, okay!' He sighed in frustration. 'I just want him to admit what he's done!'

'Him admitting what he did, and I'm not sure why he would'—Orson raised his eyebrows—'won't change what happened.'

'For fuck's sake, Orson, we've talked about this!' Terran groaned.

Orson shuffled in his seat. 'No, Ter, we haven't. Not in a way that's realistic. You think this is traumatic for *us* to deal with? Think about what this will do to Farao when he finds out. Let alone being *confronted* with that guy.'

'Exactly.' Terran sounded stubborn. 'Which is why he doesn't need to know just yet.'

'Terran…' Orson sighed.

'And!' Terran interrupted, suddenly seeming to remember something. 'Amit said this guy could be a donor, right? So, if we find him, we can see if he's a match. See? This could save Farao's life!'

Kendrik threw Terran a dubious look, not sure what to say to bring his brother to see reason, and no longer clear himself on what the reasonable thing to do was.

'He said it was still a slim chance.' Orson shook his head. 'There's no guarantee.'

'But it's still worth a try,' Terran persisted.

'So,' Kendrik said slowly, 'you want him to not only admit to something criminal he did seventeen years ago, but also to put himself through surgery for someone he's never met?'

'We won't give him a choice!' Terran exclaimed.

'Listen—' Orson started, but Terran didn't give him a chance to continue.

'No, *you* listen! Am I the only one who's taking this seriously, or what? Can you stop fighting me on this, and can we at least *try* to find this guy?'

'But what good will it—' Kendrik said quietly, more to himself than to the others.

'No!' Terran cut across him too, raising his hands in protest. 'Enough! Help me, don't help me, that's your call, but *I'm* looking into this, alright?'

Kendrik caught Orson's eye, and Orson shook his head. All Kendrik felt was confused and overwhelmed. He understood Terran's desire for revenge, and Orson's need for caution, but he struggled to figure out where he stood in all this.

Orson let out a long breath. 'Fine, we'll try to find him, but...' He threw Terran a warning look. 'When we do, we *will* be talking about all this calmly and reasonably. We're not dragging Farao down in a vendetta he's not ready for and might not even want. Deal?'

Terran nodded once. 'Fine.'

'I mean it, Ter,' Orson insisted.

'Me too.' Terran held his gaze for a moment.

Kendrik watched his brothers in silence. He found himself wishing he could curl up on the couch and sleep forever, only to wake up when everything was right again.

'Alright then.' Orson cleared his throat, reaching towards the coffee table for his laptop. 'Let's get started.'

Chapter 21
Orson

They agreed that Terran would head over to the hospital in the morning to check on Farao when he woke up, whilst Orson and Kendrik both took the day off and stayed back to start tracking down the man. They had his name and the details of the RAF base, so they started from there. They did a few internet searches on him, coming across a handful of articles and old archives about his military career. The dates of his posting at the base definitely overlapped with their father's, and his appearance matched the vague description their mother gave in the letter, reinforcing their conviction that this was the man they were after. The more they found, the more Orson felt sick. He scrolled down the article he was skimming through.

'Thank God for the internet,' he sighed, closing the tab he had open. 'How did people even do this kind of stuff before Google came along?'

Kendrik simply shrugged. He was going through some of the papers they had set aside the previous night.

'I think we'll just have to call the base,' Kendrik said absentmindedly. 'It doesn't look like this guy is listed anywhere...'

Orson pondered this for a moment. He'd been toying with the idea too, but he wasn't sure how to go about getting such personal information, especially over the phone. Whatever they came up with, they'd need an iron-clad story to justify getting those details. He rubbed his eyes, starting to feel the lack of sleep. They hadn't gone to bed until late the night before, and the emotional rollercoaster they'd been on was starting to take its toll.

'I think you're right,' Orson yawned, reaching out for the coffee pot and refilling his mug. 'We just need to come up with a convincing reason why they should share that stuff with us...'

'We could tell the truth?' Kendrik suggested.

Orson snorted. 'That we're accusing one of their most decorated veterans of rape and we want to track him down, possibly to beat the shit out of him? Yeah, I'm sure that'll work...'

'I meant...' Kendrik rolled his eyes. 'Some of the truth. Like, we can say our father worked with him, and... I don't know... We're looking for people who knew him.'

'Mmm,' Orson mused. 'That's actually not a bad shout...' He stood up, coffee cup in hand, and started pacing around the kitchen, thinking. 'Maybe we could say... That we're putting together an homage to our father... For our younger brother, who's never known him... Maybe for his birthday or something?' he said, thinking out loud. 'And that we're looking for people who knew our dad well to help paint a picture... And that our dad really looked up to that guy, or something...'

'Play the sentimental card.' Kendrik nodded.

'Mmm.' Orson thought again, leaning against the kitchen counter, then he added with a mischievous smile, 'Well, if there were ever a time to utilise my being incredibly charming, I think this is it!' He sat back at the table, ignoring Kendrik's eye roll. 'Let's get our story straight. The key to a convincing lie is in the details…'

They noted everything down, making sure it all lined up and they had their facts straight. When they were done, they looked at each other.

'So, we're doing this?' Kendrik asked.

'Yep.' Orson pulled his phone out of his pocket, gearing himself up for a good performance.

He dialled the base's number, trying to ignore the nerves building at the back of his mind. A receptionist picked up the call almost immediately.

'Royal Air Force Saint-Blaise, this is Tiffany speaking. How may I assist you?'

Orson took a deep breath, and dived right in.

'Hi, Tiffany.' He smiled into the phone. 'My name is Orson Dhawan. My father was a squadron leader at the Saint-Blaise base back in 2004. I wonder if you could help me with something. See, the thing is…' Orson kept his voice measured, with a hint of emotion. 'I have three brothers. Our dad passed away when we were all very young, but our youngest brother, Farao, was only six months old when he died. So, he never knew him.'

There was a pause at the other end of the line.

'And with our brother turning eighteen later this year,' Orson continued, as convincingly as he could, 'we wanted to do something special for him. So we're trying to find some of our father's old friends and colleagues, hoping they can share pictures and memories they have of him. To give our brother a better idea of who our dad was.'

'That's… A lovely story, Mr…' Tiffany said tentatively.

'Dhawan. But you can call me Orson.'

'Mr Dhawan,' she repeated. 'That's all well and good, but I'm not sure what I can do to help you with that.'

'Well…' Orson took a breath. 'It would be a huge help if you could give me the contact details of some of the people who served with him, back in the day? I'd love to talk to them about the time they had with him.'

Another pause on the line.

'I'm sorry,' Tiffany apologised, her voice stiff. 'But I'm afraid I can't disclose that kind of information.'

Orson's heart sank.

'Tiffany, please,' he pleaded. 'There must be *something* you can do.'

'All of our records are confidential, we're not at liberty to share them with anyone. Especially not with civilians.'

'I…' Orson threw Kendrik a desperate look.

He felt their chance slipping away from him, and he wasn't sure how to salvage it. Kendrik rounded the table and searched frantically amongst the papers, fishing out the old photograph and turning it around, pointing at the list of names and mouthing, 'What about them?'

'Listen, Tiffany.' Orson heard the begging in his voice. 'I understand that you can't tell me how to contact the people who served with him, but can you at least tell me if any of them are still at the base today? Like…' Orson scanned the list. 'Aurelius Johnson-Bowles, John Stemming, Charles Farrington, Henry Miles, George Colester…'

'Wait a second,' Tiffany interrupted. 'Let me put you on a hold for a moment.'

'Sure,' Orson breathed, his heart thumping, as classical music started playing at the other end of the line.

They waited tensely for a few minutes that felt like hours, before Tiffany's voice came on again.

'Mr Dhawan?'

'Yes, I'm still here.'

'I've just been authorised to let you know that Group Captain Farrington is still here at the base.'

Orson's heart skipped a beat.

'I can't promise you anything,' Tiffany said carefully. 'But let me see if I can reach him. I'll put you on hold for a minute.'

'Thank you,' Orson breathed. 'So much.'

The same piece of music started on the phone, and Orson covered the receiver and pulled the phone slightly away from his mouth.

'One of these guys is still there,' he explained to Kendrik. 'She's going to see if she can get him on the phone.'

'*The* guy?' Kendrik mouthed.

'No, this one.' Orson pointed at one of the names on the back of the photograph.

They waited for a few more minutes, the classical notes resonating in Orson's ear like a fanfare. In front of him, Kendrik was absentmindedly cracking each of his knuckles, his gaze fixed on him.

'Mr Dhawan?' Tiffany's voice came back shortly after.

'Yes?' Orson responded immediately.

'I'm afraid Group Captain Farrington is in training today and tomorrow, so he won't be able to come to the phone. But I can pass on your details and ask him to get back to you when he has a moment?'

'Yes,' Orson said quickly, a little disappointed. 'Yes, that would be great. Thank you.'

'Is the number you're calling from the best number to reach you?' Tiffany asked, her voice a little more businesslike now.

'Yes,' Orson nodded. 'Yes, it is.'

'Very well, Mr Dhawan. I'll pass on the message for you. Was there anything else I could assist you with today?'

'No, that was everything. Thank you so much for your help, Tiffany.'

'My pleasure, have a nice day.'

'You too.'

Orson hung up the phone and shrugged.

'And now…' He sighed, looking at Kendrik, running a hand though his hair. 'We wait.'

Chapter 22
Farao

When Farao awoke, he knew only one thing for certain: he was feeling like *shit*. There was a soreness in his abdomen that made it uncomfortable to lie down, but he didn't feel like he had the strength to sit up either.

It took him several moments to remember where he was and why he was there. He turned his head to one side and his eyes found Terran in the armchair beside his bed, fast asleep. He gave sitting up another try, and slowly, carefully, propped himself higher up his pillow.

'Hey,' Terran said groggily from the chair.

'Hey,' Farao said, settling himself. 'What time is it?'

Terran glanced at his watch, and let out a broad yawn.

'Eight thirty in the morning.' He stretched his neck. 'How are you feeling?'

Farao tried to shrug, but that too felt unpleasant.

'Like shit,' he responded.

'Yeah, you and me both,' Terran grumbled, standing up from his seat and wincing.

There was a moment of silence as Terran walked to a side table and picked up a small water bottle, drinking almost half of it in one go.

'Did you sleep here?' Farao asked, his mind slowly waking up to the situation.

'No.' Terran rubbed a hand over his face. 'I got here about an hour ago. I must have dozed off...'

'Where are Orson and Ken?'

'Home,' Terran answered. 'They'll be here in the morning. Well... Later in the morning.'

Terran paused and gave Farao a long, searching look. Terran looked older, somehow, and worried. Farao shifted against his pillow. He couldn't fully read the expression on his brother's face, but he was definitely not awake enough for a long heart-to-heart conversation.

'Jeez, Ter, lighten up,' Farao groaned, looking away. 'It's not like I'm fucking dying or anything.'

Terran coughed heavily mid-drink, spluttering water down his tee-shirt.

'Shit!' Terran swore, looking around for something to mop up the mess.

Farao watched him pat himself dry with a handful of tissue paper from the bedside table for a moment.

'Hey, Terran?'

'Mmm?' Terran looked up, distracted, balling the tissue in his hand and glancing around for a bin.

'What's going on?'

Through the cloud of confusion covering most of his brain, Farao thought Terran had frozen for a second before he walked off towards the waste bin at the other end of the room.

'What do you mean?' Terran asked over his shoulder.

'They haven't told me what's wrong with me.' Farao wanted to stay alert, but he couldn't help a yawn. He was *so* tired.

'Oh, yes.' Terran came back to sit on the chair by his bedside. 'Nothing serious, apparently.'

'Like what?'

Terran seemed to still himself. 'There's something wrong with your kidneys. Caused by tiredness and bad diet apparently. Nothing to worry about.'

Farao frowned, incredulous. 'Tiredness and bad diet?'

'Yeah.' Terran shrugged. 'Turns out we have a history of dodgy kidneys in the family, so those things can happen. Means your body can struggle a little if you overload it. I guess you just eat more junk than we do.' He gave a small smile.

Farao considered his brother for a moment. He supposed he didn't have the healthiest of lifestyles. He'd never really looked after what he ate, and he didn't exercise. He yawned again, wondering why he was still so incredibly exhausted, since all he'd done since he got to the hospital was sleep.

'Why am I here, then? If it's not serious.'

'Well.' Terran leant back in his chair, crossing one ankle on one knee. 'Because you're genetically preconditioned for kidney problems, they want to run a few more tests and keep you under observation for a while, to make sure it flushes out all of the toxins it needs to properly. It's just a precaution, really.'

Farao's eyelids felt so heavy, and the more complicated words Terran used, the more he just wanted to go back to sleep.

'Mmm,' he mumbled, stifling another yawn. 'Guess it sort of makes sense… Kinda feels like overkill, though.'

'Well,' Terran said again, giving him a tired smile, 'better safe than sorry.'

'Yeah. I guess.' Farao rolled his eyes, settling back against his pillow, vaguely wondering if he should ask any more questions, but realising he didn't have it in him to process it all.

At that moment a nurse walked in, one that Farao hadn't seen before, and who introduced herself as Amanda. She asked Terran to step out for a moment whilst she completed some routine checks. Farao had the feeling Terran was relieved to have an excuse to leave, but he wasn't alert enough for the thought to linger. Amanda reviewed the monitors around his bed before checking the bag hanging over his head and the tube linking it to his hand. She made light conversation as she went, but Farao felt she wasn't truly listening to his mumbled answers as much as trying to distract him from the dry routine she was engaged in with his equipment. When she was satisfied everything was okay, she put on a pair of medical gloves and probed around his stomach, asking him whether or not it hurt, and where. Farao winced almost every time she touched him. Amanda clipped a small glass bottle onto the IV tube attached to the top of his hand, standing watch over him until it all went through, giving him a motherly sort of smile as he sighed and laid his head back against his pillow. He didn't bother asking what was in the bottle. His brain wasn't in any condition to digest much information, swimming as it was still in a light fog of drugged exhaustion and confusion. Amanda unclipped the little bottle of medication and mechanically turned around to drop it into the dedicated bright yellow waste bin at the far end of the room. She asked him whether he needed anything, but by then Farao's mind had started to blur again and he wasn't sure he could move his lips to answer. He had fallen back to sleep before she'd closed the door behind her.

Chapter 23
Kendrik

It was another two days before they heard anything back from the Saint-Blaise base. Kendrik knew they'd said they shouldn't expect to hear anything soon, but the wait was still agony. Kendrik, Orson and Terran were home one late afternoon, having just returned from the hospital, when Orson's phone finally rang from an unknown caller. Orson slid his thumb across the screen, picking up instantly.

'Hello?' His voice was shaking a little.

Kendrik and Terran exchanged a glance. Kendrik couldn't hear the voice on the other end of the phone, and he found himself fidgeting on the spot, impatient to know who it was.

'Yes, speaking.' Orson nodded, then paused, listening for a few seconds. 'Yes, Group Captain Farrington, hi,' he added, throwing Kendrik and Terran a meaningful look. 'Thank you so much for calling me back.'

Orson motioned to the others to come closer, pressed the speaker button and popped his phone at the centre of the kitchen table for them all to hear.

'I'm sorry it took a while to get back to you.' Charles Farrington's voice came bursting out of the phone. 'I've been away in training for the last few days.'

'That's no problem at all, sir,' Orson said.

'I hear you're after information about your father?'

'Yes.' Orson nodded. 'We're putting something special together for our younger brother's eighteenth birthday, and we were hoping to get stories about our dad from people who knew him.'

'I knew your father really well,' Farrington said. 'I served under him many years ago. I was really sorry to hear he passed. He was a good man. And a great leader.'

Orson, Terran and Kendrik exchanged a smile laced with pride and sadness.

'Thank you for saying that, sir,' Orson said, his voice breaking a little.

'So, what did you want to know?'

'We were hoping to reach out to several people who were with him at the base, people who knew him, and speak to each of them, and we wondered if you could help.'

'I see,' Farrington mused. 'Well, we don't generally give out contact information for our officers, as I'm sure you understand…'

Kendrik felt his face fall. Looking at Terran and Orson, he could see the disappointment hit them too.

'But,' Farrington added, 'I had huge respect for your father. And it would be a shame for his boys not to know the kind of man he was.'

Kendrik held his breath, listening intently.

'So here's what I'm going to do,' Farrington continued. 'I still have pictures and mementos from that time somewhere. I'll look through my things, I have no issue sharing that with any of you. For the others, I can reach out to the people I'm still in contact with to pass on the message. Beyond that, the ones I've lost touch with, I'll need to make sure we're definitely allowed to provide that kind of information. I think I can make a case for it, but it might be classified information. Once I hear back, I'll let our office know about our conversation, and get them to contact you with whatever details we're able to provide. They will need to run an ID check, so they'll ask for some paperwork and a copy of your passports. Possibly birth certificates, too. To confirm you are who you claim to be,' he added. 'Just protocol. Provided we get the go ahead, once that's all done, I'll make sure they cooperate. That's the best I can do.'

Orson and Terran's faces lit up.

'Sir…' Orson breathed. 'Thank you so much, we're really grateful for your help.'

'I know this is what your father would have wanted,' Farrington said solemnly. 'I'll go through my things, fish out some old photographs for you, and we can plan another call for me to answer any questions you have once we've passed the ID check.'

'Absolutely. Thank you,' Orson said again, his voice charged with emotion. 'Thank you, sir.'

When the call ended, they all looked at each other.

'One step closer,' Terran said quietly. 'It's happening.'

***

The following day, they got a call from the base requesting proof of ID, each of their birth certificates and their parents' marriage certificate, which they scanned and emailed the moment the call was over. They'd been told it might take a few days to complete the checks, but that someone would be in touch to confirm whether everything was in order.

It was several days before they heard back from the base. Their office had needed to contact their father's former colleagues to get consent for their details to be shared. The base would only be allowed to pass on information for those who had no objections. When the operator listed the names they could provide information for, including Aurelius Johnson-Bowles, Kendrik thought he might faint with trepidation. There was a sort of giddy lightness in the air as Kendrik slumped beside Orson on the couch after he hung up the phone. He could almost feel that everything would turn out okay. He didn't dare think of what would happen if it didn't.

Their contact at the base had informed them that, as a security measure, rather than email the list to them, they would send it via private courier, and it might take another day or two to arrive.

They waited impatiently for the next couple of days, ensuring one of them was always there to receive the post when it was delivered. The doorbell finally rang one morning, when the three of them all happened to be home. Orson tore the envelope open the moment he'd closed the door on the delivery man, a young uniformed officer who'd nodded at them solemnly as he handed the package to them. Kendrik scanned the documents over Orson's shoulder. There was a postal address listed for Johnson-Bowles.

'Marseille…' Orson said aloud. 'I guess that's where we're headed…' He looked up, giving Terran a questioning look. 'If that's still the plan?'

Terran hesitated for a second, then nodded, a new sense of resolve glinting in his eyes.

'Yes,' he said firmly. 'Yes. That's still the plan.'

'So.' Orson's tone was careful, eyeing Terran with apprehension. 'Can we talk about this reasonably now?'

'Sure.' Terran nodded, his voice level, as though he'd been preparing for this. 'We have the guy's address. We go and find him. We make him fess up to what he did. We get him tested to see if he can be a donor, which is the least he can do given the circumstances. And then we come home.'

Orson gave a mirthless laugh. 'Sure, Ter. Come on, be serious.'

'I *am* serious,' Terran insisted.

Here we go, Kendrik thought, suddenly feeling more exhausted than ever.

'And I'm sure he'll be welcoming us with open arms when he hears why we're there, and comply without any objection.' Orson rolled his eyes.

'We won't give him a choice,' Terran insisted. 'We'll camp outside his house if we need to. We won't give him a fucking choice!'

His voice reverberated around them and ricocheted against the walls.

'What about Farao?' Kendrik said quietly, finally finding his voice.

'What about him?' Terran frowned.

'How do we explain us disappearing for however long this will take?'

'We'll take him with us!' Terran retorted. 'We'll all go!'

Orson and Kendrik exchanged a glance, and Kendrik knew they both wondered if their older brother had lost his mind.

'Ter.' Orson shifted in his seat. 'I don't know if it's a good idea for Farao to go anywhere in his condition.'

'It'll be fine.' Terran's tone was escalating. 'Amit said he'd be ok with the right medication for a while.'

'Terran—' Kendrik started.

'No!' Terran exclaimed, his face contorted with anger and hurt. 'No! We are *doing* this, you hear me? I don't care who this guy is or how many fucking medals he's got, but Farao's our brother. Our little *brother*. And we have to do something. We have to do something *now*. We *have to*, okay? Because I…' Terran's voice broke. 'I can't live with this. Not like this. We have to do *something*. I need to know. And Farao will too, when he finds out. We owe him that. We owe *ourselves* that.'

Orson shuffled forward.

'Ter...' he said softly.

'Orson, please,' Terran said, his cheeks flushed, his eyes glistening with a mad look. 'I need this. I *need* to know.'

'I don't know if taking on such a journey at this time is—' Kendrik started.

'Is what?' Terran rounded up on him. 'Is *what*, Ken? What's the alternative? We go on with our lives knowing we didn't even try?'

They said nothing, because there was nothing any of them could think of. A long moment passed.

'Fuck it.' Orson finally nodded. 'Let's do this.'

Kendrik couldn't believe his ears. 'What are we going to tell Farao?' he asked.

'I don't know...' Terran shrugged. 'That we're taking a holiday or something.'

'A holiday?' Kendrik stared at him, frowning. 'Now? In the middle of his school term? He's never going to buy that.'

There was a loaded pause.

'Or... Maybe he will.' Orson's face lit up, and he placed a hand on Kendrik's shoulder. 'Because we all want to celebrate your promotion!'

'My promotion?' Kendrik stared at him, dumbfounded.

'Affirmative.' Orson nodded, and there were vague traces of his old bravado in his voice now. 'What better to celebrate this great achievement of yours than a random trip!'

'We've never taken a holiday like that.' Kendrik said. 'He's going to get suspicious.'

'I know we haven't, Ken,' Orson added with the tone of one explaining something very simple to a particularly stupid child. 'But you have to admit, that's just *the* perfect cover-up, isn't it?'

'If you say so,' Kendrik groaned.

'Shut it, you two,' Terran interrupted, but there was a small smile playing on his lips now. 'Let's get planning.'

Kendrik breathed in, soaking in the sudden shift in his brothers' mood. He himself felt a huge wave of relief. It was odd, because they hadn't fixed anything yet. But the knowledge that they had a plan, a way forward, that they would work together, as brothers, lifted him and gave him more strength than he could explain. He shivered. Until that point, they could still have backtracked. They could have decided not to pursue it any further. They could have accepted what had happened and simply let it be. But in that instant, as they looked at each other, acknowledging the choice they were making, Kendrik knew there was no going back. They were in this together, proceeding with their mission to bring themselves closure, to avenge their mother and seek justice for their family.

Kendrik fidgeted in his chair. Next to him, Orson was humming to himself:

'*Oh, ma France… Ce pays qui a vu passer mon enfance…*'

Kendrik smiled. It had been their mother's favourite song.

Chapter 24
Terran

Amit popped by the hospital the next day as Terran was sitting vigil over a sleeping Farao and insisted on dragging him to the cafeteria to get something to eat. Terran followed him, though he knew he wouldn't be able to stomach anything. The tension, anxiety and excitement of the past week had considerably dampened his appetite. He was too fidgety to be hungry. He was exhausted too, but he couldn't bring himself to relax. They were embarking upon a journey that might well alter the course of their lives, and he wouldn't rest until he knew for certain they would all be ok. He'd thought of calling off their plan more than once, but he knew he couldn't. He had to do this. For himself, for their family, for the pain their mother had endured. They had to do it for Farao. He knew he'd forever regret it if they didn't even try. He couldn't live the rest of his life knowing he'd let that injustice linger without trying to make it right.

'So,' Amit started cautiously, as they waited for their drinks at the end of the counter. 'Orson told me about your plan…'

Terran gave Amit a shifty look, but said nothing. He could guess what was coming next.

'Terran, you can't be serious.'

'I am,' Terran said numbly.

Amit stared at him in disbelief, his eyes wide, his mouth slightly ajar.

'Terran.' Amit shook his head. 'You can't make Farao travel all that way in his condition. And for what? Revenge? For something that happened almost twenty years ago? That's ridiculous.'

'Ridiculous…' Terran whispered, taking the disposable coffee cup the barista was sliding towards him. 'Is that what you're calling our mother getting assaulted?'

'*What?*' Amit frowned.

'You think it's ridiculous to want to make this guy fess up to what he did to her?' Terran repeated mutinously. 'What he did to our family?'

Amit gaped at him.

'You know that's not what I said.'

Terran said nothing. The lingering anger that had been waiting sneakily just under the surface for the past week was threatening to take over again.

'Terran, please, be serious…'

'Amit, I *am* serious.' Terran's jaw tensed. 'What's the alternative? We stay here and do *nothing*? When this guy is getting on with his life like nothing happened. Did you know he's a decorated veteran? They're fucking *celebrating* that arsehole!'

'I never said it was right.' Amit placed a hand on Terran's shoulder, his voice level. 'Or that what this man did was pardonable. But think about it, *please*. What do you think you'll achieve by going all the way there? By dragging your brothers into this. And do you really think taking Farao on a trip like this at this time is the best idea?'

Terran shrugged Amit's hand off, spilling some of his coffee in the process. He swore under his breath.

'Listen,' Amit sighed. 'Why doesn't just one of you go? What's the need to take Farao with you? You could go and see what this man says and be back within a few days. How about that?'

But rather than soothe Terran, Amit's placating tone only aggravated him.

'We're not splitting up. This is a family matter, we have to be together.'

'For crying out loud, Terran, why are you being so stubborn?' Amit called out in exasperation, making the two cashiers behind the counter turn to look at them in surprise. 'I'm telling you, finding this guy won't do anyone any good. What's the point in stirring up the past, and putting Farao through all this, when he doesn't even know the whole story? Have you thought about what this will do to him? He might not want to meet this man. This could destroy him. Is that what you want?'

'Of course not!' Terran spat back. 'But he should have the choice. We should *all* have that choice. We'll tell him everything once we're there, and he can decide for himself what he wants to do.'

'What about Farao's health?' Amit pleaded. 'He needs to rest.'

'We'll go when he's well enough. You said yourself his condition is stable, and that with the right medication he'll be fine for some time, didn't you?'

Amit didn't respond.

'Didn't you?' Terran insisted.

'Yes, but...'

'And you said that once he's under the right medication there's nothing we can do but wait for news on the donor list?'

'Yes, but...'

'And,' Terran added quickly, 'we can also check if that guy's a viable donor. It's a small chance, but it's worth checking. Otherwise, all we'd be doing here is waiting! Why not use this time rather than sit around hoping we get a donor?'

'Terran.' Amit's voice was stern, his palms raised in front of him to stop Terran's tirade. 'I know it isn't ideal, but this is the way these things go. You have to have some faith.'

'Faith,' Terran snorted in derision. 'Because that's served me so fucking well in life so far, right?'

'You know what I mean…' Amit winced.

'No, Amit, I don't know what you mean.' Terran's tone was cold. 'Nothing's ever come to me, to my family, without pain and hard work and action. You don't understand. We *have to* do this. We *all* need this. And Farao needs this too, even if he doesn't know it yet. And if anything happens… If we don't get a donor… If Farao…' He couldn't bring himself to say the words. 'If something happens and I didn't do everything I could to give him justice… And closure… And help him come to terms with everything that's happened… I'd never forgive myself. No, Amit.' Terran raised his voice, seeing Amit ready to interrupt him again. 'We're doing this. That's the only plan we have. And we have to give it a shot. Now, we can do it without your help if we need to, but we *are* doing this.'

Amit said nothing for a few minutes, his eyes searching Terran's face.

'What if we find a donor whilst you're away?' He frowned.

Terran exhaled sharply. 'Then we'll be back immediately. We'd only be a day's travel away, at most.'

'You realise this is insane, right?' Amit shook his head again.

Terran felt his resolve on the brink of faltering, but he was determined to go through with the plan. He was holding on to it with a sort of mad desperation he'd never felt before. This would work. It had to. His family had suffered too much.

'I know,' he said.

Amit watched him, and simply nodded. 'Well, if I can't stop you from going,' he sighed, 'then I'll see what I can do to help you. We can't move Farao yet anyway, he'll need at least another week under observation. Let me see what needs to be done.'

'Thanks, Amit.' Terran gave him a feeble smile.

'You know all I want is for you all to be safe, right? You know that?' Amit cocked his head to one side, his face a little constricted.

'I know,' Terran mumbled. 'That's all I want, too.'

'Good.'

Later that day, as Terran sat in Farao's room, watching the slow, regular rise and fall of his chest with each breath he took, he thought of what Amit had said. He knew it *was* madness. Deep down he knew Amit was right. But that was nothing in the face of the fear of losing his brother and the wild hope that the trip could be the only way to fix the horrors of their past. *It'll be fine*, he kept repeating to himself, over and over again. It simply had to.

Chapter 25
Farao

'We're doing *what?*' Farao asked incredulously, staring at each of his brothers in turn as they stood around his bed.

He had been in the hospital for a little over two weeks now, and though the doctors and nurses insisted there was no cause for alarm, for some reason they preferred to keep him under observation. Farao felt much better now, almost back to normal, although his stint in the hospital had been the most boring time of his life. Despite the television in his room, his brothers' regular visits and Nick dropping in a handful of times with schoolwork and the latest gossip, there was little to do around here but marinate in his own thoughts—and that was never something he enjoyed at the best of times. Nick had relayed that both Serena and Mel were asking after him. More than once, Farao had pictured Serena in tears, kneeling at his bedside, her hands clasped around his, declaring how much she fancied him. His visions of Mel, however... Well, these generally took a different turn, reminiscent of their time skipping class together. But that was all fantasy, and even all his daydreaming was starting to get old. Farao hadn't seriously entertained the idea of letting either of them see him in this state—according to Nick, they'd both asked if he was receiving visitors. He was getting fidgety being cooped up in here for so long, and he couldn't wait to get out. But at that very moment, listening to what Terran had just announced, all thought of getting out had vanished out of his head, replaced by a sense of absolute consternation.

'We're going on a holiday,' Terran said lightly. 'I think we all deserve it.'

'A *holiday*? What about school?' Farao simply couldn't believe his ears.

Perfect, play-by-the-rules Terran was suggesting bunking off for a random trip? It made no sense.

'Well,' Orson chimed in, 'we never got a chance to celebrate Kendrik's promotion, and we all know how big a milestone this was for him. And with everything we've all gone through in the last couple of weeks, I'd say we've earned some time off.'

Farao looked at his brothers, and his gaze fell on Kendrik, who looked downcast, his eyes on the floor. He had the air of someone who hadn't slept in a long time. He was unshaven, which was uncommon for him, and his usually neat hair and clothes were dishevelled. He didn't look like someone ready to celebrate anything.

'Are you guys pulling my leg or something?' Farao frowned.

'Of course not,' Kendrik said, looking up to meet Farao's gaze. 'It's been a bit of a rollercoaster these past two weeks, no thanks to you...' He gave Farao a wry smile.

'Jeez, it's not like I fucking planned this...' Farao rolled his eyes.

'I know, I'm only joking.' Kendrik shook his head, forcing another smile.

'And so,' Orson added with a grin, 'the Dhawan brothers come together on this impromptu journey! We've all been able to book some time off. As long as you don't mind missing out on school for a short while…'

'No,' Farao said, a little too quickly, though something told him this was too good to be true, 'I don't care. I mean. I'm fine with it.' He smiled, not wanting to be left behind.

He couldn't believe his luck. No school, and for once he wouldn't be the one at fault for bunking classes. Now, that was one thing he could definitely make his peace with.

'Where are we going?' Farao asked eagerly, thinking for a moment he saw Terran and Orson exchange the briefest of looks.

'South of France!' Terran smiled. 'Marseille. Ken's choice. And we thought we'd make a road trip out of it. You know, for the spirit of adventure.'

Farao frowned a little.

'Are you kidding me?'

'Nope, little brother,' Orson said brightly, 'we are not *kidding* you. In fact, we're very seriously roping you into the road trip of a lifetime! Think about it…' He struck a dramatic pose. 'Four brothers, with nothing but the open road ahead of them. Heading out into the unknown…'

'Please tell me 'the unknown' is an actual hotel room and not a tent in the middle of nowhere…' Farao rolled his eyes.

'But of course!' Orson exclaimed. 'What do you take us for? We're not animals! We've rented a villa overlooking *les Calanques de Marseille*. It'll be glorious, little brother, absolutely *glorious!*'

'Ok, ok, I hear you.' Farao grinned. 'Just stop calling shit "glorious", alright? When are we leaving?'

'Well.' Terran cleared his throat. 'You're getting discharged today, and I've cleared it all with your school, so we're ready to hit the road tomorrow morning.'

Farao frowned again.

'Fucking hell, what's the rush?' he snorted, and this time, there was no mistaking the look that passed between his brothers. 'What? What is it?'

Terran, Kendrik and Orson said nothing.

'Erm, well...' Terran started.

'It's nothing.' Orson jumped in, leaning in towards Farao conspiratorially. 'The truth is, we got a great last-minute deal on the villa, but it was a limited time offer for specific dates only. So, we thought it was the perfect excuse to be spontaneous!'

Farao looked at his brothers, suspecting there was more to this, but unable to put his finger on what it was. He knew Orson to be the *spontaneous* kind, but he'd never known Terran or Kendrik to do anything like this.

'Ok...' he started saying, squinting at them.

'Well.' Terran shrugged. 'If you'd rather be here and go to school, that's your call. You can stay with Amit. But the deposit on the villa is non-refundable, and we've already got the time off work. So *we*—he gestured at Kendrik, Orson and himself—'are definitely going.'

'No, no!' Farao said quickly. 'I'm coming!'

He couldn't quite believe it, but he didn't want to let his chance slip away nonetheless.

'Fabulous!' Orson declared with a flourish, wrapping an arm around Kendrik's shoulders. 'Picture this... Four brothers,' he repeated theatrically, sweeping his free arm in front of him, 'on the open road...'

'Oh, shut up,' Kendrik, Terran and Farao all groaned at the same time.

And just like that, it was settled.

They were going on an adventure.

Chapter 26
Terran

Terran heaved the bags into the back of the ancient light-blue SUV that had once belonged to their parents. It had seen better days but replacing it would have felt like betraying his parents' memory, so they had made do with it, even when it had started to need more and more mending and patching up as time went on.

The boot, though spacious, was almost full. They had told Farao they were going away for a couple of weeks, but they didn't truly know how long they would be gone for and how much to pack. Orson came jogging down the driveway, carrying his guitar case.

'Is that really necessary?' Terran rolled his eyes, as Orson slid the case on top of the rest of the luggage.

'Of course, it is! A man never travels without his instrument! One never knows when they'll be in dire need of a good serenade!'

'Fine, fine,' Terran groaned, cutting him short, not wanting to hear any more at such an early time of the morning.

They had agreed to leave before the London traffic started clogging the roads, and had booked the five o'clock passage on the Eurotunnel. Terran had barely slept, playing and replaying everything in his mind.

It had been a tough week all around. They had managed to track down the man they were after, not without some difficulty, but the strain of keeping the truth from Farao whilst planning what had to look like an innocent family trip had taken a toll on all of them. Terran knew Kendrik was struggling the most, and nothing Terran or Orson could say or do made a difference. But they didn't have a choice now, they had to keep going.

Without thinking, he pulled out his backpack from behind the driver's seat and opened it, checking for the hundredth time he had all of Farao's medicines. They'd had to tell a lot of white lies on that front, too, though the medical staff at the hospital were reluctant at first. Terran had never had to play the 'legal guardian' card as much as he had in the past week. Eventually it was agreed, and two months' worth of Farao's treatment had been provided in clear little plastic containers, labelled only with the dosage instructions. Terran breathed in deeply. If his lies helped them all get closure, and possibly a donor to save Farao's life, then he would happily walk himself straight into hell.

As Terran zipped up his bag, Farao descended the front steps to the car groggily, a pillow under his arm, sleep still etched on his face.

'Good morning.' Terran forced a smile, shaking the dark thoughts away from his mind.

''ning...' Farao grunted inaudibly, climbing into the back seat, settling the pillow against the window and going straight back to sleep.

We're doing this, Terran told himself as he climbed into the driver's seat and took a sip of coffee from his travel mug. *We're doing this. It's happening. No going back now.*

***

145

It was still dark when Terran slid the car into the queue waiting to board the Eurotunnel carrier. The drive to Folkestone had been uneventful, with Orson and Farao fast asleep in the back and Kendrik wide awake, but very quiet, on the passenger seat beside him. Terran put the car in park and stepped out to stretch his legs. The morning air was crisp and the freshness of it felt nice on his skin. He yawned widely and pulled his phone out of his pocket. There was a text from Amit wishing them a safe journey and reminding him to keep him posted of their progress. Terran shot a quick text back to let him know where they were.

When he settled back in his seat, Orson and Farao were awake, chatting and sharing a family-sized pack of salt and vinegar crisps.

'It's not so much *what* you say,' Orson was saying, 'but also *how* you say it. It makes all the difference.'

Farao nodded, taking this in.

'And that's your secret, now, is it?' Kendrik jumped in, smirking.

'Well,' Orson beamed, '*one* of my secrets, yes. My being incredibly charming and handsome obviously also helps.'

'And modest, obviously,' Kendrik laughed.

'Obviously,' Orson repeated, chuckling, helping himself to more crisps.

'I'm almost afraid to ask.' Terran glanced at Orson in the rear-view mirror as he put the car into drive and slowly followed the moving line of vehicles in front of him. 'What did I walk back into, exactly?'

'Nothing much, dear brother, I was only imparting some of my worldly knowledge onto Farao.'

'Are you sure your *worldly knowledge* is a suitable topic to be sharing with your younger brother?' Terran squinted suspiciously.

'Ah,' Orson exclaimed, 'but he's a man already, he needs to know these things! And truth be told,' he added, leaning forward and pointing at Terran and Kendrik in turn, 'both of you could probably do with a lesson or two, as well!'

'I'm good, thanks,' Kendrik grumbled from the passenger seat.

'Yeah, I think I'm ok, too,' Terran smiled.

Orson inclined his head towards Farao conspiratorially.

'See, Farao, lesson number one: if you're in denial about your lack of skills, you will never, *ever* be able to improve.'

Chapter 27
Orson

They took a break shortly after reaching French soil. Orson's stomach was growling loudly, and he was desperate for a coffee and something to eat. The morning was bright, so they sat down at a table outside the service station. Terran put down the tray he was carrying, which was laden with a pile of freshly baked croissants and four cups of fuming black coffee—Orson already realising that French motorway stations knew very little of the fancy oat flat whites and cappuccinos he was used to back in London.

There was a sort of lightness in the air between them, and it occurred to Orson that he couldn't remember the last time they had spent so much time in each other's presence, just the four of them, out of the confines of the house. A time when there was no call from Farao's school to argue about, no bland piece of news from Kendrik's office to hear of, and no immediate life logistics to sort out. Since their parents had died, holidays had always been an avoidable expense. What

Orson could feel in the atmosphere now was different. It felt like a promise. Like hope. Like the universe reminding them that, whatever happened, they had each other.

Orson took a sip of coffee and winced.

'You alright there, coffee snob?' Kendrik teased.

'I'm not ashamed of having decent standards, if that's what you mean.' Orson raised his eyebrows at him. 'Maybe you should take a leaf out of my book sometimes—I don't know how you can tolerate this rubbish.'

'Mmmm.' Kendrik took a long gulp of coffee, swallowed ostentatiously and grinned at him. 'Lovely!'

'Ken, you amaze me sometimes.' Orson shook his head.

'Are we going to have to referee your nonsense all day,' Terran cut in, yawning and stretching, 'or can we hope for some peace and quiet from time to time?'

'Take a chill pill, bro.' Orson rolled his eyes.

'Oh'—Terran swivelled around to grab his bag—'speaking of...'

He handed several pills and a small bottle of water to Farao.

'Why do I still need all these?' Farao grumbled. 'The doctor said I'm fine...'

'They said there's a slight risk of infection in the next couple of months whilst your kidneys recover,' Terran said confidently. 'This helps prevent it.'

Farao shook his head and sighed dramatically but didn't argue, and Orson watched as he swallowed the medicine and washed it down with another croissant, his gaze on the screen of his phone.

Orson kept watching Farao from the corner of his eye, checking for any sign that something was amiss, maybe a hint that the treatment was no longer working. He wanted to be on the lookout. As much as Terran was determined to see the plan through, Orson knew that Farao's health, though temporarily restored through the strong doses of medication he was given, was now a ticking time bomb. He watched his younger brother, his eyes taking in the thin jaw, the light brown fringe falling over the furrowed brow.

Before Orson had known the truth, in what now felt like a parallel universe, it had never occurred to him that Farao's appearance had concealed something sinister. There'd been so much of his mother in Farao's thin stature, in the chestnut shades of his hair and his lighter skin tone, Orson had never really thought about it. No matter what he looked like, Farao had been his brother, period. On the rare occasions the thought had crossed his mind, he'd only assumed that, out of four children, the genetic lottery was bound to favour his mother's DNA at some point. But after he'd learnt his mother's secret, he'd sometimes found himself looking at Farao with a fresh pair of eyes. How much of his brother was from their mother... and how much was from the other side of the equation? Had his mother's eyes been that exact shade of blue, or was that something Farao had inherited from... Orson could barely think the words without wincing—his biological father? What about his hair? The shape of his nose? Orson had driven himself mad at times, trying to paint a picture of the guy in his mind, based on tiny details from Farao's looks that didn't seem to fit with what he remembered of his mother. But the exercise had proven pointless—no matter how far he allowed himself to spiral on the topic, all that Orson could see at the end of the day when he looked at Farao was his brother. His blood, and nothing else.

Orson wondered what his mother would have said if she could see them now. He liked to think that she would have understood why they had embarked on this mission, although something at the back of his mind told him she would have wanted them to be upfront with Farao. She would have wanted them to be honest. She would have wanted them to let go of the spirit of revenge that fuelled their endeavour. But, Orson thought painfully, she wasn't there to guide them anymore, and all they could do was their best. Whether or not that was enough, they'd have to see. Only time would tell whether they'd made a mistake dragging Farao on this crazy journey.

Orson stole another glance at Farao and tried hard to tell himself that, regardless of their actions, their intentions were legitimate, and that had to count for something. Surely that made the lying, the deceit and the manipulative scheming okay... didn't it? But even as he forced another gulp of the disgusting coffee mixture down his throat, wincing again at its bitterness, he feared the day they'd have to tell Farao the truth and answer for what they'd done.

Chapter 28
Kendrik

They were making good time and Kendrik was starting to feel they might reach the hotel they had booked near Dijon, their halfway point, ahead of schedule. That simple fact, as innocuous as it was, made him feel a little more positive. He needed even the smallest things to be going right.

He had taken over behind the wheel to give Terran a chance to get some sleep, and he had settled into a comfortable speed. In the back seat, Farao had plugged his earphones in, pulled his hoodie on, and leant against his pillow again. His eyes were closed, his chest moving at a regular pace. Kendrik hoped he was asleep. He knew the medicine would tire him more than usual, and he wanted him to get as much rest as he needed.

Next to Farao, Orson was awake, staring out of the window, his elbow propped on the armrest, his head resting against his knuckles. Kendrik knew better than to disturb him.

He straightened up in his seat and checked his rear-view mirror. The road wasn't too busy yet, their early departure giving them a bit of a head start before they met with morning traffic. Kendrik yawned widely, shaking his head in an attempt to stir himself back to attention. *Focus*, he told himself. *For crying out loud, just* focus. But he had found focusing a terribly difficult thing to do lately. Ever since the revelations at the hospital, his attention span had reduced to only a handful of seconds.

Farao's ill… Seriously ill… Eight months to live, a year at most… He's not our father's son… And their mother… *That letter she wrote…* The thoughts kept swirling round and round in his head, floating there like poltergeists, haunting every second of his waking life, and every rare sleeping moment he managed.

It was too much for Kendrik's brain. He simply couldn't cope. He wished he had Terran's resolve, or Orson's banter. He wished he was doing better. But all he had been able to manage was to keep himself functioning, just enough to get himself from one day to the next.

He thought of his phone conversation with Scott, the day they had decided to attempt the impossible. He remembered Scott's bewildered reaction on the other end of the line. Kendrik couldn't blame him. Never in his entire life had he taken as much as a sick day. So this sudden request to take a month off must have come as quite a shock. Scott had done his best to sound understanding, because what else can people do when you invoke a 'family emergency', but Kendrik could tell that his manager was displeased. The worst thing was, Kendrik had barely been able to care. By that point, he was already feeling so numb he had almost resigned on the spot. He'd switched on his out of office the instant he had gone off the call with Scott, then buried his phone in a drawer in his bedroom. He hadn't wanted to be reached. He hadn't wanted to know about anything else other than the mountain they had to climb and the fire they had to cross and the storm they had to survive before he could feel even remotely human again.

***

'Hey.' Terran's sleepy voice emerged from the passenger seat, some time later.

'Hey.' Kendrik glanced sideways at him. 'Did you manage to get some sleep?'

But Terran didn't respond. His eyes were stuck to the map on the navigation system attached to the dashboard.

'Erm, Ken,' Terran said tentatively, '*where* are we?'

'What do you mean?' Kendrik frowned.

Behind them, Orson was leaning forward in between the two front seats to listen in.

'Well,' Orson chimed in, 'unless I'm very much mistaken, I don't think Metz is on the way to Marseille…'

'Are we lost?' Farao called out from the back seat.

'Fuck,' Kendrik seethed under his breath, as realisation struck him. 'Fuck, fuck, FUCK!' he yelled, hitting the wheel with clenched fists.

'Hey,' Terran called out. 'Easy, Ken. It's fine. We'll just find our way back to the right motorway, ok? Calm down.'

But Kendrik was anything but calm. His hands were clasped so tightly on the steering wheel his knuckles were turning white. He felt he had let his brothers down. And that was a feeling he could hardly cope with at the best of times.

They drove in complete silence until the next service station. The moment they were parked, Kendrik stormed out of the car, slamming his door shut behind him and stomping out onto the parking lot. He cried out in frustration. He felt so angry, so furious with himself and with the circumstances he could have screamed all day and not managed to let go of his anger.

Terran ran after him, concern clear on his face. When Terran tried to wrap his arms around him, Kendrik fought back, tears now rolling down his cheeks. But Terran didn't give up. Eventually he managed to engulf Kendrik into a tight hug, and Kendrik was able to finally let go. He felt exhausted.

'I can't do this, Ter. I can't do this…' he sobbed into Terran's shoulder.

'I know,' Terran said soothingly, keeping a strong grip around him. 'It's ok… I know.'

'I can't do this…' Kendrik kept repeating, his heart breaking all over again, into so many tiny pieces he didn't know whether he ever would be able to make it whole again.

Chapter 29
Farao

'Wow,' Farao said, as he stood by Orson's side, watching Kendrik fall apart. 'All that over a small detour... He's really taken this whole thing to heart, hasn't he?'

There was an odd, pained expression on Orson's face and he was quiet for a moment.

'Yeah,' he finally said. 'Yeah, I guess he has... Come on.' He turned to Farao. 'Let's just give them a moment. We'll go and get some food.'

They walked to the service station, one of those large ones spreading over two floors. Orson disappeared towards the men's bathroom. Farao wandered over to one of the coffee shops and ordered himself a coffee and a four cheese toastie. He only spoke broken French, never having lived in the country or spent much time conversing with his mother in her native tongue, like his brothers had. The fact had always bothered him.

He sat at a table in the area outside the coffee place and pulled out his phone. He had a text from Nick, who had been worried sick since that day he'd found Farao lying down on the bathroom floor, two and a half weeks ago. *Two and a half weeks,* Farao thought. *Gosh.* It felt like a lifetime. He opened the text.

'Hey, mate. How's the trip going? You're not missing much here, same old shit going on. Serena asked about you. I gave her your number. Hope you don't mind.'

Farao stared at the screen. *Serena asked about you.* She had *asked.* About *him.* He re-read the text a second time, and a third. She had asked for his number. He checked his inbox and skim-read through the pointless group WhatsApps and the avalanche of texts from Mel asking how he was doing and when he'd be back at school. He briefly scrolled through his text history with Mel, which was pretty much a one-sided stream of worried messages she'd been sending him daily. As he often had in the past few days, he started typing a response, but he never knew what she wanted to hear, or what to say, or how to say it, and it seemed easier not to answer. Closing the chat with Mel, he looked through his inbox again, but there was no text from Serena. *She has my number, though,* he told himself. *She might text. She wouldn't have asked for it if she wasn't going to use it. Right?*

'You look happy.' Terran's voice sounded from above him, and Farao looked up, so surprised that he dropped his phone and poured some of his coffee onto his lap.

'Shit,' Farao swore, standing up suddenly, grabbing his phone to make sure it was ok and looking around for a napkin to mop up his trousers.

'Sorry.' Terran grimaced, handing him a paper towel. 'Didn't mean to scare you.'

'It's fine,' Farao mumbled, thinking that even this couldn't dampen the amazing thought that Serena had asked about him and that, any moment now, she could text.

They were almost done with their food and drinks when Kendrik joined them, his expression sombre but his demeanour much calmer. He just nodded at them and sat down, and Terran slid a sandwich and cup of coffee towards him, which Kendrik took with a silent nod.

Half an hour later, the three of them were waiting by the car, but Orson was nowhere to be seen. Terran had gone around the service station looking for him but hadn't managed to find him, and all of their calls ended up going to voicemail. Eventually they had agreed that the best place for them to wait for their brother was the car, but still he hadn't showed up.

Terran was starting to look really worried when, in the distance, Orson's silhouette finally appeared, walking at a leisurely pace towards them.

'What the…' Terran groaned.

And Farao could see what was unnerving his older brother. Orson wasn't alone. He was dragging a small suitcase and talking animatedly to a slender blonde. Both of them were headed straight in their direction. Farao's gaze immediately glanced over the woman. She was petite, with light brown eyes and the lean frame of someone who exercises a lot. She was very, *very* pretty. She was wearing tight leggings and a white low-cut jumper which accentuated the tone in her shoulders. Her sleeves were rolled up, showing several tattoos on her forearms.

'Oh, for fuck's sake, Orson…' Terran moaned.

But Farao could only smile, because this was so typically Orson, and he couldn't help but admire his cheek. Who picks up a pretty girl in a random service station in the middle of nowhere? Orson did, and Farao was in such awe that it almost made him want to burst out laughing.

'Well, hello there!' Orson exclaimed, coming to a halt in front of the car, not reacting to the dark look Terran was throwing at him.

'Orson…' Terran growled, his voice threatening to break.

'Now, now. Ter, let me explain.'

'Explain *what*, Orson,' Terran pleaded. 'Seriously, what *is* this?'

'It's not what you think…' Orson started.

'Really? Because I'm pretty sure it's *exactly* what I think it is.'

'This charming young lady,' Orson continued as if Terran hadn't spoken, 'is hitchhiking her way to Aix-en-Provence. That's *literally* on our way. What sort of gentlemen would deny assistance to a damsel in distress?'

'Orson, this is *not* the time…' Terran groaned.

'Come on,' Orson said. 'I've already offered, we can't take it back now. And I'm sure Farao and Ken don't mind, right?' He turned hopefully to his brothers.

Kendrik simply shrugged, but Farao gave Orson a wide grin. He had a soft spot for Orson's wacky schemes.

'Yeah, I don't mind.'

'See?' Orson turned to Terran. 'It's all *fine*. Chillax, bro,' he added, slapping Terran on the arm.

'Don't you fucking tell me to chillax, *bro*, when you're the one picking up random strangers,' Terran growled, and he stormed away to climb into the driver's seat, closing the door forcefully behind him.

'Well…' Orson grinned at Farao. 'I'd say that went well, didn't it?'

The young woman shuffled closer to Orson, eyeing Terran cautiously, sounding uncertain—given Terran's outburst, Farao couldn't blame her.

'Are you sure it's ok?' she asked Orson in a slight French accent, glancing at Terran, who sat mutinously in the car, his fingers tapping the steering wheel.

'Of course, of course!' Orson smiled at her, picking up her suitcase and carrying it to the boot. 'Dhawan brothers, this is Juliette. Juliette, this is Farao, Kendrik. And the grumpy one over there is

Terran. He's really much more charming when you get to know him, I promise.'

Juliette gave them an embarrassed smile, which Farao returned, feeling suddenly too awkward to speak.

'Are we done?' Terran called out. 'Can we get a move on, please?'

'*En voiture, mademoiselle,*' Orson exclaimed, opening the door for Juliette to take his place by the window whilst he slid in the middle seat, between her and Farao.

Terran drove the car out of the parking lot and sped on to rejoin the motorway, backtracking away from Metz in the correct direction.

'Listen,' Juliette said after a short while, a pained look on her face. 'I'm really sorry if I intruded on your holiday. I can get off at your next stop, really.'

'Nonsense, Juliette, nonsense.' Orson smiled at her broadly, and lowered his voice a little, so only she and Farao could hear. 'Listen, my brother is just in a bad mood right now, but he's alright, really. Just ignore him.'

Juliette looked doubtfully at him, her gaze darting toward the back of Terran's head.

'You're really sure?'

'Absolutely, *belle demoiselle,* absolutely! Now,' Orson continued, 'Farao, did you know Juliette here is a personal trainer?'

Farao leant slightly forward. 'Oh,' he said, feeling stupid for not knowing what else to say. 'Erm, that's cool.'

'Extremely cool indeed!' Orson nodded vigorously. 'Maybe you can help me get this one into shape, Juliette, because it's a struggle even getting him out of his room at the best of times,' he added, pointing a thumb at Farao.

'Ah, shut up.' Farao felt himself blush furiously.

He could have punched Orson for throwing him under the bus like that. But somehow he could not find a witty retort.

'You know'—Juliette looked at Farao—'most of the time it's only a matter of finding the right form of exercise for you. It helps with motivation.'

'Such wise words indeed,' Orson agreed. 'So, Juliette, tell me more about this festival you're going to in Aix-en-Provence?'

'Oh.' She smiled widely at him, clearly excited. 'Yes, it's a wellness festival my friends and I are attending. In fact, I'm teaching there on the second and third day. One of them was supposed to pick me up from the service station—we'd made this whole plan—but her car broke down on the way and she doesn't know how long it will be until it's fixed. Anyway.' She pushed a strand of strawberry blonde hair away from her face. 'This festival. It's *amazing*! They have healthy food, all vegan of course, and all these classes. Everything! Fitness, yoga, meditation…'

But Farao didn't hear any more. His phone buzzed in his pocket and, upon pulling it out and checking the screen, he saw a text from an unknown number waiting to be opened. He unlocked the screen and read the message. His heart skipped a beat when he realised it was from Serena. He stared at the message, reading it over and over again.

'Well, well, well…' Orson's voice came whispering just inches away from his ear, and Farao jumped with fright, dropping his phone, which slid under Terran's seat.

'Fuck, Orson. You're such a prick!'

But Orson was smiling broadly at him, and Farao knew from the devilish look on his face that he had read the text over his shoulder.

'Who's Serena?'

Chapter 30
Terran

Terran was fuming. Absolutely and positively *fuming*. He knew Orson had his eccentricities, but this was too much. With Kendrik in the state that he was in, and Farao's health and the already difficult mission they had set for themselves, what was he doing loading them with yet another problem to deal with? Could he not just keep it in his pants for one second whilst they focused on saving their family?

A string of swear words flowed through his mind, and it felt good to think them, which was the next best thing to stopping the car right there on the motorway, stepping out on the side of the road and saying all these words out loud.

He stole a glance in the rear-view mirror at the back seat, and his eyes found the girl. Juliette. She caught his eye, the intensity in her gaze taking him by surprise, and he immediately looked away. A moment later, she'd turned back to Orson. He couldn't hear exactly what she was saying, but from some words he was picking up in the conversation, she seemed to be talking about some hippie festival she was going to. She was attractive, very attractive even, there was no doubt about that. But *honestly*, was this the time for Orson to get up to his usual antics when they had so much going on? Terran felt the anger rise within him again, and he diverted his eyes back onto the road, checking the satnav to make sure they were on the right track.

The next time he looked into the rear-view mirror, he met Orson's gaze. He felt his anger fade away almost instantly, because there was so much sadness and such a sincere apology in Orson's eyes that Terran knew he'd been too harsh. He let out a sharp breath. He nodded once at him, and he saw Orson let out a sigh of relief, then turn around to keep talking to Juliette.

Terran refocused on the road. Could he blame Orson? Could he truly berate him for wanting to act normal? For needing, if only for a moment, to feel like his old self? Terran exhaled slowly. Who was he to judge? Wasn't that was he was craving, too?

He looked at Kendrik, who seemed to be asleep, and found himself wishing that they could all hit pause. That for just a few hours, they could all take a break from this madness and not worry about what came next. He swallowed hard. Maybe he should let go of such wishful thinking, because if his life story was anything to go by, nothing had ever come to him from just wishing things were different.

***

Because of their detour, it was late afternoon by the time they reached the hotel they had booked for the night. Juliette stepped out of the car to go and get herself a room whilst they unloaded their bags. Terran went to pick up his backpack. Behind him, Farao was saying something he couldn't quite hear. Terran lifted his bag from where it was wedged under the driver's seat, turning to look at Farao and ask what he was on about. But as he hoisted his bag onto his shoulder, something slid from the top of it and fell onto the tarmac, hitting the ground with a shattering sound.

'No! No, no no,' Farao shouted, rushing past Terran and pushing him aside, crouching down. 'Shit! Shit. Shit. SHIT!'

'Farao, what…' Terran frowned, confused.

'My phone!' Farao exclaimed. 'It fell down when we were driving. Fuck!'

Terran leant over to assess the damage. The screen had shattered in the fall, and Farao was desperately trying to switch the phone on, but to no avail.

'Nooooo!' Farao moaned out loud, looking upwards.

Orson and Kendrik came running around the car, looking worried.

'What happened?' Kendrik breathed, a queasy expression on his face.

'Nothing, he's fine,' Terran started.

'I'm not fine!' Farao screamed, jumping to his feet, brandishing his phone. 'My phone! It's dead! Look!'

'Oh,' Orson said, with a look of recognition, 'and you hadn't responded to Mystery Girl yet, had you?'

'No, I hadn't!' Farao groaned. 'Fuck!'

'What did we miss?' Kendrik looked puzzled. 'What mystery girl?'

'Our young brother here seems to have a secret admirer. A lovely lady by the name of Serena.' Orson gave him a cheeky grin.

'Oh, piss off, ok!' Farao roared.

Orson took a step towards Farao and placed both hands on his shoulders.

'Listen to me, and listen carefully,' he said, very seriously. 'This is lesson number two: give her a chance to miss you. A chance for her to wonder whether or not she likes you. And how will she *ever* get a chance to ponder the nature of her affection for you if you don't give her a little time to think it over?'

Farao looked suspiciously back at Orson.

'Jeez, Orson, who says shit like that...' Terran groaned.

'Ter, *this* is exactly the reason why, of the four of us, I'm the one with an active sex life. This isn't *shit*. It's the rulebook on how to play the game.' Orson turned back to look at Farao. 'Farao, take my word on this one. This is the best thing that could have happened. Tomorrow, we'll go and buy you a new phone, and in the evening, you may respond to her.'

Someone behind them cleared their throat, and they all turned around. Juliette was standing looking at them.

She winced. 'I'm sorry. I didn't mean to overhear, but tomorrow is Sunday. You won't find any shops open in France on a Sunday...'

Farao's face fell, and he looked, panicked, at Orson.

'Even better!' Orson exclaimed. 'On Monday then, we'll get you a new phone, and by then she'll be so glad to hear from you, she'll be primed and ready for a good text flirtation!'

'Ok, well, before you completely corrupt him with your dodgy tactics,' Terran butted in, 'let's go in, shall we?'

Chapter 31
Gabrielle

It all happened so quickly, sometimes I can't even remember how.

But it did happen. There's no doubt about that.

I instantly saw on his face that he was drunk. His cheeks were reddened and his gaze dangerously out of focus.

When he saw me, his eyes narrowed and then widened again, as though something had just occurred to him.

Before I could back away, he had crossed the space between us, swaying on his feet, and grabbed me by the arm.

I wanted to push him away, to scream, to do anything, *and to this day I can't explain why I didn't. All I remember was the fear. The all-consuming, paralysing fear that kept me still and rooted to the spot, incapable of making a sound.*

He pulled me into the room and slammed the door shut. My legs were like jelly and still I couldn't find my voice or my strength. My brain, struggling through the haze of the few drinks I'd already had, was refusing to respond.

My pen lifts off the sheet of paper in front of me. Although I don't want to impose the details of everything that happened in that room on my boys, I can't help the memories from rushing into my mind. I close my eyes, willing myself to shut them out—but there's no point even trying.

He pushed me towards the desk and forced me to bend over onto my front. I heard him fiddle with his belt, and finally I felt my body regain control.

I started struggling against him. I tried to push him away, and I tried to scream, but he had one hand on my back and one against my mouth. I tried to bite him, and felt his hand slam against my cheek.

When he was finished, I heard him pull his trousers up and buckle his belt. He grabbed his half empty glass from his desk and downed the brown liquid in it in one go.

Then, without a word, he opened the office door and left, leaving me bent over the desk with my dress over my back, immobilised with pain and horror.

Chapter 32
Orson

The hotel was an idyllic white-stoned French noble house in the countryside, a short drive away from Dijon, in the middle of a generously sized estate. If Orson hadn't been so preoccupied, he might have appreciated the beauty of where he found himself.

Terran and Kendrik settled in their own rooms whilst Orson, under the pretext that the hotel had been fully booked at the time Terran made the reservations, was sharing a twin room with Farao. They didn't want to take the risk of leaving him on his own. Farao didn't complain at this arrangement, and Orson knew he was still distracted by the disaster of his broken phone.

They agreed to meet down at the hotel restaurant for dinner, after they'd all had a chance to rest and wash. Terran, Orson noticed, had made a point of inviting Juliette to join them later, which he suspected was an attempt at apologising for his rudeness earlier that day. The expression on Juliette's face, the disarming way in which she looked at Terran and the tentative smile that spread over her lips as she accepted his invitation had sent Orson's spidey senses tingling. *Could it be...* he wondered. He supposed he'd have a chance to find out sooner or later.

Orson was lying down on his single bed, wondering whether he should squeeze in a quick nap before dinner, when Farao's voice reached him from the other bed.

'Orson...' Farao was staring at the ceiling, and his voice was low.

'Yeah?'

'Doesn't this seem a bit... *weird* to you?'

'Weird?' Orson turned his head to look at Farao.

'Yeah...' Farao frowned. 'I mean, don't get me wrong. I'm all up for skipping school and all... But this whole trip... It really seems a bit... I don't know. Something seems off. And isn't this supposed to be some sort of celebration for Kendrik's job or whatever? He doesn't really seem to be too happy about it.'

Orson swallowed hard, glad that Farao was still looking up at the ceiling, because he was certain his face would have given him away.

'What do you think?' Farao insisted, propping himself on his elbow and looking at Orson.

'I think...' Orson said slowly, buying himself some time. 'I think that Kendrik's going through a tough time. He's working through some stuff. And yes, he's acting a bit out of character,' he conceded.

'A *bit*.' Farao raised his eyebrows. 'That's the understatement of the year...'

'But,' Orson insisted, 'whatever's wrong with him, he needs us. I know we all bicker sometimes, but at the end of the day, we're brothers. We're all we have. And we'll always go to the ends of the earth for each other.'

Farao lay back down on his bed and resumed staring at the ceiling.

'Yeah…' he said eventually. 'I guess you're right.'

There was a short pause.

'Hey, Orson…'

'Mmm?'

'Are you *sure* about the whole texting thing?' There was real concern in Farao's voice.

'A hundred percent,' Orson smiled, and yawned. 'If this doesn't get you at least one hot date, I'll eat my guitar.'

'Mmm…'

A few moments later, soft snoring sounds from the other bed told him Farao had fallen asleep.

***

They went down for dinner a little after seven. Orson had managed a short nap and, coupled with a long shower, he was feeling refreshed after the day's drive. The hotel's dining area was set in a large circular room lined with tall French windows on one side, overlooking a stone terrace and the estate beyond. The evening was pleasant and the autumn air mild, so they sat by one of the open windows. They had just taken their seats when Juliette joined them. Orson stood up and walked around the table to pull out her chair for her, and she gave him a surprised but delighted smile.

A young waiter wearing a black apron came to take their drinks order and hand over their menus.

'This place is beautiful,' Juliette breathed, looking out the window.

'It is, isn't it,' Orson agreed. 'I'm almost expecting some sort of French duchess to come prancing into the room at any time!'

Juliette gave a hearty laugh. 'Yes,' she smiled. 'I suppose that's one way of putting it.'

They all reviewed their menu, and placed their order to the young waiter who came to deliver their drinks.

'Let us raise our glass.' Orson lifted his cocktail. 'To brotherhood. And to new friends,' he added with a wink at Juliette.

'Hear, hear,' Terran chimed in.

They raised their glass, and each took a sip of their drink.

'Actually...' Terran added, suddenly looking embarrassed. 'Juliette, I'd like to apologise for my behaviour earlier... It was completely uncalled for. I'm sorry.'

'It's ok.' Juliette shook her head. 'Really. I'm the one who's sorry for butting in on your trip.'

'No, it's totally fine.' Terran raised his hands. 'That's no problem at all.'

'Ah,' Orson sighed. 'Here's the Terran we know! Juliette, didn't I tell you he was much more charming when he wasn't behaving like such an arsehole?'

'Oh, shut up,' Terran groaned, but there was a half-smile at the corner of his mouth.

They talked for some time about nothing in particular until their starters arrived. Juliette promptly picked up her phone and clicked a picture.

'So, Juliette,' Orson asked, tucking in to his plate, 'we know where you're going, but where do you come from? What's your story?'

Juliette smiled apologetically as she swallowed the mouthful she was chewing.

'Well, as you can probably hear, I'm French.' She grinned. 'I grew up in Brittany, but I moved to England when I was in my early twenties. Now I live down south.'

'Really?' Terran asked. 'Whereabouts exactly?'

'I have a house by the beach in Brighton. I moved there three years ago, after I started my PT business.'

'What's the personal training scene like around there?' Terran took a sip of wine.

'Oh, it's alright. Most of my content is online.'

Their starters were cleared, and shortly after, their mains arrived. Orson noticed Juliette taking a picture of her plate again before tucking in. Conversation flowed easily between them, although mostly led by him, Juliette and Terran. Kendrik was still very quiet, eating his food in silence. Orson could tell by the look on Farao's face that he was only half listening, and he wondered whether his mind was back on the mysterious Serena.

By the time their plates were cleared a second time, night had fallen, and Orson saw someone walk around the terrace, placing lit candles on each table, their soft light glowing in the semi-darkness.

'*Bonsoir, messieurs-dames. Excusez-moi de vous déranger.*' A man was standing by their table, older and more important-looking than the waiter who had attended to them so far.

They all looked up at him, and Orson recognised the hotel manager who had welcomed them on their arrival.

'*Mademoiselle Rochet?*' The manager was addressing Juliette directly in rapid French. 'I am Monsieur Moreaux, the hotel manager here. It is a pleasure to have you with us today. My apologies that we did not realise this before.'

'*Ne vous en faites pas.*' Juliette smiled warmly at him.

'If you will please accept a complimentary dessert,' the manager said, and he added in strongly accented English to the whole table, 'on the house. If you would like to make your way to the terrace, I will send someone with the dessert menus in just a moment.'

'*Merci beaucoup.*' Juliette nodded. '*C'est très généreux de votre part.* That would be lovely.'

When Monsieur Moreaux had gone, Farao leant in towards the group.

'Erm, what was *that* about?'

'It would seem...' Orson gave Juliette a quizzical look. '...that we have a celebrity among us!'

Juliette blushed and looked down, visibly embarrassed.

'It's nothing, really.' Her cheeks were bright red. 'I just posted about them on my Instagram story. They must have seen I have a bit of a following...'

'Define "a bit"?' Terran cocked his head at her.

'Just... a bit.' Juliette shrugged dismissively, standing up from her chair. 'Shall we?'

And she led the way to the terrace.

'Well, that was fucking weird,' Orson heard Farao mutter behind him as they all followed her outside, and Orson had to agree.

None of them, however, had a problem with free desserts, and they all indulged in a generous selection of miniature pastries—small *éclairs*, *tartelettes de fruits*, *tartes au citron meringuées* and chocolate *religieuses*. Finally, the last of the coffee *éclairs* had vanished and the manager came to personally deliver their tea and coffee, which they drank in comfortable silence. Orson's stomach was full and a sense of contentment had spread over him. The night air was light against his skin. Somewhere in the grounds, he could hear the wildlife going about their nighttime business. He glanced over at his brothers. Terran was gazing out into the darkened lawn. Kendrik was looking up at the starlit sky. Farao had his eyes closed. Orson's eyes found Juliette's profile. She was sitting beside Terran, a gentle smile resting on her lips. She'd pulled her chair just a little closer to Terran's than it really needed to be, their forearms almost touching. *How about that...* Orson silently mused, smiling a little, a tingle of hope blooming in the pit of his stomach.

For that one moment, those handfuls of seconds, life was good. He was fed, rested and in good company.

'What this is missing,' Orson said out loud to the group, and the others lazily turned their heads to look at him, 'is some acoustic guitar...'

He heard Kendrik mumble something, but he ignored him, and went back to his room to grab his case.

Back on the terrace, he settled himself into his chair, his guitar nestled in his arms, and he started playing, allowing his fingers to find whatever tune they wanted. The music filled the air around them, and he could almost feel them all breathe it in, allowing the notes to permeate their lungs.

After a while he stopped playing and nudged Farao with his toes. Farao opened his eyes and looked at him.

'Come on.' Orson handed him the guitar. 'Why don't you play us something you've been practicing?'

Farao hesitated for a second before taking hold of the guitar and adjusting it in his arms. He played a few tentative chords and cleared his throat. When Orson looked back at him, Farao's eyes were closed again, his hands expertly navigating their way over the strings. The notes to a song Orson couldn't place rang through the air, and he leant back in his chair, his head titled upwards, lost in the starry night sky.

As Farao started singing, his voice rang through the quiet evening.

'*I've travelled far... Come all the way... But now I'm lost... Can't find my way...*' Farao's voice was soft and low.

Orson took in a sharp breath. He recognised the tune as one he'd taught Farao long ago, an original he'd written right after their mother had passed away. Farao had slowed down the pace of the song, giving an acoustic rendition of it that was so raw and so piercing it gripped at Orson's insides like an iron fist. Farao sang, speaking each bit of the lyrics with so much emotion that Orson soon found it hard to breathe.

'*Now tell me why... Am I still here?... Now tell me why... you've disappeared?*'

Orson closed his eyes, because he knew that any moment now, he might start crying. That song... Those words... They brought everything to the surface. Like salt on an open wound.

'How can I live... How can I be... When all that's left... Are shards of me?

Orson inhaled slowly, and as he exhaled a wave of sadness engulfed him. He wasn't sure he could do this anymore. He could no longer ignore the fact that his baby brother was dying. That he didn't even know it. And that they had embarked on this impossible journey in the wild hope that they could do something to fix things. Orson felt his body go numb. He could no longer see the way out. He realised now how powerless they all were on the face of Destiny, and he couldn't bear to confront this new reality, this world in which Farao was going to die and there was nothing he could do about it.

Chapter 33
Kendrik

Kendrik didn't know how long they stayed there, listening to Farao playing. It felt like much, much later when the hotel manager came to tell them they were closing the restaurant, apologising profusely for asking them to vacate the terrace. Terran and Juliette had to assure Monsieur Moreaux that no offence was taken, and they walked back to their respective rooms without much talking.

Kendrik met Terran and Orson's eyes as they ascended the stairs to their floor, and he saw that, for all of their determination and strength of character, this evening his brothers were feeling exactly how he was feeling. Dejected. Exhausted. Terrified. He gave them a curt nod, because that was all he could manage.

Alone in his room, Kendrik lay fully dressed on his bed staring at the ceiling, the enormity of what they were doing dawning on him more than ever before. The hurt he'd seen in Terran and Orson's faces tonight, rather than reassuring him that he was not alone in his pain, had scared him. He needed them to be strong. He needed them to carry this forward, because *he* sure as hell didn't feel like he could do this without them. He fell into an agitated sleep. When the phone on his bedside table rang with a wake-up call from the front desk, it felt like no time at all had passed. He dragged himself out of bed and into the shower, willing himself to attention.

Breakfast was a light-hearted affair. Terran and Orson seemed to now be making a point of pulling themselves out of the previous evening's slump by acting as positively as they could. Juliette joined them for breakfast too, and she and Orson were talking about the classes she was leading at the festival she was headed to. Farao still seemed half asleep, his head bent over a cup of black coffee.

They stored their bags back in the car, and the manager insisted on personally checking them out, giving Juliette a little bow of the head as he asked her what she thought of her stay and suggested she gave the hotel a review. Kendrik thought this behaviour a little odd, but he let it slide. He wasn't quite awake enough for much mental deliberation on what Monsieur Moreaux's deal was.

They all climbed in the SUV, Kendrik conceding the front passenger seat to Juliette, who, after some polite back and forth, climbed in next to Terran. The doors were closed, seatbelts were fastened, and Terran turned the key into the ignition. Once. Twice. Three times. Nothing happened. On the fourth attempt, the engine gave a little raspy cough, then a shudder, and was quiet once more.

Chapter 34
Terran

'You have *got* to be joking!' Terran exclaimed, throwing his hands in the air, undoing his seatbelt and stomping out of the car.

He lifted the hood and peered inside. He didn't know exactly what he was looking for, but the slim stream of smoke emanating from the engine told him something was definitely not right. He gave a cry of frustration. Orson and Kendrik came rushing out of the car, Juliette on their heels. Farao's head stuck out of the open window.

'What's wrong?' Orson asked.

'I don't know...' Terran groaned.

Juliette took one look under the hood and hurried up the stairs back to the hotel reception, returning a moment later with Monsieur Moreaux in tow. The hotel manager pulled up his sleeves, bent over under the fuming engine and poked at a few wires, muttering to himself.

'*Bon*,' he finally said, standing up and turning to look at them all. 'I think you need a *garagiste... Comment vous dîtes en Anglais?* What do you say? Ah, a mechanic. Yes, a mechanic. For your battery. See, *la batterie*, here? *Là?* It is broken. It needs to be replaced.'

His words were met by silence as Terran took in their implication. From the corner of his eye, he caught Orson and Kendrik exchange a meaningful look.

'But, not to worry,' Monsieur Moreaux added quickly, '*ne vous inquiétez pas*. My cousin's husband, he is a mechanic. Tomorrow, I will call him and he will come to replace the *batterie*. No problem.'

'Tomorrow?' Terran said feebly. 'Can't it be done today?'

'Today!' Monsieur Moreaux chuckled, then added, apologetically, 'But today, *Monsieur*, it is Sunday. Everywhere is closed! No, no. It will be tomorrow. But I promise you, tomorrow morning, your car is fixed. *Voilà*! As good as new!'

Terran felt his legs threaten to give way, and he went to sit down on the stone steps to the hotel front door, his head in his hands. *This can't be happening,* he thought, his mind instantly spiralling into the dozen ways he could have prevented this. He could have taken the car for an MOT before they'd left. He could have gone for a long drive before they'd set off on this journey to make sure the car could handle the distance. He could have learnt more about car maintenance so he'd know how to fix a dead battery. *Coulda, shoulda, woulda.* He shook his head, silently berating himself, feeling like, once again, no matter how hard he tried, it never seemed to be good enough.

'Why, God, why…' he whispered under his breath, and he looked up when he felt a hand on his shoulder, to see Orson standing above him.

'It's okay, Ter,' he said quietly, his face serious. 'I know what you're thinking. But a day won't make a difference. There's nothing much we can do about it right now…'

Terran slowly nodded, feeling his throat constrict.

'Listen, listen.' Monsieur Moreaux came striding towards them. 'Don't worry, it is all fine. *Ça va aller.* I will take care of it. We will give you a room again tonight, free of charge! And you can borrow some bicycles and enjoy the day around here. The area, it is beautiful. *Magnifique!* Yes?'

But Terran couldn't respond. His voice had disappeared somewhere in his oesophagus, and he could not let out a single word of thanks. Juliette came to the rescue.

'That's very generous of you, Monsieur Moreaux. *Merci infiniment.*'

'Not at all! Not at all!' Monsieur Moreaux exclaimed, leading her back towards the front desk to sort out the logistics.

'Well,' Orson said jovially when she returned, 'when life gives you lemons and all that. Let us make the most of this day, shall we?'

Terran simply shrugged, but inside he was screaming. On a rational level, one that was buried under layers and layers of guilt and shame, he knew there was little he could have done to prevent this. He even knew, deep down, that this wasn't the end of the world. But he also knew the voice of reason never won at times like these. All he could see was that he'd failed, and try as he might, he couldn't let it go.

Half an hour later, with their luggage back in their rooms, they set off on the borrowed bikes down the path Monsieur Moreaux had indicated to them, which would take them on a scenic loop around the estate and back to the hotel. He had asked for the baskets affixed to the bikes to be filled with enough snacks and drinks for a picnic. Juliette had thanked him over and over again, though he had simply waved her off with a paternal smile.

'*Mais non, voyons.* Not at all, not at all,' he repeated. '*Ce n'est rien.* Enjoy your *balade!*'

***

A large earthy track had been cleared, leading right into the woods through the estate, and continued along a little stream, beyond which the countryside stretched as far as the eye could see.

Terran felt his bad mood slowly dissipate as they cycled further and further along the path. He liked this setting, a place unpolluted by human activities. A gentle breeze ruffled through the leaves, mingling with the soft songs of birds calling out to each other, and the sound of it all was as soothing as anything Terran had ever heard.

He found himself recognising some of the vegetation around him—ferns, oak trees, a few pines and birch trees. It reminded him of being out in the woods with his parents and brothers, a long, long time ago. Orson, Kendrik and him playing cowboys and Indians, building makeshift huts out of sticks and branches, feathers stuck behind their ears, pretending to be explorers. The sun was peeking through the trees, giving the greenery around them a soft golden glow. It was quiet here. Peaceful. A little piece of heaven away from everything. For a second, he contemplated staying there forever, the bike ride going on for all of eternity, in a place where he never had to face what came at the end of the road.

The general atmosphere in their group was pleasant, largely due to Juliette's presence, which forced them all to stay on their best behaviour and distracted them from the troubles of their own minds.

'*On avançait sur les chemins, on s'en allait tous les matins.*' Orson sang the first line of the song they had heard their mother sing so many times in the past.

'*Sur nos bicyclettes!*' Juliette joined in, beaming at him, and together they sang the parts that they remembered, exploding with laughter when they reached the end.

A little while later, they came by a grassy meadow where the stream slowed down and gathered in a small pool of clear water. They decided to take a break there and laid out their picnic on one of the blankets stored in their baskets. They delighted in the delicious-looking selection Monsieur Moreaux had provided for them, and sat down to eat.

After some time, Farao grabbed a blanket and went to lie down a short distance away. Kendrik was sitting by the water's edge, his naked feet in the clear stream. Orson was lying on his back, arms bent behind his head, humming gently.

'So,' Terran asked Juliette, helping himself to a second serving of cheese sandwich and lemonade, 'how did you get into personal training?'

'Ah,' she said with a smile. 'It's kind of a long story.'

'Great!' Orson exclaimed, giving her a wink. 'Long stories are the best stories.'

'That's true,' she laughed. 'Well, it all happened randomly at first. I was very sick as a child. No matter what my parents did, I was never completely fine. I just remember spending a lot of time at the doctor's growing up. I was always taking all these different kinds of pills. Some of them made things worse, some of them sort of helped, but none of them ever had an impact on the underlying condition. My parents tried everything, but I'd always be collapsing at birthday parties, or be taken ill at school events. I was one of these kids that never really got to take part in things because everyone was worried I was too fragile to take it.'

She paused, and Terran watched her pull a few blades of grass from the ground and shred them. She spoke of it all in such measured tones, but he could see it must have been a lot to go through at such a young age. There was something in her expression he thought he recognised. Resignation, maybe, or acceptance? Something that told him that she'd grown used to telling the story, and that she'd managed to let go of the pain she might have once felt because of it.

'That must have been really lonely,' Orson observed, his voice full of kindness.

Juliette threw the shreds of grass aside and gave him a small smile. 'It was,' she sighed. 'But I guess it could have been much worse. It taught me to listen to my body and my inner voice from a really young age, which is more than can be said for a lot of people.'

'True that.' Orson nodded.

'Because I spent so much time on my own, I got used to reading a lot,' Juliette continued. 'As a teenager, I read this book about nutrition and how simple changes you can make to your diet influence how you feel... And it started from there, really. I read up on nutrition, then on exercise, and started to incorporate both into my life. It seemed to help.' She looked over at the stream. 'And it worked for some time... Then, after university, I started working an office job, and suddenly I didn't really have time or energy to eat well or work out, and I started getting sick again.' She grimaced. 'I spent some time in the hospital, but back then they couldn't figure out what was wrong with me. My symptoms were all over the place. Tests always came back inconclusive. No one thing ever made sense of everything that was going on with me. It wasn't until years later that they figured out the diagnosis.'

'What was it in the end?' Terran frowned.

'I'm diabetic. And on top of that, I have a perfect storm of food intolerances and hormonal imbalances that just make everything worse. It took finding the right doctor, someone who was able to look at the bigger picture. It's a lot easier to manage now that I know what I'm dealing with and have the right medication. But back in the day, I didn't have a clue what was wrong with me. So I started forcing myself to get back to the routines that had worked for me before. Eating healthy and keeping fit made me feel better, and so this time I kept it up. I started training some of my friends... And the freelance work grew from there, really. Now I do it full time.'

Terran looked at Juliette, trying to put words on what he was feeling. It was a mixture of awe and affection, he thought, an all-encompassing tenderness that made him simultaneously want to wrap his arms around her and worship at her feet. He couldn't help the wave of admiration coursing through him at the idea of what she'd had to live through and her determination not to let it bring her down. He knew better than anyone how hard that was. And despite her struggles, she carried herself with grace, with a self-assurance and presence that he knew he didn't possess. How odd, he wondered to himself in amazement, he barely knew her, and yet there was a powerful pull inside him that told him to hold on to her and never let go.

'That's impressive,' was all he could say.

Orson nodded silently, too.

'Is it?' Juliette shrugged. 'I don't know… I just did what I could to feel better. The nutrition and exercise was just a way to help myself. I didn't want to spend my life being that same sick kid sitting on the sidelines all the time. But it morphed into something else of its own accord…'

Orson sat up to face her. 'Everything you did, you worked to make it happen. And that, in itself, is really impressive. Regardless of why you started in the first place.'

'That's very kind of you to say.' Juliette smiled.

'Well, I did warn you when we met.' Orson gave her a cheeky grin. 'We are an extremely charming bunch.'

Juliette laughed, and the sound of her laughter filled the air. Terran thought he'd never heard anything more alluring in his life.

'Yes,' she admitted. 'Yes, you *did* say something like that.'

She lifted her gaze and she met Terran's eyes. For a brief moment, they simply looked at each other, smiling. Terran was first to look away. He cleared his throat.

'So, should we head off?'

'What's the rush?' Juliette cocked her head at him. 'We just got here!'

She stood up, took off her shoes and held out her hand to him.

'You, mister, need to learn how to relax...' She gave him a knowing smile.

'I'm extremely relaxed!' Terran protested.

Behind him, Orson snorted loudly, and Terran turned around to give him a stern look.

'What?'

'Oh, sorry,' Orson said in mock innocence. 'Was I being too subtle? Ter, you're the least relaxed person I know. I doubt you even know the meaning of the word.'

'Come on.' Juliette grabbed hold of Terran's arm and forced him to his feet. 'Shoes off and follow me.'

He obeyed and followed her to the edge of the stream, where she motioned to him to advance into the water.

'I'll get my jeans wet...' he complained, and she rolled her eyes at him.

She pulled up her leggings and motioned to him to do the same. He imitated her, rolling up his jeans, and came to stand beside her, the water reaching halfway up his calves. She beamed at him.

'Now what?' Terran asked.

'Now...' Juliette leant in towards him, a secretive look on her face. 'Now, nothing.'

He looked at her blankly.

'Terran,' she said calmly, speaking to him as though placating a difficult child. 'Breathe. Look around you. Look at how beautiful this place is. It's all there to be enjoyed, if you'll just give it a chance...'

He raised his eyebrows at her, but did as she said and looked around, taking in a deep breath. She was right, he had to admit. The place truly *was* beautiful. The sun was peering through the canopy of trees, glittering against the surface of the water. Beyond the stream, fields of yellow and green expanded in a colourful canvas to the horizon. The air around them felt crisp in a delicious sort of way. The water was cool and refreshing against his skin. He wiggled his toes. He couldn't remember the last time he had forced himself to stand still for more than a few seconds. There was always something to attend to, something to worry about, something to solve. And in the midst of all that, he never took the time to just pause and breathe.

'So?' Juliette probed, watching out for his reaction.

He looked at her, grinning. 'Yeah… It's alright.'

'Just alright? You're a tough crowd…'

'Yeah, I've heard that one before…' He sighed.

He felt his phone vibrate in his pocket and he picked up, seeing Amit's name flash on the screen.

'Sorry.' He gave Juliette an apologetic look. 'I have to take this.'

'Of course,' she said, but he'd already trodden away.

'Amit,' he said cautiously into the receiver, glancing back at Juliette and then at the others to make sure he couldn't be heard. 'Any news?'

There was little point beating around the bush.

'No,' Amit sighed on the other end of the phone. 'It doesn't mean it's over,' he insisted, 'these things just take time. How's everything on your end? How was the drive?'

They spoke for a few minutes, Terran filling Amit in on their journey. He hung up and slid his phone back into his pocket, a familiar feeling of lingering dread taking hold of him. Juliette was watching him in silence from where she still stood, knee-deep in the clear stream. She looked as though she was about to say something.

'Hey, love birds!' Orson called out from behind them. 'Shall we get going?'

Terran gave Juliette a brief smile and turned around. Whatever moment he had been granted to take in the scenery, he knew it had to end. Reality always caught up with him sooner or later. When all this was over, when Farao was saved, when this was all behind them… Maybe *then* would he take the time to stop and smell the roses.

Chapter 35
Farao

Back in the hotel room, Farao pulled his phone from his pocket out of habit, only to find it was still irrevocably broken. He swore under his breath, and his thoughts travelled back to Serena. He wondered what she would think, seeing the text she had sent him as read but still without a response. He hoped Orson was right, and that he wasn't ruining his only chance to make a good impression with the girl he'd fancied ever since he had first laid eyes on her.

Of course, a lot of guys at school fancied her too, because she was absolutely gorgeous, and Farao had never thought he even stood a chance. He'd watched her from afar, trying to make the most of the smallest of interactions he got with her, but never gathering enough courage to ask her out. Mel often teased him about it, and he got the impression she was jealous of Serena and the attention she attracted. The more he thought about Serena, the more he felt his body respond. He pictured her soft figure, the delicate roundness of her chest showing through her school uniform, her long legs. Another image, of Mel this time, wormed its way into his mind, a vivid depiction of one of their snogging sessions behind the shed, that one time when she'd...

Orson poked his head through the door, dragging Farao away from his silent reflections, making him jump a metre into the air and almost fall down from his bed.

'Dinner in ten minutes.'

'Shit, Orson,' Farao croaked. 'Sure, sure. I'm coming.'

Orson gave him a quizzical look but didn't linger, and a moment later he was gone. Farao took a moment to catch his breath. He shook his head, trying to calm his body down. *Dead puppies*, he said to himself, sitting on the side of the bed, willing the blood to rush away from his groin.

A huge pile of shit. Old grannies. A slimy fat naked guy. Dead baby penguins.

Slowly, the age-old trick worked, and giving himself one last look into the full length mirror, still slightly red with embarrassment, he made his way down to dinner.

Chapter 36
Orson

Orson watched Terran closely over dinner, wondering if his earlier suspicions were correct. His brother looked different. For the first time, there was a softness in his gaze that Orson had never seen before. The thought pleased him, because he wanted so much for Terran to live a little. Orson had seen how he'd set everything aside to look after his brothers, and he'd rarely seen him falter since.

But the walls he'd seen Terran erect around himself had also meant he kept himself closed up to anything else around him beyond their family. And this, of all things, made Orson feel guilty for being able to enjoy his life as much as he did. Today, however, looking at Terran's eyes light up with every smile Juliette sent his way, and the attentive gaze he gave her when she spoke to him, Orson felt hopeful. Maybe, just maybe, something good could flourish from all of this mess.

Dinner was as delicious as it had been the night before, and Monsieur Moreaux was all thoughtful attention towards them. He seemed to have taken to this odd group, stranded as they were in his hotel. After their plates had been cleared up, they made their way again to the terrace, where they were brought a warm pot of fresh mint tea. Orson grabbed himself a cup, and motioned to Kendrik and Farao to join him at a table a little distance away from where Terran and Juliette were deep in conversation. When Kendrik gave him a questioning look, Orson quietly tilted his head towards their elder brother, signalling that they should give them some space. But Kendrik, far from looking pleased, sat down grumpily and noisily onto a chair. Farao and Orson exchanged a look. Farao simply shrugged and shook his head, but Orson turned his gaze to Kendrik again, watching him closely.

Kendrik's mouth was in a hard line, his whole face set into a cold expression. Orson frowned. Something didn't feel right, he thought. Kendrik wasn't the angry type. He got frustrated when he was stressed, of course, but didn't they all? This sort of reaction though, out of proportion and seemingly fuelled by pettiness, felt at odds with Kendrik's nature, usually so conciliatory and mild-mannered.

'You alright there, Ken?' Orson asked in a low voice.

Kendrik huffed, but didn't respond, crossing his arms in front of his chest.

'I guess that's your answer…' Farao rolled his eyes.

'Fuck you,' Kendrik seethed.

'Whoa, whoa, whoa.' Orson turned to Kendrik sharply, but tried hard to keep his voice as quiet as he could. 'There's no need for that.'

'No need? No *need*?' Kendrik blabbered on in an angry whisper. 'We're right here, alright? In this… In this… In *this*. And he's over there like a… Like…' He struggled for words. 'What about fucking brotherhood!'

'Jeez, Ken.' Farao frowned at him. 'Chill.'

'Don't *you* fucking tell me to chill, of all people,' Kendrik growled.

'What's that supposed to mean?' Farao retorted coldly.

Orson stood up and took Kendrik by the elbow, pulling him to his feet.

'Alright,' he said with a finality in his voice he hoped would reach Kendrik. 'I think someone's ready for bed.'

Kendrik tried to protest, and Terran and Juliette turned around at the sound.

'Everything ok, there?' Terran asked.

'Fantastic, dear brother,' Orson said in a jovial tone, 'Ken over here's just ready to turn in.'

Orson gave Terran a pointed look and Terran frowned, but seemed to get the message.

'Come on, Farao, let's go,' Orson added. 'Night, night, guys!'

Orson led his two brothers up the stairs and told Farao to go ahead to their room, whilst he accompanied Kendrik to his. The moment Orson closed the door behind them, Kendrik exploded, and the force of his outburst took Orson by surprise.

'What the fuck, Orson! What the absolute *fuck*! I'm not a fucking child!'

And with those words, he strode across the room, grabbed his bag and hurled it across the room in anger.

'Well, you sure seem intent upon acting like one right now,' Orson said quietly.

Kendrik marched towards him, stopping just inches away from Orson, his face distorted with fury. Orson forced himself to remain calm, although everything inside him was ringing with alarm bells. He'd never seen Kendrik like this before—*ever*—and the sight of him in such a state chilled him to his core. *Breathe*, he kept repeating to himself, *just breathe, so you can get him through this.*

Kendrik's cheeks were reddened with anger, his nostrils flared, tears building up at the corners of his eyes. For a split second, Orson thought Kendrik was going to hit him. In that moment he felt suspended in time, the tension stretching between them to breaking point. Kendrik's pupils were dilated, his teeth clenched and his breathing heavy. Orson glimpsed Kendrik's fists clenching by his sides, and he braced himself for the blow. *If that's what it takes*, he thought, cringing, hoping Kendrik wouldn't get his nose. But slowly, like a balloon deflating, Kendrik's face fell and his entire demeanour changed. His shoulders sagged and he lowered his head. He started sobbing loudly. Orson wrapped his arms around him and held him tight.

'I'm sorry,' Kendrik cried. 'Orson, I'm so sorry... I think I'm going mad... I can't deal with this... Farao... Mum... It's too much, I don't know how to deal with this... I'm not as strong as you, or Terran... I can't deal with this...'

Orson felt the hot tears soak the fabric of his tee-shirt and he held Kendrik tighter. He couldn't leave him like this. Nor was he comfortable leaving Farao on his own for too long. He thought of Terran, sat comfortably outside on the terrace with Juliette, and a painful dilemma emerged in his mind.

When Kendrik finally calmed down, Orson led him into bed and pulled the covers over him. Kendrik's eyes closed almost immediately. Then Orson took a seat in the armchair in the corner of the room and rested his head against the high back, feeling suddenly drained. It felt to him like as long as he was moving, he could cope. But it was in moments like this, where there was complete stillness and silence, that the truth caught up with him.

It had taken him years to come to terms with what had happened to his mother, although 'coming to terms' with it was probably overselling it. All he'd managed was getting to a point where he knew how to brush the thought aside without feeling like he was about to vomit. If he pushed it away fast enough when it popped up, most of the time he could get on with whatever else he was doing. As the years passed, he'd learnt to bury the truth so deep inside of him that there were moments he could almost forget it was there.

At the very beginning, he'd briefly wondered if it would make him feel any different about Farao, but he'd soon realised that, if anything, it made him feel even more protective of his younger brother. He categorically refused to think of Farao as his half-brother. He'd never seen him that way, and he knew he never could. Farao was his brother, end of story. The thought that Farao might no longer be with them… Orson swallowed hard. The mere idea of it felt like having his heart wrenched out of his chest with hot pincers.

On the bed, Kendrik turned sleepily on his side. Orson looked over at him from the corner of the room, but Kendrik didn't stir again. Orson closed his eyes. On one thing he hadn't been able to reach a conclusion: how his father had felt about the whole situation. His mother's letter was clear on that topic, their father had known everything. Orson wished more than anything that he could have asked his father about it. About how it had affected him. About whether that was the reason he'd… Orson shook his head. He couldn't go back there now. He neither had the courage nor the energy for it right now. But under his breath, the lyrics to a long-buried song surfaced to the tip of his tongue, and he found himself muttering them in the darkness.

'I wander like a ghost… For proof that I still feel… But all I find is pain… How can I know that's real…'

Minutes ticked by. Orson waited for Kendrik's breathing to fully slow down, suggesting he had fallen into a deep sleep. He knew what he needed to do. He wished he didn't have to ask Terran to choose between his own happiness and his duty towards his brothers, but he also knew that, given the choice, any of them would always show up for the others, no matter what.

Chapter 37
Terran

Terran breathed in deeply. On the seat next to him, Juliette was sipping her tea, her gaze upon the starry sky. A comfortable silence had settled between them, one that made Terran feel at peace with himself. Apart from his brothers, he'd never met anyone with whom he felt comfortable enough to be himself completely. But the more time he spent with Juliette, the more he was realising how easy it was to be around her.

He remembered his father once telling him that he'd known their mother was the one the moment he'd laid eyes on her. For a long time, Terran had thought that this was the same for everyone. That when he met his ideal life partner, he'd know instantly. Obviously that hadn't happened so far. And even now, enjoying his time with Juliette more and more, he couldn't say that he'd fallen for her the way his father always described falling for his mum. He liked Juliette, that much was becoming clear to him, though he didn't truly know what to make of it, but he was lacking the instant certainty his father had described that she was made for him. He had lived enough by now to know that love at first sight was more of an exception than a rule, but deep inside him the belief that it should have been that way for him too was hard to change.

'Penny for your thoughts?' Juliette smiled at him in the semi-darkness.

Terran smiled back at her, apologetic. 'I don't know if they're worth even that...'

She looked at him with such intensity, like she could see right through his pretence, that he found it hard to hold her gaze.

'Do you sometimes wish,' she whispered, turning her face towards the night sky once more, 'that you could pretend your life is a movie... And that at any time you could get out of character, check the script and know what all the next scenes have in store for you?'

Terran let out a breath, leaning back into his chair, gazing at the stars.

'I wish...' He sighed. 'Oh, how I wish...'

'I used to think I could,' Juliette continued, lost in contemplation of the spectacle above them. 'When I got sick, I used to tell myself I was really just an actress enacting a story, and that the end had already been written. I used to picture myself flicking through the pages to know exactly how it all ended...'

'And?' He glanced at her, but her eyes were still resolutely looking up. 'Did it ever work? Or make a difference?'

'Sort of.' She grinned at him. 'At the end of the day, I was still sick. But it gave me faith. It helped me believe that I could write my own ending. That I wouldn't spend the rest of my life in and out of hospital. That there was another way. And that made a whole world of difference.'

Terran considered her for a moment. 'Sort of a "mind over matter" thing, then?'

'In a way, yes.'

Terran looked down into his cup of tea, swirling the now lukewarm liquid against the edges of the fine china.

'Sometimes…' he started, his hands shaking a little. 'Some things you just can't change. No matter how much you want to believe differently.'

Juliette's brow furrowed, but she said nothing. Terran felt it then, the need to say more. The burning desire to have someone else share his truth and help him carry the hardest thing he'd ever had to deal with. But the words didn't come. The moment was there, ripe for him to seize, but he couldn't let the words out. He couldn't let himself be helped. He felt himself clinging to his duty with more fervour than ever, comforted in the familiar knowledge that it was his and his only. That he alone could make it right. That his brothers' welfare, their safety, their happiness depended on him. Because the day this was no longer true, the day he no longer needed to carry it all on his shoulders, after years of making it his life's mission… what would he have left? Who would he be then? Did he even know who he'd be if he let go of the biggest part of himself?

'Some things you just can't change,' he repeated, a tone of finality in his voice.

She didn't probe. She didn't contradict him. She didn't try to tell him he could, in fact, write his own ending, if he'd only let himself open up to the possibility. A small part of him, one that was buried so deep under the surface it was nothing but a faint murmur, wished she would. But Juliette said nothing. Instead she nodded slowly and went back to staring at the sky, her face pale and soft in the moonlight.

Behind them, the door to the terrace creaked open and Terran turned around to see Orson standing in the doorway. Terran knew immediately from the look on his face that something was wrong.

'Sorry to disrupt your evening, guys.' Orson grimaced. 'But, Terran… You're needed upstairs.'

Terran was on his feet instantly, a sense of dread spreading through him like wildfire. *What now?* he thought. Did he only ever need to look away for half a second for something to go wrong?

'Is everything ok?' Juliette asked with concern.

'Of course, my lady.' Orson gave her a little bow. 'Nothing to worry about.'

'Well.' Terran waved awkwardly at Juliette, impatient to get going. 'Goodnight.'

He strode back into the hotel, barely hearing's Juliette 'goodnight' in return.

'What happened?' he asked Orson when he was sure they were out of earshot.

'I don't know.' Orson shook his head, leading the way up the stairs. 'It's Kendrik. He sort of... lost it.'

'Lost it?'

'Yeah, we were talking and... I don't know...' Orson repeated. 'I've never seen him like this. Anyways. He's asleep now. But I'm not sure we should leave him alone.'

Terran nodded. They came to a halt in front of the door to Kendrik's room, which was adjacent to Orson and Farao's.

'It's fine, I'll stay in his room tonight,' Terran sighed. 'I'll see you tomorrow.' And with one last nod at Orson, he stepped into the darkened room.

He paused for a moment in front of the bed, assuring himself that Kendrik was still asleep. Then, sitting in one of the armchairs, he took off his shoes and socks, realising he was suddenly very awake and wondering how on earth he was going to manage falling asleep now. He sat, hunched forward, watching Kendrik's chest rise and fall. The sense of guilt taking over was overwhelming. *This all happened on my watch. I should have been there. I've been distracted.* He wasn't sure what he could've done to help, but that was beside the point. He had let his guard down, and Kendrik had needed him, and he hadn't been there. Terran rubbed his eyes with his fists, wishing he could catch a break, and knowing that wasn't on the cards.

He stood up and walked to the balcony, the cold stone sending shivers through his bare feet. Orson was leaning against the stone ledge on the adjoining balcony, sipping a Stella Artois. He looked up when he saw Terran, and smiled as though he'd been expecting him.

'Well, fancy seeing you here.' Orson gave him a weak grin and handed him a second bottle of beer.

Terran smiled back. He never knew how Orson did it. All he knew was that he was always ready to catch each of them when they fell.

'Thanks,' Terran said, taking the bottle and resting his elbows on the stone ledge in front of him.

They let the silence stretch, each sipping their beer, gazing out into the grounds in front of them. Terran tried to reason with himself, to calm his busy mind, but the guilt was eating up at him.

'Don't worry about Kendrik…' Orson said quietly, reading Terran's mind.

Terran turned to look at him, but said nothing.

'He's a sensitive boy, our Ken.' Orson nodded. 'Underneath it all. But he'll figure it out.'

Terran shook his head. 'I don't know, Orson. I mean… Are we missing something here?'

'We just need to…' Orson shrugged. 'Be there for him, I guess.'

They fell quiet again. To Terran, the silence rang with the thousands of worst case scenarios he knew he was powerless to fight.

'Do you ever wish…' Terran whispered. 'Do you ever wish you could… You know… Step out of it all. Just for a while.'

Orson gave him a sideways glance. 'I used to…' he said after a moment. 'Quite a lot. I used to resent Mum and Dad for being dead…' He gave a sad chuckle. 'How stupid is that…'

Terran didn't say anything, but he thought it was anything but stupid.

'But now,' Orson continued. 'Now, I just try to make the most of it. And again,' he added like an afterthought, 'I don't have nearly as many responsibilities as you do.'

Terran groaned. 'Yeah... I'm guessing you don't want to switch places?'

'Nah, I'm good, thanks.' Orson smiled and shook his head, taking another sip of beer.

'I just...' Terran gazed up at the sky. 'Sometimes I just want to take a break, you know...'

But even just saying the words felt like a betrayal, and he stopped himself from saying any more. Orson turned towards him, his face suddenly serious.

'Terran,' he said. 'It's ok to think it. And it's ok to say it. It doesn't take anything away from everything you do.'

Terran looked at Orson, his jaw tense.

'It shouldn't be all on you,' Orson continued. 'It's *not* all on you.'

'Isn't it, though...' Terran murmured.

'Terran...'

'And yet.' Terran ignored him, feeling his chest tighten, speaking the words before he could stop himself. 'It's *you* she confided in...'

Orson said nothing, and they let the words float in the air between them. Terran knew there was little to be said. As much as he was the one in charge, the one picking up the slack, the one who tried his hardest to keep their lives running smoothly, at the end of the day, none of that made a difference. In her final hours, it wasn't him his mother had entrusted with her darkest secret. And, more than anything, it was the truth of that fact that made Terran feel like his entire existence was a lie.

Chapter 38
Juliette

Juliette watched the two brothers disappear through the dining room door, leaving her alone on the terrace. She nestled her cup closer to herself, bringing her knees into her chest. She shivered, even though the night wasn't all that cold. She took a deep breath, forcing her heart rate to slow down, wondering what on earth was happening to her.

This is all insane, she thought. All of this, everything that had happened since Marianna had called her to say she could no longer pick her up and drive her to the festival. Orson approaching her with his cheeky grin and extravagant manners. She'd been reluctant to engage in conversation at first, concerned as she had been to figure out how she'd make it to her destination. But there'd been something about Orson that had made her feel at ease. Something beyond his obvious charisma. Something so real, so innocent, almost childlike that had told her, in the deepest parts of her gut, that she could trust him.

Who would have thought that this random stranger, unexpectedly stranded at the same service station, would happen to be going in the same direction she was headed? And who would have thought he'd have a spare seat?

The odds of it all were insane. The word kept buzzing around Juliette's head like a talisman. *Insane.* Just *insane.* But what sent her mind racing was that that hadn't even been the wildest part of it. The wildest part was *him.*

Terran.

She'd taken one look at him and she'd known, the electric current of body recognition coursing through her like a thunderbolt. She'd never met him, didn't know a thing about him, and right at that point he'd looked less than happy to see her, but she'd *known.* Her body knew. Her entire self knew with absolute certainty. *There you are*, her soul had whispered. *There you finally are.* She'd never felt that way about anyone before.

She could tell that, although he'd made an effort to be welcoming after his initial reluctance, Terran didn't feel the same way about her. Or that, if he did, he wasn't aware of it yet. But that didn't matter. Juliette knew these things weren't always perfectly synchronised. She wasn't even sure she understood it herself. So she'd taken it slowly, gently, realising that it'd take a lot for Terran to open up. She'd need to be patient, and that even then it might never happen. But she couldn't live with herself without giving whatever was happening here a chance to flourish, no matter how slim.

So, for the time being, she'd do nothing. She'd let the brothers deal with whatever tense situation was obviously unfolding between them, which they tried so hard—and failed—to conceal to the world. As she swallowed the rest of her tea and stood up to retire to her room, she hoped that, once again, she would be granted the chance to write the end of her own story.

Chapter 39
Kendrik

When he woke up, Kendrik felt numb and empty. He could barely muster the strength to open his eyes. There was warm daylight seeping into the room through the open curtains. He looked slowly around and his gaze found Terran's figure, fully dressed, asleep on the other side of the double bed.

Kendrik took a moment to awaken, the memory of the previous night sending a fresh wave of pain and shame through him. He dragged himself to the shower and turned the jet onto the coldest setting, the icy water slapping him to full consciousness. He forced himself not to move away from it. A few minutes later, he stepped back into the room, a towel wrapped around his waist, to find Terran had woken up.

'Hey,' Kendrik said.

He felt so embarrassed, but he didn't know where to start with his apology.

'Terran...' he started.

'It's ok,' Terran said simply, placing a hand on Kendrik's shoulder. 'Ken. It's alright. We're here for you, ok?'

Kendrik could only nod, but the gratitude that shot through him warmed up his insides.

'I'll just go and get ready,' Terran yawned. 'I'll see you at breakfast.'

Kendrik nodded again and watched his brother walk through the door. With a shake of the head, he forced himself into motion. Packing his bag and getting dressed, he swore to himself that, from that moment on, he would do better.

Chapter 40
Gabrielle

I didn't try to find Anand.

I just couldn't face him. I couldn't face anyone.

I don't know how I found my way out of there. I don't know how I got home. All of it is a blur. All I know is that I came to in our little bathroom, crouched on the tiles of the shower cubicle, fully dressed, with the water running over my head.

I must have gone home fine. I must have relieved the babysitter of her duties. I must have, but I have no memory of it.

As my hand hovers over the letter I know I need to finish, I recall that time with such accuracy it's almost as if I'm there.

I sat under the burning hot water, as hot as the tap would go, until my skin felt as much on fire from outside as it did from inside.

I almost tore my dress off my body, never wanting to see it again. I grabbed the bar of soap and frantically rubbed it against every single inch of my body, over, and over, and over again. I felt dirty. Filthy. Disgusting. I wanted to wash the evening away from reality. To erase it from my memory.

I don't know how long I stayed in the shower, but it must have been some time, because when Anand stormed in, a long time later, in a panic, I was still there. The hot water had run out a long time ago, but I hadn't noticed.

Anand said something about the babysitter calling the base asking for him, that she'd been worried when she saw me, and he had hurried home.

He took one look at me and instantly knew something was wrong.

I wouldn't let him touch me. I couldn't let him anywhere near me.

My stomach lurched and I vomited everywhere on the bathroom floor, the acid burn at the back of my throat almost feeling like a relief.

He asked what had happened, but I think that deep down, that night, he already knew.

Hearing it from me, when I was finally able to say the words, only confirmed his suspicions.

The first chink in the armour of us appeared that night.

A few weeks later, I found out I was pregnant, and we broke completely.

Chapter 41
Terran

First thing in the morning, the mechanic came and replaced their battery, and they were ready to hit the road again. When Terran climbed into his seat, he noticed that, once again, Orson, Kendrik and Farao were sat in the back, leaving the passenger seat for Juliette. He caught Orson's eye in the rear-view mirror. Orson winked at him, and Terran felt his cheeks heat up.

Was it so obvious? Had *he* been so obvious? He had very little experience of these things. He'd never found anyone he wanted to get to know as much as Juliette, though in truth he had never looked very hard. He'd been too busy being the head of the family. He glanced at Orson in the rear-view mirror again, and his brother gave him a broad grin. Had Orson guessed how he felt? Did Orson think Juliette was interested, too?

He drove the car through the little roads. They had the windows open, and the fresh morning air was flowing all around them.

By his side, Juliette had taken off her shoes and was sitting cross-legged on her seat. She'd switched on the radio and found a station playing an old Adele song. It was more prompting than either she or Orson needed, and before anyone could stop them, they were singing at the top of their lungs, roping Farao in midway through.

It wasn't the most harmonious bit of singing Terran had ever heard, but he couldn't help himself. As he took a right turn, ready to speed up onto the motorway, he burst out laughing, and once he'd started he couldn't stop himself. It took hold of him and brought him almost to the brink of tears. His laughter spread through the car and, one by one, they all joined in, even Kendrik. Farao was bent over double with laughter, nursing a stitch in his side. It was some time before they all calmed down and Terran found he could breathe a little easier than before.

'Well, for what it's worth,' Juliette announced, tears of joy gleaming at the corners of her eyes, 'I'm really glad I ran into you guys. I mean, this is the most bizarre and exciting adventure I've ever been on!'

Terran gave her a smile, and she smiled back at him, sending his insides on a sudden backflip.

'My dear,' Orson exclaimed, 'the best things in life *are* weird and wonderful and extremely random. If only one allows oneself to embrace them…'

Terran knew the last few words were directed at him, but he kept his eyes on the road.

'They sure are,' Juliette agreed with a sigh, looking out the window. 'Actually,' she said tentatively, turning around to look at them. 'Why don't you guys come to the festival?'

A moment of silence greeted her words.

'We…' Terran started, but Orson interrupted him.

'What. An. Amazing and *glorious* idea, Juliette!' he declared, then turned to Farao and Kendrik. 'Guys, isn't a glorious idea?'

Farao adjusted his pillow against the window. 'I'll agree to anything as long as you stop calling things "glorious",' he groaned.

'Fabulous! Ken?'

Kendrik looked uncertainly at Orson, then at Terran through the rear-view mirror.

'I don't know, Orson,' Terran said slowly. 'That wasn't the plan.'

'Ah, yes, yes, the plan.' Orson waved him off. 'But plans are made to evolve, aren't they? And that festival won't be too much of a detour, right?'

'It's on your way,' Juliette piped up. 'And it's only three days. I can get you passes.'

Terran hesitated. The idea of spending an extra three days with Juliette was alluring, but he had to remind himself that they weren't there on an actual holiday. They had a mission on their hands.

'Come on,' Orson pleaded. 'Three days. That's all it is—it'll make no difference to the plan,' he added. 'Come on. We can just... Step out of it for a bit,' he added with a loaded look that brought Terran right back to their conversation the previous night. 'Take a break.'

Terran felt his grip tighten on the steering wheel.

'What about my phone?' Farao whined. 'We were going to get one in Marseille!'

'Oh, for the love of God, little brother, *here.*' Orson rolled his eyes, and pulled his phone out of his pocket. 'Use mine, if this lady friend of yours means so much to you.'

'I don't have her number,' Farao groaned. 'It's on *my* phone.'

'You have Facebook, don't you? Or Instagram? Or whatever it is you young people use these days. Reach out to her there. But.' Orson held the phone up, away from Farao's hand. 'You will not be contacting her before tonight. We had a deal.'

'Fine,' Farao snapped, but he eagerly grabbed Orson's phone.

Terran gave his brothers a final glance in the rear-view mirror: Farao's furrowed brow as he browsed through the phone, Orson's excited face and Kendrik's tired expression. Surely they could all use some fun. He peered sideways at Juliette. She was looking hopefully at him.

'Ok, fine,' he finally conceded. 'But just a day or two, and then we're back on the road.'

But no one heard the rest of his sentence, because his voice was drowned out by Orson and Juliette's cries of delight.

Chapter 42
Farao

Farao was surprised Terran had agreed to the idea of popping by the fitness festival. It wasn't like Terran to deviate from a well-defined, agreed-upon, sensible plan. But this time, the plan *had* been changed. Farao suspected it had something to do with the pretty Juliette.

The drive to Aix-en-Provence was uneventful. Farao, though at first dubious about the whole endeavour, had found himself rather enjoying this time on the road. He couldn't remember ever spending this sort of quality time with his brothers, and it made him realise how very little he knew them. He'd spent the most amount of one-on-one time with Orson, of course, but he had never had these types of interactions with the other two. Far from the mundane logistics of daily life, he realised, Terran was actually alright. And Kendrik, when he wasn't obsessing about work or being all prim and proper, was pretty bearable, too. For the first time in his life, Farao got a glimpse of the life his three brothers had shared, back before he was born, when their parents were alive. The idea made him envious of the childhood they'd had, so different and so much more joyful than his own.

He tried to shake the thought from his mind, but it had lodged itself there, like an unwanted weed, worming its way through the darkest corners of his insecurities. They had shared so much, experienced so much, lived through so much happiness and carelessness. He, on the other hand, had known nothing but tension and grief. By the time he was born, the happy and carefree times were gone, as if his arrival into the world had set off a chain reaction that had made his entire family combust.

Farao breathed in deeply, trying hard to unhook himself from the downwards spiral. He pulled out Orson's phone, and logged into his Facebook account. He gingerly typed in Serena's name in the search bar. Her profile popped up instantly. He checked her wall. Her profile picture showed her in trainers, denim shorts and a black tee-shirt, smiling broadly, posing on the top of a hill, with the countryside spreading behind her as far at the eye could see. Farao scrolled down her updates and photos, and his eye caught a green dot at the bottom of the screen. She was online. Right now. At this very moment, she was in front of her screen, and if he messaged her now, she would see it.

Farao hesitated. Next to him, Orson was dozing off, his head tilted back, snoring lightly. Should he message her? Just to tell her he'd got her text? To say he'd been thrilled that she'd reached out? He breathed in again. Orson had assured him he should wait at least till the evening, and if anyone knew anything about dating, it was Orson. Farao knew he wouldn't mislead him on purpose. He breathed in again, willing himself to resist the temptation.

A message popped up, but it wasn't from Serena. It was Mel.

'Where have you been?????'

Farao sighed, and typed a response.

'It's a long story.'

'What the fuck Farao!!! Why didn't you answer my texts????'

Farao closed his eyes. He *had* seen Mel's texts, which had started trickling in since after he had been rushed to the hospital from school, but he hadn't answered any of them. At first, he'd been too groggy to really keep up with his virtual correspondence, and he'd found the time away from all the notifications actually relaxing. But then, when it had come to it and he'd gone through Mel's messages, he wasn't really sure what to say, so he'd simply said nothing. It had been easier to pretend the texts weren't there than to figure out how to respond to the flurry of worried enquiries she was sending.

'I told you, it's a long story,' he typed again.

He watched the three dots showing that Mel was typing appear on the screen. Then go away. Then appear again. And go away again.

'I'm sorry,' he typed. *'It's just complicated.'*

He pressed send and his message immediately showed as read.

She started typing and Farao watched the three dots flash on the screen.

'Fuck off Farao. JUST FUCK OFF YOU FUCKING ARSEHOLE!!!!!'

And she went offline.

Well... Farao thought. That was even worse than he'd expected. When he checked Serena's status, he noticed that she, too, had gone offline.

***

They arrived at the festival late in the afternoon. It was set in a large field, surrounded by wheat and lavender-covered hills, a little way outside Aix-en-Province. They found a spot in the giant car park and made their way to the reception area, where they were to get their badges. Juliette had assured them that she could sort out passes for them, despite their late arrival at a completely sold out event. They were attended to by an excited-looking young woman, who introduced herself as Harriet. Harriet was wearing a bright pink tank top marked with the bold letters STAFF, and skin-tight yoga pants. She was positively bouncing on the spot and speaking in a high-pitched voice that Farao thought would become really irritating really quickly.

'Ohmygodohmygodohmygod!' Harriet squealed. 'Juliette Rochet! It's *such* an honour! I'm *so* excited to finally meet you! I've been following you for*ever*! I've done all your programs, I'm *such* a huge fan!'

Farao exchanged a glance with his brothers. What the hell was going on here? Juliette was acting very cool about it, thanking Harriet for her warm welcome and for sorting out her friends' access, and posing with her for a selfie, before Harriet consented to guide them to their tent. They walked past reception onto a path going through a wooded area. Everywhere he looked, Farao saw people dressed in swank workout gear, some with flower crowns in their hair or glitter paint on their faces and bodies. Brightly coloured garlands were hung through the trees, leading the way down the path into a large clearing. When he took in the view, Farao gasped.

They stood on top of a small hill on the edge of the trees, and below them a gigantic grass-covered clearing held the festival. There were tents everywhere in the main area, some large, some extra large, hundreds of them at least. Beyond the first clearing there was a field filled with small camping tents of all shapes and sizes. There were food trucks spread through the main clearing and several rows of portable toilet cubicles at the far end. At the centre of it all stood a huge stage set in front of a long, untouched stretch of grass. The grounds were buzzing with people by the thousands.

'Impressive, isn't it?' Harriet chimed in, noticing the brothers' stunned faces. 'We've got five thousand people attending this year, and that's without counting the staff. It's doubled since last year!'

Harriet led them down a winding path to the grounds, and guided them around the edges to a cordoned-off area. On the way, they were stopped by more people asking Juliette for photos, exchanging a few excited sentences with her, asking her for a hug. Juliette indulged them all gracefully. Harriet showed the security personnel their badges and they were let in to the private area. The section they were in now was like a smaller version of the main clearing. It held about twenty large tents—*yurts*, Harriet corrected—which housed the senior organisers and their top lead instructors.

'*Obviously*,' Harriet said to them very seriously, 'we couldn't let Juliette Rochet camp outside!'

Juliette tried to say it really wasn't necessary, but Harriet dismissed her, and Farao and his brothers were left exchanging yet another incredulous look. Harriet showed them to the yurt they would be sharing. It was more spacious than Farao might have guessed from the outside. There were three double beds arranged along the edges, facing a circular stone altar at the centre of the yurt. It was decorated in shades of white and cream, with fur rugs on the floor and a small door leading to a private bathroom. Farao gaped at it. It was unlike anything he'd ever seen, and judging by the looks on his brothers' faces, he could tell they were impressed, too.

Harriet handed them welcome packs, and when she eventually left them, there was silence in the yurt. Terran, Kendrik, Orson and Farao were all staring at Juliette, who was looking a little embarrassed.

'So.' Orson cocked his head to one side, taking out the programme from his welcome pack and staring at Juiette's picture on the front page. 'When you said you had *a bit of a following*... How big is "a bit" exactly?'

Juliette gave him an awkward smile and shrugged.

'A bit,' she said, and turned around, walking to one of the beds to unpack her bag.

***

'Shit, Juliette, you're *huge*!' Farao exclaimed.

He had pulled Orson's phone from his pocket and Googled Juliette's name. The results had made his jaw drop.

'Ah, come on...' Juliette rolled her eyes.

'Show me.' Orson came to peer over his shoulder. 'Wow!'

'Guys, please, it's nothing.' Juliette was taking some clothes from the piles she had taken from her bag.

'*Nothing?*' Orson repeated in disbelief, taking the phone from Farao and turning the screen towards her. 'You have two and half *million* followers on Instagram!'

They all stared at her in astonished silence, but she didn't turn to look at them.

'Listen,' she said slowly, her back still to them. 'I just get so much attention all the time... Not that I mind, of course, that's part of the deal. And I'm thankful for the success I have. I really am. And I wasn't trying to hide anything... It's just... hanging out with you guys... It's been nice to be anonymous for a bit...' She finally turned to look at them, then looked directly at Terran. She had an odd, apologetic look on her face. 'I'm sorry...'

'Hey,' Terran said, crossing the yurt to stand in front of her. 'You have nothing to apologise for. Really. I guess I... *We,*' he corrected, 'weren't expecting that, that's all.'

'Are you kidding?!' Orson exclaimed. 'We're prancing around with fitness royalty! This is the best holiday *ever!*'

Farao nodded—even he had to admit it was pretty cool.

Juliette's smile broadened. 'So,' she said, with one last look at Terran, her voice turning bright and excited again, 'I'm not teaching till tomorrow, and it looks like they have some music on the big stage tonight. Who's up for a party?'

Chapter 43
Orson

They showered and changed, and Orson was glad he'd packed for the occasion. Although, he thought to himself with a grin, it wasn't like he'd planned on meeting a social media celebrity whilst taking a random detour on the motorway to find themselves at a health festival, ready to paint the town red. But he was nothing if not prepared for every opportunity life put his way. He tied his hair into its usual ponytail, pulled on a fresh pair of black jeans and one of his light fabric shirts. He rolled up his sleeves. *Tonight*, he told himself. *Tonight is out of time.* It existed beyond the reality they'd have to face again tomorrow. Tonight, they weren't orphans. Farao wasn't ill, and Kendrik wasn't heartbroken. Tonight, Terran would get a chance to put himself first. *Tonight*, Orson thought, *I'm not guilty of keeping anyone's secrets.* Tonight, they were just the Dhawan brothers, out in the world on a beautifully random adventure.

Juliette emerged from the bathroom, looking ravishing in a strappy red dress, and Orson suppressed a smile when he saw Terran do a double take.

They headed out into the breezy night. All around them was excitement and anticipation. There were people everywhere Orson looked, gorgeous, happy, smiling people dressed in all manners of sports outfits, bright colours and fancy dress. There was glow paint on every limb, glitter on every face and flowers on every head. Orson breathed it all in. The surreal experience gave a spring to his step.

A band had started playing on the huge stage at the other end of the clearing, and he took in the vibrations of the music in the air as they queued for their mocktails—no alcohol allowed on the site, Juliette explained. They toasted each other and sipped their drinks on the way towards the stage, the music growing louder and louder around them. The crowd was getting thicker too, as more and more people started to dance.

Juliette downed her drink and popped her glass in a bin. Then she took hold of Terran's hand and led him deeper into the dancing mass.

'You stay with Farao,' Terran mouthed at Orson before disappearing in the crowd.

Orson watched Terran go, a sudden lightness in his stomach and a smile on his face.

'I'm not a kid…' Farao grumbled.

Orson turned to Farao and smiled more broadly when he saw his sulking expression.

'Ah, Farao.' He wrapped an arm around Farao's neck and pulled him towards him, rubbing the top of his head. 'You know you'll always be my baby brother!'

Farao protested, half laughing, and pulled himself out of Orson's grip.

The three of them wandered off through the crowd, checking out the different stalls, Orson taking care of most of the conversation. He was wondering which food truck to queue by to treat themselves to a snack when he noticed, a little further away in the distance, a group of people sat in a circle around a campfire. Forgetting about the food, he motioned to Farao and Kendrik to follow him, and walked to where the group was settled. There were a couple of people with guitars, one with a violin, one with a percussion box. A woman was singing an acoustic version of Lady Gaga's 'Shallow'. The group arranged around the fire was listening, and Orson noticed a small audience spread around them on the grass nearby, swaying gently to the rhythm of the music.

Orson tilted his head and led Farao and Kendrik towards empty seats around the fire. They sat there, listening to a few songs. Orson closed his eyes, his fingers playing an invisible guitar along with the band, wishing he'd brought his case with him. There was very little that live music couldn't fix, in his opinion, and he sensed himself shiver with every note the band played.

When the next song ended, he felt a nudge against his arm and opened his eyes. One of the guitar players was looking at him, smiling.

'You play? You play the guitar?' the young man asked, his voice thickly accented.

Hispanic, Orson guessed.

Orson nodded and smiled when the young man handed him his instrument.

'Come on, your turn,' the man said, bringing the audience to a quiet stand-still as they all watched the newcomer settle the guitar expertly in his arms.

Orson glanced at Farao, who nodded at him, and cleared his throat. He was wondering which song to play, when he realised with a jolt of surprise that his fingers had started playing of their own accord. He felt strangely detached from his own hands as he recognised the first chords to Jimmy Rhodes's 'Ghost'. Orson swallowed hard, the notes resounding in the night around him. He closed his eyes again, because his heart was feeling suddenly very heavy, and he worried that he might choke. He took in a deep breath and, in a voice that sounded distant and foreign, he started singing.

'I wander like a ghost.
For proof that I still feel.
But all I find is pain.
How can I know what's real?'

The lyrics felt like they were scraping the back of his throat raw. His voice was hoarse, almost painful. Total silence had fallen around the circle, although he felt so far away from it all he couldn't really tell with certainty where he was anymore. Such was the power of the song, and the Pavlovian reflex it triggered. The lyrics he knew by heart pierced him like a hot blade. He tried as hard as he could to keep the memories they threatened to unleash buried deep inside him.

And suddenly, as he sung, he was no longer there, sat around the fire at his brothers' side, surrounded by strangers. He was a little boy again, looking at his father's back as he stood facing the fireplace...

There was a prickle on his skin, an uncomfortable energy that made the hair on the back of his neck stand on end, reminding him of all of the secrets he'd had to keep, and all of the hurt he'd had to carry. He was vaguely aware of Farao's body, tense and rigid beside his, and of the eerie silence greeting every word he sang.

'I weave the threads of lies.
Sat on this burning throne.
I watch my life go by.
I feed on dust and bones.'

Almost as soon as it had started, it was over, though Orson only realised the song had ended several moments after it happened. The audience had stayed deadly silent, and all that could be heard was the crackling of the fire and the festivities going on in the distance. Orson opened his eyes slowly and gave the young man next to him a pained smile, handing him back his guitar. There was sorrow and sympathy on the young man's face as he took the instrument from him. The music resumed, the band launching into a more cheerful tune, which Orson was grateful for. It took some time for his heartbeat to slow down, and for him to shake off the icy chill the song always plunged him in.

'You ok?' Farao asked quietly.

'Yeah.' Orson nodded, clearing his throat. 'That song… Gets me every time.'

Farao threw him a questioning look, but Orson didn't respond. He felt something vibrate in his pocket, and he pulled out his phone. Several Facebook notifications popped up and he unlocked the screen, frowning as he read through message after message. He looked up at Farao.

'Who's Mel?' Orson asked, bewildered. 'And what the hell did you do to her to piss her off so much?'

Farao's eyes widened and he paled in the firelight.

'Shit, Orson, give that to me.' Farao lunged at him, trying to get a hold of the phone.

But Orson was quicker, and he lifted his hand high in the air, out of Farao's reach.

'So if *this* is Mel, who's Serena?' he teased. 'Have you been getting more action than I've given you credit for, little brother?'

'Orson, you prick! Give it back!' Farao groaned, the embarrassment and annoyance on his face making Orson burst out laughing.

'You and I,' Orson concluded, chuckling, 'need to have a conversation.' And he slid the phone back into his pocket.

Orson looked around him, the smile on his face slowly fading into concern. He stood up and took a few steps away from the campfire. He spun on his heel, looking over the bobbing heads of the crowd.

'Where's Kendrik?'

Chapter 44
Terran

Terran couldn't remember the last time he'd gone out dancing—if one could really call the awkward side-to-side swaying he was doing 'dancing'. In front of him, Juliette was moving to the Latin beats with such grace it made him feel like a stick man in comparison. Her eyes were closed and there was a contented smile on her face. The bright colours of the spotlights around them reflected on her skin, giving her a light glow. The inviting roll of her hips kept catching Terran's eye, and he had to try hard not to reach out a hand to pull her towards him.

He'd been attracted to other women before, of course—he wasn't made of stone. But he'd never been this interested in anyone. The physical pull he felt whenever he was near her was something completely new to him, and he didn't quite know what to make of it. Could it be just lust? After all, it'd been a long, *long* time since he'd got any action. On that front, Terran thought bitterly, Orson's constant teasing was absolutely on point.

Juliette opened her eyes, locking her gaze with his. She beamed at him, knocking the wind out of him. That smile. That alluring and gorgeous smile. He couldn't take his eyes off her lips, the way they stretched and curled up, the dimples that formed in her cheeks. He wanted more than anything to run a finger on those lips, to feel their softness, to lean forward and taste her. Juliette's eyes stayed on his, her smile shifting into something a little mischievous, and for a wild moment he had the feeling she knew exactly what he was thinking. More than that, something told him she wanted nothing more than for him to go ahead and do it.

He took a step forward towards her, his body mere inches from hers. He could almost feel the heat emanating from her skin. The music enveloped them like a cocoon, wrapping around them like nothing else in the world existed. Slowly, deliberately, Terran inched closer towards her, sliding his arms around her waist, gently pulling her into him. She let him lead, still holding his gaze with an intensity that made his skin prickle. The moment her body nestled against his, Terran's stomach gave a flutter, sending a shiver through him, making every hair on his body stand on end. The feeling was electrifying, the firmness of her against his chest sending his head spinning. He tightened his embrace.

Their faces were so close now it would have taken nothing at all for him to bring his lips to hers, to give in to the impulse and kiss her. But the thought of it was as scary as it was invigorating. Because the moment he gave himself to her meant opening up something inside him that he'd tried hard to bury. Try as he might, he couldn't get past it.

He sighed and pressed a kiss to her forehead instead, pulling her tighter against him. She snaked her arms around his torso and buried her face in his neck. The feel of her breath on him was so good it was almost unbearable. He closed his eyes and, unable to stop himself, he leant in, resting his head against her shoulder, the smell of her skin calling out to him like a drug. He traced his nose against the crook of her neck, up to her ear, over the sensitive spot at the base of her jaw. He felt her shiver in his arms, her hands in fists on the back of his tee-shirt. He had one hand firmly against her lower back, the fingers of his other hand wandering of their own volition up her spine, sliding off the silky fabric of her dress to meet her exposed flesh. The skin-to-skin contact sent a delicious sort of burn against his fingertips, and he kept his touch featherlike, delicate, savouring every instant of it, until his hand reached all the way up, to the side of her face. His fingers followed the line of her jaw, cupping her cheek. His thumb caressed her bottom lip, and he watched in delight as her eyes closed and she leant her head back ever so slightly, inviting him in.

He wanted her. He wanted her so badly and so ferociously the intensity of his desire took him by surprise. He was sure she would be able to feel how strongly his heart was beating, pounding against his chest. He buried his nose in her hair and inhaled her scent, pulling her closer still against him, knowing she too could sense his body's response. He traced her jawline with his mouth, hovering over her skin, stopping millimetres away from her parted lips. He could feel her breathing hard against him, her body moulding itself to his. He was only half aware that they weren't alone. The crowd around them was like a barrier between this magical moment and the outside world. It shielded them, breathing life into the myriad of possibilities of what kissing her might bring to life. He almost wished she would stop him, that she would step away and take the choice away from him. The craving he had for her was so strong he thought he might not be able to resist it on his own. *One kiss*, he thought. *What harm can it do?* One moment of freedom. One moment of living just for himself.

Something buzzed in his pocket. It happened a second, third and fourth time, and he was slapped back to reality. He immediately pulled away from Juliette, the moment broken, the music suddenly frustratingly loud and the crowd suffocating. Taking his phone out of his pocket he saw Orson's name flash on the screen and an instant sense of dread filled him. This, he knew, *this* was his warning. The dark reminder that his life wasn't his to own. That if he ever tried to step away from his duty for even a second, something terrible would happen and *he* would be responsible for it. He slid his thumb across the screen to answer the call, but Orson's voice was drowned in the noise around him.

Terran turned around, making his way frantically through the dancing mob, the phone pressed to one ear, one finger in the other, calling out in the receiver, straining to hear this brother's muffled voice. When he finally emerged out of the dance floor, Orson had hung up, but there was a new text in his inbox. Terran flicked it open, and reading the words was like having a bucket of ice water poured over his head:

'We've lost Kendrik.'

Chapter 45
Kendrik

Kendrik looked around him, and he had to admit to himself that he was lost. No matter where he looked, nothing looked familiar and he couldn't see his brothers anywhere.

'Great,' he groaned.

He started walking, with no particular destination in mind, weaving in and out through the flow of people all around him. He wandered aimlessly, thinking he might as well find their tent again and wait there, but he must have taken a wrong turn because he couldn't find his way. He had reached a slightly secluded area on one side of the clearing, nestled against the edge of the woods. There were several tents arranged in a semicircle, looking like a Bedouin settlement. A small group of people sat around a fire. *Great*, Kendrik thought grumpily, *another campfire...* This really had to be a health and safety hazard. The people around the fire were wearing the type of indie hipster outfits which Orson could have easily pulled off. A couple of them carried instruments, and soft music was playing. Kendrik spotted a sitar and tabla. Someone, an older man wearing long white robes, was singing, and his deep, soulful voice filled the night. There was an otherworldly sort of atmosphere there, Kendrik thought, which made even the loud buzzing of the festival feel like it was miles away. Kendrik paused a little way away from the group of people, standing in the shadows, unable to tear himself away from the man's voice. He wasn't singing in any language Kendrik recognised, but the timbre of his voice, the depth of emotion he managed to convey in every sound, was enough to glue him to the spot.

When the song ended, Kendrik wasn't sure how long he'd been standing there. It was the strangest of sensations. It might have been minutes, or hours, or days. His body felt numb but his insides, his heart, his soul, were screaming. It was like the man's eerie song had awoken something inside him that had long been buried. Kendrik shook his head slowly and made to leave, but a strong, deep voice called out to him.

'Come over, young man, join us.'

Kendrik looked back over his shoulder to see who the voice was talking to, but there was no one there. He turned back to look at the man in white robes. He must have been in his late fifties, his dark hair sprinkled with strands of white and grey. The rest of the group was younger, in their twenties and thirties maybe, and Kendrik could tell the man had a higher standing, because they all looked up to him with reverence as he spoke.

'No, it's fine.' Kendrik shook his head again. 'I was just leaving.'

'But you don't have anywhere to go yet,' the man said simply. 'So why not share this part of your journey with us?'

Kendrik stared at him, dumbfounded. *What* had he just said? He looked at the group sat around the fire. They were all looking at him, some very seriously, some with polite consideration, some with welcoming smiles.

'I don't know…' Kendrik started, a feeling of uneasiness growing in his stomach.

'All you need is one step into the light, son,' the man said. 'Take one step into the light, and all will reveal itself.'

Kendrik frowned, but as he was about to retort that, no, thank you very much, he was fine walking away right now, he found that his feet had quite a different plan. Before he knew it, he had come to the fire and taken the seat the man had cleared by his side.

The music resumed, as if they all knew the interlude was over, and the man started singing again. The unknown and incomprehensible words he was singing felt ancient and full of wisdom. Kendrik closed his eyes and took them in, letting the aura of the scene permeate through him, seep into the pores of his skin. It made his entire body vibrate. He found himself almost on the edge of tears. He felt tired. So incredibly tired. His body was just so heavy all the time, so slow, shrouded in a cloud of lethargy he couldn't shake. He couldn't remember the last time he'd slept properly. He was just exhausted, knackered by the pretence, by the effort of going on.

But most of all, he felt sad. A huge, overwhelming wave of sorrow was building up inside him, rising through his throat and threatening to drown him completely. He rubbed his hand on his face and realised he was crying. When he opened his eyes, he looked around him and noticed everyone else in the group had their eyes closed. The music had stopped. Instead, they were humming, one low, rumbling hum, in unison, and its vibrations rose through the circle. The man in white robes bent over the fire and picked up a large clay pot from the flames. It was full of a dark brown silky liquid. He pulled a little pouch from a bag next to him and sprinkled a pinch of red powder on top of the brown liquid. He held the pot towards the sky and spoke a string of words in the same strange language as before, something that sounded like an incantation. His words rose through the night. Then he poured a little of the liquid in small clay cups and passed them around the circle.

When one of the cups reached Kendrik, he tried to refuse, but the woman sitting next to him nodded her head solemnly at him, and he eventually took the cup from her. The clay was warm underneath his fingers, and the aromas emanating from the cup reminded him of chocolate and chilli powder.

Around the circle, people were drinking the contents of their cups, then sliding off their seats and lying down, some on their side in a foetal position, some on their backs. Kendrik looked around him, until his eyes met the man's eyes.

'I don't...' Kendrik started, trying to give him back the cup.

'It's ok, son,' the man said in his deep, rumbling voice, but not taking the cup from Kendrik. 'This is your choice.'

Kendrik looked at the man, at the fine lines on his face which gave his look a twinkle. The man was gazing straight at him, with such depth and intensity that Kendrik felt he was scanning his entire soul.

'You've come a long way,' the man said. 'And you've carried a heavy burden.'

Kendrik didn't reply.

'You're worried about your brother,' the man added after a pause. 'But he will be fine, in the end. And when that time comes, who will you be? Will you keep carrying your heavy burden, or will you finally start living?'

Kendrik's eyes widened. He couldn't believe what he was hearing.

'What...What...' he stuttered.

'There is a great pain in your heart, a deep sadness which existed since the beginning. Until you shed that pain, you cannot shed your skin of sorrow and come out into the light. You are not the burden. You are not the pain. And you are not the sadness. Step into the light, son. Rise and step into the light.'

Kendrik couldn't find anything to say. Somewhere far, far away, at the back of his head, something was telling him to leave and not look back, but that voice was so small and so low it was easy to pretend it wasn't there. Slowly, very slowly, his eyes never leaving the man's face, he brought the cup to his lips and drank the warm liquid in one go.

***

It's the middle of the night. Kendrik is lying down in his bed. It isn't the bed he sleeps in in the big London house. It's the bed he had as a child in the apartment they lived in in the south of France. The covers are crumpled at his feet. He's hot and thirsty, and he really wants a glass of water. In the other beds in the room they share, his brothers are asleep, the sound of their breathing distinguishable in the silence. Kendrik slides out of bed. He's wearing his favourite pair of pyjamas, the blue ones with the shapes of dogs all over them. His mother bought them for him on his last birthday, and the fact that she chose this gift for him herself makes it extra special. Kendrik tiptoes out of the bedroom, his bare feet quiet on the cool, tiled floor. He wonders if the babysitter is still here. He's forgotten her name now, and what she looks like, but he knows his parents said she would look after them for the evening, and the nice lady gave them ice cream and let them watch cartoons on TV.

At the end of the corridor, the living room is plunged in darkness, and he's a little scared to walk through it to the kitchen. Then, he spots a ray of light under the bathroom door. He walks to it in silence, pushes the door open a sliver and peers through the crack.

He's not entirely sure what he's seeing. His mother is crouched in the shower cubicle. She's fully dressed, and water is running over her head. She's crying. She's crying so much that Kendrik doesn't know what to do. He's never seen his mother so sad. What does one do when a grown-up is this sad?

'Maman?' he whispers, but she doesn't hear him.

He pulls the door shut as quietly as he can and walks back to his bedroom. He comes to a halt next to Terran's bed and he tries to shake his brother awake.

'Terran...' Kendrik murmurs. 'Terran, wake up.'

But Terran just rolls in his bed and falls back asleep. Kendrik walks over to Orson's bed and prods him gently.

'Orson, Orson wake up. Come on, wake up.'

'Mmmm... Go away, Kendrik, it's late.' And he, too, turns around and goes back to sleep.

So Kendrik stands there, in the dead of night, unsure what to do, feeling too powerless and too young to act. Eventually, with one last look at the door, he walks back to his bed, pulls the cover over his head, and goes back to sleep.

When he wakes up in the morning, he has no recollection of his nighttime wander.

***

'It's ok,' said a deep, low voice, resonating from far away. 'Keep going, son.'

***

It's a little while later, and Kendrik is watching television with Terran and Orson. It's one of these weekend evenings where they're allowed to have veggie burgers and fries with loads of ketchup and mayo, and cookies and ice cream for dessert. They're watching an X-Men movie for the umpteenth time, their absolute favourite. They each have their individual little tray on their knees.

The movie has just started when Kendrik realises he's forgotten to take pickles from the fridge. He's the only one who eats them, so no one had realised they're not there. He pops his tray on the coffee table and walks to the kitchen, his gaze back over his shoulder so he doesn't miss anything on the screen.

But as he nears the kitchen, he hears the low voices of his parents. It sounds like they're arguing. Kendrik stops by the door, not wanting to walk in on them when they're having a row. He can hear every word of their conversation.

'You're what?' His father sounds angry.

'Anand...' His mother's voice is almost a whisper, and he can hear that she's crying.

'What are you going to do about it?' his father growls.

There's a pause.

'What do you mean?' his mother pleads.

'Don't tell me you're keeping it!'

There's another pause.

'Anand... It's too late... The doctor said...'

'I don't give a damn about what the doctor says!' His father's voice resonates in the kitchen.

'Anand... The boys... Keep your voice down...'

'Are you listening to me?' His father sounds more mad than Kendrik has ever heard him. 'We are not bringing this... this... this thing, this monster, into our home!'

Silence stretches, and Kendrik stands rooted to the spot.

'This monster...' His mother's voice is hollow. 'Anand, neither of us asked for this. And the baby didn't ask for any of this either...'

'Don't call it that!' His father seethes under his breath.

'Anand, please.' His mother is sobbing again.

There's the noise of a commotion in the kitchen, and the sound of someone striding to the door. Before he can move, Kendrik finds himself face to face with his father, whose expression softens when he sees him. His father crouches down, bringing his face to Kendrik's level, placing both his hands on his little shoulders.

'Kendrik,' his father says, very seriously, 'whatever you do, don't you ever grow so soft-hearted and delusional that you forget what truly matters. There is no one and nothing else that is more important than your family. You hear me?' His father's voice is more pressing now, and Kendrik nods frantically to show he understands.

Without another backwards glance, his father stands up and marches out of the flat, slamming the door behind him. Kendrik looks up at his mother, who is leaning against the kitchen counter, one hand on her stomach, the other hand on her *face. She's crying uncontrollably. He doesn't know what to do. Eventually his mother seems to remember he's there, and she forces a smile onto her face.*

'Maman...' *Kendrik says.*

'It's ok, mon chéri. Everything's ok.' *She passes her fingers absently through his hair, turning him back towards the living room.* 'Why don't you go and join your brothers.'

But later, long after Terran and Orson have fallen asleep, long after they're done discussing which X-Men character they would each rather be—Terran is Professor Xavier, Orson is Storm and Kendrik, Wolverine—as he lies in bed staring at the ceiling, all that Kendrik can think of is that he never grabbed the jar of pickles from the fridge.

***

'It's alright,' the low rumble of a voice said to him. 'Keep going.'

***

It's much, much later, on a crisp winter morning, and Kendrik is studying in his room for a big exam the next day. His door is open, and he can hear his mother cough in the other room. She's been on bed rest for weeks now, growing weaker and weaker every day. Kendrik can hear Orson's voice, and he wonders if he's reading to her again. Since speaking started to make her tired, he's taken to picking up her favourite books and reading them aloud to her till she falls asleep.

Normally Kendrik doesn't care, and he finds the sound of Orson's reading enjoyable white noise. But today, on the eve of his finals, Kendrik can't take any of it. He can't take Orson's reading or his mother's coughing. He can't take the cracking sounds of the stairs as Farao stomps down to the front door. There's been some kind of problem at school and Terran has to go and drop him, to meet with the headmistress and Farao's teacher. Their mother would have gone, but she's in no condition to go anywhere.

It feels to Kendrik that the whole house and everyone in it is determined to see him fail his exam, and every single noise he hears adds fuel to the fire. Suddenly, in a fit of annoyance, he picks up his books and his things, grabs his backpack and storms out of his room. When he passes his mother's room, her voice calls out to him through the open door. She's calling out his name, but he doesn't even stop to listen. He mumbles something about heading out to the library, and being back later.

'Kendrik?' his mother's voice calls out, almost pleadingly from her bedroom.

'Later, Mum,' Kendrik calls back pointedly, frustrated, from the bottom of the stairs, not even pausing for a second.

He's sitting in the library when he finally checks his phone, a long time later. He had put it on airplane mode so as not to be disturbed. When he switches it back on, a barrage of texts and missed calls floods his phone screen.

They're all from Terran.

His mother has died.

Later, as it turned out, was too late.

***

'It's ok, son.' The low, faraway voice was soothing now. 'It's ok.'

Kendrik shook his head violently. 'It's not! It's not ok!' He could hear his own voice whining, but he couldn't feel his lips moving.

'There was nothing you could have done.'

'That's a lie!' Kendrik heard his voice exclaim, interrupted by heavy sobs. 'I should have guessed, I should have known! I could have helped her… I should have known…'

'There was nothing you could have done,' the deep voice repeated.

'I didn't help her…' And to his own ears, Kendrik's voice sounded distant and faded. 'I should have helped her…'

'Shed your pain, son. Walk into the light,' the voice said, it too, fading away.

But Kendrik was burning from inside, as if his entire body had been ignited. He still couldn't move a single muscle, and all he could do was endure the pain, feeling the burn eat him up. There was boiling water trickling down his face and into the neck of his shirt, but he couldn't shake it off. The pain was agony now, and he wished it would all just stop. He wished he could die so that he didn't have to feel the pain, but all he could do was lie there and let the flames wash over him.

'Step into the light, son,' the voice said again.

But there was no light. There was only darkness. There was only pain. There was only the weight of the guilt he'd been holding on to since he was a child. The knowledge that when his mother had needed him the most, he had done nothing. He had let her suffer. He hadn't even listened to the last words she'd wanted to say to him. He'd failed her so many times, he felt undeserving of calling himself her son. And he had broken his word to his father. He hadn't put his family first. He was sobbing so hard now his entire body was shaking. The sorrow he felt was gripping him at the guts. There was a scream of agony building inside of him, tightening around his chest, threatening to swallow and suffocate him.

'Shed your pain, son. Step into the light,' the voice was repeating, over and over again.

Kendrik wished he could go back, back to that first night when his mother had been crying in the shower, and that he could do it all over again. He wished he'd run to her and held her tight. He wished he'd screamed at Terran and Orson to wake up and help him hold her, to prevent her from falling apart so completely. And in his mind's eye, a new scene unfolded. One in which he had known what to do. One in which he was somehow older, and stronger. One in which he drank his mother's pain like it was his own and took it away forever.

And in that new scene, his mother's smiling face looked up at him, and she hugged him and kissed his cheeks. He could hear her voice now. She was telling him what a good boy he was. How strong he was. How much she loved him. How much she wanted him to be happy.

Through that vision, slowly, tentatively at first, a ray of light appeared, and Kendrik felt himself be lifted onto his feet and walk towards it, letting go of his mother's hand, taking in her smile.

I love you, he told her silently. *I'm sorry.*

But she kept smiling, ruffling his hair. Kendrik walked towards the light, which grew wider and more intense as he approached it. He was no longer scared. He didn't turn to look back. He knew his mother was not there anymore.

And, with one last breath, he stepped into the light.

Chapter 46
Terran

'What did they do to him?' Terran asked, watching Orson pull the duvet over Kendrik's sleeping figure.

'I don't know…' Orson shook his head. 'I couldn't get a straight answer out of any of them, but it looks like some sort of hallucinogenic. I've heard of ayahuasca ceremonies before, it looked a bit like that.'

'Is he going to be ok?' Farao asked quietly from beside Kendrik's bed.

'Of course,' Terran heard himself say, and he hoped beyond hope that he was right—he'd never seen Kendrik in this state before, and the sight of it scared him to his core. 'Of course he'll be fine,' he said, a little louder, trying to convince himself, too. 'He just needs to sleep it off.'

The entrance panel to the tent lifted and Juliette walked in.

'Oh, good.' Relief spread over her face. 'You found him.'

They stood in silence for a moment, watching Kendrik's face, and Terran thought he looked more peaceful than he'd seen him in a long time.

'I could definitely do with a coffee...' Juliette murmured, sounding drained, her arms tight around herself.

They had been looking for Kendrik for several hours before they found him, lying unconscious on the ground next to the smouldering remains of a campfire.

'You guys go,' Orson said, and it took Terran several seconds to realise he was addressing him. 'Farao and I will stay with him.'

Terran frowned. 'Are you su—'

'Go,' Orson insisted, cutting him off. 'If anything changes, I'll call you.'

Terran hesitated.

'*Go*,' Orson repeated. 'We've got it covered here.'

Terran nodded and followed Juliette out of the yurt. It was the middle of the night now, and the festivities around them were winding down slowly. They walked through the maze of tents and festival-goers for some time in silence, Juliette leading the way. She stopped at one of the food trucks and showed her pass to the young man standing half asleep behind the counter. He jerked to attention, read her pass and took her order for the complimentary coffees all staff and organisers were entitled to.

Juliette took the disposable cups from the young man and motioned to Terran to follow her to a quiet spot a little way away, where large beanbags were laid out. They each took a seat, and Juliette handed Terran one of the cups. He sipped his coffee absentmindedly, his thoughts back in the tent, with his brothers. He'd never seen Kendrik like that. Kendrik simply wasn't the kind of person to stray too far away from the trodden path, let alone be convinced into doing drugs. But again, Terran thought, Kendrik's state had deteriorated so quickly and so intensely since that day in the hospital, maybe they'd just missed the signs that their brother really needed their help. He'd known he was struggling, they all were, but he hadn't realised he was so far gone. A familiar ball of guilt lodged itself in Terran's throat at the thought that he might have been so focused on one brother he'd failed the other.

'He'll be fine…' Juliette said softly.

Terran turned to look at her.

'Kendrik…' She gave him a weak smile. 'He'll be fine.'

'I don't know…' Terran sighed. 'I just don't know anymore…'

'Who are you referring to now, Kendrik… or Farao?' Juliette asked.

Terran considered her for a moment. They hadn't spoken a word of Farao's condition to her, not explicitly. How could she possibly know?

'Something's going on, isn't it? With Farao?' Juliette probed.

Terran looked at her, at the concern in her eyes, the gentle lines of her face, the softness of her lips. He wanted so badly to tell her everything, to have someone to share his burden, one that he could never pass on to his brothers. His sense of duty forbade him from letting them see how difficult it was, how much he doubted and struggled. And, looking at Juliette, right there, he suddenly felt exhausted. He was tired of being the strong one. Tired of carrying the weight of responsibility, tired of holding everyone at arm's length because there was no room in his life for anything other than his family. He wanted so badly to go to sleep and wake up the next day to find his parents still alive and in charge, and to be able to plan his own life without anyone else's interests coming before his own.

But just as soon as the thought popped into his head, he knew there was no point. Life was what it was; he didn't have a choice in the matter. He couldn't let his brothers down. It would have been betraying his parents' memory. He had to keep going. He had to make it all ok, because if he didn't, even for a second, terrible things would happen.

'Terran?' Juliette said quietly.

He turned to look at her, opening his eyes, only realising then that he'd closed them. He took in Juliette's worried expression, but he could also see something else. Something he hadn't seen, or hadn't allowed himself to see, in someone else before. It wasn't pity. It wasn't judgement. She *cared.* More importantly, he was letting her care. He'd never let anyone so close before.

Before he could stop himself, the words came pouring out of his mouth, and he told her everything. He told her about his parents, about growing up in France, about moving to England and about life after they died. He told her about the day he heard of his father's accident, and the day he found his mother's body. He told her about his brothers, about how he had to carry them through life no matter what. He told her of Farao's condition, and of the truth about his parentage. He told her about the letter his mother had left behind. He told her about the shock and the fear, and his ruthless determination that he would fix this. He told her of their trip's true purpose. He told her everything, and it was like the first word he uttered had opened the gates to a lifetime of repressed confessions. He talked until there were no more words to speak.

Juliette never interrupted him. She never said a word. She just listened. When he was done speaking, she looked at him in silence. There were tears streaking down her cheeks, but still she didn't say anything. She simply leant over, took Terran's hand in hers and squeezed it. He was crying now, years and years' worth of unshed tears, but he let them pour out of him without trying to stop them. Juliette kept her hand on his and stayed with him, sitting quietly.

Eventually, the tears dried up and his breathing softened. They sat there, hand in hand, in silence. But the silence had a different quality now. It was almost peaceful. It was precious. The secrets Terran had shared floated lightly in the air around them, in shared understanding that it was ok to let them be there, to let them be seen. They no longer felt like ghosts.

Juliette gave a shiver and Terran turned to look at her. She gave him an apologetic smile.

'Little cold.' She shrugged.

Without thinking about it, Terran opened his arms and motioned for her to come in. She stared at him, uncertain, for the briefest of moments, as if asking whether he was sure.

'Come on.' He patted the spot next to him, scooting over on the beanbag. 'Hop on.'

Slowly, carefully, as though not to scare him, she took a seat, her body nestling into his, and he closed his arms around her. He thought he heard her gasp, or maybe it'd been him, he couldn't even tell. The moment they came into contact, his skin burst into flames, prickling with longing for her, for keeping her close, for never, ever letting her go. She leant her head into the crook of his neck and he rested his cheek against the top of her head. The scent of her fuelled him. He felt her shiver again, and worry instantly flooded his brain. *Shit.* He hadn't thought this through, which was very unlike him. Was he making her uncomfortable?

'Is this ok?' he whispered.

'Yeah.' She nodded. 'It's ok.'

Relief washed over him, and he held her a little tighter, feeling her relax into his embrace, moulding her body against his, her hands sliding their way along his forearms, locking him into place. His heart was pounding a hundred beats a minute, and he was certain she'd be able to feel it thumping against her back. She fitted into him perfectly. This felt right. He'd never felt so at peace with the world in his entire life.

He watched the festival around them shut down for the night, until all around them was quiet and still. He felt calmer now. Tomorrow would be a different day, he told himself, but just for now, just for a moment, he gave himself permission to be. The sense of freedom it gave him was almost overwhelming. He breathed the night in and soaked in the warmth of Juliette's skin against his. The world around him seemed to be moving a little slower, and he wished he could press pause on this moment, hold it there for a while, until he was ready to face his life again.

Chapter 47
Gabrielle

I've known for a while that I'm dying. In truth, I think I've known it for some time, long before the many appointments, and before the long list of test results came back positive.

You'd think I would be scared. I thought I might be terrified of death. The reality of it, though, is that I'm not.

I'm not scared. In fact, I'm a little relieved.

I don't want to leave my boys behind. I know it would be hard for them. I wish it had been enough to make me want to fight harder. But I can't do it anymore. Part of me surrendered long ago.

I'm tired. Tired of lies, tired of secrets, tired of wishing life had turned out differently. Tired of the guilt that, despite it all, despite the horrors I've endured, I still love all of my sons equally. I was never able to tell Anand, he never would have heard it anyway. But Farao is mine, too. And he's never asked for any of this. None of us did. It happened how it happened and there was nothing we could do to change it.

Now that the end is near, I needed to tell someone. To explain all that happened.

The lengthy letter I leave for my sons will come as a shock, but I want them to know the truth. I don't want it to die with me. My last act of cowardice is to write it down, because I can't bear to see the pain in their eyes.

My darling boys. My everything. The most amazing achievement of my life…

All I hope is that they will find peace, find the happiness they deserve. For them not to make the mistake their father and I made, and let this ugly truth define them.

I wish I could see them all grow into the wonderful young men I know they are bound to become.

I've grown too weak. I am ashamed to admit it, but it is time for me to go. I am sorry that I couldn't fight harder. I wish I'd been stronger. I hope that, in time, they will forgive me.

Chapter 48
Farao

Farao lay on one of the beds, the inside of the tent illuminated by a couple of large electric candles at its centre, bathing the space in a warm, soft glow. Outside, he could hear the party starting to quiet down. Occasionally, bursts of voices travelled through the entrance of the tent as people walked by outside.

He looked over at the bed next to his, where Kendrik lay motionless except for the soft rise and fall of his chest underneath the duvet. He wasn't sure what to think. Kendrik had always been so... proper. So incredibly boring in Farao's eyes. He'd have expected something like this from Orson, but not from either of the other two. What the hell was going on with his brothers, he thought, that they were all losing it at the same time? First this weird-ass trip, then a hitchhiker, and now *this*? *What the hell?* he thought again, shaking his head.

'Orson?' He turned to glance at his brother, who was sitting on the floor, his back against the wooden pillar at the centre of the tent, staring into space.

'Yeah?' Orson looked up at him.

Farao opened his mouth to speak, but to his dismay, the question that came through his lips wasn't the one he'd intended.

'What happened the day Mum died?'

Farao felt his eyes widen, shocked at his own words. They'd never spoken about that day. Although Orson had been with her in her final moments, he had never volunteered much information, and Farao had never asked. He hadn't realised how much he'd wanted to know, but now the question was hanging in the air, he found himself desperate for an answer.

Orson was still looking at him, fear, hurt and concern on his face.

'I'm sorry,' Farao mumbled, suddenly regretting that he'd asked. 'I shouldn't have said...'

'No,' Orson interrupted. 'No, it's not that... I just...'

They looked at each other, and Farao had never seen Orson look so unsure. He always seemed so confident, so certain of everything; it was odd to see him falter. Orson patted the floor next to him, and Farao stood up, coming to take a seat by his side.

'What do you want to know?' Orson said in a quiet voice.

'I don't know...' Farao shrugged. 'Did she say anything to you? Before...' His voice choked up. 'You know.'

Orson took a deep breath, resting the back of his head against the wooden pillar. When he finally spoke, it was in a low, careful tone.

'She said she knew.' Orson swallowed hard. 'That she knew she was going to die. That she'd known for a while. She said she was sorry...' He paused. 'She said she loved me. That she loved all of us. She told me to look after you. To make sure you'd be ok. She wasn't very coherent after that... At one point,' Orson croaked, clearing his throat, 'I think she thought she was talking to Dad...'

Farao said nothing, letting the words sink in. He could almost see it. Picture it. He could almost hear her words resonate in the night around them. He remembered her voice. He remembered its softness. The kindness in it. He remembered her smile, the one that always seemed a little sad.

'And how was it when... You know...' Farao said after a pause.

Orson glanced at him briefly. He seemed unsure whether or not to respond, but Farao held his gaze.

'Maybe we shouldn't...' Orson started.

'Please, Orson. I want to know. I *need* to know,' Farao insisted. 'I can't even really remember those days, you know. Whenever I look back... Nothing's there. It's just a huge black hole. I think I can remember the pain and the fear... but they're more like echoes of what I must have felt then... but it's this huge missing piece. It's...' He shook his head. 'It's so confusing.'

Orson exhaled sharply. 'I didn't know...'

'I never told you.' Farao shrugged.

Orson shook his head. 'I should have asked.'

'Yeah, well...' Farao wrapped his arms around his legs. 'I guess you didn't. It's fine.'

'It's not. Not really.' Orson reached out and squeezed Farao's arm. 'I'm sorry, Farao. I'm sorry I wasn't there for you.'

Farao gave him the briefest of glances, a little taken aback. 'You were there. In other ways. I guess nobody's ever perfect.'

'I guess not...' Orson agreed, letting go of Farao's arm.

They sat in silence for a moment, both looking over at Kendrik, who'd started to snore lightly. Then Farao turned towards Orson, who heard his unspoken request.

'It happened pretty fast...' Orson closed his eyes, a tear rolling down the side of his cheek. 'She gripped my hand really tight...' he gulped, shuddering, his voice barely audible now. 'I can still see it… Her body gave, like, a final gasp, and then it sort of… released. Like I could see her soul floating out of her. Her hand went slack. And then she was… gone.'

Farao sat frozen, wishing he hadn't asked. More than the knowledge of her mother's final moments, it was the realisation that Orson had had to endure this on his own that gripped his insides and made him want to puke. Orson had been younger than Farao was now, and he'd had to face this alone.

'Orson…' Farao whispered, but he didn't have the right words.

Orson angled his face towards him, opening his eyes, his smile full of sorrow. 'It's ok…' Then he added, seeing Farao's frown, 'No, really. It's ok. I've made my peace with it. I got to be there with her. I got to hold her hand. Much better than her dying alone…' He gave a pained smile. 'If that's the price I had to pay, then I'd pay it a hundred times. For her. And I'd do it for any of you.'

Farao opened his mouth, then closed it again. He was annoyed at himself for not knowing what to say. Orson was always the one with the right words, who always knew how to handle those situations, and it hurt not to be able to do the same for him.

'So…' Orson said after a moment, forcing a smile, nudging Farao with his shoulder. 'Are you finally going to tell me what's going on with all these girls sliding into your DMs?'

***

When Farao awoke the next day, the yurt was bathed in warm morning light. He stirred under the duvet and, turning around on his side, noticed that Orson's spot next to him was empty. He sat up, rubbing his eyes, and glanced around the room. Juliette's bed was empty and neatly made. There was no sign of Terran either. In the third bed,

Kendrik was lying on his back, his eyes wide open, staring at the ceiling. Kendrik turned to look at him.

'Morning,' Kendrik said, and his voice sounded calm, and lighter than it had in weeks.

''ning.' Farao yawned. 'Where is everyone?'

'Dunno.' Kendrik shrugged.

Farao studied Kendrik's face. He looked rested, and his jaw was relaxed.

'You alright?' Farao asked uncertainly.

Kendrik paused for a moment before answering, considering the question.

'Yeah...' he finally said, sounding almost relieved. 'I'm good.' He smiled at Farao.

'Cool.' Farao nodded, leaning over to pick up Orson's phone from the bedside table. He unlocked the screen and navigated to his Facebook account. The memory of Mel's written outburst the previous night made him wince. Orson had refused to hand the phone back over till Farao had told him the full story, not that he felt there was much to tell. But he'd seen Orson's eyes widen as he kept talking.

'Ah, little brother,' he'd said, shaking his head in disbelief when Farao was done. 'There is *so* much you don't know about women...'

Listening to Orson's advice, Farao could sort of see why Mel was so angry with him. According to Orson, their snogging sessions had meant more to her than they had to him. He'd never for a moment thought how hurt she might be if she realised he was treating her like a placeholder till someone better came along—Orson's words, not Farao's.

Farao scrolled through Mel's messages again. Orson had advised a heartfelt apology, but no matter what Farao started typing, it never seemed to come out right. A notification popped at the top of the screen, and Farao froze. It was an instant message. From Serena. With trembling fingers, he clicked on the small banner and read her message:

'Hi Farao, I don't know what's going on with you and Melissandre, but I never meant to come between you two. It was never my intention. I just hope you're feeling better.'

Farao stared at the words.

'What the...' he mumbled, reading the message again.

What is she on about? he thought, unable to make sense of what she was saying. He racked his brains, trying hard to remember if he'd ever mentioned his situation with Mel to Serena, which he knew he never would have. So how could she know? And why would she think she was in the middle of anything?

Unless... Farao frowned as realisation dawned on him. Unless, instead of keeping Mel at arm's length, his silence had only goaded her into spreading rumours about them. Anger rose in the pit of Farao's stomach at the unfairness of it. Screw what Orson had said, he'd never made any promises to anyone, and he was certain Mel knew of his interest in Serena. All her casual mentions of 'the new girl'. She had known *exactly* what was going on, and it was her problem if she'd deluded herself into thinking it was something else, not his. He groaned with frustration, and in a furious impulse, he threw the phone across the tent. It crashed into one of the wooden poles keeping the yurt erect with an ominous sound of bursting glass.

'Shit, shit, shit, shit.' Farao panicked, jumping out of bed and rushing to where the phone had fallen to the floor. The screen was completely cracked, and try as he might, the phone was no longer switching on.

'Nice one,' Kendrik's voice called out from the other side of the room, where he was sitting up in bed, watching Farao.

'It was an accident!' Farao whined. 'I didn't mean to—'

'You didn't mean to throw the phone across the room into a wooden pillar and trash it?' Kendrik laughed, and for a second, Farao was taken aback at the sudden lightness in his brother's tone.

He turned to glare at Kendrik, but seeing him grinning, trying hard not to laugh again, made his anger abate a little.

'Yeah…' Farao admitted with an awkward smile. 'I guess I sort of meant it.'

'What was that about, by the way?' Kendrik asked, adjusting the duvet around him.

'Don't ask…' Farao grunted, bending over to pick up the phone pieces from the floor.

'What happened here?' Orson's voice boomed behind them as he came into the tent, his eyes taking in the scene.

Terran and Juliette were right behind him, holding a tray of coffee cups and breakfast muffins.

'It was an accident!' Farao repeated, dropping the pieces he was holding in surprise.

'Yeah, I heard that one before,' Kendrik chuckled.

Farao turned to Orson. 'I'm sorry, Orson. I really didn't mean to, I just…'

'Let me guess,' Orson said, 'the hate mail from all these scorned ladies wasn't looking any better in daylight?'

There was a moment of silence. Farao felt his face heat up, and he tried to ignore the fact that all eyes were on him.

'Wait a second,' Kendrik said. 'Can someone fill me in here? What's the deal with Farao's love life?'

Farao spun on his heels to look at him.

'Just shut up, ok? There's nothing to fill in,' he snapped.

'Ah, little brother.' Orson came to wrap an arm around his shoulders. 'Heartbreak is the perfect moment to share your sorrows and bond with your brothers.'

'I'm not fucking heartbroken, ok? Let go of me!' He tried to shake Orson's arm off, but his grip was tight around him.

'I'm lost—is there more than one girl?' Terran chimed in, distributing the coffees around. 'I thought Sarah was the one he liked?'

'It's *Serena*!' Farao barked, finally managing to push Orson away. 'And it's none of your business, so piss off, all of you!'

'Ok, now *I'm* confused.' Kendrik took his coffee cup from Terran, frowning. 'Is there another girl, then?'

'I said PISS OFF!' Farao yelled.

'Brothers, brothers,' Orson said in a placating tone, raising his arms. 'Let us not embarrass our younger sibling any further. All I shall say,' he added with a cheeky grin, 'is that he's actually much more popular than we thought with the ladies.' He winked at Farao.

'You... I... You can't...' Farao was lost for words, the anger and shame building up inside him jumbling the response he wanted so desperately to throw at them. 'You're such a bunch of arseholes!' was all he could think of. 'I'm out of here.'

And he stormed out of the yurt, leaving his brothers dumbfounded behind him.

He stomped through the cordoned-off restricted area and made his way out into the main field, where festival-goers were slowly awaking. There was the scent of sunshine and freshly brewed coffee in the air. If Farao hadn't been in such a foul mood, he might have appreciated the loveliness of the scene he found himself in.

But he couldn't. He was furious with Orson. How could he have thrown him under the bus like that, in front of the others? He knew how delicate the matter was—why would he give it such little consideration all of a sudden?

Farao swore loudly and kicked at a pile of moss, which went flying in all directions. He walked towards the big stage and found a seat on one of the large beanbags scattered around the grass. He crossed his arms in front of his chest, determined to hold on to his bad mood as long as he could.

'Free breakfast?'

Farao looked up to see a young man in rainbow-coloured hot pants and an elaborate unicorn headdress towering over him. He was carrying a large wicker basket held by a thick leather strap around his neck and shoulders. The basket was full to the brim with disposable cups, a bottle of oat milk, a fuming pot of what smelled deliciously like fresh coffee, and a pile of blueberry muffins.

'Free breakfast?' the unicorn man repeated with a broad smile when Farao didn't respond. 'You sure look like you could use it!'

Farao opened his mouth to tell the weirdo to piss right off, but held himself back just in time. He actually could do with breakfast, and he didn't have any money on him.

'Yeah, sure.' he shrugged. 'Thanks.'

The unicorn man's smile widened. He handed Farao a muffin, and poured him a cup of coffee.

'Milk?' he asked.

Farao shook his head, and took the cup he was handing him. The unicorn man stood there for a second, watching Farao intently.

'Erm,' Farao said awkwardly. 'Thanks.'

'No problem! Enjoy!' the man said brightly. 'And remember…' he added before walking away, 'whatever it is, it can't be *that* bad.'

The unicorn man waggled his eyebrows at him and turned around. Farao watched him approach the next group of people. He shook his head. He wanted to swear to himself some more, but somehow he could no longer find the energy to be annoyed. He took a bite of his muffin. It was incredibly good. As he watched the unicorn man hand over breakfast around the field, his smile so wide you'd think it was the happiest day of his life, Farao realised that, maybe, he had a point. Maybe, just *maybe*, things weren't quite as bad as he'd thought.

Chapter 49
Orson

Orson looked at the door of the tent, through which Farao had disappeared.

'You should not make fun of him like that,' Juliette said quietly, handing Orson his coffee and breakfast.

Orson looked at her and smiled. 'It's good for him,' he nodded absently. 'He needs to learn to stop taking himself so seriously.'

Juliette frowned at him. 'So, this is part of some bigger plan or something?' She looked unconvinced.

'It is, my lady. It most *certainly* is.' Orson gave her a wide grin, taking a sip of coffee.

They all went to sit outside at a wooden picnic table overlooking the fields below. Orson took a bite of his muffin, realising only then how starving he was. He hadn't eaten much since the previous day, having spent most of the evening searching for Kendrik and then the biggest part of the night standing vigil at his bedside, talking to

Farao. He glanced at Kendrik, who was opposite him with both hands wrapped around his cup, gazing into the distance. Orson couldn't put his finger on what it was, but he noticed Kendrik looked... What was it exactly? Calmer? More settled? There was a rested glow on his face which hadn't been there for weeks now. The dark circles around his eyes, though still visible, seemed a little less puffy than before. The tension that had kept his mouth and jaw constantly clenched of late had evaporated.

Kendrik caught Orson looking at him, and raised his eyebrows.

'You look...' Orson started, searching for the word. 'Different.'

Kendrik smiled at him, and Orson thought he looked younger, too.

'Yeah,' Kendrik sighed softly. 'I feel different.'

Orson studied his brother. Maybe that was the right word. He looked *different*. In a good way.

'I feel lighter,' Kendrik added, bringing his cup to his lips and taking a gulp of coffee.

'Gosh, Ken, had I known that's what it would take, I'd have got you on hallucinogenics long ago!' Orson chuckled.

'Orson, that's not funny,' Terran cut in, his tone stern.

'It is a *little* funny,' Orson said, raising his eyebrows at Juliette, who was watching the scene in silence.

'Kendrik.' Terran turned towards him, and it sounded like he'd been bottling this up all night. 'This was *not* ok. We were worried sick about you. We looked for you everywhere. It was hours before we found you. And completely unconscious, at that. Think what example this is setting for Farao.'

'Whoa, whoa, whoa.' Orson interrupted him. 'Easy, tiger. Everything's fine. No one was hurt. And, let's be honest, Farao can set his own bad examples for himself. He doesn't need anyone's help.'

'No,' Kendrik said quietly. 'Orson, Terran's right. It wasn't right. I didn't mean for it to end up that way, but that's no excuse.'

Terran looked at him in silence, his face impassive.

'You know,' Kendrik continued. 'Since we were told that Farao... That he...'

'It's ok,' Orson said, placing a hand on Kendrik's arm. 'We know.'

But Kendrik shook him off, taking a deep breath.

'No,' Kendrik insisted, his voice determined. 'You don't. Even I didn't know. And I have to say this.'

They all fell quiet.

'Since we learnt of Farao's condition, and of all that history, I haven't been able to cope. I mean, I've been a mess. I haven't been able to think properly. I haven't been able to sleep. I just couldn't deal with it. And I didn't understand why.' Kendrik was speaking very fast now, like he was scared that if the words didn't come out now, they might never be said. 'Of course I was affected by Farao's illness, but so were you two, and you weren't as much of a mess as I was. I just felt so guilty, it was crushing me. Last night... Last night I realised something. I think I might have known all along...' He looked up at them, and there were tears in his eyes. 'Well, maybe I didn't know exactly what was going on, but I might have put some pieces of it together.'

Orson sat glued to his seat, not daring to even blink. He listened as Kendrik told them of the memories he'd buried without knowing how to make sense of them. Of the times he wished so hard he had extended a helping hand to their mother.

'And then, one fine day, it was too late.' Kendrik's voice was breaking now. 'I just wasn't there for her. I never did anything to help her... And now Farao... And I haven't been there for him either. What if he, too...' He shook his head. 'What if something happens and I haven't done anything to help him?'

Orson caught Terran's eyes, and he knew that he, too, had been caught off guard. He saw the pain in his older brother's eyes, and he saw his own guilt reflected on his face. Orson gave a shudder. In his effort to plough on, to save Farao, to keep some lightness in their new gloomy reality, he had been blind to how deep Kendrik had sunk.

'Kendrik...' Orson whispered.

A movement at the corner of his eye caught Orson's attention. Juliette had stood up from the bench and made her way to Kendrik, kneeling in front of him, placing her hands on each side of his face, forcing him to look at her.

'Hey,' she said, her voice gentle. 'Kendrik. Look at me.'

After a moment, Kendrik looked up.

'Kendrik,' Juliette repeated. 'This wasn't your fault. You hear me? This *wasn't* your fault. There is nothing you could have done to help your mother.' She spoke a little louder now, as Kendrik shook his head and tried to extricate himself from her grasp. 'You were just a child, there is no way you could have known what any of it meant, or what to do with that information.'

'But later,' Kendrik choked harder than ever, 'later I... I didn't...'

'It wasn't your fault,' Juliette repeated. 'You couldn't have known. It. Wasn't. Your. Fault,' she said again softly, pulling Kendrik into her arms and hugging him tightly.

Kendrik let himself be held, and they stayed there until, eventually, he stopped shuddering and his breathing slowed down.

'I'm sorry,' Kendrik mumbled, leaning out of the hug.

'*Don't* apologise.' Juliette shook her head. 'Better out than in.' She gave Orson and Terran a meaningful look, then glanced at her watch. 'I have to go and set up, but I'll see you guys later, ok?'

They nodded and watched her go. None of them spoke for some time. Orson was trying hard to find the right thing to say, but there was a ball of hurt and guilt lodged in his throat which prevented him from speaking.

'Ken,' Terran said quietly, 'she's right, you know. It wasn't your fault. We were just kids. None of us could've known...'

Kendrik simply nodded.

'And this time is different,' Orson said, finding his voice at last. 'You're here for Farao. We all are. We won't let anything happen to him.'

Kendrik nodded again. He seemed calmer now.

'Yeah,' he breathed. 'Yeah, you're right.'

'*And*,' Orson added with a small smile, 'now we have a great story to keep us warm in our old age.' He pulled his best senior citizen impression. 'Remember that time we ended up at a random festival and Kendrik got high on magic cocoa?'

Kendrik and Terran gave a short laugh. They sat together, sipping their now lukewarm coffee, looking out onto the festival in the field below.

Orson took a deep breath. The air around them felt clearer somehow, and a little lighter. For a moment, he felt like everything would work out. Like nothing could possibly go wrong with their plan. They were invincible as long as they were together.

He wanted it so badly to be true.

Chapter 50
Kendrik

By the time Farao rejoined them, it was almost lunchtime. He seemed to have calmed down since he'd stormed out on them. They made no mention of his morning outburst. They walked around the festival site, but very soon, Farao said he felt like lying down, and they accompanied him back to the tent. Kendrik saw Terran and Orson exchange a look of understanding as Farao swallowed the pills he was given without a word and got into bed. Farao had seemed mostly ok since they had left England, albeit a little quicker to tire than usual, but otherwise it might have been easy for an outsider not to notice anything was wrong. But something *was* definitely wrong, and moments like this were a painful reminder that they shouldn't be fooled into thinking otherwise.

Terran motioned discreetly to Kendrik to stay with Farao, before disappearing out of the tent again with Orson close behind him. Kendrik nodded to say he understood, and went to lie down on his own bed. When he turned to look at Farao, he saw his eyes were open and he was staring into space. It occurred to him that he barely knew his younger brother. They'd never spent that much time together. Neither of them had really ever made an effort; they seemed to have just accepted they probably didn't have much in common. In truth, Kendrik realised now that he had gone about his business without paying much attention to Farao. He'd been so busy trying to make a life for himself he hadn't stopped to get to know him. All he saw was how disobedient and difficult Farao could be, how much trouble he caused Terran, how ungrateful he was.

Kendrik saw things differently now. He realised he simply didn't have a clue who Farao really was, what he liked or whether he was happy. He didn't know what kept him awake at night or what troubled him. But he wasn't going to fail this time; he refused to let history repeat itself. He racked his brains for something to say.

'So…' Kendrik started. 'What *is* going on with these girls?'

'Oh, for fuck's sake,' Farao hissed.

'No, Farao,' Kendrik said quietly, propping himself up on one elbow. 'I'm not making fun of you. I'm just asking. It seems like a lot to handle, that's all…'

Farao turned to look at him, a look of mild surprise on his face. He seemed to be trying to decide whether or not Kendrik was pulling his leg.

'Well,' Farao finally sighed, readjusting the duvet around him. 'It's all just a mess, to be honest. I've kind of fucked up…'

Kendrik remained quiet, listening to Farao, amazed once more at how little he knew about him. It wasn't like Kendrik's own experience with girls was much more extensive than Farao's, so he didn't think he had much advice to impart upon him, but he found himself glad that Farao was sharing it all with him.

'Mmm…' Kendrik nodded when Farao had finished talking. 'It does sound messy… What are you going to do about it?'

'I dunno…' Farao yawned, blinking slowly. 'I haven't figured that out yet… I just don't get girls, you know? Or why it has to be so complicated…' He turned on his side and closed his eyes. 'To be honest this is already more hassle than I signed up for…'

It wasn't long before he'd fallen asleep. Kendrik waited a few moments, listening to his slow, steady breathing. When he was certain Farao wasn't waking up, he slid out of bed and stepped out of the tent. Terran and Orson were sitting on the grass a short distance away. They looked up when they saw him approach.

'He's sleeping,' Kendrik said, sitting down with them.

'Good.' Orson nodded.

Kendrik looked at each of his brothers in turn. They looked preoccupied.

'So,' he asked tentatively. 'What's the plan?'

'We should get going,' Terran responded, absent-mindedly pulling blades of grass from the ground and shredding them to pieces.

'Yeah.' Kendrik nodded. 'I agree…'

There was little more to be said, and they sat watching the crowd go about their day around them, occasionally glancing back at the tent entrance, as though to reassure themselves it was still there.

There was so much they had to do, Kendrik thought, so much they needed to get right. The drive was only a fragment of the journey. The easiest part, in fact. What would happen once they got there? They had the man's address, but was that enough? What if he refused to see them? What if he denied everything? As someone who had built his entire comfort zone around being prepared and knowing what was coming next, Kendrik now felt like a fish out of water. So much of it was outside of his control, and there was nothing he could do to change that fact.

He found himself wondering what his father would have done. His father would definitely have known what to do. He was the bravest man Kendrik had ever known. Much braver than he had turned out to be.

Kendrik remembered the day the news about his father had come, because that was the day his life had lost its colour. He had been very young at the time. It was the lunch break at school, and the deputy head had come to fetch him, Orson and Terran from the canteen, where they had just sat down to eat. She had asked them to follow her, and they had obeyed, throwing side glances at each other, wondering what she could possibly want with them. Kendrik remembered how solemn the deputy head looked. He couldn't even remember her name, or what she looked like, but he could recall with exact precision the look in her eyes. Pity. It had definitely been pity. She had led them to the school gates where, to their surprise, Amit was waiting to collect them. They climbed into his car, baffled by this odd and unprecedented turn of events. Amit had driven them in near silence for some time. Eventually, he had parked the car and they had walked a short distance to the South Bank, where Amit bought them ice cream and they sat at a little table facing the troubled waters of the Thames.

And then Amit had told them. His voice had been gentle but his words had resonated clear as day in Kendrik's mind.

Their father had been in an accident.

Something had gone wrong with his plane.

He was dead.

Everything around Kendrik had stopped. His father was dead, and there was nothing in the universe that made sense any longer.

The rest of the day had been a blur. The rest of the week, even. There was a wake, though Kendrik learnt later that given the state of the crash site, on the edge of a small lake in the heart of Somerset, no one had been able to recover the body, so they hadn't been able to arrange a proper funeral.

Kendrik had lost a huge part of himself that day. His father had been his hero. His best friend. And now there was life before that day, and the half-life that came afterwards.

Kendrik often thought he saw so much of his father in Terran, and he despised himself for how envious it made him. But it was the truth. He wished so much he'd taken after the great and handsome Anand Dhawan. Maybe if he had... Maybe then he might have been there for his mother, and he might have been stronger for Farao.

Kendrik shook his head. He couldn't change the past, as much as he wished he could. All he could do now, he reminded himself, was do better and show up for his family like his father would have done. *Yes*, Kendrik thought, that was something he could do to make amends, and as the thought crossed his mind an idea occurred to him. It seemed simple enough, one thing he *could* do in an ocean of things that were irremediably out of his control.

'Ter,' he said, and his voice was much calmer than he felt inside. 'Can I borrow your phone?'

Terran gave him a questioning look but didn't ask, simply pulling his phone out of his pocket and handing it to him. Kendrik stood up and marched into the tent, looking around for Terran's backpack. He found it resting by Terran's bedside table. He rummaged in it for a few seconds until he found what he was looking for. Then, settling himself on the floor, he logged into his personal email and got to work.

Chapter 51
Amit

Amit pulled onto the motorway and sped up, slotting his Audi expertly into the incoming traffic. He found his cruising speed and adjusted himself against the leather seat. In the background, the radio was playing a political debate. Not that he was paying it much attention.

In his mind, he was replaying the last conversation he'd had with Terran over the phone, that very afternoon. When he'd first heard about it, he'd been a little alarmed at the news that the brothers had picked up a random hitchhiker and made a detour to a hippie festival, but he had tried not to sound too admonishing. The last thing Terran needed was to have someone on his back, and Amit wanted him to feel he could tell him anything. He needed to stay in the know about what they were doing. He had to make sure they were alright.

Amit glanced at the satnav on the digital screen on the dashboard, though he knew the way by heart by now, having made the journey so many times in the past. His mind travelled back to his conversation with Terran. They'd decided to move on and continue to their destination, not that Amit had much hope of them finding what they were expecting—and he still wasn't too clear on what it was they were hoping for. He doubted even the brothers knew. The possibility that the man could be a donor for Farao was merely an excuse, Amit knew, nothing more than something to further justify this ridiculous trip they'd embarked on. Amit had warned them that even if they found Farao's biological father, and even if they convinced him to check if he could be a donor for Farao, there was little chance he would be a viable option. Barely a chance in thousands. In fact, the man would need to have two impeccably healthy kidneys himself, and with the disease being a dominant genetic anomaly, the chance that his body would be in bad shape was high.

But Terran had not budged; he'd latched on to the idea with mad desperation, and somehow he'd convinced his brothers to embark upon the journey with him. Amit had offered to come along but Terran had refused. Amit hadn't pressed the matter, knowing Terran to be strong-minded when he wanted to be. Besides, there were other responsibilities he needed to be around for on British soil. The familiar pang of guilt struck him, as it always did, when he thought of the deception he had taken part in. He forced himself to push it away, something he had grown somewhat adept at over time. With a sigh, he increased the volume on the radio and made himself pay attention to the debate, quashing his conscience for the millionth time.

Amit drove for three hours without stopping. He knew the route well enough, and he didn't want to delay his arrival, hoping he could drive back to London that same day and catch a few hours' sleep before he had to be back at work the following morning.

He exited the motorway and emerged on an empty country road. He sped down the rough tarmac, watching out for vehicles ahead. A short distance away he spotted a tractor coming towards him and he reduced his speed, driving his car in slow motion as close to the edge of the road as he could, letting the tractor pass him by, before speeding up instantly the moment it had gone. *Not long to go now*, he thought, suppressing a yawn. Finally he spotted the familiar sign, turned left onto a narrow cemented lane lined with trees and through a set of large iron gates. He kept driving along until the outline of the large country house appeared in the distance. The sight of the majestic building always took his breath away, no matter how many times he saw it.

He left the car in the visitors' car park and marched to the front door. He smiled at the receptionist, who greeted him by name, and walked down a large corridor to a side room. Two people, a man and woman, both wearing pale lilac scrubs, smiled at him. They, too, knew his name. But again, he'd got to know them all after so many visits. He made some enquiries and listened carefully to the updates he was given, checking the paperwork and notes in the file they handed to him.

Amit thanked the nurses and stepped out of the room, walking back along the corridor and climbing the large marble staircase two steps at a time, making his way through the building he knew like the back of his hand until he arrived in front of the door he was headed for.

He took a breath, wedged the file under his arm and knocked on the door. On the other side, he heard a man's voice invite him in.

Amit turned the handle and pushed the door open. He stepped into the familiar space, a well-furnished carpeted room adorned with a stone-carved fireplace. Several framed photographs, all gifts from Amit, were arranged on the mantelpiece. The room boasted a set of large windows offering a stunning view of the gardens around them. And, by the window, sat a man in a wheelchair. He didn't turn around when Amit came in. In fact, he barely acknowledged his presence, and Amit knew from experience that this was to be one of *these* days. He left the file on a side table and walked to the man's side, placing a gentle hand on his shoulder.

'Good afternoon,' Amit said softly. 'Anand-*bhai*.'

Chapter 52
Terran

It was with a heavy sense of dread that Terran went to find Juliette to tell her about their change of plans. He wished he'd had more time. He'd wanted so much more time to be around her, to find himself relaxing in her presence, to hold her against him and pretend the world was no longer swirling around him. Instead, he forced himself to shove down the feelings he could sense bubbling at the pit of his stomach. It'd be easier to act as though none of it existed.

As he walked into the main clearing, he saw Juliette by the main stage, talking to someone with a bright pink 'staff' tank top and an iPad. The expression on her face when she caught sight of him told him she knew exactly what he had to say. She motioned to him to hold on for a moment, and he waited to one side, his hands in his pockets, glancing around without really seeing anything. He knew that getting on with their trip and leaving Juliette behind—with all the hope and promise she'd awakened in him—was the right thing to do. But at the back of his mind, he wondered why doing the right thing so often made him feel hollow and miserable.

'Hey,' he said as Juliette came to stand next to him.

'Hey.' She fixed her eyes on him, and all he could do was look away.

He took in a breath, bracing himself, but the words weren't coming.

Juliette studied him for a moment, then said calmly, 'you're leaving.'

'Yeah.' He nodded, finally lifting his gaze to meet hers. 'Farao's... He's... you know.' He hated himself for making such little sense. 'We've just got to get going.'

Juliette was quiet for a moment. He could see she was trying to be supportive, though the quiver in her jaw told him of her disappointment.

She gave him a gentle smile. 'It's ok. I understand.'

'Thank you,' he sighed.

There was another heavy pause. He wanted to find the words to express how grateful he was for her, for how easy she was making this on him, for how her presence filled him with reassurance that everything would be ok. But nothing came. *I can't*, was all he could think.

'Say goodbye to the guys for me, please?' she finally said, motioning behind her. 'I don't think I'll get the chance. I have to hop on for a class in a moment.'

'Of course I will.'

'And, Terran?'

'Yes?'

'Keep me posted, ok?' Juliette cocked her head to one side. 'On how you get on?'

'I will.' He nodded.

She looked at him expectantly for a moment, then let out a soft laugh.

'Give me your phone.' She held out her hand to him, smiling and shaking her head.

'Ah.' He caught on. 'Yes, of course...'

He pulled his phone out from his pocket, unlocking the screen and giving it to her. He watched as she typed her contact details in and gave herself a missed call.

'Now you have no excuse not to keep me posted,' she teased, handing him back his phone.

'I will,' he repeated. 'I promise.' And he wanted more than anything to live up to that promise.

'Good.' There was a glint in her eye as she looked at him, and a smile playing with the corners of her lips. 'Because I may have to track you down and kick your arse if you don't.'

Terran felt his stomach flutter, and before he could help himself, he stepped forward and pulled her into him. She wrapped her arms around his waist and let out a long exhale, resting her head against his chest. Just like the previous night, her closeness seemed to spark him alive, igniting his body like a bonfire. It wasn't just desire—although he wanted her with a passion that was hard to control—it was *longing*. A craving for all of her—body, heart and soul. The thought of going away, of no longer seeing her smile or hearing her laugh... He swallowed hard, closing his eyes. The mere idea that this might be the very last time he got to be around her terrified him. He held her tight, allowing himself one more instant of relief before he knew he'd have to let her go.

Come on, Terran, he thought to himself after a long moment. *Get a grip.* He felt his insides go numb as he dragged himself back to reality and pulled slowly away from Juliette. He didn't have time for this now, and his guts gave a lurch as a little voice at the back of his head sniggered that he probably never would. Juliette took a step back, seeming to sense the change in his demeanour.

'Goodbye, Terran.' Her voice trembled a little.

'Bye,' he breathed, taking in the sight of her for one last time.

Then, before he could say anything else, his heart sinking, he turned around and walked away. *Get a grip*, he told himself over and over again. *Just get a fucking grip.*

By the time Terran joined the others in the tent, Kendrik and Orson had packed the bags and Farao was just waking up, his tired face looking confusedly at the pile of luggage on the floor. Orson gave Terran a searching look, but Terran turned away. He couldn't face Orson's knowing gaze right now. He walked to his bed and opened his backpack, checking its contents, more for something to do than anything else.

'Are we going somewhere?' Farao mumbled, rubbing his eyes, a gesture which made Terran picture a much younger Farao, one who used to curl up into Terran's arms and cry himself to sleep.

'Yeah.' Orson's voice was forcefully bright. 'After Ken's adventure yesterday, we thought it might be better to get on with our road trip. You know, before he becomes an addict or something,' he added with a grin.

'Seriously?' Kendrik rolled his eyes. 'Don't you think that's a bit of an exaggeration?'

'Darling brother.' Orson punched Kendrik softly on the arm. 'These are the famous last words uttered by every single drug addict on the planet. Better have our intervention early on than risk you joining yesterday's magic trip club.'

Farao had slid out of his bed and was putting on his shoes. Kendrik looked as though he had an answer ready, but Terran handed over their bags and ushered them all out of the room.

'Guys, come on, you can continue this fascinating argument in the car…'

'How right you are, Terran,' Orson exclaimed with a flourish as he stepped out of the tent. 'On and on we go! Four brothers, on the road, ready for the adventure of a lifetime...'

'Doesn't this guy come with an off button?' Kendrik groaned, making Farao laugh.

'If you find it, let me know.' Terran shook his head. 'I've been looking for it for years.'

But looking at Kendrik, Terran saw that, like him, his brother was smiling.

***

The drive to Marseille from Aix-en-Provence was short and they found their rental easily. Terran had booked a house, the back garden of which opened straight onto a private stretch of beach, with azure blue sea beyond as far as the eye could see. It had been more money than they really should have spent, but one look at the pictures of the place on the listing and Terran hadn't been able to resist. If their lives were going to crumble in the south of France, he'd thought, then at least it would be with the stunning blues of the Mediterranean in the background.

They dropped their bags in the hall and walked around the house, each picking a bedroom, before gathering in the small manicured garden. A wooden gate slotted in between two thick green hedges separated them from the beach. Looking into the distance at the soft ripples of the waves, Terran felt he could have stayed there forever.

'Well, if that's not heaven, I don't know what is...' Orson sighed, staring out towards the sea.

Terran nodded his agreement. This *was* heaven. Or it could have been. Had they not been here on such a dark occasion.

They decided to order pizzas for dinner, and Orson, whose French was the best out of them all, placed the call using Terran's phone, informing them as he hung up that their delivery would be another forty-five minutes.

'Give or take,' he added with a shrug. 'The French aren't best known for their punctuality…'

They walked out past the little gate and onto the beach, leaving their shoes behind them in the garden, strolling all the way to the water's edge. The beach was deserted. The early evening sky was starting to colour with pastel shades. The soothing sound of the waves was a reassuring melody. A little further up the beach, there were several large logs arranged in a semicircle around the remains of a campfire, and Terran motioned towards it. Kendrik jogged back to the house and came back shortly after with a few small logs under his arm, some newspaper and matches, which he had seen in the utility room when they had toured the house. Terran lit a fire, and they watched the flames grow as the evening sky slowly darkened. None of them was speaking much, but Terran found he rather enjoyed their shared silence.

'You know what this is missing,' Orson announced after a short while. 'Music!'

Farao gave an approving grunt and stood up. 'I'll go get your case,' he said, looking at Orson. 'Is it in your room?'

Orson nodded, and they watched Farao disappear out of sight back through the gate and into the house.

'How are we going to do this?' Kendrik said the moment Farao had gone, in a voice so low it was barely audible.

Neither Orson or Terran needed to ask what he meant.

'I don't know,' Terran said. 'I haven't thought it through that far.'

There was a pause. They had all focused on getting themselves to this point, and Terran had assumed that by the time they got here he would have figured something out. But now, there they were, and he was none the wiser on what to do next. The night had almost fallen around them now, and the sound of the waves reverberated softly in the darkness.

'I guess…' Terran said tentatively after a pause, 'I can go and meet this guy tomorrow and see what he says…'

'No way.' Kendrik was staring at him in disbelief.

'You're not going there alone,' Orson said firmly, shaking his head. 'For all we know, he could be dangerous. I mean, clearly he is…' He shuddered, his gaze on the crackling fire in front of them.

There was another pause.

'What then?' Terran probed. 'We can't bring Farao along, and one of us at least needs to stay with him.'

'And what are we going to tell him?' Kendrik murmured.

'Well, I was thinking…' Orson started, but with one glance at Kendrik's face, he suddenly stopped and turned around.

Terran looked up and saw Farao's silhouette approach them. He instantly knew something was wrong, though at first he couldn't say what. When he got a glimpse of Farao's face in the light of the fire, his heart constricted. Farao's face was white as a sheet, his jaw tense, his mouth thin with silent fury.

Slowly, Farao lifted a hand and Terran saw a sheet of paper clenched in his fist. In his other hand was an envelope which had been roughly torn open. The envelope was marked with Farao's name.

Terran recognised it instantly.

The second letter.

The one their mother had left for Farao, and entrusted to Orson to hand over to him when he felt he was ready to know the truth.

'Shit,' Orson breathed in horror.

'What. The. *Fuck*,' Farao snarled, waving the crumpled letter in front of him, his voice quivering with anger, every word sounding like it took a gigantic effort to enunciate, 'is *this* about?'

Chapter 53
Farao

Farao stared at his brothers, who stared back at him in shock. Their mute silence sent his blood boiling even more.

'What the *fuck* is going on?!' he yelled, and he saw Kendrik flinch.

It was when he'd popped Orson's guitar case open that Farao had noticed it. Something poking through a small hole in the torn fabric lining. Without thinking, he'd traced his fingers around the hole, and he'd felt something flat underneath it. The sharp corner of a piece of paper. Curiosity had got the better of him, and he'd leant over the case, inspecting the edges where the lining met the hard material, looking for a bigger hole. He found what he was looking for, though someone had tried to patch it up with glue. Glancing over his shoulder, he'd pulled on the fabric, reopening the hole. He'd slid his fingers in it, giving the case a shake to direct the piece of paper towards his hand. Eventually he'd managed to extract it, and to his amazement, had held an aged envelope to his face—his name written clearly on the front, the handwriting eerily familiar.

With shaking fingers, he had torn the envelope open, and read the single sheet of paper inside it. He'd got to the end of the letter and frowned. Then he'd read it again. And a third time. But all he felt was confusion. None of it made any sense. He'd turned the letter around, but the back of it was blank. He'd torn open the entire lining on the guitar case, but no other treasure was hidden in it.

Then, as he'd stared at the letter for a long moment, confusion had been replaced by something else. Anger. What was this doing hidden in Orson's case? This was *his* letter, clearly addressed to *him*, so why had he not known it existed until this moment?

And, most importantly, what on earth did any of its contents mean?

Forgetting about the guitar, fury boiling at the pit of his stomach, he had stomped down the stairs and run out to the beach.

And now, seeing the looks of agony on his brothers' faces, Farao knew one thing for certain: they knew *exactly* what the letter was about.

'Farao…' Terran whispered with a pained expression.

'TELL ME WHAT'S GOING ON!' Farao yelled louder, tears burning at the corners of his eyes.

His brothers exchanged a look and Farao felt like, any second now, he might throw himself at them and hit them.

'Sit down, Farao,' Orson said calmly.

'I'M NOT FUCKING SITTING DOWN!' Farao screamed, and he saw Kendrik flinch again.

'Ok, ok,' Orson said in a placating voice. 'But please, hear us out.'

'What have you been hiding?' Farao found himself screaming again, but his voice no longer sounded like his own. 'What is it that…'

He glanced down at the letter again, his vision blurry with angry tears. '…that *I should not feel is my fault*? What is she talking about?'

He looked from each of his brothers to the next, feeling like he might implode with rage.

'Farao, please.' Orson's voice quivered. 'Please sit down and we'll tell you everything. Just… Please, sit down.'

Farao hesitated for a moment, then, slowly, he sat down on one of the logs. No one spoke for a few seconds, and he shivered with frustration. He was about to open his mouth to speak when Orson started talking.

'Before Mum died,' he said quietly, sounding like he was measuring every word before saying them, 'she left two letters. One for the four of us… And one for you.'

'What the…' Farao's eyes were wide.

'Hear me out, please,' Orson pleaded, and he took a deep breath. 'She wanted me to keep them safe, and to share them with the rest of you when the time was right…' He paused, his voice lowering to an agonised whisper. 'I read the first letter. And I waited for the right time… But it never seemed to come…'

'Did you know?' Farao snapped, looking at Terran and Kendrik, who shook their heads.

'We didn't know…' Terran said. 'Until a few weeks ago.'

Farao's head shot back towards Orson.

'Why did—' he started, but Orson interrupted him again.

'It happened when you were taken to the hospital from school.' Orson's gaze was on the flames, the fire reflecting in his eyes. 'We…'

There, Orson paused, and glanced up at Terran, as though silently asking for help.

'We…' Orson said again, his voice breaking.

Another pause. Farao felt his temper rising again.

'Farao,' Terran looked straight at him. 'There's something you need to know. And I hope you'll understand why we did what we did…'

Farao froze. Though he didn't know what was coming, the fear he heard in Terran's voice paralysed him. A moment passed, an agonisingly long moment where Farao watched the silent exchange between Orson and Terran across the fire. Meanwhile, Kendrik just sat there, his head in his hands. It was Terran who started to talk, with Orson jumping in when Terran's voice faltered.

Farao remained frozen as he listened to them recount everything.

He listened as they told him the news they had received at the hospital, not just of his illness, but of the secret Orson had been forced to reveal. He listened to the words that came out of their mouths, but they didn't seem to make any sense.

Critical.

Rare genetic disorder.

Life threatening.

He listened as they told him of their mother's letter and explained the plan they had formed. Words started rushing through his mind, completely out of control.

Assault.

Pregnancy.

He listened, his eyes mesmerised by the burning fire, to their apologies. He listened as they begged for his forgiveness.

He listened until he wasn't really listening anymore, and their voices were just a buzzing noise in an ocean of dread flooding over him. He knew they must be talking, but he was no longer really there. He was far, far beyond their reach. His mind was a mess of thoughts and emotions he couldn't untangle, numbing him completely.

'Where's the letter?' he heard a low voice say in the distance, realising with a jolt the voice was his own.

He looked up slowly, his face impassive, and he saw Terran's face constrict. Orson reached into the inside pocket of his jacket, and without a word, he handed Farao an envelope. Farao opened it and extracted several sheets of paper bearing the familiar handwriting.

There was nothing but the sounds of the waves and the crackling of the fire as he read every word of his mother's confession. He read until he reached the very end of the letter. Then he sat there, immobile as a statue, for what might have well been the rest of his life. The world around him had stopped turning. The air had grown so stiff and heavy he could no longer breathe.

His mind had stopped working, too. Nothing made sense anymore. His entire life had been a lie. A big *fucking* lie. His coming into the world had been a cause for pain and destruction. He wasn't one of the Dhawan brothers. He wasn't his father's son. He was the son of a monster. He was the child of the most evil act known to mankind. He hadn't been wanted. His father—no, not *his* father, his *brothers'* father— must have hated him. He must have wanted him dead. And now, he was dying, and maybe this was the universe's way of rebalancing things, of correcting the horrible mistake that had been committed.

He looked around slowly, but everything he saw was a blur, the scene suddenly becoming distorted. He thought he saw Terran's lips move, but he couldn't hear a single sound coming out of his mouth. All he could hear was the pounding of his heart.

A touch on his arm snapped him suddenly back to attention and he jumped to his feet.

'Don't fucking touch me,' he seethed, and there was so much venom in his voice that Orson recoiled.

Farao's head spun around madly. The world, which had seemed so still a mere moment ago, was now spinning uncontrollably. His breathing was accelerating and the panic in his chest grew so dense he could no longer breathe. The words from his mother's second letter flashed in his mind. *Don't ever think any of this is your fault.* But wasn't it? *His fault?* His very existence, from the moment he was conceived, had wreaked havoc in his parents' happy life. He had destroyed his family from the inside, like a parasite, poisoned everything that they had shared. How could he not feel this was his fault? How could he bear to exist knowing what he knew now?

His hands were trembling, and he dropped the letter. He couldn't stand looking at his brothers. *Half*-brothers, a snide, harsh voice in his head echoed. He couldn't see the expressions on their faces. He couldn't see their disgust. He couldn't bear it.

This couldn't be happening. This couldn't be true. It had to be a nightmare. He felt his heart breaking under the soul-crushing, filthy truth. He wrapped his arms around himself and fell to his knees. A silent cry was rising within him, consuming him, scraping his insides raw, but when it reached his throat, no sound came out.

Suddenly he couldn't take it anymore. He couldn't be here. He simply couldn't. He stood up, and without another glance at the others, he turned around and started running.

Chapter 54
Orson

It was a few seconds before Orson realised Farao had bolted. By the time he reacted and got to his feet, Farao's figure had almost disappeared into the night. He started sprinting after him, Terran and Kendrik on his heels. They called out Farao's name but he wasn't answering, and their voices echoed desperately through the darkness.

Orson felt the sense of panic expanding his stomach, fear such as he had never known before. All he could picture in his mind's eye was Farao's face as the dread and realisation sank in and agony took over. Orson swallowed hard, the back of his throat burning. If only he had told them the truth before. If only he had let the secret out long ago… This was all his fault. They had to find Farao. They had to make this right.

They ran down the beach, and the further they got from the fire, the darker it got, until they were running completely blind.

'Farao!' Orson screamed.

Terran and Kendrik's calls resonated behind him, but Farao didn't respond. Then Orson heard a noise in the night. Had he imagined it? He called out to the others to be quiet and listened hard. Had it been the sea? He perked up, his body rigid with attention. Then the noise came again.

A sob. A heart-wrenching sob.

Orson turned around, listening for the sound, walking frantically towards it until, finally, he could make out the vague outline of a body, sat hunched on the wet sand, a short distance away. Terran and Kendrik were by his side in an instant, and together they approached the small figure.

Now that he'd stopped running, Orson's eyes were slowly acclimatising to the night, and he was able to distinguish the lines of Farao's face. He was crying, his body convulsing. He didn't react when Orson sat beside him. He just kept crying.

There they were again, Orson thought with a pang, sitting together in the dead of night, Farao inconsolable, and Orson feeling like he'd failed his younger brother beyond forgiveness.

Orson felt Terran and Kendrik take a seat next to him.

'Farao…' Orson whispered.

'Leave me alone!' Farao cried, jumping to his feet.

'We can't do that…' Orson said.

'You lied to me! You all *lied* to me!'

'We just…' Terran stuttered. 'We didn't…'

'You what? Huh?' Farao seethed, gesticulating wildly. 'You *what*? Everything. All of it. You didn't think I deserved to know? Oh, poor little Farao, who's always such a huge pain in the arse, let's not even fucking bother to let him in on the biggest fucking secret of his entire life!'

'Farao, it wasn't that…' Kendrik stood up, and the rest of them imitated him.

'What was it then?! You think I didn't know? Huh?' Farao screamed. 'You think I didn't already know I'm not like you? That I'm not one of you? That I don't belong here? And now, *this*! All this while you were plotting behind my back and fucking play-acting happy family?'

'Farao, listen...' Orson pleaded.

'No! I won't fucking listen! You took the biggest...' Farao shook his head, his eyes wide with fury. 'The most important thing there was and you made it into a fucking joke! And there I was like an absolute moron thinking... Thinking that finally... Finally we could...'

'Farao, we weren't play-acting.' Terran took a step forward but Farao moved away from him instantly. 'Please, you've got to believe us. We were trying to protect you...'

'Protect me?' Farao sounded almost delirious now. '*Protect* me! Are you fucking kidding me? Protect me from *what*? The truth? Well, big news for you, Terran.' His tone was full of derision. 'You can't fucking *protect* me, alright? No one can! It's over!'

'Don't say that, please.' Orson's voice was raw.

'You don't understand!' Farao shouted, shuffling further away from them. 'You don't *get it*!'

'Farao...' Terran started, his voice almost a whimper.

'No!' Farao screamed louder still. 'You don't get it! I'm... I'm a...' He was crying harder now. 'I'm a *monster*! I should be *dead*! And I *will* be dead! Soon! You don't fucking get it!'

'Farao!'

They all turned around towards Kendrik, whose voice had boomed so sternly it made Farao fall quiet.

'You're *not* a monster,' Kendrik said in a commanding, icy tone. 'You're our *brother*. You *are* one of us. And you are not dying! Not on our watch.'

The finality in Kendrik's words echoed around them and bounced through the night. For a moment they all froze on the spot, no one daring to break the spell.

'Well, you don't get to decide.' Farao seemed to deflate. 'I'm not like you… I'm not… How can I…'

But he appeared to have run out of words. He went quiet, falling to his knees on the sand and burrowing his head in his hands. Orson felt powerless before Farao's distress. He didn't know how to make it alright. He didn't know what to say. He simply sat down, leant in and wrapped his arms around Farao's slumped shoulders.

'Get off me.' Farao pushed him away. 'I said get off! Don't fucking touch me! I hate you! I fucking hate you!' he roared.

The words rang through the night, bouncing around the deserted beach. Orson didn't dare make another move. He didn't know how long they stayed there, sitting side by side on the sand, facing the sea, with nothing breaking the silence other than the soft whooshing of the waves and Farao's muffled sobs, which eventually died away.

Minutes merged into hours as they sat with each other without speaking. There was so much to say, which, in Orson's mind, boiled down to very little. Despite the secrets they'd unearthed, and whatever their parents had endured, at the end of the day, they were brothers. The Dhawan brothers. And nothing else mattered beyond that.

Gazing out to the dark horizon, a half-forgotten memory came back to Orson. His mind made his way back through the scene as though through a dense fog, which slowly dissipated. He was getting ready for school. They had just had their breakfast and his mother was putting the dishes into the dishwasher, humming a tune to herself. Baby Farao was asleep in his basket. Kendrik and Terran were upstairs. Orson slid off his chair at the dining table and walked out of the kitchen, checking his bag in the entrance corridor. He wanted to take his Spider-Man action figure with him today, because Chase Meltin was bringing his Batman, and they had planned to meet up at recess to swap them.

Looking into his bag, he realised the action figure wasn't there. He must have forgotten to put it back when he took it out the previous evening. He walked to the living room, glancing around for the action figure, when his father's silhouette caught his eye.

His father was leaning against the mantelpiece with his back to him, and it was a moment until he noticed Orson was there. Orson stood on the spot for a few seconds, because something in his father's demeanour told him something wasn't quite right.

'Dad?' Orson said timidly.

His father turned around to look at him, and Orson noticed he was crying. He'd never seen his father cry before.

'Orson,' his father had croaked, his voice sounding a bit rusty. '*My* son.'

As he said the words, his face contorted into a grimace, and Orson frowned.

'Dad, are you ok?'

'Of course.' His father forced a rueful smile. He looked everything but.

On the mantelpiece, Orson spotted his figurine clasped in his father's hand. He heard his mother call out to him that it was time to go.

'Go on, son.' His father motioned towards the door. 'Time for school.'

But Orson stood there, looking between his father and his figurine. His father followed his gaze and gave a sad chuckle.

'Oh, yes,' he said, bringing the action figure to his face and studying it before handing it to Orson. 'There you go. Keep him close, maybe he'll be able to protect you.' And then he added in a whisper, 'maybe *he* won't fail.'

Orson had taken the figurine, but he had stayed rooted to the spot. There was something wrong with his father's smile. His gaze seemed unfocused, and there was a trembling in his hands that Orson had never seen there. Somewhere in the background, the radio was playing Jimmy Rhodes' 'Ghost'.

What is left of me,

When all's said and done?

Where my ghost may be.

So, too, will be my crown.'

'Be good, Orson. Can you do that for me?' His father bent down to ruffle Orson's hair, then he stood up, swaying a little, and walked unsteadily out of the room.

Looking up at the mantelpiece, Orson noticed his parents' large tequila bottle was open. A used glass laid next to it, some of the brown liquid still in it. Orson walked towards it and smelt the glass. It had the same smell his father's breath had had, a moment ago, when he'd come close to him.

His mother called out to him from the entrance again. Slowly, and without knowing why, Orson screwed the tequila bottle closed and took the glass, hiding it behind a row of books on a shelf. Then, without another look, he ran out of the room, his Spider-Man in hand, and left for school.

At lunchtime that day, the deputy head came to get him and his brothers in the cafeteria, and Amit bought them ice cream on the South Bank.

Their father had died.

He'd crashed his plane in a routine training exercise.

***

The first rays of the rising sun took Orson by surprise, because he'd completely lost track of time. They watched the glorious morning light expand across the sea, scintillating against the waves and bathing the beach in a warm glow. It started gradually at first, and then all of a sudden the sun broke out of the line of the horizon, illuminating everything around them.

Then, slowly, and still without a word, they stood up and walked back to the house. Orson only realised then how far they'd come. Farao, Terran and Kendrik made their way inside, but Orson went back to the campfire, which had long gone out now. He picked up his mother's letters, folding the first one into its envelope and storing it back inside his jacket pocket. Then he took the second one, Farao's letter, and dusted the sand off it. It was a bit crumpled, but still perfectly legible. His heart heavy, he read his mother's words:

> *My Darling Farao,*
>
> *If you read this letter, it means you finally know. I have dreaded the moment when you will find out, because I never wished for you to live with the weight of what happened.*
>
> *I want you to know that you are loved. That, despite it all, you are my son, and nothing can ever change that. I hope that you can hear the truth and be able to let it go. It doesn't define you. Don't ever think any of this is your fault. None of it is. I pray you won't let your anger get the better of you.*
>
> *I want you to be happy and to become the wonderful young man I know you will be. I know now I won't be there to witness it, and I can only hope that you and your brothers will find your way. I will be watching over you, always.*
>
> *My darling boy. My son.*
>
> *I love you,*
>
> *Maman*

Chapter 55
Anand

He was sitting by the window, looking out into the garden without taking in much of the view. He winced as he felt something in his legs twitch, though he knew that it was all an illusion. The waves of phantom pain came and went, and he had long stopped fooling himself into believing they meant anything.

Behind him, there was a knock at the door, but he didn't respond. Whoever it was, they would come in anyway. This was the way things were here. He recognised Amit's cautious step without needing to turn around to look at him.

'Good morning, Anand-*bhai*.'

Anand gave a sharp nod of the head, and Amit came to stand beside him.

'Is it done?' Anand asked.

He noticed the side glance Amit gave him, and the hesitation in his manner.

'Is it done?' Anand repeated, his tone more forceful.

'The lab's got your samples,' Amit sighed. 'We'll know in a day or two.'

'Good.'

Amit was looking at him now, and Anand knew what was coming before he even started speaking.

'Anand-*bhai*.' Amit's voice was almost a plea. 'Are you sure about…'

'Yes,' Anand said firmly, and his voice left little room for further discussion.

Amit fell silent for a moment. 'Why not meet them, then?' he whispered. 'They need you.'

Anand refused to look at Amit, his hands clenching on the armrests of his wheelchair.

'They don't need me,' he seethed. 'What they need is a donor. They're managing perfectly well without me.'

'Anand-*bhai*, if they knew that you were alive…' Amit begged.

'No!' Anand snapped. 'Their father is *dead*. You will say nothing to them, you hear me?'

He turned his head sharply to look at Amit, who wore a constricted and pained expression. He looked like he was about to protest, but taking in Anand's glare, he seemed to think better of it. Amit simply shrugged.

'I can't stay long,' Amit said, 'I have to get back to work.'

'Fine,' Anand growled. 'Go, then.' And he turned to look the other way.

He felt Amit's eyes on him, but refused to look at him.

'Call me when you have the results.'

Amit acquiesced, and without saying anything else, he left the room. Anand heard the door close behind him. He massaged his thighs. The pain was growing more intense by the second, but he knew he would just have to ride it out.

He closed his eyes. Amit didn't understand. Good, gentle, sincere Amit, who had never once failed him. He didn't get it. He probably never would.

There was nothing Anand could ever ask of Amit that he would refuse, and although he'd never abused that before, everything had changed after the accident. Anand never knew how he had survived the crash. He still remembered vividly how he'd lost control of his plane and how the nose had dived forward, plummeting towards the ground at unimaginable speed. The rest was a blank.

It wasn't till much later that he'd pieced it together. He'd come to in the cockpit, moments after the crash, bleeding and in agony. All around him was just fire and smoke, the flames already licking at his legs and quickly spreading. His foggy brain had known he only had moments to act. His survival instinct must have kicked in, because he'd had enough sense to trigger his ejector seat, and his body had been thrown from the plane, through the blaze, sending him flying in a ball of flames into the woods, a considerable distance away from the crash site. It was a miracle he had survived.

Back then, however, all he knew was that, weeks later, he had awoken from a coma in a countryside hospital, covered in bandages, severely burnt, with his legs no longer working, incapable of coherent speech and with no memory of what had happened. At first, he could barely remember who he was. By the time his rescuers had gone back to the spot they'd found him, looking for clues, the RAF had already cleared the site. The fire had destroyed the little that could have helped him be found—his fingerprints, his uniform, and most of his face. The hospital staff had been unable to identify him, and with no one coming to claim him, they had moved him to one of the long-term recovery wards. He'd become another John Doe. It was months before Anand was able to speak again, and even longer before the jumbled memories in his mind rearranged themselves into a semblance of coherence.

Eventually, almost a year after the accident, he had woken up one morning with Amit's name flashing like a bright light in his mind. He had asked for someone to find him and, sure enough, a few hours later, Amit had dropped everything and made his way to Anand's side. Amit had wanted to telephone Gabrielle and the boys immediately, but Anand had forbidden it.

During his convalescence, Anand had had plenty of time to think. Time to remember the reason why he'd suddenly lost control of his plane on a simple routine flight he'd done hundreds of times before. He'd been drunk. So completely and utterly drunk his reflexes had been muddled and his neural pathways blocked. And before he'd known it, he couldn't remember how to pilot the fighter plane that was falling towards the ground, or how to pull out of a dive.

And Anand had plenty of time to remember why he was drunk in the first place. Every time he thought about it, his entire body shuddered. The time before it happened felt like an eternity ago, like a distant dream, as though it'd never existed. He knew at some point his family had been happy, but that time was so long gone he could no longer picture it.

All the memories he now seemed to have revolved around what had happened to Gabrielle, and how it had burnt any trace of happiness from their lives. All Anand could see in his mind's eye when he tried to think back to their time together was Gabrielle's expanding belly, and that *thing* growing inside her. The final nail in the coffin of their marriage had not just been the news of her pregnancy, but their inability to do anything about it. Gabrielle had said the doctors affirmed it was too late to terminate it, but Anand had always known how she felt about abortion, and he suspected she might have lied rather than go through with one.

That, Anand knew, that was the day he truly died. Whoever he was before then, that man was gone, buried under a mountain of grief and pain and hatred. They'd tried a change of scenery. They'd moved to

England, faithful Amit arranging everything for them. But their life in London was only more of the same, the same agonising pain, the same ever-growing wedge between them, only against a different backdrop.

Anand had started drinking. With every passing day that Gabrielle's pregnancy progressed, so had his resentment, until he could no longer get through a day without a drink. The night Gabrielle went into labour, Anand was passed out at a bar. It was Amit, once again, who had come to the rescue, taking care of the boys whilst she recovered. Anand hadn't come home for over a week, dreading the moment he would have to face the truth. That the child she'd pushed into the world wasn't his. The constant living and breathing reminder of what she'd endured, and of his failure to come to her rescue when she'd needed him most.

So, when he'd come to realise the world thought him dead, Anand had felt relieved. It was easier that way. He'd had Amit submit all the required paperwork to change his name, wiping Anand Dhawan officially from the face of the earth. Erasing his name from all records cut himself off entirely from his old life. It took away the possibility that he might one day be found. That his sons would know he'd survived. He knew that, and he'd made the decision in full consciousness. It was the only path he could see.

***

Two years after the accident, Anand had been discharged from the hospital, and Amit had found him a room in a convalescence home in the Somerset countryside. This had been his place of residence ever since.

Amit came to visit regularly, bringing him news of Gabrielle and the boys, which Anand listened to with a sting of pain in his chest. But he had stood firm on one point: they should never know he had survived. He couldn't bear them seeing him in this state. It would have broken whatever little fragment was left of his heart. He had made Amit swear on his father's memory that he would never, ever break his vow of silence of the matter, and, ever so reluctantly, Amit had eventually consented.

When Gabrielle had died, Anand had doubted himself. He'd second-guessed his vow to stay out of his sons' life. His heartbreak at Gabrielle's passing had weakened his resolve, and he'd almost changed his mind. *Almost*, but not quite. Instead, he had watched from afar as Terran stepped up as the head of the family. Despite his grief, he'd never felt prouder of his eldest son. He could see so much of himself in him. That pride had blinded him for a long time. It wasn't until much later, when Anand caught a glimpse of Terran's daily struggles through all the things Amit wasn't quite saying, that he'd truly appreciated the burden he'd imposed on his son by remaining in the shadows. But by then, anything he could have done was too little, too late. He'd missed his chance, he told himself, and he'd convinced himself it was a justifiable excuse to remain hidden forever.

Far from his duties and responsibilities, Anand had allowed himself to indulge in his bitterness, letting his regrets consume him, burning down every last remnant of who he had once been, until all that connected him to his past life was the loyal Amit. He lived a half-life, he knew that, but he was long past caring.

Then, one day, Amit had come unexpectedly, bringing him news that *the boy* had been taken to the hospital and that tests results had come positive for a rare form of genetic disease. They knew, Amit had said. Orson, Kendrik and Terran knew everything. Amit told him of the letter Gabrielle had left, the one Orson had held on to all these years.

Amit had called him daily after that, informing him of the brothers' desperate plan to save the boy. All Anand could think of was his sons' determination to rescue him, the lengths to which they were prepared to go to help him.

But somewhere in his subconscious must have existed a better man than his awake self, because one fine day, Anand came to and finally realised what he should have seen long ago. The boy was part of their family. Whilst he'd spent years hating him and despising his very existence, his sons had grown up by his side as brothers. *And Gabrielle…* he thought with unbearable guilt and agony, Gabrielle might still have considered him her child.

The thought had planted the seed of realisation, and it had grown rapidly over the following days, until one fine morning, Anand opened his eyes to find the fog had lifted. He saw his life in a different light all of a sudden. He realised how selfish and foolish he'd been. He knew he'd failed them all, and the hurt was so strong he wished he'd truly died in the ball of flames that had engulfed his plane when it hit the ground.

Slowly, as he lay in bed hour after hour, waiting for news from Amit on the boys' progress, an idea had formed in Anand's mind. The boy needed a transplant. *What if,* he thought. *What if… What an ironic twist of fate that would be…*

He'd instructed Amit to see whether *he*, of all people, was a compatible donor. Amit had been stunned at the suggestion. He'd tried to talk him out of it, but his mind was made up. He had been warned that a donor would need clean cells, and that the heavy painkiller treatment Anand was subjected to daily disqualified him. So Anand had requested for the morphine and the meds to be taken away, against Amit's heavy protests.

It had been hell. The aches and pains in his body, some phantom, and some very, very real, had hit him with full force. But he'd gritted his teeth and coerced Amit into arranging for the tests to be done.

He knew he could never make up for what he'd done. But if there was one thing he could do to redeem himself, then this was it.

There was one chance in thousands he would be compatible, Amit had warned, but if he *was*... Maybe he could save his sons the pain, after all they had been through. After he had so often failed them.

And, maybe, finally, *the boy* would carry a piece of him, too.

Chapter 56
Juliette

'Well done, everyone! You all did great!' Juliette announced in the hands-free microphone she was wearing, clapping at the crowd amassed in front of her.

As she was the headline act for the festival, her classes ended up gathering the largest attendance. As always when she realised how many people knew about her and wanted to follow her workouts, she felt humbled. She still couldn't quite believe how far she'd come.

She waved at the class and stepped off the stage, thanking the supporting staff as she handed them back her headset. She strode back to her tent, smiling back at people who recognised her on the way. She normally took the time to talk to everyone, to give them the satisfaction they all seemed to get from talking to her for a moment, and pose for selfies, but today she couldn't face it. She'd left her phone charging in her tent, and she couldn't wait to go and check whether she had any messages or missed calls.

She'd heard from Terran when they'd arrived at their rental, though he'd turned out to be a man of fewer words in text than he had been in person. And then, since the previous night, nothing. She'd followed up, checking up on him a couple of times, but none of her texts had shown as read. Not all morning, not over lunch, and now the afternoon had elapsed too. She had finished her last class of the day, and found herself hoping fervently that she would return to her tent to find an update waiting on her phone.

One glance at the screen, however, proved her wrong. There was nothing. Not a text, not a call, and all of her previous messages were still showing as maddeningly unread. Juliette swore loudly. She didn't get it. Had something happened? Should she be worried? Knowing that neither Orson nor Farao had working phones anymore, and since she didn't have Kendrik's number, Terran's phone was her only link to the brothers. Were they alright? Or had something gone wrong with Farao? Before she could stop it, her mind was spiralling.

She put her phone down, walked once around the tent, shaking her arms, then picked up her phone again and opened her chat history with Terran. She started typing something. Then erased it. Then started again. Then erased that too. What should she say? Should she even say anything?

The lingering doubt that had wormed its way into her mind earlier that day was snaking its way through to the surface now. What if Terran simply didn't *want* to hear from her? Was he glad he didn't have to deal with her now they'd moved onto the next part of their journey? Had she imagined the chemistry between them? Could it have been all in her head?

No, it can't be. Maybe he wasn't the most expressive, but she had seen the way he looked at her. *And that dance…* Juliette shivered at the recollection. That dance had been real. She was certain he'd felt it too. They'd both felt it. They'd both wanted it, and she was sure he'd been as disappointed as she had that they were interrupted.

But now, in the light of day, could he have been feeling different? He always tried so hard to be responsible for his family; he seemed to think it meant he wasn't allowed to enjoy his own life. Or... maybe she simply wasn't enough to tempt him.

'Stop,' she said out loud, shoving her phone into her handbag. 'Enough is enough.'

She wouldn't become one of *those* women, whose self-worth was reliant on a man's attentions. *Screw you, Terran Dhawan*, she thought angrily as she exited the tent. But a moment later she checked herself again. Because she didn't want to be one of *those* women either, the ones who grew bitter upon facing rejection. She sighed, thinking once more that she simply didn't get it, and hoping as hard as she could that the brothers were ok.

She weaved her way through the tents into the main festival field. All around her the world was going on with its business, not caring that she no longer knew what to do with herself.

It was all unbelievable, really. She barely knew the brothers, but in the short time she'd spent with them, she'd grown disproportionately fond of them all. Being around them had been the most natural thing in the world. It had felt like being with family. She didn't have any siblings, but for the first time in her life she'd had a glimpse of what having brothers might have felt like.

Well—she rolled her eyes—her feelings towards Terran had most definitely been rather unbrotherly. She had been in love before, a couple of times, but each time her affection had grown slowly and subtly, fuelled by shared moments and memories, before it mutated into something akin to love. With Terran though, it was anything but slow and subtle. It had hit her with full force and without any warning. Before she realised it, her entire body was attuned to his, moving as he moved, her eyes searching out for him constantly, looking for any interaction she could get with him. She'd never experienced anything like it. *And that night...* It jolted her body even now, just thinking about it.

With newfound resolve, she took out her phone from her bag and typed a message to Terran: *'It's ok if you don't want to talk, please just let me know you're all ok.'* She pressed send before she had a chance to overthink it, and watched as the double grey ticks appeared next to her message, showing it had been delivered. She held her breath for a moment in the mad hope that the double ticks might turn blue, or better even, that he might respond. Of course, that didn't happen, and the disappointment was stronger than she'd expected it to be.

Then, suddenly, her phone buzzed, and Terran's name flashed on the screen. Juliette was so surprised she was unable to move for a few seconds before shaking herself back into action and answering the call.

'Terran?' she said, uncertain.

'Hey Juliette,' said a voice she wasn't expecting to hear. 'It's Orson.'

'Oh.' She knew she sounded disappointed and hated herself for making him think she didn't want to talk to him. She took a breath. 'Orson, is everything ok? Are you ok?'

'I don't know...' Orson sounded tired, and his voice was a little hushed. 'Define "ok"...'

She heard a door open and close, and the sounds of the outdoors—*was it the sea?*—on the other line.

'I'm sorry we didn't keep you posted,' Orson said, his voice no longer muffled now. 'I had a suspicion that Terran wasn't keeping in touch... I was using his phone, and I just noticed he didn't even open any of your texts.'

'Oh, it's alright...' Juliette responded instantly, too quickly to be believable, and she knew she wasn't fooling anyone.

'No, Juliette,' Orson sighed, 'it's not alright. I know Terran cares about you, but I don't think he knows how to let you in...'

'Yeah... I'd sort of noticed.'

'Please don't hold it against him. He might be the oldest, but when it comes to matters of the heart, he hasn't got a clue.'

Neither of them said anything for a moment.

'How's Farao?' Juliette finally asked.

Orson let out a dark chuckle. '*How's Farao...*' he croaked.

'What? What happened?' Juliette insisted, worried that her earlier suspicions that something had happened might have been true.

'Well... We're in a bit of a pickle over here...' Orson's voice was breaking with emotion, though she could hear he was trying his best to sound light. 'It's a long story... We fucked up, Juliette... I fucked up...' His voice was barely a whisper.

Orson felt silent again.

'Where are you?' Juliette asked when he didn't continue.

'In Marseille.'

'I know that,' she said calmly. 'Where *exactly*? Can you text me the address?'

'Juliette.' Orson's voice was soft. 'You don't have to come here. Really. It's not a pretty sight.'

'Text me the address. Right now,' she repeated as firmly as she could. 'Please.'

'Juliette, are you su—'

'I'm sure,' she insisted.

Orson was quiet for a moment, and her phone buzzed with his incoming text.

'Ok.' She sighed with relief. 'I have to be at the festival for two more days, but then I'm coming to you, ok?'

'Ok...' Orson breathed, and she wasn't sure whether his lack of further protest was a good or a bad sign.

'It'll be fine, Orson. Farao will be fine.'

Orson groaned an unintelligible response.

'I'll be there soon. Keep me posted, please.'

'Ok… And, Juliette…'

'Yes?'

'Thank you,' Orson whispered, sounding suddenly exhausted.

Juliette smiled. 'It's ok. Just hang in there, I'll be there soon.'

When she hung up the phone, she felt both better and worse. Better because she now knew where the brothers were, where Terran was. But knowing they were struggling and that she wouldn't be able to do anything to help until the festival was over was unbearable.

Soon, she told herself, taking in a deep breath. *Soon.*

Chapter 57
Terran

The next couple of days passed in a daze. Farao spent most of the time in bed, buried under the thick duvet. He hadn't said a word since the night on the beach. He took the pills he was given with a blank expression on his face. He was barely eating, and so docile it terrified Terran.

Orson, Kendrik and Terran took turns standing vigil in Farao's bedroom, watching over him as he lay with his back to them. None of them knew what to say or how to make things right. Terran's heart was breaking slowly, excruciatingly, a little more every day. How was he supposed to fix this? Where was the handbook for a situation like this? He'd tried to talk to Amit about it on the phone but the words hadn't come out, and he'd ended up glossing over most of the details of what they were going through. He felt completely and utterly powerless, seeing Farao's state deteriorate from one day to the next as he closed himself off to the world around him until there was barely any light in his eyes. Terran felt he could have handled anything else. He could have handled Farao's anger, his outrage; he could have taken one of his usual outbursts. That, he thought, he'd know how to deal with.

On the fourth day, the doorbell to the house rang. Orson, who was sitting in the living room with Terran, stood silently and went to the front door, ignoring's Terran's questioning look. Terran heard voices from the corridor. When Orson walked back into the living room and Terran looked up from staring into space, his heart skipped a beat. He instinctively stood. Juliette was standing by Orson's side, a stricken look on her face.

'How…' Terran asked, his breath suddenly catching in his throat.

'Orson…' Juliette said, as though it explained everything, and Terran nodded.

Of course. He let out the breath he'd been holding.

For a moment, their eyes locked, and Terran felt his stomach flutter despite himself. She dropped her bag on the floor and crossed the space between them, wrapping her arms around him. He felt himself instantly relax in her embrace, realising only then how tense he'd been, just sitting there. He snaked his arms around her waist and held her close. From the corner of his eye, he saw Orson quietly slip out of the room.

'It's ok…' she whispered. 'I've got you.'

Those simple words, murmured softly against his cheek, threatened to make him break down completely, and he tightened his grip around her. Juliette held him, one hand stroking the back of his head, saying nothing. He allowed himself to let go, the strain of the past few weeks engulfing him entirely.

'I'm sorry…' he murmured, leaning away from her, when he finally calmed down a little.

He rubbed his face.

'Don't be silly,' she said quietly. 'You have nothing to apologise for.'

She looked around, and her gaze fell on the view of the sea out the large window.

'Come on,' she said, holding out her hand to him. 'Let's get some air.'

Terran slid his hand in hers and followed her without a word. They exited onto the beach, walking to the edge of the water. They let go of each other's hands, and Terran popped his into the pockets of his jeans, looking down at the sand, suddenly feeling extremely self-conscious. He could feel Juliette glancing sideways at him, but he couldn't bring himself to look at her. It occurred to him that he'd been ignoring her messages over the past few days. He had neglected his phone after the dramatic night they'd spent on the beach, and hadn't opened any of her texts after that. He hadn't been able to deal with it, not when everything and everyone around him was on fire. But he had to say something now; he owed her an explanation.

'I...' they both said at the same time.

Terran smiled.

'I'll go first,' he said, pausing and turning to face her, but as he uttered the words he realised he didn't know where to start.

She waited patiently for him to speak.

'I'm sorry I haven't responded to your messages,' was all he could find to say. 'It was just... So much to handle...'

'It's ok.' She shook her head. 'I understand.'

'But still,' he insisted, 'I shouldn't have ghosted you like that. I just didn't know...' He paused.

'You didn't know how to deal with a crazy French girl on top of your younger brother having a massive breakdown from learning something really traumatic?' She cocked her head, an apologetic smile on her face. 'Yeah, I get that.'

He looked at her, startled, then laughed. The sound felt almost foreign to his ears.

'Something like that…' He turned back to look out towards the sea.

They walked in silence for a bit, Terran increasingly aware of how close her body was next to his.

'I'm glad you're here,' he said softly.

'Me too.' She smiled at him.

Terran paused, and looked towards the line of the horizon, feeling awkward, wishing he knew what to do and say next. But nothing came to him and they just stood in silence, their gaze on the gentle waves.

'What can I do to help?' Juliette eventually asked, her voice soft.

Terran turned to look at her.

'What do you mean?'

'How can I help you guys?' Her eyes were on his, earnest and determined. 'What can I do?'

Terran shook his head.

'You don't have to do anything.' He turned back to face the water. 'This isn't your fight. It's kind of you to offer, but you don't have to be here.'

He saw Juliette give him a shifty look and take a sharp breath.

'I know I don't *have* to be here.' Juliette's arm was on his, forcing him to turn to look at her again, and there was a steely note to her voice. 'I *want* to be here.'

'Why?' Terran frowned. 'Why are you doing this?'

Juliette's face clouded with annoyance and Terran instantly regretted his words.

'I mean…' Terran tried to backtrack. 'I appreciate you being here, and wanting to help, but…'

'But *what*?' Her eyes were boring into his with an intensity that almost made him take a step back.

'I... I just...' Terran stumbled on the words.

Juliette glared at him for a moment longer, then her face softened and she shook her head slowly, rubbing a hand against her cheek.

'Ah, Terran...' She gave him a wry smile. 'I just... I just care about you guys, ok? And I want to do something to help. What more of an excuse do I need to give you?'

Terran felt stupid. He wished he could take back his outburst, but all he could do was nod, which he knew was highly inadequate.

'Well...' He shrugged. 'Thank you. But there's nothing anyone can do right now...' He sighed, and turned around to start walking back towards the house.

'Orson said Farao's not talking?' Juliette fell into step next to him.

'Yeah...' Terran nodded, his chest constricting painfully at the thought. 'I don't know what to do... I'm completely out of my depth here...'

'You're doing everything you can, Terran.' Juliette placed a light hand on his arm again, and he felt his skin prickle under her touch. 'Don't beat yourself up.'

'That's not good enough though, is it,' he huffed.

'Terran.' Juliette's voice was firm, and she tightened her grip on his arm. 'It's not in your power to fix this. You have to let Farao process everything he's learnt. When he's ready, he'll come out the other end.'

Terran jerked his arm out of her grasp, a sudden and inexplicable wave of anger making his hands tremble. 'Listen, I appreciate all the wisdom, but you simply don't get it,' he growled. 'There is *no time*, ok? There isn't time for him to process all of it because, in the meantime, he's fucking dying!'

Juliette looked at him, completely unfazed, her face stern. 'What is it that you're so angry about?' she asked simply.

'*What?*'

'All this anger you have. What is that really about?'

Terran opened his mouth to respond, but no words came. He wanted to lash out some more, he wanted to yell at her, to yell at the world, to scream his fury into the sea, but he found himself suddenly speechless. What *was* he so angry about? She was right. He had so much anger inside him. Anger that had been fizzing just under the surface, waiting for the smallest of opportunities to explode out of him since that day at the hospital. Had he been in a calmer state of mind, had his brother not been dying, had his family not been breaking apart... maybe then he could have observed the matter rationally and seen that Juliette had a point. But he wasn't calm. His family was on the verge of imploding and Farao's life was at risk. And the last thing he needed right now, the last thing he wanted to do, was to introspect. He needed the anger. He needed it to fuel himself. He thought he might crumble without it. And since Juliette was here, since she insisted on standing in his way, then she'd just have to take the brunt of it.

'I don't need your cheap therapy right now, ok?' he snarled. 'I don't need you to save me, or whatever the hell it is you think you're doing. *Fuck*,' he groaned in frustration, his hands balling into fists.

Juliette was watching him impassively, letting his words reverberate around them.

'I really don't appreciate your tone,' she said coldly after a minute. 'And you guys really have to stop swearing so much,' she added as an afterthought.

And with these words, she turned on her heel and walked back to the house, her arms crossed in front of her chest, not looking back even once to see if he was following. Terran watched her go, his anger disappearing as quickly as it had come, leaving him feeling like the world's biggest prick.

***

When he made his way back into the house, Terran found Juliette and Orson in the kitchen, setting the table. There was something bubbling on the stove which smelt delicious, and Terran felt his stomach grumble.

Juliette threw him a quick, distant look as he walked in, then announced she was going to check if Kendrik and Farao were coming down, and left the room.

'What did you say to her?' Orson asked, frowning after Juliette.

'What?' Terran snapped.

'What did you say to her?' Orson repeated pointedly, looking at him from the stove.

'Nothing.' Terran rolled his eyes, marching to the sink to wash his hands.

'Sure doesn't seem like nothing…' Orson raised his eyebrows.

'Why would it be something *I* said, huh?' Terran said with frustration. 'Couldn't it be something *she* said?'

'Mmm.' Orson seemed to consider the matter. 'It's possible, but unlikely. You and I both know she's an angel.'

Terran threw the towel he was drying his hands with moodily on the kitchen counter.

'She's a stranger, Orson! Why is she even here? Why does she even want to help?' His anger was rising again, inexplicably, at the pit of his stomach.

Orson blinked, once, twice, then turned slowly to face him.

'Terran,' Orson said, considering him carefully, as though gauging how to say something delicate. 'I know this is scary. You've always guarded yourself. You've never let anyone get close. And I know why you did that. But don't let fear get in the way of something beautiful when it finally comes your way. You don't have to push it away.'

Terran stood, gobsmacked, staring at Orson. 'What are you on about?' he blurted, trying with all his might to push down the bubble of emotions blocking his throat.

Deep down he knew, but he couldn't think about that now. He couldn't deal with any of it. He couldn't let himself *feel*. He just wanted to pretend there was nothing to feel. It was easier that way, safer.

'My dear brother.' Orson gave him a small smile and shook his head. 'You're so helpless, it would be cute if it wasn't so dramatic. Just…' He sighed, shaking his head again. 'Be nice to her, alright?'

Orson lifted the pot from the stove and placed it on the dinner table. Terran felt his mouth open, and close, and open again, but no words came out.

'I'm always nice…' Terran mumbled after a moment, which was all he could manage.

'Of course you are.' Orson patted him distractedly on the back. 'Now, be a dear and go get everyone. Dinner's ready.'

Chapter 58
Farao

There were sounds coming from the kitchen downstairs, where the others were having dinner. Juliette had suddenly appeared earlier that evening, but even her gentle manner and soft pleas hadn't managed to coax Farao out of bed. He turned onto his side, with his back to the door, and pulled the duvet further up over his head.

Farao closed his eyes, hoping for sleep to carry him out of his state of consciousness, but nothing came. The moment his eyelids closed, all he could see were the words of his mother's letter, and the mental pictures of the ordeal she'd endured. Farao shivered, despite the warmth of the cocoon he was wrapped in. He couldn't tell if he was feeling cold. There wasn't much he was feeling anymore.

At first, he'd been angry. Angry with his brothers for hiding the truth from him. Angry with his mother for her confession, angry with the world for forcing it on him. He'd been so furious it had almost consumed him. He felt he could have set himself on fire with the sheer power of his fury. But eventually the wave had passed, leaving an ocean of sorrow in its wake. A sadness so profound and so limitless he had drowned in it. He'd felt lost, completely and utterly lost. The world as he knew it, the life he'd taken for granted, everything had disappeared. He was falling apart, and he didn't know anything anymore. He didn't know who he was, or what to do.

He instinctively curled into a foetal position, pulling his knees tight into him. He opened his eyes and peered over the duvet, his gaze falling on the window. The sea spread all the way into the horizon, glittering softly under the moonlight. He wondered what it would feel like to step into the water and walk, and walk, and keep walking until he was pulled under, until there was no turning back. He wondered if it would be easier that way. Easier for him, easier for the others, so that none of them had to deal with any of this anymore. A sob rose deep within his chest, gathering speed and intensity as it made its way up his throat, making his entire body convulse as it came out. The tears came rolling onto his cheeks before he could stop them, burning his skin like acid as they trailed down onto his chin and neck. He hugged his knees tighter, trying to contain the pain and wondering fleetingly if he should just stop trying to fight it and give into it once and for all.

In the past few days, he'd tried hard to remember anything his mother might once have told him that would have hinted at the reality of things, but the more he tried to remember, the more he questioned everything his mind came up with. He no longer knew the woman he'd thought of so often, the one parent he'd felt he could identify with. He thought of the suffering she had endured, of everything she had gone through because of him, and it made him sick to his stomach. He couldn't bear it. And his father... His brothers' father... He'd known all along. Had he hated him for it? He must have wished Farao had never been born. And that thought, on top of it all, made Farao want to scream at the top of his lungs. How often had he felt excluded from the bond that united his brothers, because they had shared so much before he was born, and they looked so much alike, whilst he was as different from them as it was possible to be? But Farao had reasoned with himself that, though he looked different, he was still one of them. The Dhawan brothers. And all along he'd been an outsider.

And then there was the other side of the truth… That his father, his *actual* father was a monster. A rapist. A drunkard who had assaulted his mother without even blinking. This, Farao thought as his stomach gave another lurch, *this* was his origin story. How was he ever supposed to live with that?

It was all too much to handle. He hadn't even started to think about the fact that he was dying. The words swirled in his head, stubbornly refusing to make sense. He was dying. He was dying. *He was dying.* Part of him thought it was only fair. Maybe he deserved it. Maybe the Dhawan clan would be better off without him in it. He only ever created trouble. His brothers reminded him of it often enough. Maybe he'd just lie there in bed until they ran out of medicine and he just died.

There was a dull pain in his stomach. Whether it was hunger or something more sinister, he couldn't tell. He'd been feeling worse and worse as the days went by, and he'd started getting accustomed to the aches prickling all over his body. He felt exhausted, but he didn't want to close his eyes again. He didn't want to see the images that crept up on him when he did. It wasn't just the letter anymore, or his condition, or what had happened to his mother that haunted him. There was more. It was as if the shock of everything he'd learnt recently had unlocked other memories, too.

That day. In all its gory, paralysing, blood-chilling details.

In his mind's eye, he was running up the stairs with Terran to his mother's room. He felt the fear hovering around him like a poltergeist. He saw the look of horror on Terran's face as he reached the landing and stood in the doorway. And there it was. The reality Farao hadn't wanted to face. His mother was dead. But it was one thing to know it, and it was quite another to see it with his own eyes. Because he could see it now, clear as day, as though he was there. His mother was lying on her bed. Her eyes were closed, but he knew she wasn't sleeping. She was too still. Too quiet. Too… *dead*. Her face was a weird shade of grey, her hair spread dully around her head, her mouth slack. Orson was kneeling by her side, clutching her hand, sobbing.

And now, lying in this foreign bed in a foreign house, years later, what Farao could remember most clearly wasn't the sight of it, or the sound of Orson's crying. No. What he remembered best of all was the smell. The stench of piss and shit that floated in the air. It had clutched at his throat and pulled at his insides, assaulting his senses. Much later, in biology class, he'd learnt that bodies do that, when people die. The sphincters relax and every bit of fluid, urine and excrement it contains starts leaking out.

It broke Farao's heart that, after years of failing to grieve, what came to him most specifically wasn't the stillness of her. It wasn't the peaceful way in which her face had relaxed, after weeks of cringing with pain, or the fact that her fingers were still intertwined with Orson's. It wasn't how beautiful and heartbreaking Orson's final moments with her had been. No. How fitting, Farao thought bitterly, painfully, that in the middle of the shit-storm he found himself in now, what he most remembered of the day his mother breathed her last was that she really did smell like death.

Farao waited for the memory to hurt. He waited for the pain he expected to come as he relived that moment. He waited, and waited, but it never came. After the anger and the sadness, he could feel something else coming. Something that felt more final and more real than any of the rollercoaster he'd been on so far. The emptiness. The absolute, all-encompassing sense of numbness which settled in, gluing him to the mattress.

There was nothing he could do. He couldn't change the past. He couldn't fix the present. And he couldn't face a future in which he was the son of the man who had forced himself on his mother and destroyed his family forever. He was powerless. He was at the bottom of a hole so deep and so dark he could never climb out. This was the end, he knew it. Just like his mother had known she was dying, and she'd understood there was nothing she could do to change it, maybe this was his time, too. Maybe she had shown him the way, shown him it was easier not to fight it, that it was better for everyone if he let himself go rather than endure a lifetime of hardship. At this point, any ending felt more appealing than going on like this. He closed his eyes as tightly shut as he could, wishing he could be dead in the morning and not have to face another day.

Chapter 59
Orson

A week went by, and their group had settled into an odd routine, set around the pace of keeping vigil at Farao's bedside, and the food Juliette and Orson insisted on making rather than letting them all live off pizzas and takeaways. There was a weird vibe in the beach house, Orson often thought, because try as they might to pretend there was some normalcy in their life, they were all tiptoeing around the ugly reality of Farao's degrading state.

The sight of Farao's limp body and hollowed cheeks made Orson feel sick. This was on him, he knew. The way in which Farao had come to learn the truth, so far from what he'd hoped for, had been his doing. By keeping the truth for so long and refusing to face the hard conversation he needed to have with his brothers, he'd brought this upon them. He'd failed his mother, but more than anything, he'd failed Farao. Once again. One too many times, in fact, because it started to look as though Farao might never recover. If the state of depression he had sunk into didn't bury him alive, then sooner or later the illness would catch up with him. There would come a time where he might be too ill to travel, and how were they going to give him the treatment he needed then?

When he sat in Farao's room in the dead of night, watching his brother die a little more each day, Orson wondered about the mission they had set for themselves. He knew they'd had a reason for setting off on this mad adventure, but he no longer knew what it was. The reasoning and rationale for driving all the way had evaporated the second he'd seen the look of understanding on Farao's face that night on the beach. It had bulldozed everything in its path, leaving no more room for Terran's personal vendetta, Kendrik's meltdowns and epiphanies or Orson's deluded wishful thinking that everything would somehow turn out alright. They hadn't broached the subject of the air commodore again, and Orson wasn't in a hurry for that conversation to come up. In his books, that was so far down the list of priorities they might as well abandon the endeavour altogether. He wanted to hate the man. He wanted to want to meet him and beat him up and make him acknowledge what he'd done. But he couldn't get there. The truth was he no longer cared, because all he felt was that overwhelming sense of guilt that, regardless of what the man had done, the tragedy of their present situation wasn't his fault. It was Orson's. He'd done this by never manning up enough to break the truth to Farao when he should have. *That...* That was all on him and he embraced the blame like it was his lifeboat.

Juliette had stuck around and turned out to be their saving grace, the one presence in the house which prevented them all from combusting with pain and powerlessness. She made Orson want to believe that Farao was going to get through this, that they all would, and that it wouldn't be too late. She sat with Farao, reading him some of the books she found around the house, a battered copy of *The Great Gatsby*, followed by a French version of the fourth Harry Potter book. She reminded Orson of himself when, once upon a time, he'd sat reading to his mother, even when he wasn't sure she could hear him. Sometimes he sat with Juliette as she read, leaving her to settle in the comfortable chair while he took a seat on the floor against the wall, his head resting back, his eyes closed, forcing himself to focus on every word she spoke so that his agonising mind wouldn't spiral out of control of its own accord. He found solace in hearing her read in French; it brought some balm to his aching heart, and brought back long-gone memories of his mother reading to them when they were children.

Orson knew why Juliette was there, of course. He'd seen the look on her face when she watched Terran, when she thought no one noticed. Not that Terran was paying much attention, choosing to retreat every day a little further into his shell, barely speaking to her, seeming to find it easier to block her off than deal with more emotional upheaval. Kendrik, on the other hand, had taken to sitting on the beach, facing the sea, for hours at a time. It felt like Farao's muteness was becoming contagious. In the midst of the chaos, Orson was grateful for Juliette's patience with them all, and he tried as much as he could to help her keep them all afloat.

But how much longer? he kept thinking. How much longer would they have to keep this up? How much longer until Farao emerged and rescued them all from drowning? Or how much longer until... until... Orson couldn't bear to think the words. Until it was *too late*. But he mustn't think like this. *Positive thoughts*, Juliette reminded him. He was at risk of no longer knowing what the words even meant anymore. All he knew was he'd failed. And he couldn't change any of it. If Farao died, it would be his fault, and he'd have to forever live with the knowledge that he'd let it happen.

Chapter 60
Amit

Amit listened intently to the person talking on the other end of the phone.

'Alright,' Amit said warily, when he'd heard the other man out. 'Thank you, John. I owe you one.'

He put his mobile down on the desk in front of him and rubbed his temples with his fingers, breathing out heavily. He took a seat in the large leather chair and sighed. The news was good news. Or as good as possible given the circumstances. He still wasn't convinced the whole idea was worth the risks, but he'd had very little choice in the matter, as always. At the end of the day this was yet another decision that wasn't in his control, and one secret that wasn't his to reveal. He glanced at his watch, realising only then how late it was. He would have to wait until the morning to make the phone call he knew he couldn't avoid.

Amit swirled around on his chair, facing the window, glancing out at the night sky, illuminated by London's most iconic landmark. In all his years at St Thomas' Hospital, he'd never quite got used to the sight of Big Ben that greeted him every time he turned his head. But there it was, as permanent and as solid as ever. The good old reliable clock, ticking away the minutes come rain or shine, never missing a beat. As if it knew it had a job to do. As if it knew it never had a choice anyway.

Amit sighed again, and turned away from the window. He stood up and walked around his desk, grabbing his phone and his jacket on the way, and left his office without a backwards glance.

He made his way through the maze of busy hospital corridors, nodding at members of staff on his way, only managing to return greetings with a half-hearted, tired smile. Night or day, it didn't matter, healthcare never slept, especially in one of the busiest care centres of the capital.

When he finally reached the street, Amit allowed himself a stretch. He'd been bent over an operating table all day, a complicated procedure that had required his undivided attention, and his back muscles were now complaining. He rubbed the side of his neck and his shoulder with one hand, wincing a little at the soreness he felt there. He really could have used a break, he thought wryly, knowing full well that wasn't on the cards anytime soon.

With a wide yawn, he started walking, joining the Thames Path and heading west. He could have hailed a cab, but the stroll back to his apartment in Nine Elms was less than a half hour, and he fancied a bit of fresh air.

His thoughts turned to his last conversation with Terran, a few days before. Amit could tell something was wrong, but he hadn't been able to wriggle any information out of him. In the end, he had satisfied himself with confirming Farao's health was still stable, which he supposed was the most important thing. *Soon*, Amit thought, soon they'd be able to get Farao the procedure he needed. The stars seemed to be aligning, although there was still a little way to go.

Amit had tried to dissuade Anand from proceeding. After all, there was very little chance of a match between him and Farao. And even if Anand *was* a match, he would need squeaky clean kidneys, which was far from the case. He would first need to be weaned off the medication he was taking to be considered for a donation. This meant taking away painkillers, anti-inflammatories, anti-depressants and every single pill that kept his broken body afloat. In the beginning, he'd doubted Anand had truly realised what it implied. It wasn't just the amount of pain he'd have to face. Coming off the meds meant Anand's condition would be quick to deteriorate and that, Amit had tried his hardest to hit the point home, meant signing off his own death sentence. Anand had not budged, and after a while, Amit had let it go, assuming that the low probability of the match didn't warrant the argument.

When the results had come back positive, however, Anand had not wavered, and nothing Amit could say was able to change his mind. Rather than make him doubt his decision, the sheer luck of the match had only confirmed Anand's belief that this was meant to be and, having never prayed a day in his life, he'd suddenly taken this as divine instruction that this was his destiny.

And so Amit had had to go along, as he knew he must. As it always was. He'd spend every spare moment he had pulling every string he could and every favour he was owed to make it happen. Because, as it turned out, getting a mentally unstable invalid off the vital medication he needed to survive and straight into a cold turkey situation so that he could donate his kidney and most likely sentence himself to die wasn't the easiest scenario to make a reality. Based on his own research and the second opinion of every surgeon he knew, Amit was confident that if they could wean Anand off his medication and gave his kidneys a chance to purge themselves from the chemicals, they would have an organ in good enough condition for a transplant. Still, it needed to be fast-tracked to work, and this had taken official medical expert recommendations, psychiatrist evaluations and legal recourse to get to a point where the surgery could be considered. They were getting there, Amit knew, and all they needed was a final stamp of approval from the local court to give them the green light. According to the lawyer friend he'd put on the case, John, it was just a matter of a few days until they got the verdict.

The night breeze made Amit shiver. He turned his jacket collar up and quickened his pace, ignoring the buzz of the evening crowd milling around the Thames' illuminated banks.

If this all worked out, Amit thought bitterly, at least it would give Farao a fighting chance, which was what they all wanted. Amit wished he could have shared this with the brothers and confide in them what was going on in the shadows. But he knew this would never happen. Anand would never allow it, and what Anand Dhawan said was as good as the word of God.

Amit still remembered his father clutching his hand on his deathbed and making him swear he would uphold the family honour by continuing their pledge to serve the Dhawans in any way humanly possible. These were the last words his father had ever spoken to him, and for the longest time Amit had resented the Dhawans for taking away his final goodbye. They'd taken his father's entire life, up until his very last breath, then it had been his turn to take up the job of answering their every beck and call. It was just the way things were, and his last promise to his father prevented him from ever defaulting on his duty. Amit's life had had to mould itself to the pace of Anand's comings and goings as he'd joined the RAF, and left for France, and came back, and spiralled into alcoholism, and crashed his plane, and left his entire family in Amit's care.

And then one day, long after they'd held Anand's token wake, a call had been put through to Amit's office at the hospital, one that shook him to such an extent his legs almost gave way. He had answered the summons immediately, clearing his schedule on the spot, and driving up to the country to confirm it with his own eyes. And there he was. In the flesh. The family hero. The incredible father that the boys were still mourning and the man Gabrielle was heartbroken over. Anand Dhawan. Except he was no longer the man Amit had once known. He was broken, physically and mentally. He was filled with bitterness and resentment and anger. And he ordered Amit to help him disappear for good.

Amit hadn't had a choice in the matter. As much as he'd wanted nothing to do with the scheme, he couldn't refuse Anand. If he was honest with himself, a selfish part of him didn't want Anand back in their lives anyway. So he'd arranged for Anand to go into hiding. He'd submitted Anand's paperwork to legally change his name and give him the anonymity he demanded. He'd dealt with the life insurance provider once they'd discovered the man they'd just released a large payout for was, in fact, very much alive, and had requested a full pay-back. It was Amit who'd discreetly handled all the paperwork, handled the money, remortgaged his own flat in the process to keep providing for the family. Anand hadn't much cared. He had seemed much beyond caring the lengths Amit had to go to to cover for him.

When Gabrielle had passed away ten years later was the only time Amit had thought he might not be able to manage. There was no time for his own grief because the boys, Gabrielle's sons, her everything, needed him more than ever.

And so life had gone on, with its twists and turns, its difficulties, and Amit had stuck around. For her. For the memory of her. Because even after she was gone, he could never stop loving her with everything he had. Because he knew that her sons had been her biggest pride and joy, and that he couldn't let her down.

Amit quickened his pace, striding past the impressive MI5 building, feeling suddenly very small in the face of everything that was yet to be done. There was nothing more he could do tonight other than rush home and crash into bed. *Tomorrow*, he thought with a heaving sigh as he passed the new builds overlooking the Vauxhall Bridge, tomorrow would be another day, and he prayed it would bring him the strength to continue his mission. He had to. The boys needed him.

'Don't worry, Gabrielle,' he murmured under his breath, a pang of longing piercing through him. 'I won't let you down.'

Chapter 61
Anand

The pain. The pain was excruciating. It was as if his entire body was submerged in acid. A scorching sort of sensation that kept scraping the deepest layers of his skin every second of every day.

It had tested his resolve. Of course it had. No one could get through this amount of pain and not have to reconsider why they were doing this to themselves. But far from deterring him from his purpose, it had only convinced him further that his decision was the right one. He deserved the pain. He had to feel it. He had to atone for his past mistakes. He had to carry the amount of pain he had inflicted upon others. He *had* to, and it was that thought alone that helped him keep his sanity in the worst moments.

Amit had tried to dissuade him countless times. He had offered to restart his treatment. He had begged for the boys to be told what was really going on. But as tempting as the promise of morphine sounded, Anand had stood his ground. He wouldn't cave. He'd gone too far down the rabbit hole to crawl back. Amit had said there wasn't long to go now, and Anand clung to that promise with fervent desperation. He wasn't sure how much longer he could take it. He wanted to be done with it all, one way or the other.

At times when the pain was so maddening it sent him spiralling, feverish and delirious, he thought of his sons, and random memories from their past together surfaced in his mind.

Terran's sixth birthday. They'd spent the day on the beach, playing cricket on the wet sand, Gabrielle watching them from the picnic blanket, cheering them on. Gabrielle's carefree smile and musical laughter.

Kendrik's debate society contest at school. The first time he'd won. He'd carried his medal and certificate carefully home as if they were made of glass. Anand had felt his heart fill with pride, and he'd helped Kendrik pin the certificate to the living room wall, right above the cabinet where they kept their occasion plates. Kendrik had worn the medal every day for three weeks straight after that.

Orson's first steps. How he'd launched himself towards his father, hands outstretched, as though desperate to reach him. The giggle of joy that had escaped his little mouth when he'd crashed into Anand's arms.

There'd been so much love. So much laugher. So much happiness.

And then there'd been *the boy*. In his disturbed stretches of sleep, Anand watched himself as though through tainted glass. He saw over and over again the moment he'd first laid eyes on him. He'd stumbled home, blind drunk, in the middle of the night, reeking of sweat and alcohol, a week after Gabrielle had given birth, when he couldn't avoid going home any longer. Everyone had been sleeping. Amit was snoring softly on the living-room couch. The baby was sound asleep in his basket by his side. Anand had stood there, towering over the infant like a deadly shadow, staring at it like it was a cockroach. Amit had woken then, and his sleep-filled eyes had taken a moment to fully absorb the scene. Anand knew he'd been found out. He could see the dread on Amit's face. Amit had stood slowly, his eyes never leaving Anand, his stare ice-cold, and Anand had never seen such defiance in Amit before. The idea of it had unsettled him. Without a word, Anand had swayed away into the night, letting the front door slam behind him on his way out.

So, yes. The pain was his punishment. It was all he deserved now. He would make amends for what he'd done. He would make things right, or die trying.

Chapter 62
Kendrik

Kendrik sat on the beach, digging his toes into the sand, feeling the coolness of the under layers against his feet. He looked around. The sky was a clear blue, the gentle waves a stunning turquoise. In a different life, he would have thought of this place as paradise. A little way away, he spotted a couple, hand in hand, walking their golden retriever. The dog was zooming around them in frenzied joy, pausing here and there to sniff or dig, then launching himself into the water with loud splashes. Kendrik watched it run out of the water again and shake wildly on the wet sand, spraying water all around him, then rushing back to his owners, a wide goofy smile on his furry face. *Such a simple life*, Kendrik thought longingly.

He stretched, his back complaining at the night he'd spent on that damned armchair in Farao's room. Every bit of him was sore, but he supposed that was the least of his worries right now.

He closed his eyes. It was only morning, but it was pretty mild already, and it would only get warmer as the day went on. *The day*, he sighed. All these long hours of nothing, of waiting for something to happen—though what, he wasn't too sure. He glanced at the sea again, his body releasing ever so slightly.

There was a different pace of life here. Everything felt slower. Gentler, in a way. It felt a little like being out of space and time, in a completely different parallel universe, one that resonated only faintly with echoes of the life he'd once lived with his parents in the south of France, a million years ago.

For now there wasn't much to do—eat, sit on the beach, watch over Farao, sleep, repeat—but Kendrik found there was a beauty in this simplicity that, despite everything, was almost soothing. For the first time in his life, he spent time just being. There was nothing to be done for now, no action to be taken, and he was finally able to hear himself think. He knew nothing was resolved. If anything they were worse off than when they had set off from London, but in an odd way this trip had given him a sense of peace and freedom he'd never experienced before. This place, on the white sandy beach facing the clear blue sea, had a way of making him feel like everything would turn out ok. Like life was a string of endless possibilities. Like it could be filled with excitement and joy, whatever happened. Like Farao would wake up from his stupor and come back to them, that he would be ok and they would all heal together. Kendrik didn't want to lose that sense of quiet certainty. He wanted to carry the feeling with him wherever he went.

He looked over at the horizon, trying to capture it all, what it felt like, and imprint it in his memory. The sounds of the waves with their rhythmic reassurance. The soft colour palette of the beach. It fitted into him perfectly. It felt like it belonged to him, or he belonged to it, whichever way he looked at it. And he tried with all his might to hold on to how grounding it was.

He heard the soft crunching sound of feet on sand behind him, and he turned around, feeling everything he'd been trying to grasp slipping through his fingers. The moment was gone. Juliette came to take a seat next to him, handing him a cup of coffee.

'Thanks,' he breathed, stealing a glance at her.

She looked tired—but then he figured they all did. He could see dark circles under her eyes, and he guessed that her worries weren't all to do with Farao. He'd long figured why she'd come back. He was grateful she'd stuck around, but part of him felt she didn't have a place here. Not with the way Terran was behaving, at least.

'Have you thought of going home?' he asked. He was long past beating around the bush.

She threw him a brief look. 'A hundred times…' she sighed.

'And yet…' He raised his brow. 'Here you are.'

It wasn't an accusation, and he hoped his tone would convey his meaning. He didn't want to see her getting hurt, and he could see that the way Terran was acting was doing just that. Her face was set, and he couldn't be sure what she was thinking.

'Here I am…' she murmured.

He took a sip of coffee, wanting her to understand what he was trying to say.

'You know he won't stop being a dick, right?' He looked at her, and saw her face fall. 'Not anytime soon, anyway. I don't think he can handle it at the moment.'

Juliette nodded, not looking at him. 'Yeah,' she said. 'I know.'

'And yet…'

'And yet.' Her smile was sad. 'Here I am.'

He reached out to squeeze her shoulder, and she nodded again.

'Thanks, Kendrik.'

'I just don't want to see you getting hurt, that's all.'

'I know.'

The sound of someone walking up behind them made them both turn around. Kendrik saw Terran's gaze take in Kendrik's hand, still on Juliette's shoulder and his eyes narrowed. He said nothing, but Kendrik let go of her, and she got to her feet and walked back to the house without another word.

Terran's eyes followed her silhouette through the small gate to the back garden before he sat down next to Kendrik. Kendrik took in the look on Terran's face.

'What?' Terran snapped.

'Nothing.' Kendrik took a swig of coffee.

A moment of silence passed.

'I just can't do this right now, alright?' Terran breathed, exasperated. 'I just *can't*.'

'I didn't say anything.' Kendrik shrugged.

'Yeah. Well… Say that to your face,' Terran grumbled under his breath.

'What's wrong with my face?' Kendrik turned to him in surprise.

'I know, ok?' Terran growled. 'I know I'm not treating her well. I know I'm being an arsehole. I just… I just *can't*, ok? I just can't!'

'If you say so.' Kendrik shrugged again.

'Oh, don't you get started on me, too!' Terran exclaimed. 'First Orson, now you. I don't need all the lectures, alright?'

'But I didn't say anything!' Kendrik protested.

Terran huffed, wrapping his arms around his knees.

'Ter…' Kendrik said softly, but Terran refused to meet his eyes. 'What if you could?'

He felt Terran tense next to him, his mouth opening to defend himself again.

'No.' Kendrik raised his hand to stop him. 'Listen. I hear you. I understand. I promise. I *get it*. It's not easy letting go. Jeez, I would know! But even then… What if you could?'

Terran made no sign to show he'd heard him, but Kendrik saw the slightest droop in his shoulders. Then, slowly, with a look of maddening sadness on his face, Terran shook his head. Kendrik nodded, wishing he could tell his brother about how peaceful it was on the other side. He wanted to tell him that facing the wave of darkness was the scariest thing he'd ever done, that he'd thought he'd drown in it. But that he hadn't, and that what awaited him on the other end was what life truly is about. Peace. Kindness. Love.

He knew the journey couldn't be forced. He also knew Terran would get there eventually. He only hoped it'd be in time not to ruin the best thing that had ever happened to him. Juliette, Kendrik knew with absolutely certainty, was Terran's saving grace. Whatever karmic energy had come together to bring her on their path had been for a reason. It had been to give Terran a ticket to live and Kendrik a route to explore his demons. She'd been the lightness Orson needed to keep carrying them all and a grounding force for Farao ever since they'd met her. She almost felt like the sister they'd never had—if you excluded whatever was going on with her and Terran, of course. But she, too, had her limits, and it was unfair to ask her to be a pillar for them all when Terran was treating her so poorly.

Kendrik downed the rest of his coffee and, standing up, he patted Terran on the shoulder. *One day*, he thought as he walked back into the house. *One day he'll step into the light, too.*

Chapter 63
Orson

Orson was sitting in Farao's room one evening after dinner at the end of their second week, his guitar propped against his chest, his fingers absentmindedly stroking the strings, his gaze on Farao's sleeping figure tucked under the duvet. His hands found their way to a well-known pop tune, one he hadn't played in a while. The words reached his lips before he could stop himself. He was singing softly, almost to himself, in a barely audible murmur.

'Drowning again... I'm drowning again... I'm drowning...'

His voice broke. He closed his eyes when he felt the tears coming, allowing them to fall freely, too tired to pretend he wasn't forever on the verge of crying anymore.

'I'm drowning again...'

But the words were too much for him to say, the truth of them cutting through him. He brought a hand to his face, and started sobbing, because there was nothing else left to do. There were no more words to be said or songs to be sung. It was over. It was all over.

'You must really have hit rock bottom if you're playing me that kind of boy band crap...'

The voice was hoarse from lack of use, and sounded more tired than Orson had ever heard it, but it was unmistakeable. His head suddenly jerked up, shock freezing him in his seat, as his eyes found Farao's face. He was awake, lying on his back, his gaze on Orson. They stared at each other for a long moment in silence, Orson's jaw quivering a little under the sheer relief he felt at hearing his brother's voice. He swallowed hard.

'It...' He breathed in slowly, forcing the shadow of a smile onto his face. 'It's not boy band crap, little bro. It's the great Colton Smiles!'

'Who's the lead singer in a stupid boy band,' Farao scoffed, coughing a little.

'*Was*,' Orson corrected, his voice trembling slightly. 'They all went solo a long time ago. He's an artist in his own right, now!'

'You only say that because you fancy him...' Farao rolled his eyes feebly, and the sight of such a typical expression on his brother's face made Orson's heart skip a beat.

'That's true.' He gave a weak grin. 'He truly is a gorgeous man. I definitely wouldn't say no, should the occasion present itself...'

Farao shook his head slowly, but there was the ghost of a smirk on his lips.

'What's going on here?' Terran appeared in the doorway, shortly followed by Kendrik.

There was a pause, one terrifying instant in which Orson feared the spell would be broken, and the glimmer of hope he'd felt at seeing Farao emerge from his trance might vanish. The air around the room grew thick with expectation as Orson watched Terran and Kendrik take in the situation, and he saw the same relief hit them.

'Well,' Orson finally said tentatively. 'Farao here's complaining about my choice of bedtime lullabies.'

Terran and Kendrik remained standing uncertainly in the doorway.

'Really? I thought you guys had similar taste in music...' Terran cleared his throat, and Orson knew he was being careful.

'We did,' Farao said in a raspy voice, 'until he played me some bloody Colton Smiles...'

'Who's Colton Smiles?' Kendrik asked, frowning.

'See?' Farao said. 'He's not even worth knowing about.'

'Nonsense,' Orson declared. 'You guys just have no standards.'

'Orson fancies him,' Farao said to Terran and Kendrik knowingly, his eyebrows raised.

'Ah.' Terran nodded, as though that explained everything, and took a cautious step into the room, coming to sit on the corner of Farao's bed.

'Is everything alright?' Juliette's concerned face appeared behind Kendrik's shoulder.

'Juliette,' Orson called out to her, 'please help me talk some sense into these guys. Colton Smiles? Yay or nay?'

Juliette stared blankly back at him. 'Colton *who*?' she asked, making a face.

'See, I rest my case,' Farao chuckled softly, and the sound of his laughter sent such joy through Orson, he could have jumped with happiness.

'You guys are useless,' Orson managed, shaking his head and putting his guitar down on the floor against the wall, his voice breaking.

He forced himself to breathe, but inside his emotions were all over the place. There was an overwhelming sense of relief and hope and panic frantically pulsating under his skin. He found himself almost too terrified to blink, worried that if he did it would all go away, and Farao would have stepped out of reach again.

'Is there something to eat?' Farao asked a moment later. 'I'm starving.'

Orson met Terran's eye, and he could see his own turmoil reflected in his brother's gaze. *Stay calm*, he told himself. *Be strong.*

'Of course.' Juliette nodded. 'I'll go make you a plate.'

'Thanks, Juliette.' Farao gave her a small smile, which she returned before heading out of the room.

Silence settled between them. For the first time in his life, Orson couldn't think of a single thing to say. Nothing he came up with felt right—it was all too serious, or not serious enough. He could sense the tension emanating from Kendrik and Terran, seeping into the quietness of the room. He worried that if they didn't come up with something soon, they might miss their chance, that they might lose Farao all over again. The thought of it paralysed him.

'Relax, guys.' Farao sighed, straightening up against his pillows. 'I'm fine.'

Kendrik snorted, then, looking up at the others, seemed to instantly regret his reaction. 'Sorry,' he mumbled, a glimmer of panic in his eyes.

Farao breathed out a small laugh. 'Ok, maybe not *fine*.' He rolled his eyes. 'But I will be. Eventually.'

'We just...' Terran started, but his sentence trailed off.

'I know.' Farao nodded slowly. 'But you don't need to worry about me. Not like that, at least.'

'Is there anything we can do?' Orson asked quietly, just as Juliette came back into the room carrying a tray of leftovers.

'You can start by *not* all staring at me whilst I eat.' Farao looked at them pointedly. 'I'm not a circus animal.'

'Good to see someone's not lost their attitude,' Orson smiled, his heart beating a hundred times a minute inside his chest.

'Guess I learnt from the best.' Farao cocked his head, raising an eyebrow.

'Guess you did.' Orson winked, feeling himself slowly start to relax. '*And*, you're welcome.'

He leant back, grabbing his guitar again and settling back into his seat. He threw Terran a sharp look to tell him he had this covered, hoping he'd get the message. Unsurprisingly, it was Juliette who caught on first.

'Alright,' she smiled, motioning to Terran and Kendrik. 'We'll let you eat. Just shout if you need anything else, ok?'

Orson started to play, watching from the corner of his eye as Farao polished off the tray of pasta, yogurt and fruit in front of him. Farao didn't start the conversation again, and Orson followed his lead, the silence between them familiar and comfortable. At the back of his mind though, Orson was on edge. He was so scared of losing Farao again, he didn't leave his spot on the chair in the corner of the room. He stuck around, watching Farao fall back into a deep sleep, almost holding his breath, for fear that when Farao woke up again he would have sunk back into his previous mute torpor.

Time went by, and Orson lost track of how long he sat there. He had a vague sense that it was late, way past midnight. He still hadn't replaced his phone, and he wasn't wearing a watch, so he had no way of knowing.

He was staring into space, his fingers knotting and unknotting on his lap, his head feeling heavy, when Farao's voice sounded in the semi-darkness.

'Orson?'

Orson shifted on his seat, straightening up. Farao was lying on his back again, his arms resting on top of the duvet, hands together, looking up at the ceiling.

'Yes?'

Farao was quiet for a second before he spoke again.

'How am I...' Farao swallowed audibly. 'How am I supposed to live with all this?'

Orson's throat constricted and he winced in the dark.

'I don't know, little bro…'

Farao exhaled sharply, and was quiet once more.

'What I *do* know,' Orson said, pulling his chair closer to Farao's bed, his voice soft, 'is that we'll be right here with you to help you figure it out.'

Farao glanced at him sideways, and returned his gaze to the ceiling.

'I don't know who I am anymore…' Farao's voice was just a murmur. 'I don't know anything anymore…'

Orson looked at him, wanting more than anything to rush towards him and hold him, but the incredible sadness of Farao's words glued him to his seat.

'Farao,' Orson whispered. 'You're still you. You're *our brother*. Nothing can ever change that.'

Farao snorted, but said nothing.

'No, Farao,' Orson insisted, his tone suddenly urgent. 'Whatever happened, whatever secrets… That doesn't change anything.'

'It changes *everything*,' Farao interrupted harshly, raising his voice a little.

'No, it doesn't change *anything*,' Orson repeated, leaning in closer.

'Orson.' Farao turned to look at him, and his expression was hard, 'I'm the bastard child of a rapist. Mum only had me because it was too late for her to get an abortion. Don't you see? It changes *everything*.'

There were tears glistening at the corners of Farao's eyes, and Orson felt his heart break a little further.

'You should have told me earlier,' Farao said after a long pause, his voice level.

Orson looked at him, his jaw quivering. 'I know…'

'I can sort of see why you didn't… But still… you should have told me earlier.'

Orson nodded feebly, his head low. 'I'm sorry, Farao. I'm so, so sorry,' was all he could say.

There was a pause.

Eventually, Farao shrugged. 'To be honest, I don't know if I'd ever have been able to take it well... But learning about it the way I did... It made everything worse.'

Orson's head fell in his hands. He knew Farao was right; he'd been telling himself the same thing all along, but it wasn't any better hearing him say the words.

'I still don't know how to process all this...' Farao sighed. 'But I guess I've had enough of lying in bed feeling sorry for myself...'

'I'm glad to hear it.' Orson gave him a half-smile, looking up.

'Yeah...' Farao turned to look at him. 'You know what did it?'

Orson shook his head, and Farao propped himself up on his pillow.

'Juliette's reading... It reminded me of you reading to Mum. Towards the end, you know? And I guess... I guess it made me think that, at that point, she'd already given up. I mean, she was writing to us knowing for a fact that she was going to die. She didn't fight it. She didn't even try... Even if not for me, then for you guys.' Farao's jaw tensed. 'And that just made me angry. That she didn't see enough of a reason to try.'

Orson tried to speak, but he found himself speechless, so he only nodded. Silence fell between them again, disturbed only by the soft sounds of the waves reaching them through the open window.

'Orson?' Farao said again after some time. 'It'll be fine... right?'

Orson took in Farao's expression, the fear and uncertainty in his eyes, and his silent plea for reassurance.

'Of course,' Orson smiled, squeezing Farao's hand. 'Everything will be just fine... Better even... It'll be *glorious*.'

And the sight of Farao rolling his eyes at him, with the hint of a smile brightening up his tired face in the darkness, was the best thing Orson had ever seen in his entire life.

Chapter 64
Juliette

Juliette opened the sliding door leading into the small garden, her hand clasped around her mug of ginger tea, and stepped out into the gentle morning breeze. She left her flip-flops in the garden and headed barefoot straight to the little gate that opened onto the beach. The sun was starting to peer over the horizon, and she breathed in the scene, the warm colours of the sunrise soothing her. She walked closer to the water's edge and sat down on a spot of dry sand, pulling her knees into her chest, wrapping her fingers around her hot mug and looking out to the sea.

As she watched the golden half-globe of the sun glittering over the waves, her thoughts wandered back towards the house. After seeing Farao resurface the previous night, the collective relief that had washed over the house had been the best feeling in the world. And yet... She sighed. And yet she was left feeling a little disappointed. She didn't need to think about it for too long before she could pinpoint why. Part of her had thought that when Farao came back to them, Terran's attitude towards her might improve. They had barely said a word to each other since their heated exchange on the night she'd arrived, and they'd skirted around each other ever since.

And what *were* her feelings for Terran now, anyway? She'd felt so strongly about him at first, so intensely, but with every passing day of his keeping her at arm's length, her emotions towards him grew ever so muddled. She knew she'd fallen for him, there was no denying that. She'd known it from the very beginning. And she knew that some part of him reciprocated that. She'd felt it. But his behaviour was increasingly hard to overlook. She understood he had a lot going on, and she got that his knee-jerk reaction at having so much to deal with was to shut her out completely, but even with that knowledge she was running out of excuses for him. In her entire life she'd never let anyone treat her that way, and she wasn't about to start now. She owed it to herself not to allow him to get away with this so easily, to think she would be available to him on his terms, as and when he was ready.

She was hurt and she was angry, which was never a great combination at the best of times. She wanted him to step up, and then wanted not to care whether or not he did. And in the odd moments when she caught a glimpse of him and she saw the pain he carried, she wanted nothing more than to go to him and wrap her arms around him. Of course she never did, and every time he failed to take a step towards her felt like a slap in the face.

So, slowly, one day at a time, she'd worked on folding her feelings for him neatly into a box in her own heart and tucking it away somewhere where it all felt less painful. She'd focused on the others. Farao, Kendrik and Orson. She resented the fact that she still found herself hoping that Terran would come round and that some part of her still wanted him to let her in. She resented even more the crushing disappointment that predictably came every moment they looked at each other and he looked away, closing off a little more.

'Hey.' A voice behind her made her turn around.

'Hi.' She gave Orson a small smile as he came to sit next to her.

They sat in silence for a moment, both facing the azure of the Mediterranean.

'You okay?' Orson said after a while, leaning towards her and nudging her with his shoulder.

She gave him a weak smile. 'Yeah, I'm fine.'

Orson considered her for a few seconds. She peered at him sideways.

'What?' she said.

Orson looked at her for a little longer without saying anything, seeming unsure how to say what he wanted to say.

'I know it doesn't excuse his behaviour...' he started, and Juliette's heart thumped in her chest. 'But I know Terran. I can see how much he cares for you...'

'So you say...' Juliette huffed, turning her gaze back onto the sea. 'He's got a funny way of showing it...'

'I know,' Orson repeated. 'And you shouldn't have to take any of this.'

'No, I shouldn't,' she retorted, a little too quickly, her voice hard.

She waited for a moment, desperate to say the thing that had been on her mind for the past few days, but scared that speaking the words out loud would make them too real to bear. She stilled herself, bracing herself for impact.

'Kendrik thinks I should leave.' She spoke quietly, and the moment she'd said it, she knew there was no turning back.

'Why don't you?' Orson asked.

She shrugged. 'I guess...' She sighed. 'I guess it feels that as long as I'm here, it all actually happened, you know? That it wasn't all in my head. All this...' She gestured around. 'And...' She exhaled deeply. 'And everything with Terran.'

Orson gave a knowing nod. 'I get it.'

She fell quiet. She could feel the tears prickling at the corners of her eyes.

'Maybe…' When he spoke again, Orson's tone was soft. 'Maybe it's enough to know that it did happen. I saw it, too. It was real. And whatever happens afterwards doesn't take anything away from what it was.'

She closed her eyes for a moment, centring herself, before gazing back out at the sea.

'If I leave…' Her voice was quivering. 'It's like it's really… you know…'

'Over?' Orson finished.

'Yeah…'

Orson watched her for a few seconds. 'Maybe that's the risk you need to take if you want to give him a chance of finding his way back to you.'

Juliette swallowed. She knew he was right. She'd known it for a while, but the fear of losing the one thing that had made her feel more alive than she had in her entire life had prevented her from accepting it. She nodded.

Orson seemed to hesitate for a brief moment, then shuffled closer to her and wrapped an arm around her shoulders.

'Come here.' He pulled her in, and despite her resolve to be strong, she leant into him and rested her head against him, feeling herself deflate almost immediately. 'I know you must be disappointed. As clearly as I can see how Terran feels about you, I can see how much you care about him.' Orson gave her shoulder a squeeze and she closed her eyes. 'I know he's acting like a jerk. He doesn't mean badly, but that's no excuse. You deserve so much better than that…'

Juliette suppressed a sob, the disappointment that had been growing inside her for days now bubbling up to the surface, and Orson gave her shoulder another squeeze.

'You're magnificent, Juliette,' he continued, and she smiled despite herself, sniffing back the tears. 'A warrior goddess. And if Terran can't see that clearly enough to stop behaving like an arsehole, that's his loss.'

Juliette nodded and rubbed a tear off her cheek.

'I'm here for you, okay?' Orson said softly. 'And, for what it's worth, I'm so glad you're here. I don't know about him, but I sure as hell couldn't have faced all this without you.'

'Thanks, Orson,' Juliette whispered, leaning out of the hug and taking a slow sip of her tea.

'It's my pleasure, kiddo.' He grinned at her and patted the top of her head, making her burst out laughing.

'You did *not* just pat my head,' she giggled.

'Actually, I think I just did!' he laughed.

'What am I?' She rolled her eyes. 'A dog?'

'Mmm.' He observed her in mock seriousness for a second. 'Actually you're much more feline than canine. But not quite a house cat... Maybe a lioness. Or a cheetah.'

'Orson,' she sighed, shaking her head, feeling better already. 'Please, whatever you do, never *ever* change.'

'You're in luck, I don't *ever* intend to!' He winked at her.

'I wished I'd had a brother like you growing up...' she mused, looking out over the beach.

'Ah.' He nodded. 'It's probably better we didn't grow up as siblings.' Then he added, in response to her questioning look, 'We're the perfect partners in crime. We'd have caused way too much trouble!'

'Yeah, you're probably right.' She smiled.

And, taking another sip of tea, she felt that, despite the tensions with Terran, despite Farao's condition, despite all of their broken hearts, this... *this* was exactly where she was meant to be. And because it was so precious was exactly the reason she had to let it go.

Chapter 65
Kendrik

That afternoon, Juliette packed her bags and left. Kendrik could see that she looked heartbroken, but she also looked determined. They gathered up in the living room to say goodbye, Orson, Kendrik and Farao each giving her a hug, Terran pointedly standing back. When she turned towards him, they exchanged a look. Her face was set, emotionless. For a moment Terran seemed disarmed, unsure, almost like he wanted to say something or take a step towards her, but before he could do or say anything she'd turned back and walked out of their lives. And just like that, it was the four of them again.

The following days passed in a daze. The suffocating fog that had surrounded them had finally lifted now that Farao was out of bed. He was still quieter than usual, but he was taking steps towards them, slowly but surely, and Kendrik was finally starting to see a light at the end of the tunnel.

With the hearty and wholesome food Orson kept making for them, Farao slowly started to regain some of his colour, the hollows in his body filling up again, one meal at a time. Their third week in the house fell into a new rhythm. They took a walk on the beach every day, taking regular breaks, sitting down facing the sea when Farao needed to catch his breath. Their days were punctuated by the regular pace of Farao's medicine intakes and the long, frequent naps he took. They seemed to have reached a tacit agreement that they were all waiting for the right moment to speak of the unspeakable, when Farao was ready, and until then, all they could do was wait.

On their fourth week, as the four of them were sitting on the beach late in the morning, looking out to sea, Farao finally brought up the topic.

'What's the plan now?' he asked, and his voice was uncharacteristically steady.

Kendrik turned to look at the others, but neither of them answered.

'We got this far.' Farao studied them. 'What were you planning to do next?'

'Well…' Terran said uncertainly, but he didn't seem to have the words.

'Come on, guys,' Farao sighed. 'The time for sugar-coating is over, don't you think?'

Kendrik swallowed hard and turned to Terran, who was observing Farao from the corner of his eyes.

'I'm growing roots here…' Farao rolled his eyes, and Orson gave a chuckle.

'We have the guy's address…' Terran finally said. 'Which is as far as we'd planned, really.'

'What? To meet him or something?' Farao frowned.

'Meet him… Confront him…' Terran shrugged.

'Punch him in the face... Kick him in the balls...' Orson added.

'All of the above,' Kendrik concluded.

Farao nodded silently.

'But we don't have to do any of it if you don't want to,' Terran said calmly. 'I guess it wasn't really our call to make in the first place.'

'Maybe not...' Farao said. 'There isn't really a precedent for that kind of stuff, is there.'

'If there is...' Orson cleared his throat. 'We didn't find the rulebook.'

Farao gave him a small smile. A few minutes passed before Farao spoke again, his gaze on the glittering waves in front of them:

'I think we should go today.'

They all turned to look at him in surprise. Farao shrugged.

'We've come all this way, haven't we? Let's get this over with.'

'Are you sure?' Orson asked after a pause.

Farao nodded, giving them a sideways glance. Kendrik thought he looked much older than his years.

'I know you meant well,' Farao said quietly. 'I know that... To be honest I don't know what I would have done if I'd been in your shoes...'

Kendrik held his breath. This was the first time they'd broached the subject since the night their mother's second letter had surfaced.

'I still don't know what to do with all this.' Farao shook his head. 'With what happened to her... With what's happening to me... But I know you were only trying to help,' Farao's gaze found Orson and he addressed him directly. 'I know you weren't trying to hide anything. I know you were probably just scared of what would happen if you let out the truth. That I'd freak out or something...' He gave a dark chuckle, gesturing at himself. 'Case in point.'

Orson reached out to Farao, squeezing his hand.

'So,' Farao sighed, 'I think we should just finish what we started. At least we'll know… I least I'll see… I don't know…'

He fell quiet, the words hanging in the air around them.

'Ok,' Terran said after some time. 'Let's go.'

They stood up and walked back to the house. Ten minutes later, the four of them were in the car, on their way to meet the man who had started it all, and Kendrik wondered how he would be able to face such a monster.

***

Terran parked the car in front of a two-storey mansion, and they all looked out of the window, taking in the delicately pruned front garden and the expensive-looking white-stone building. Everything Kendrik saw reeked of wealth, and for some reason it made his stomach lurch. He looked over at Farao, whose face was impassive.

'Are you sure?' Kendrik asked, and Farao gave a curt nod.

They stepped out of the car and walked up the path to the front door. Terran rang the bell, and they waited. Kendrik felt nauseated, but he forced himself to keep his composure. A few moments elapsed, and he was just wondering if no one was home when the sound of approaching footsteps made his stomach give another unpleasant spasm. There was a bad taste of acidic bile at the back of his throat.

The door opened and they found themselves face to face with a woman who must have been in her late sixties. She was impeccably dressed with a tidy hairdo and a row of white pearls hanging around her neck. She gave them a look of polite enquiry.

'*Messieurs, en quoi puis-je vous aider?*' Her voice was soft.

And then her eyes found Farao, and her face fell, in almost comical slow motion. Her expression morphed into something else. It wasn't confusion. It wasn't even surprise. It was a look of recognition.

With a pained grimace and without another word, she stepped aside and gestured at them to come inside. Kendrik frowned, but followed his brothers through the door.

She let them down a wide, richly adorned corridor into a large room at the back of the house lined with French windows. There was a young man sitting in an armchair, his body wrapped in blankets, and when Kendrik saw his face, he gasped. He recognised the light hair, pale eyes and fine jaw. The young man looked thin and unwell, and there were dark circles under his eyes, but apart from a few details, he was almost Farao's carbon copy.

'My son,' the woman said in perfect English. 'Aurélien.'

Meeting her gaze, Kendrik was struck by the sorrowful look in her eyes.

'I know why you are here.' Her voice quivered. 'But I'm afraid I cannot help you.'

***

The woman, who introduced herself as Odette, disappeared into the kitchen and emerged several minutes later carrying a tray with a teapot, teacups, a milk jug and biscuits. She served the tea with shaking hands. They watched her in silence. Kendrik noticed Farao couldn't tear his eyes from Aurélien's pallid, skinny face.

'Odette,' Terran finally said. 'We wanted to…'

'I know why you're here,' Odette interrupted him softly. 'You are not the first ones to knock on our door… I knew this was coming when Saint-Blaise contacted me, asking for permission to share our contact details with the children of one of my husband's former colleagues.'

The four brothers exchanged confused looks, and Odette nodded.

'Yes,' she said, nodding again. 'I made it possible for you to find us. But I'm afraid we cannot help you.'

Kendrik felt like the air had been punched out of his lungs.

'My husband'—Odette looked at them with watery eyes—'passed away several years ago. He died from the same condition my son is suffering from. He was named after his father... I expect the information you were provided with didn't make the distinction...' she sighed.

Of course, Kendrik thought bitterly, the man who would not think twice about forcing himself on a non-consenting woman would also be enough of a megalomaniac to name his only legitimate son after himself.

'Aurélien carries the same condition my late husband passed on to every single one of the children he fathered... He himself never received the right treatment.'

Behind them, Aurélien winced and shuffled in his armchair. Odette made as if to stand but Aurélien raised a frail hand to stop her, shaking his head slowly. Kendrik took in Aurélien's sallow face, the dark circles under his eyes and the tremor in his arms. A thought flashed in his head, unbidden and terrifying, that this might be Farao before too long. His ears were ringing. Their journey had been in vain. It was over.

'You knew?' Terran's voice sounded hollow and distant.

Odette gave him a stricken look.

'I never knew for certain. I thought my husband was having affairs, but I never suspected... I never thought...'

Aurélien gave a cough, and Odette got promptly to her feet, wiping his mouth with a handkerchief she pulled out of the pocket of her cardigan. She readjusted the blankets around his shoulders. A few seconds later, he seemed to have fallen asleep.

'I only discovered the truth just before he passed away,' she continued after she had sat down again. 'When the first one came.'

'The first one...' Orson repeated in a whisper.

'The first of several.' Odette lowered her gaze. 'I learnt the truth then, but there was nothing we could do to help.'

A sense of numbness spread through Kendrik's body as Odette kept talking.

'Maybe this is the price I have to pay for my lenience. I never confronted him, when I thought he was keeping mistresses... Maybe it made me complicit... And now I'm losing my son...' she added, her voice breaking a little, looking at Aurélien's sleeping figure.

Kendrik stared at her. She looked devastated, and he wondered how she could bear to go through this conversation over and over again. He knew only too well how easily guilt could latch on to one's conscience, and how hard it was to shake off.

'It's not your fault.'

Kendrik snapped out of his train of thoughts. Farao's voice had been soft but perfectly audible.

'It's not your fault,' Farao repeated, looking straight at Odette. 'You didn't know. If there had been anything you could have done to stop it, maybe you would have.'

Odette gave a little whimper. 'I'm so sorry,' she said slowly, 'to all of you. I wish there was something I could do.'

'There isn't,' Farao said, with a note of finality in his voice, standing up from his seat. 'But thank you for seeing us.'

And with a final, shifty glance at Aurélien, he walked out of the room. Kendrik gave Odette an apologetic look before rushing after Farao, Orson and Terran behind him. Outside, Farao was leaning against the car, his head in his hands, his shoulders slouched forward. Suddenly, he doubled over and vomited loudly on the pavement.

'Farao!' they all called out as one, running towards him.

Terran caught him just before he fainted. They lifted him into the car, laying him down on half of the back seat, and Terran drove back, somewhat erratically, to the beach house. They carried Farao to the couch and shook him gently to his senses, long enough to make him swallow his medicines. Then they laid him back down, covered him with a blanket and settled themselves around him, still shaking with shock. None of them spoke. Kendrik took in Farao's paleness and Terran and Orson's ashen expressions. He looked away quickly, fearing that he would only see his own panic reflected on his brothers' faces. He didn't think he could have taken it.

'What the…?' Terran mumbled, and Kendrik finally glanced up. Terran was scrolling down his phone, looking dumbfounded.

'I have fifteen missed calls from Amit…' Terran said, pressing a button on his screen and bringing the phone to his ear.

Amit picked up on the first ring. Kendrik and Orson watched intently, though they couldn't hear what Amit was saying on the other end of the line.

'Ok… Mm-hm…' Terran was nodding dumbly, gazing into space, his eyes out of focus. 'What… Ok… Of course… But how… No, I understand… Ok. Yes, I'll keep you posted… See you soon.'

Terran hung up the phone and looked at them. He seemed lost for words.

'What happened?' Orson pressed him.

'They found a donor…' Terran's voice sounded disbelieving. 'A perfect match. He says he'll explain when we get there.'

Kendrik and Orson gaped at him.

'Guys…' Terran finally seemed to shake himself back into attention. 'We have to go back. We have to go back *now*.'

Chapter 66
Terran

Terran never knew how they managed to pack all of their bags in record time, or how they were able to carry a still sleeping Farao into the car without waking him, nestling him against a folded duvet they had grabbed from one of the bedrooms—somewhere at the back of his head, a practical voice wondered if that'd come out of their deposit, and it amazed him that he was still able to think about something like this at such a time. All Terran knew was that, less than an hour after ending the call with Amit, they were on the road again. He drove for four hours straight until Lyon, at which point Orson forced him to stop at a service station. Terran wanted to keep going, but he was starting to feel sleep threatening to send him dozing off, so he didn't argue.

Farao had awoken by then, and they filled him in on the new development. They grabbed a coffee and some food to go, and before long, Kendrik had popped behind the wheel, and they were moving again. They made another pit stop a little before Troyes, Kendrik's driving stamina almost reaching its breaking point. They couldn't stop for longer than half an hour. Amit had been insistent that they should come back as soon as possible, and though he hadn't given him more details over the phone, Terran had sensed the urgency in his voice.

It was another three and a half hours before they got to Calais and slotted the car into the queue, ready to board the Eurotunnel carrier. Terran felt drained. Night had fallen by then and he had barely slept the entire journey. He stepped out of the car, waiting for the line of vehicles to move forward, stretching his legs. He pulled his phone out of his pocket to text Amit, and noticed another text. From Juliette. His eye gave an involuntary twitch. He couldn't do this. He couldn't cope. He hadn't been able to do it so far, and he still couldn't do it now. He sent his update to Amit and slipped his phone back into his pocket without checking Juliette's message. The cars at the start of the queue were starting to move and he sat back behind the wheel, following the flow of traffic.

Orson took the final driving stretch to London, with Terran, Kendrik and Farao all dozing off in their seats. It was past one in the morning when they finally got to the hospital. Amit was waiting for them at the reception, looking stressed and overworked but relieved to see them.

'We found a donor,' Amit said, 'but the transplant needs to happen quickly. We're not sure whether he'll be able to hold on much longer.'

'What?' Terran snapped. 'What's wrong with him?'

Amit flashed him a quick uncomfortable look.

'Nothing, at least not in any way that matters. His kidneys are healthy, and that's all we need at this stage.'

'Amit, what—' Terran insisted.

'Terran, there is no time,' Amit said severely, a touch of impatience in his tone. 'Do you think I would let this happen if I hadn't made sure everyone had done their due diligence? Don't you trust me?'

Terran felt a pang of shame.

'Of course,' he said apologetically. 'Sorry, of course I trust you.'

Amit talked them through the next steps. The hospital had been gearing up to receive Farao, and the staff were ready to take him through for a full examination. If everything looked good, they would be prepping him for surgery right away.

Before long, Farao was taken to a room, and they were back where they had been a mere few weeks before, waiting nervously outside his door, hoping for the best. There was nothing else they could do but wait.

Chapter 67
Orson

As he sat in the hospital's waiting room, Orson thought that he'd had enough of this to last him a lifetime. It wasn't so much the hospital itself that got to him, or the odd, otherworldly atmosphere that reigned within its walls, it was the waiting. The never-ending stretch of time ahead of them, the indefinite amount of seconds, minutes and hours that spread as far as the eye could see. With it came a mind-numbing sort of exhaustion, one that started in the deepest recesses of your soul and spread across your being until you could feel the strain of it in your muscles. The weight and tension of being left hanging, of not knowing and only imagining the worst—because what else was there to do?

Amit had explained they needed to check everything—blood samples, kidney function, heart and liver health—anything that could cause complications during the surgery, before they could proceed. When every test result eventually came back all clear, they were told that

Farao was now being readied for surgery but that they would be allowed to speak to him for a few minutes before he was taken to the operating theatre. When they walked into Farao's room, they found him lying on the sanitised bed, looking a little queasy. Orson tried to speak, but no words came out. He looked at Farao, who gave him a feeble smile. Terran squeezed Farao's hand.

'We'll be right here the entire time,' he said quietly.

Farao simply nodded.

'It's ok.' Terran squeezed his hand again. 'It'll be ok. We'll see you on the other side.'

Farao nodded again and squeezed Terran's hand back. Orson wanted so badly to say something, but he had lost his voice. Farao met his gaze.

'Hey,' he groaned, rolling his eyes, 'don't you go sentimental on me now.'

Orson made a sound halfway between a chuckle and a sob.

'We'll see you soon,' he croaked, ruffling Farao's hair.

Farao nodded again and patted Kendrik's arm as the nurses wheeled his bed out of the room. They followed and watched him disappear behind the double doors at the end of the corridor.

The hours that followed were the longest Orson could ever remember experiencing in his life. Amit had assured them that, though the transplant was a complex procedure, the surgeon in charge of the operation was highly experienced and trustworthy. They sat in the waiting room with Amit, none of them talking, anxiously waiting for news. Farao had been gone for a little over three hours when the surgeon emerged to meet them, informing them the transplant had gone well and they were keeping Farao under observation for a little longer until he came round.

The relief that flooded Orson was like a concentrated shot of adrenaline, waking up every single cell in his body at once. It would take a few days, possibly a week or two, to make sure the transplant had been successful, the doctor warned, but for now everything looked promising.

They fell into each other's arms. They had made it. Orson felt so elated he could have run a marathon. Farao would be fine. Everything would be ok.

As he stepped out of Terran's embrace, Orson peered over his shoulder. A little way away, the doctor stood with Amit, their heads close together, whispering. The doctor's face was grave, and Amit's expression was unreadable. Orson frowned and nudged Terran, who turned to look too, and they exchanged a glance. Without a backwards look, Amit followed the doctor through a set of double doors and disappeared from view. Orson felt his stomach sink.

'What was *that* about?' Terran said, his frown deepening.

'I don't know...' Orson shook his head. 'You don't think... Farao...'

'Mmmm,' Terran said, his gaze on the door Amit had just gone through.

'No,' Kendrik said firmly. 'They just told us he was fine. He wouldn't lie to us like that.'

Chapter 68
Amit

Amit rushed down the corridor after Mark, who was still wearing the scrub cap he'd worn during the surgery. He listened as Mark launched into a summary of how the operation had gone. The *other* operation, as they had come to refer to it.

'We almost lost him halfway through,' Mark said in the professional medical tone Amit knew only too well. 'We managed to stop the haemorrhage, but his vitals have dropped. He's stable for now, but I have to warn you'—Mark threw Amit a serious glance he recognised at once—'he doesn't have long. Now would be a good time to make sure his affairs are in order.'

Amit nodded once. They had stopped in front of an open door, and Mark stepped aside to let Amit in.

'I'll be at reception if you need me,' Mark added, walking away swiftly.

Amit walked into the small room and his eyes fell on the figure of the man lying on the bed. There were tubes poking out of his hand and wires connecting him to several monitors. He seemed to be asleep. Amit checked the graphs, but they told him nothing he didn't already know. His mouth was suddenly very dry.

'Anand-*bhai*,' he whispered.

Anand's eyes flickered open, and he turned his head to look at him.

'Amit,' Anand wheezed. He coughed, and Amit rushed to his side, kneeling on the floor, but Anand gave a feeble wave of his hand. 'Did it work?'

Amit suppressed a sob and nodded. 'Yes,' he said. 'Yes, it worked. He's recovering now.'

'Good,' Anand whispered, turning back to face the ceiling.

Amit wrapped his hand around Anand's fingers.

'Amit…' Anand said again, the tremor in his voice making Amit shiver. 'Am I dying?'

Amit looked down, the tears now flowing down his cheeks.

'Just tell me,' Anand insisted.

Amit took a breath. 'There were complications during the surgery…' he said quietly. 'Because you haven't been taking your medicine for several weeks now, your body is struggling to cope with the stress of the operation…'

'Mmm…' Anand nodded slowly.

'Anand-*bhai*,' Amit pleaded, the words tumbling out of his mouth before he could stop them. 'The boys. They're here. I can call them in. They would want to…'

'No!' Anand's objection resonated loudly around the room, sending him into a fit of coughing.

'Anand-*bhai*,' Amit begged, squeezing his old friend's hand.

As hard as their relationship had been, as much as it had weighed on him, Amit knew their fates had been linked, and the prospect of losing Anand felt like... He swallowed, the words flashing unexpectedly into his mind: like losing his brother.

'No,' Anand said again firmly. 'They cannot see me like this...'

Amit fell quiet.

'Amit,' Anand said, his voice quiet again. 'It's ok. They will be ok. They'll be ok now...'

But Amit couldn't look up; his eyes were glued to the floor, his body quivering with grief.

'Look at me,' Anand said, his voice feebler still, and Amit lifted his gaze. 'I never knew... Why I stayed alive. I never knew... Why I didn't die. All these years...' Anand winced, but he seemed determined to keep talking. 'All these years I thought I should have died. But this... *This* is why I've been surviving all this time. You said there was one chance in thousands of finding a matching donor, didn't you... What were the odds...' He gave a feeble cough. 'I've done wrong... I failed them all. For so long... But now... Now my debt is paid. And when I see Gabrielle again'—he pointed weakly towards the ceiling—'maybe now she'll forgive me...'

Amit held Anand's hand tightly.

'You've always done so much...' Anand's voice was just a murmur now. 'You're the real hero... Amit-*bhai*...'

And, with a great shudder, Anand's body convulsed, then moved no more.

Chapter 69
Farao

When Farao eventually came to, it took him several minutes to remember where he was and why he was feeling so groggy. He was sore everywhere, as if he'd got into the losing side of a violent fight. His mouth felt dry and itchy, and there was a stinging pain at the back of his throat every time he swallowed. He glanced around the room he found himself in, and his eyes immediately fell on the silhouettes of his brothers, huddled in one corner, talking in low whispers.

'What time is it?' he called, his voice hoarse.

Not that it mattered, but it was the only thing that had come to his mind. Terran, Kendrik and Orson stopped talking and turned around, coming to stand nearer his bed.

'It's seven thirty-five in the evening,' Terran answered, checking his watch.

Farao tried nodding, but the motion sent his head spinning, so he stopped instantly.

'How are you feeling?' Orson asked.

'Like shit…' Farao grumbled. 'Thirsty.'

Kendrik walked to the side table and brought him a glass of water and a straw, holding it out for him whilst he drank.

'The surgery went well,' Terran said softly. 'They say it'll take a few days to confirm whether it's fully worked, and they'll keep you under observation here until they're satisfied you're recovering. It could be a couple of weeks.'

'Ok…' Farao said, not daring to move his head too much again.

'Can we get you anything?' Orson asked, looking relieved to see him awake. 'More water? A magazine? A hot nurse?'

Farao snorted a laugh and winced at the ripple of pain that went through his upper body.

'Orson.' He coughed, the soreness in his ribs making him grimace. 'You prick.'

But Orson was smiling broadly back at him. 'There he is, our little bro,' he said with a wide grin. 'Now at least we know they haven't cut the grump out of him!'

A nurse walked in, and Farao heard her exchange a few words with his brothers. Though he tried, he couldn't really pay attention. He felt tired. His vision was blurring, and his awareness drifting away. A moment later, he had fallen asleep again.

***

It was a further two weeks before the doctors declared themselves satisfied with Farao's progress and announced that he should be able to go home in just a few days' time. Farao couldn't wait. He'd had enough of the hospital, of the tasteless food, and of the constant comings and goings of people in and out of his room. He'd had enough of being probed and poked for a lifetime. Although, judging by the lecture one of the nurses had given his brothers on the care and attention Farao would need once he got home, he gathered there was more probing and poking to come, especially when it came to helping him use the bathroom and shower for the next few weeks. Farao tried hard not to think about it, though the idea didn't bother him as much as it might once have. They had travelled a long way together lately, his brothers and him. Things were different now.

Farao was in bed one morning reading a magazine Kendrik had dropped off earlier that day, when Orson popped by, a mysterious smile on his face. Farao frowned, because anything that made Orson grin like a Cheshire cat rarely boded well.

'Orson,' Farao started, unable to keep the suspicion out of his voice. 'What's going o…'

He stopped abruptly when he recognised the person standing awkwardly behind his brother. Mel walked into the room and came to stand a little way away from his bed, not meeting his gaze.

'You have a visitor!' Orson exclaimed with a wide smirk. 'Well, I'll leave you two to it,' he added, apparently delighted, and winked at Farao. 'Don't do anything *I* wouldn't do.'

And with those words, Orson marched out of the room, humming a chirpy tune, and closed the door behind him. An excruciating silence fell between them, and Farao found himself suddenly very glad that he was wearing one of his own tee-shirts and not the stupid gown he'd had to wear for most of his hospital stay. He looked at Mel, thinking something about her looked different. He'd rarely seen her out of her school uniform, which she always wore a little dishevelled, but today her tight jeans and simple white tee-shirt gave her a completely different appearance. Her short blonde hair, usually arranged stylishly around her head, fell more naturally around her face, framing it like a halo.

'Erm…' he started, not sure what to say to a girl he'd been so intimate with before, and then royally ignored for weeks on end. 'Hi.'

'Hey…' Mel answered, finally looking up at him.

There was silence again.

'I brought you class notes… and the homework you missed…' Mel said, and he'd never heard her sound so shy before.

'Oh, thanks.' Farao simply nodded, not having the heart to tell her that Nick had already dropped by to share his lesson notes.

She gave him a small smile and pulled a thick folder out of her bag, which she dropped on his bedside table. He picked it up absentmindedly, more to give his hands something to do, and started flicking through the pages.

'Wait. These are *your* class notes?' Farao asked. 'You went to class?'

He was astonished. He recognised her handwriting, but it seemed so unlikely, given that she normally missed more than half of the classes in their timetable.

'Yeah…' Mel looked away again and winced. 'I thought you might need them… You know… Since you weren't there.'

Farao studied her. She was barely wearing any makeup at all—which was very unlike her. It brought out the pale green of her eyes more than usual. It suited her, he thought. He wondered how he'd never noticed how pretty she was before. He supposed he'd never really looked at her properly, and given all the time they'd spent together, the idea made him feel a little ashamed. In a parallel universe, he was extremely aware of the other Farao, the version of him that hadn't gone through what he had endured, and how confused he would have been. That other Farao, the clueless, emotionally impervious boy he once was, wouldn't have known what to make of this. But that wasn't who he was anymore. He'd changed when everything had changed. All he could see now was how stupid he'd been, how thoughtless. He couldn't for the life of him understand how he'd missed so much before.

'Mel,' he said, his voice coming out much softer than he'd expected. 'Listen… I'm so sorry.'

She looked up at him again, and her face was set.

'I was an arsehole to you,' he continued, watching with discomfort the moisture build in her eyes. 'I never meant to hurt you, but that's no excuse. I'm sorry, Mel. I really am.'

She stared at him for some time, and he wasn't sure he should say anything else. He silently debated whether he should explain more, but the right words didn't seem to present themselves. Eventually, slowly, painfully, she shrugged.

'It's ok.' She gave him a weak smile. 'I just thought… You know…'

'I know…' He grimaced. 'I shouldn't have led you on like that.'

She shrugged again. 'You really were a bit of an arsehole, you know.'

He could tell she was trying her best to sound light, but he heard the tremor in her voice.

'I know…' He wished he had something better to say.

'So, you don't… You don't think that… You know… You and I…' Mel's voice was barely a whisper now.

Farao felt something inside his chest constrict, because it dawned on him once again how cruel he'd been. He wanted to be able to tell her what she wanted to hear. He wanted so badly to make things right, but if he'd learnt anything in the past few weeks it was that although truth was rarely an easy thing to impart onto others, it was necessary.

'I'm so sorry, Mel.' His voice was raspy with emotion. 'I just… I don't… I don't feel that way…'

There were tears building up in her eyes now, slowly travelling down her pretty face.

'I'm so sorry…'

And he found that he was. He truly, absolutely was.

'It's fine.' She shook her head, and rubbed a hand on her cheeks. 'I'll just… I have to go.' She looked at him briefly, then averted her gaze. 'Just, let me know if you need anything,' she added, pointing at the notes.

'Thanks, I really...'

But she just waved him off and before he knew it she was gone, leaving behind her a faint fruity scent he knew only too well. Farao glanced down at the thick stack of notes again, and the guilt hit him once more with full force. He knew he deserved it, but that didn't make it any easier to swallow.

***

Amit came to visit every day, checking in with Farao's doctor and nurses, making sure everything was in order. He was sitting in Farao's room one day, having sent the others home to rest and shower. The television was on in the background, though neither of them was really watching. Amit had pulled out his phone and was scrolling down the screen. Farao looked at him and it suddenly struck him how exhausted Amit looked. There were new lines along his furrowed brow, and dark circles under his eyes.

'Amit,' Farao said, and Amit looked up from his phone. 'Are you alright?'

Amit's shoulders sagged a little and his jaw tensed visibly. He gave Farao an unconvincing smile.

'Of course.' He nodded. 'Why do you ask?'

Farao cocked his head to one side. 'Because you look terrible.'

Amit laughed, but it was a hollow sort of laugh. 'Yes,' he admitted. 'I've had a lot going on lately. But I'm fine.'

Farao nodded slowly, still looking at Amit closely. Amit shifted uncomfortably in his seat. He reminded Farao of himself, once upon a time, almost a lifetime ago, sitting at the dinner table, lying to Terran about having done his homework.

'There's something you're not telling us, isn't there?' Farao said.

Amit just stared at him, and Farao had the feeling he was pondering carefully what to say next.

'When did you become so perceptive?' Amit gave him a tired smile.

'Oh, I don't know.' Farao shrugged. 'Maybe somewhere between discovering I had a life-threatening illness and realising it was passed on to me by the dickhead who raped my mum.'

Amit gasped, his eyes widening with shock and disbelief. In the background, the well-known jingle of a nineties television show sounded. The expression of mingled amazement and concern on Amit's face made Farao laugh.

'Chill, Amit.' Farao smiled at him. 'What's the point of any of it if I'm not allowed to laugh about it?'

'Is that what you want to do?' Amit asked quietly. 'Laugh about it?'

Farao thought for a moment, pondering the question.

'No,' he said finally, his voice a little sombre now. 'None of it is funny, really. But I do want to be able to look at it with some distance one day.' Then he added, remembering his mother's words, 'I don't want it to define me.'

Amit nodded. 'It's a lot for anyone to go through...'

'It is,' Farao agreed. 'But, the odd part is... I'm sort of glad it happened. How weird is that?'

'Glad?' Amit frowned.

'Yeah...' Farao's gaze fell on the television, but he wasn't seeing the images on the screen. 'You know, I spent so long feeling like I wasn't part of this family. Like I didn't belong. I've always looked different. I didn't have the experiences the others had when they were kids. All I've known is everyone's grief and struggles. I never knew where that all came from... It just didn't feel fair...' Farao glanced at Amit briefly, then looked away again. 'But knowing all this... knowing the truth... It explained everything. It meant the feeling I had that I was an outsider wasn't just in my head… It was always inside me. You see?'

Amit didn't respond; he just kept looking at Farao with sadness in his eyes.

'I always thought it was them against me,' Farao continued, lost in his train of thoughts. 'Like none of them understood me. Like I wasn't really their brother… But now, after everything we've been through… After what we've shared… The bond we have… I don't think anything else could have got us there.'

Farao turned to meet Amit's eyes.

'Look at you, all grown-up,' Amit smiled, tears glistening at the corners of his eyes. 'Your parents would have been so proud.'

'Well…' Farao smiled back. 'I don't know about that… But it doesn't hurt so much to wonder about it anymore.'

Amit placed his hand on Farao's arm.

'For what it's worth,' he said, looking Farao straight in the eyes, 'I'm extremely proud of you, Farao.'

'Thanks, Amit,' Farao said, swallowing hard.

Amit sat back in his chair, and Farao settled against his pillow, and together they turned to the old re-run on the television. *Yes*, Farao thought, with newfound calmness settling in his heart, he did feel different. He felt older, somehow. The idea that, a few weeks back, he'd been worried about lessons, and girls, and broken phones seemed risible. There was so much more to life than he'd ever realised, and it'd taken facing death to understand it. He had needed his entire world to collapse around him to notice that he'd had it wrong all along. But now… Now he knew better, and he had his whole life ahead of him to make it all worth living.

Chapter 70
Terran

A month after Farao's release from the hospital, Terran was bustling around in the kitchen, busy with dinner preparations, trying not to let his nerves get the better of him. He switched on the tap in the sink and absently washed the fresh peas under the cold jet of water. He glanced out of the window towards the street, checking for any movement outside. He checked his watch and breathed out. There was still time, and no need to assume the worst. Not yet, at least.

He stopped the tap and gave the sieve a gentle shake before stepping back towards the hob. He turned to the pan full of spiced tomato sauce gentling bubbling on the stove, checking the open cookbook propped against the bottle of oil, and added in the paneer cubes. The cumin and coriander aromas filled his nostrils. The doorbell rang, making him jump and spatter tomato sauce over the counter.

'Shit,' he groaned, wiping his hands on his apron, trying to ignore the fact that his heart had just summersaulted inside his chest.

Hearing Orson run down the stairs, Terran rushed past him to the front door.

'I'll get it!' he called out, half anxious, half excited, sprinting to pull the door open.

When he took in the sight that awaited him, his heart skipped a beat: Juliette was standing in the doorway, wrapped in a long red winter coat, her cheeks pink against the cool evening air. *There you are*, Terran thought longingly as his breath caught in his throat, and it suddenly hit him how much he'd missed her. One look at her reserved expression told him she wasn't about to fall into his arms, but he couldn't help the wave of relief that coursed through him as his eyes met hers. She held his gaze, sliding her hands in her coat pockets, her face composed.

'Look who's here!' Orson exclaimed, bounding in behind him and pushing past to give Juliette a tight hug.

'Hi Orson,' Juliette smiled.

'Juliette, I didn't know we were expecting you!' Orson threw Terran a questioning look over Juliette's shoulder.

'You didn't?' She frowned.

'Clearly Terran here forgot to mention it.' Orson raised an eyebrow, releasing her.

'Erm…' Terran's insides clenched. 'I wasn't too sure…'

Juliette looked at him shrewdly. 'You weren't sure I was actually coming.'

'Yeah… Something like that.' Terran grimaced.

'Well, that's no matter, you're here now!' Orson grinned at Juliette and ushered her inside. 'Come on in, come on in. We've missed you!'

Terran found himself suddenly speechless. It had taken all the courage he could muster to finally call Juliette a few days before, intent on apologising for being the world's biggest prick to her. It had been an awkward conversation, and for a moment he'd been worried he'd ruined things beyond repair. But although she'd sounded a little unsure and more distant than usual, she'd let herself be convinced to come over for dinner, with the promise that he'd explain everything in person.

They stepped into the hallway, and an odd silence fell over them. Terran felt nervous. He'd been dying to see her, but now she was here he had no idea what to say. Juliette seemed intent on avoiding his gaze, her face impassive. She crossed her arms in front of her, and with that simple gesture Terran sensed her bound even further out of his reach. He hadn't expected her to forgive and forget easily after the way he'd treated her, but seeing her icy demeanour hurt more than he had anticipated.

'Hi,' Terran said, wanting to say more, but not knowing what.

'Hi,' she said coolly, finally looking at him, her gaze stern.

Ok, Terran thought, *she's pissed off.*

'I…' he started. 'I just… I mean…'

He was acutely aware of how little sense he was making, but the right words eluded him.

'Ok.' Orson looked uncertainly from one to the other. 'Well, this is a bit awkward,' he chuckled. 'A *lot* awkward, actually, and quite painful to watch. Ter, why don't I take over in the kitchen, and you go and… erm… entertain our guest.'

Terran let himself be ushered out of the kitchen, and with a constricted look at Orson, he led Juliette out into the back garden. He took a seat on the stone steps that led down to the small patch of lawn, and she sat beside him. Terran gave her a side glance. She was not looking at him, and he couldn't read the expression on her face. A full minute elapsed.

'So,' Juliette finally said with a sigh, turning to glare at him. 'Here we are again…'

Terran frowned in surprise.

'Is this the point where you apologise for being horrible to me, and for ignoring my messages,' she said in a voice that was almost business-like, 'and tell me you weren't trying to block me out, and you had a lot going on, yada, yada, yada?' She looked straight at him, her face set.

Terran blinked, taken aback.

'And then, I'm supposed to tell you it's alright,' Juliette continued, 'and that I understand, and you were just trying your best, and you don't need to apologise. Right?'

Terran frowned harder. He opened his mouth to respond, but Juliette spoke again.

'Except, Terran, it's *not* alright.' Juliette shook her head vehemently, her voice rising. 'And I sort of understand, and maybe you *were* trying your best, but if that was your best then it was pretty rubbish.'

Terran stared at her, his voice lost somewhere in his throat.

'I put my life on hold for you! I was there for you,' Juliette went on, looking at him pointedly. 'For *you*, Terran. Don't you get that?'

'I…' Terran mumbled.

'And you acted like an absolute moron, alright?' Juliette's cheeks were flushed now, and her eyes wet. 'I get that you don't know how to let people be close to you, but your behaviour was just absolutely, *completely* wrong, and hurtful, and honestly borderline unforgivable.'

Her words hit him with full force. She might as well have slapped him.

Terran swallowed hard. 'I truly am sorry,' he breathed. 'The way I treated you… I know it was wrong. *I* was wrong. I thought it was easier to keep you out. I just couldn't cope. You deserved better than that. *So* much better.'

Juliette closed her eyes but said nothing.

'I know our history doesn't play in my favour,' Terran continued, 'but I promise I'll do better. I'm still learning, I know. I swear I'll never do this to you again.'

Juliette leant back to look at him.

'I'm not showing up a third time if you do.' She gave him a piercing look, and Terran could tell this was no idle threat.

'I know.' He nodded.

'You've really hurt me,' she insisted, her voice low, the words slashing painfully through him. 'Your behaviour, before... That was appalling.'

'I know.' He hung his head, ashamed.

'If we're going to be in each other's lives in any way, shape or form, you *cannot* shut me out like that ever again.'

'I won't. I promise.' He reached out to hold her hands in his. 'I've been a complete idiot.' He gave her hands a gentle squeeze. 'You're the best thing that's happened to me in a long time. I'm sorry it took me so long to see it.'

She nodded quietly, her gaze still on his, and he saw her jaw soften.

'*If* I give this another chance,' she eventually said with a sigh, 'please don't make me regret it.'

'I swear I won't.' His heart was beating with mad relief inside his chest.

She looked at him for a long time, searching his face, and Terran held his breath, hoping she'd see in his eyes how sorry he was and how deeply he meant every word he'd said. He let out a long breath.

'Alright, then.'

They looked at each other for a long while, and he didn't dare make a move, terrified that saying or doing the wrong thing would send her right back out the door. She held his gaze, her expression hard to decipher, and Terran cursed himself for feeling so inadequate. He shifted in his seat, and she inclined her head slightly, the hint of a smile playing at the corner of her lips. She reached out, gently running her fingers along his cheek, and the sensation of her skin on his sent his body into instant overdrive. He stayed quite still, suddenly incapable of moving, although all he wanted was to reach back, to pull her in and hold her. Slowly, deliberately, she leant forward, sliding her hand along his neck, pulling him into her, angling his face towards hers. She paused there for a fraction of a second, her eyes burning into his, her lips stretching into the most alluring smile, her voice a seductive whisper.

'Alright, then,' she said again.

Before he realised what was happening, she'd pressed her mouth against his and kissed him, parting his lips with her tongue. He felt himself melt—gosh, had he wanted to do this for so long, to feel her, to taste her, to let himself be free. He pulled her into him and she slid her arms around his neck, pressing her body against him. Kissing her felt as incredible as he'd imagined, as intoxicating as he'd thought it would be, her desire meeting his with equal force. She pulled back for an instant that felt like an eternity, her mouth teasing his and her fingers tangled in his hair, keeping herself just out of his reach. Her devilish grin brought a primal groan out of him and he tightened his hold on her, diverting his lips up the line of her jaw to the crook of her neck, brushing against the tender skin until she was purring in his ear. The mere sound of it sent his heartbeat out of control, and the rush of want and joy and contentment that washed over him felt momentarily overwhelming.

He forced himself to stop, although he wanted nothing more than to carry her up the stairs to his bedroom and never come out again. Terran couldn't remember ever feeling so at peace with the world as he did in that very moment, pulling his face slowly away from hers, resting his forehead against hers and allowing the moment to sink in. They sat there, wrapped around each other, breathing hard, their hair a little dishevelled.

'I'm so glad you came,' he said softly, placing a kiss on the tip of her nose.

'I'm glad I came, too,' she purred, resting her face in the crook of his neck.

She was about to add something when Orson's booming voice came calling from inside.

'Come, children! Dinner is ready!'

They both jumped in surprise, like two teenagers caught red-handed, and instantly let go of each other, turning around to look at the house. Juliette giggled as Orson poked his head through the garden door.

'You guys coming? You'll see, I've completely rescued this *mattar paneer*, it's to die for!'

'As if it needed rescuing...' Terran mumbled, getting to his feet.

'I love you too, dear brother.' Orson punched him on the arm. 'Now come along before it all gets cold.'

Terran threw a look at Juliette, who was grinning broadly, and they stepped inside. The table was set for five, and Farao and Kendrik had already taken a seat.

'Hey!' Kendrik said in surprise, noticing Juliette. 'Hello, stranger!'

'Sorry for gatecrashing your meal...' Juliette said apologetically.

'Nonsense, nonsense,' Orson declared with a flourish, pulling out a chair for her to sit down. 'First time in weeks Terran's not a grumpy git, we're not about to let that slip through our fingers!'

Farao suppressed a snort.

'What?' Terran protested. 'I haven't been a grumpy git!'

'Sure, you haven't...' Farao laughed, raising his eyebrows.

'I'm telling you,' Kendrik added, giving Juliette a resigned nod, 'if you being here is what's finally snapping him out of being all touchy and prickly, you're never leaving this house.'

Juliette gave Terran an apologetic sort of look, and he rolled his eyes.

'Are we done here?' Terran grumbled, 'or should I give you guys some more time to air your grievances?'

'Nah.' Orson grinned at him, offering the bowl of cucumber and onion *raita* to Juliette. 'I think we've made our point.'

'Great.' Terran shook his head, helping himself to an *aloo-paratha*.

'Seriously, guys.' Juliette let out a soft laugh, shaking her head. 'I've missed you!'

'We've missed you too,' Terran said softly, placing his hand on hers, watching her blush slightly.

There was an embarrassed pause around the table. Kendrik, Orson and Farao exchanged glances, all of them beaming.

'Well,' Orson said finally, 'tuck in!'

Terran looked around at the table, at Orson who kept refilling everyone's plate, at Farao and Kendrik talking about a Marvel movie marathon they were planning over the weekend. His gaze found Juliette again, and his chest swelled with joy. For the first time in his life, he felt like he had a choice. Farao was recovering well, and the bond he shared with his brothers was stronger than it had ever been. Terran didn't have to merely survive for their sake anymore. It wasn't all down to him. There was time, he thought, and it was wonderful to acknowledge it. There was plenty of time to live for himself, too.

***

When dinner was over, Terran noticed the other three discreetly disappear off upstairs, leaving him alone with Juliette to finish putting everything away. He could feel the tension in the air as she passed him the dishes to load into the dishwasher, their fingers sometimes brushing when he took a plate or item of cutlery from her. He wondered how a task as mundane as this one could feel so incredibly charged.

When everything was done, Terran leant back against the sink, feeling very self-conscious. Juliette was standing by the kitchen table, not looking at him, folding her tea towel with a little too much precision and care for it to be inconspicuous. Terran wondered why on earth this was so awkward when not so long ago, they were wrapped around each other, out in the garden. He wanted to cross the space between them and kiss her again, but something stopped him. He wasn't sure what to say or do. It annoyed him how inexperienced he suddenly felt. At the back of his mind he pictured Orson rolling his eyes at him as he silently decided to go for the first thing that crossed his mind:

'Cup of tea?'

She cocked her head at him, looking surprised, then amused.

'Cup of tea sounds good,' she smiled.

Terran put the kettle on and walked over to one of the kitchen cabinets, pulling out two mugs and rummaging in another cupboard for tea. He took out a few of the boxes they had, offering them to her, and she picked out a sachet of Earl Grey from the selection of black, green and herbal blends. He couldn't help a smile—Earl Grey was his favourite. He popped a sachet in each mug and leant back against the kitchen counter again, waiting for the kettle to boil. Juliette was perched on the edge of the dining table, her hands knotting and unknotting in front of her. He couldn't think of a single thing to say.

'Farao seems to be doing well.' She finally broke the silence.

'Yeah.' He grinned. 'He's recovering. The doctors say there's no cause for alarm, we just have to make sure he follows the rest of his treatment.'

'Good.' She nodded.

'Yeah.'

Terran wanted to slap himself. *Yeah*? Was that really the best he could do? He wanted to hold her. To tell her how much he'd missed her. He wanted to tell her that he hadn't stopped thinking about her from the moment they'd met, and that the day she'd left them in France had been excruciating. He wanted her to know how much she meant to him, how badly he wanted to start afresh, to be the man she deserved. But he didn't know how to voice any of it, or where to even begin. He worried that by saying the wrong thing he might chase her away again, and he knew he wouldn't get another chance. He felt inadequate, and that was one emotion that always rubbed him the wrong way. Juliette was watching him quietly, and he wished he knew what she was thinking.

He was saved by the kettle coming to a boil. He felt relieved to have something to do, and took his time pouring the hot water and walking over to the fridge to grab a bottle of oat milk, raising it to her in a silent question.

'Milk, no sugar,' she answered.

'Coming right up,' he smiled, pouring a dash of milk in each mug and handing her one.

He gestured into the living room, leading the way. He took a seat on the couch, inviting her to do the same. As he settled onto the cushion, the television screen flicked on, a random comedy program blaring at them out of nowhere. He rummaged behind him to pull out the remote from underneath him, pressing the mute button.

'Sorry.' He grimaced, not really sure what he was apologising for.

Juliette smiled and sat down facing him, both hands around her mug. They looked at each other expectantly.

Say something!

'So…' Terran said.

Jeez, Terran, get a grip.

'So…' Juliette grinned, a note of amusement in her voice.

They both chuckled, and the awkwardness around them started to dissolve.

'I'm sorry.' Terran winced. 'I don't know how to do this. I haven't done much of this before… or ever, really.'

Juliette gave him a look of such tenderness he felt himself shiver.

'Well,' she said, scooting over to him, 'I guess we don't have to rush into things right away. How about baby steps for now?'

She was so close he could sense the heat emanating from her body. He cleared his throat.

'I'd like that,' he sighed.

'Good.' Her smile widened, and she leant back into the couch.

The rest of the house was mostly quiet. He could hear the faint sound of music coming from the floors above them. On the television, the adverts gave way to the second half of an American show, and Juliette gave a contented purr. She nodded at the screen.

'I've seen every episode of *Friends* so many times.' She shook her head. 'I used to love it when I was younger.'

'Never seen it.' Terran shrugged, earning himself a disbelieving look from Juliette. 'I never watched that much TV,' he explained.

'Ok.' She grabbed the remote, turning the volume up, rolling her eyes. 'Then we're *definitely* watching it now. Let this be the start of your pop culture education.'

He smiled, watching her settling back against the cushions, her hair falling gracefully around her face, her eyes bright and joyful, a cheeky grin still toying with the corner of her lips. How beautiful she was. How... *perfect*.

'What?' She beamed, raising an eyebrow when she caught him looking.

Terran opened his mouth to speak, but once again, as so often happened in her presence, he couldn't find the words. So, instead, he patted the spot next to him and opened his arms, inviting her in. The surprised delight on her face sent his heart pulsing madly against his ribcage. She nestled into his embrace and he wrapped one arm around her, pulling her in even closer. On the screen, a group of people was sitting around a table in a coffee shop, talking about love and dating, but he wasn't paying much attention. He sat there, revelling in the feel of Juliette in his arms, unable to take his eyes off her. He loved the way the soft light on her skin made it look as smooth as velvet. She turned to look at him and offered him a radiant smile. Terran smiled back at her. Their eyes locked, and in an instant the atmosphere around them shifted. It was suddenly charged again, growing so heavy with electricity Terran was surprised both of them didn't just catch fire on the spot. Slowly, she placed her mug, then his, on the coffee table and turned back to face him. She closed the gap between them, her hands lifting up to his face. He snaked both his arms around her waist, his palms almost greedy, relishing the touch. She leant in towards him, their lips brushing for a second or two before her mouth met his. He pulled her in, with one hand at the back of her head, holding her tight against him.

A loud noise from the floor above them made him freeze, and he felt Juliette suddenly tense.

'What was that?' Juliette whispered.

Terran listened closely. He could hear steps coming down from the upper levels, and Orson's voice coming from the upstairs corridor. He heard a muffled conversation between Orson and Kendrik, then Kendrik's door close again and Orson's footsteps finally making their way back up the stairs. The mood around them had evaporated.

'It's just the others,' he murmured. 'I keep forgetting how thin the walls are in this house…'

She studied his face for a second and barely stifled a laugh. He thought he could never get enough of the sound of her laughter. He laughed too, resting his forehead against hers. Terran felt like a teenager, giddy with excitement and anticipation, barely able to contain himself.

'It's ok.' She caressed his forearm, leaving a trail of goosebumps on his skin. 'I'm not going anywhere. I mean…' She grinned, looking at him from the corner of her eye. 'You did try your hardest to shake me off, and even that didn't work…'

'Thank God for that.' Terran brought her hand to his lips and kissed her knuckles.

She laid her head against his shoulder. Terran closed his eyes, smiling to himself. He could feel her body relaxing against his. On the screen, in the nineties, in New York City, Ross Geller was courting Rachel Green.

'Terran?' Juliette said quietly, a little while later.

'Mmm?' He angled his face towards hers, but her gaze was still on the television.

'If you ghost me again,' she said in a low voice, 'I'll punch you in the face.'

He tried to suppress a grin. 'I know you will.' He kissed the top of her head.

'Good.' She adjusted herself in his embrace.

He couldn't tell when she'd fallen asleep, several episodes later. Terran listened to the slow cadence of her breath until he too felt himself doze off. The last conscious thought he was aware off before he fell asleep was that, for the first time in a long time, he was happy. And that was the most invigorating feeling in the world.

Chapter 71
Farao

Farao was in his room, tossing and turning on his bed, wondering if he should go and check on his brothers but unable to get himself to actually do it. He checked the time: eleven twenty in the evening. He groaned and turned onto his back. The same thoughts kept swirling in his mind, and he could only hope he wouldn't come to regret his decision. *All I can do*, he breathed, *is wait and see.* He closed his eyes and willed himself to calm down.

So much had happened in such a short time, it often felt like whoever they had all been before had never truly existed. It was March, and six months had passed since his surgery. They had celebrated his eighteenth birthday at home with Amit and Juliette. They had sat in merry banter around a Christmas feast, the six of them, and welcomed in the new year in a light and joyous atmosphere the house hadn't seen in a very long time. Farao was mostly recovered now, albeit a little tired sometimes, an expected side effect from some of the meds he was still taking.

His recovery, of course, had not been solely physical. On Amit's advice, he had started therapy. The two sessions he had every week with Doctor Zoya had been a godsend. Farao often smiled as he thought of how, in the not-so-distant past, his old self might have thought of therapy, of talking about his *feelings* with a total stranger, with contempt. But the new Farao couldn't see how he'd been able to get on with his life without it, without doing the work, without giving himself time and space to put all that had happened to him in order. He had known there would be much to unravel, but he hadn't quite realised how deeply rooted some of that stuff was. And it wasn't just everything that had happened—although that in itself was something he was still processing. It was also learning how to deal with what he now called 'the fog'.

The fog, Farao thought with a shiver. That toxic cloud that had kept him under for days on end back in the beach house. The suffocating feeling that nothing would ever be right again, that life wasn't worth living. The repetitive and corrosive thought that he'd much rather be… He closed his eyes and winced at the idea. *Dead.* In his entire life before then, despite everything that had happened, Farao had never found himself wishing to die. He'd never truly considered taking his own life. He'd never given up, not like that. But his time in France had got him to that point. It worried him that the fog could engulf him at any time. That, next time, he might not have the strength to pull himself back. He was working on it, and Doctor Zoya kept assuring him that awareness was a start, but it wasn't always easy. Some days he just felt sad. Whether he woke up that way or something shifted inside him without warning, he'd find himself slowly drowning in deep, gut-wrenching sorrow for no apparent reason. It was as if his depressive episode in Marseille had unlocked something in him, a force that was dark and ever-lurking and dangerous. It was like standing too close to the edge of a cliff, not wanting to fall but wondering if he might just jump before he could stop himself, and not knowing what to do to prevent it. It scared him to know it was there, and sometimes the thought alone was enough to trigger him. It had taken a long time and many discussions with Doctor Zoya to even start to comprehend that it was a part of him. That, far from trying to resist its presence, he should lean into acknowledging that it was there. That the day he stopped fighting and fearing it would be the day he took away its power and allow himself to heal. Acceptance, however, let alone surrender, felt like a long way away still.

Thankfully for him, Doctor Zoya was patient and supportive. She made him feel heard. Not just listened to but truly, fully *heard*. It was Doctor Zoya who had suggested that writing some of it down might help him get a sense of closure, and though Farao hadn't been sold on the idea at first, he had given it a try. He wasn't back at school yet, and he had so much time on his hands, he thought if anything it might give him something to occupy himself with. As it turned out, it had become much more than that. The moment he sat down to write, the words had come pouring out of him. He'd written fervently for hours at a time, and every word he put down on the page felt like a relief. He wrote about everything. About his parents, his family, about how he'd grown up. About everything that had happened before and after the incident that had changed all of their lives. He talked about himself, and he talked, extensively, about his brothers. He wrote about Juliette, and the random encounter which had healed their family in so many ways. He retold the story of their adventure, of everything they had gone through together, of the secrets and lies they'd had to face. And it felt good to let it all out.

He'd finished the first draft of his story in just under three weeks. He'd shared it with Doctor Zoya, who, after reading through it, had told him with astonishment that he should consider sharing it with his brothers, if and when he felt ready. He had dismissed her at the time, because that wasn't why he had started writing, but he'd kept going back to the manuscript, working on it, editing it over and over, until he had a finished version he was happy with. The real test had been printing and binding four copies and handing over one each to Terran, Kendrik, Orson and Juliette, who hadn't known what he was spending so much time on his laptop for. This had happened earlier that morning, and the wait to see their reaction when they finished reading it was agonising, sowing doubt in Farao's mind as to whether he'd done the right thing.

It was late into the night when Orson walked into Farao's room, manuscript in hand. Without a word, he sat on the edge of his bed and hugged him.

'I don't say this enough...' Orson said softly. 'But I love you.'

Farao tightened his grip on his brother. 'I love you, too.'

'I'm so grateful you decided to share this with us. I can imagine it wasn't easy,' Orson said, letting go of Farao.

'It wasn't.' Farao shuffled in his seat. 'But it felt like the right thing to do.'

'I sort of knew how hard it was for you, but I never really understood until now...'

'It was hard for all of us.' Farao shrugged. 'Not that it's a competition.'

'True.' Orson cocked his head to one side, smiling. 'Though if it were, I wonder who'd win...'

Farao laughed. 'Probably Juliette. I don't know who else could've put up with all of our shit.'

'Probably.' Orson nodded, then added, in mock conspiracy, 'Tell you what, let's put it to a vote tomorrow at dinner, see who gets the medal of honour.'

Farao looked at his brother for a moment. 'You're a bit silly, you know that?' He smiled, the tenderness in his voice taking him a little by surprise.

Orson winked at him. 'One of my best qualities!' He patted him on the shoulder. 'That said…' He turned serious again. 'You should publish this.' He jutted his chin towards the manuscript on the side of the bed. 'It's excellent. Think about it.'

Farao gave an awkward laugh, but Orson gave him a pointed look.

'Think about it,' Orson repeated, getting up and making his way out of the room.

The topic came up at dinner the next day. By then the others had progressed through their own copies too. It was odd, Farao thought, because though they had lived through it all together, they hadn't discussed it. They hadn't talked about that time, about what they had gone through individually and as a unit. But Farao's written account seemed to be opening up a door for that discussion to happen.

'Thank you for sharing this with us, Farao.' Juliette spoke first, placing a gentle hand on his. 'It means a lot that you would trust us with something so personal.'

'Yeah,' Kendrik smiled. 'Though I don't remember being as much of a stuck-up prude as you make me sound!'

Farao gave him an embarrassed look, but he was rescued from answering by Orson.

'Ken, my dear…' Orson leant in, conspiratorially. 'You were even worse. Farao here has just been sparing your feelings!'

'You're such a—' Kendrik started.

'Farao,' Terran cut in, interrupting the other two's bickering. 'I'm so impressed. I think you should put this out there. You're good at this. And I think your story will resonate with a lot of people…'

A short silence followed his words as Terran looked straight into Farao's face.

'You mean'—Farao frowned—'all the people who are also one of four orphaned siblings, who found out they're the illegitimate child of sexual assault *and* have survived a near-terminal illness?'

'Well, not quite,' Terran chuckled, 'but everything around it. I think a lot of people will relate to feeling out of place and misunderstood... And not just the younger ones, the grown-ups, too.'

Farao pondered it for a moment. Everyone around the table, without exception, was nodding in agreement. When he was to reflect on the matter, months, even years later, Farao would think of this as the moment the idea had become real. That same week, they all dove into the logistics of it with fervent excitement. They hired the services of an editor, a cover designer and a typesetter, and within a couple of months they had a book that was ready to self-publish.

When the big day finally arrived, Farao sat in front of his laptop, ready to press the submit button which would see the book added to the online marketplace's inventory, where it would be available for the world to see. Beyond the screen, he could see Terran lighting candles and Orson gathering the tequila and shot glasses into a circle on the living room floor. Except this time there were five glasses—it hadn't been too clear when Juliette had moved in with them; she had just become a permanent fixture in their lives. Farao took a deep breath and submitted the book.

They sat around the tequila bottle, their arms raised in a toast.

'To Farao's first book,' Terran said.

'To brotherhood,' Kendrik added.

'To all the royalties that will make us millionaires,' Orson said with a grin, making them all laugh.

'To the Dhawan brothers.' Juliette nodded.

'The Dhawan brothers.' They repeated in unison before chucking down their drinks.

Chapter 72
Orson

Orson smiled to himself. If only their parents could see them now, he thought, and the idea made him a little melancholic.

'Since we're celebrating,' Kendrik announced from his spot in the circle they were forming on the floor. 'I've got something to share.'

They all turned to him with interest, and watched him turn to grab something hidden behind his back. He placed a thick manila envelope in front of him.

'When we were in France, I...' Kendrik cleared his throat. 'After the night at the festival, I emailed everyone on the Saint-Blaise list.'

Orson frowned to himself. *The list?* He'd completely forgotten about that.

'The what?' Farao asked.

'The list we got from the RAF base, to try and get the details for...' Kendrik sighed. 'Well, you know.' There was a brief, loaded silence before Kendrik continued, looking at Farao. 'Erm... We actually told them we wanted contact details for people who'd worked with Dad, back in the day, to put some stuff together for your birthday.'

'I'm still amazed that worked.' Terran raised his eyebrows.

'Yeah, me too.' Kendrik nodded. 'Well, anyway, we did get a full list. So I... I actually emailed everyone on the list,' he said again. 'Asking for stories and pictures they had of that time.'

Orson's heart skipped a beat, and his eyes found the envelope by Kendrik's feet.

'Most of them responded. Some of them sent stuff through the post. A lot of them emailed a few things. I've printed everything out.' He reached inside the envelope and pulled out a pile of papers and photographs, which he placed at the centre of their circle. 'I haven't gone through all of it... But it's not just Dad, there's stuff about Mum, too.'

Orson froze, staring at the pile of documents in front of him, unable to move a muscle. He wasn't sure what was stopping him. *What the hell?* he thought. *Pull yourself together, Orson.* And yet he couldn't, and the papers seemed to stare back at him, taunting him. At the back of his mind, "Ghost" was playing in a crescendo, until he could no longer hear himself think.

"Will time work its magic... Will it erase my name... Or will I be the freak... That brought you so much pain...?"

Orson inhaled sharply, pressing his eyelids together, willing the tune to go away. Terran was first to react, leaning over and grabbing the first piece of paper on the pile, a handwritten letter with a photograph stapled in the top left-hand corner. Orson forced his eyes open again, focusing on Terran's face, refusing to let the memory get the better of him. Terran's gaze travelled over the letter in silence, his mouth set in a tight line, Juliette leaning in to read over his shoulder.

'Dear Kendrik,' Terran started reading out loud. 'I'm glad you reached out. Your father and I served together for several years, and he was one of the best men I ever knew. He was generous and fair, and an incredible pilot. Flying just seemed like second nature to him, and I know I wasn't the only one to envy his skill and discipline. But he was so much more than that. He was always first to volunteer to give anyone a helping hand, even when people didn't ask for it. He had a sixth sense for knowing what the right thing to do was, and he just went ahead and did it. He helped me out of a few tight spots back in the day, and I'll forever be grateful and honoured to have called him a friend. I was sad to hear he'd passed, because I've seldom met better men in my entire life and career. You and your brothers should be proud of calling yourself his sons, and I hope that you will carry his legacy through every one of your actions.'

Orson's throat felt tight, and he didn't trust himself to speak. Terran brought the picture to his eyes and studied it before passing it around the others. When it reached Orson, he took a deep breath and looked at it. The black and white shot showed his father and three other men, beaming, in their RAF overalls, nonchalantly leaning against a jeep. Orson's jaw clenched. He couldn't tear his eyes from his father's face, the words from the letter reverberating in his mind. He tried to shake them off but he couldn't, and every word of praise felt like a punch to the gut.

Kendrik had taken hold of the next letter and read it aloud, and the others took turn sharing the memories others had so generously taken the time to send. Orson took in the words without knowing what to make of them. He looked at picture after picture of his father, and all he felt was hurt. He found himself cringing at every recollection about the spotless, irreproachable Anand Dhawan. It was too much for Orson. There was something bubbling inside of him which he could no longer contain. He hadn't wanted to burden his brothers with it; he hadn't wanted to taint their memory of their father with the truth. He had wanted to let them believe what every letter was saying. That their father had been blameless. But his time of keeping secrets to keep them from feeling hurt was over. *We've all seen how that went down last time*, he thought bitterly.

'He was drunk,' he said, unable to hold it in any longer, interrupting Kendrik mid-reading.

They all looked at him in confusion.

'What do you...?' Terran frowned.

Orson exhaled sharply.

'The day Dad crashed his plane...' He looked up at the others. 'He was drunk.'

Kendrik's mouth fell open, and Farao stared at him blankly. Juliette looked at all of them in turn, concern on her face.

'How do you kn—' Terran started.

'I just know,' Orson said, with a note of finality. 'I saw it. He was drunk. That's why he crashed that day.'

Seconds passed, the revelation lingering painfully between them.

'Are you sure?' Farao asked quietly.

'I'm sure.'

Terran shook his head, his face tense, and looked back at the picture he was still holding.

'I just...' he said. 'I don't remember...'

'He was different after we moved.' Orson wrapped his arms around his knees. 'I don't know if you guys remember, but he wasn't really around anymore. And whenever he was... He was just...' He paused. '*Different*.'

Orson looked at each of his brothers in turn, taking in Terran's confusion, Kendrik's unreadable expression and Farao's saddened look. He could see the seed of recognition in each of their faces. He hated that he'd just told them, but he knew he'd had to. After everything they'd gone through, he couldn't have kept it from them.

'Thank you for telling us,' Terran said quietly, his voice breaking a little, as though reading his mind. 'I just…' He winced. 'I don't really know what to do with that information.'

Juliette placed a gentle hand on Terran's forearm, and he gave her a small nod.

'Me neither,' Farao breathed, shaking his head.

They turned to Kendrik, who was still silent.

'Kendrik?' Orson said tentatively.

'I can't believe it…'

There as a strange look on Kendrik's face. He looked confused, angry and… Orson swallowed hard. *Betrayed.*

'Ken…' Terran.

'I just… I need a minute.' Kendrik got to his feet and hurried across the room.

He rushed towards the garden, and he strode out into the night.

Chapter 73
Kendrik

They all hurried after him, but Kendrik couldn't stop moving. The disappointment and agony that had hit him a moment earlier were piercing through him.

'I can't believe it…' he repeated, over and over, his voice resonating in the darkness, as if saying the words would be enough to make it all untrue.

'Kendrik…' Orson approached him slowly.

'No, Orson.' Kendrik was shaking his head at him. 'He wasn't… He didn't…' he stammered, stumbling over his words, his eyes wide. 'He was a good man!' he finally cried out. 'Ok? He was a good man. A great dad. He wasn't…' He kept shaking his head, tears streaming down his cheeks.

His father. His hero. The best man he'd known. And now… And now, this? Kendrik knew that if the past few months had taught him anything, it was that no one was ever perfect. That, actually, perfection really came with a whole world of imperfections. But none of this felt like it had applied to his father, even in the light of the memories he'd so recently unlocked. He didn't know how to reconcile the memories of the father he'd adored with those of a man who'd let his family down. He didn't want to know his father had failed.

'Ken...' Terran said softly, coming to stand next to him. 'He *was* a good man. *And* a great dad.'

Kendrik gave a loud sniff, and Orson came to join them, with Farao and Juliette in tow.

'But he was only human.' Terran wrapped an arm around Kendrik's shoulders. 'He was flawed, just like everyone else.'

'I just...' Kendrik wiped his face with the back of his hand. 'I just...' he sighed.

'I know.' Orson nodded. 'It must have been so much for him to go through. All that... That's bound to take a toll on anyone. It did on Mum, too. But however they dealt with it doesn't take anything away from your memory of either of them. They were just good people who had to face something really, really difficult.'

'I mean,' Farao added, 'see how well *we* handled it...' He gestured around at them. 'I'm not surprised they struggled.'

'Shame neither of them had magic cacao, huh?' Orson grimaced. 'Seems like they could have used some.'

Kendrik made a sound halfway between a sob and a laugh. 'I just don't get it.' His voice was low. 'I don't understand how this could be the same person. It just... It doesn't add up...'

'You know,' Farao said quietly, 'if there's anything I've learnt, it's that nothing works in absolutes.' He shook his head. 'There's no black and white. There's only a billion shades of grey. Just because he couldn't deal with everything doesn't mean he wasn't an outstanding man. And...' Farao hesitated, throwing Kendrik a pained look. 'Just because he wasn't able to save himself doesn't mean he wouldn't have wanted to stay alive for you.' He placed a hand on Kendrik's arm. 'It doesn't mean he didn't love you.'

Kendrik closed his eyes and took in the words, a fresh wave of hot tears streaking behind his eyelids. The others were all silent, but he was grateful for their presence. There was a time, not so long ago, when he would have wanted to run, to hide, to conceal from anyone how badly he was hurting. But that time was gone.

They stayed in the garden for a long time, huddled together, and Kendrik allowed himself space to grieve, to feel the full force of his disappointment, to let the memory of his father start to blur and merge with this new reality he disliked so much. *One day*, he hoped, as the sobs started to subside, one day he'd be able to think about it all, to remember his father without bitterness and to love him unconditionally, for all that he'd been—flaws and all.

Chapter 74
Farao

Farao sat in the little waiting room with his brothers and Juliette, absentmindedly rolling the hem of his tee-shirt between his fingers. Everything since the book release had been a bit of a blur. Juliette had promoted it on her social medial channels and Kendrik had taken it upon himself to create the best online advertising campaign he possibly could. Before they knew it, the book was flying off the electronic shelves. Something about Farao's story and the heartfelt rendition he gave of their family's adventure seemed to resonate with people in a way that he hadn't expected. Before long, the internet was buzzing with praise of the book, of his courage, of the extraordinary journey of brotherhood they had gone on. The messages had started flooding in, from people who had survived near-fatal illnesses thanks to organ donation, children born of sexual abuse who found him inspiring, people who wanted to tell Farao how brave he was for sharing his story. But it wasn't until the interview requests and emails from agents had come in that it had become real. Farao still struggled to believe it. And so it was that, a couple of months later, he found himself in the colourful waiting room of a national radio station, waiting to go on air on their morning show.

'There you go, superstar,' Terran called out to him from afar, snapping Farao out of his silent reflection and handing him a takeaway coffee.

'Thanks,' Farao responded, taking the cup gladly.

He'd needed the caffeine. He was feeling suddenly nervous, unsure whether he could go ahead with this. It had been one thing to write all those things down. But it was quite another to be talking about them on live radio to a bunch of strangers.

'You know you can back out anytime, right?' Juliette said softly, taking a seat next to him, seeming to read his mind.

Farao simply nodded, but now she'd given him the option, he couldn't seriously consider it. He had gone this far, too far to be scared into running home to hide.

'Farao?' A young woman with a badge around her neck, a headset and a clipboard in her hands came to stand before them. 'They're ready for you, if you'll just follow me.'

Farao nodded again and, with a final look at his family, who all beamed at him, he followed the young woman through the thick door, above which the bright 'on air' sign glowed ominously. The other side of the door felt like a different world altogether, with its walls and ceiling covered in thick black foamy material. The large room was divided in two areas separated by a large plexiglass partition. On one side the production team milled around cables and electronic contraptions, following the show happening around the circular table laden with microphones on the other side of the glass. The young woman waited for a signal from a man who seemed to be in charge, and led Farao in through the small passage into the area where the show hosts were now taking a break.

'Farao.' The young woman introduced him to the two hosts, a man and a woman. 'This is Craig Bunting and Carrie Stones. They'll be leading the interview today.'

Farao shook Craig and Carrie's hands. They were both in their late twenties or early thirties, smiling at him, their manner easy and relaxed. They settled him in front of one of the empty microphones and placed a heavy headset on his head.

'Do you need anything else?' the young woman asked. 'Water? Tea? Coffee?'

'No, I'm good, thanks.' Farao shuffled on his seat.

'We're back live in one minute, guys.' The producer's voice resonated in their headsets from the other side of the glass panel.

Craig and Carrie positioned themselves again. Craig gave the producer a thumbs-up and Carrie threw Farao a friendly wink.

'And we're back after Adele's latest hit. What a great song! Isn't it, Carrie?' Craig said.

'It *is* a great song,' Carrie chimed in, 'and already top of the charts, *obviously.*'

'And speaking of top of the charts.' Craig turned to Farao, grinning. 'We have a rather special guest with us today who's also on top of the world in his own category, don't we?'

'We do!' Carrie exclaimed. 'This young man has become, in a matter of weeks, the new writing sensation the internet is raving about, and has claimed a well-deserved spot in the Amazon top ten best sellers in the UK for the third week in a row. Not a mean feat for someone who, I believe, has only just turned eighteen! We're talking of course, of the talented Farao Dhawan, who's sitting with us in the studio this morning. Hi, Farao!' she finished, looking at him and nodding encouragingly.

'Hi,' Farao answered, feeling a little awkward.

'It's a pleasure to have you with us today,' Craig said. 'We hear you've been in high demand—it makes us feel quite special!'

'I don't know about that,' Farao laughed, 'but it's a pleasure to be here. Thank you for having me.'

'Oh my *God*,' Carrie chuckled. 'So modest!'

'So, Farao, we, like thousands of others out there, have both read your memoir, *The Long Way Home*, and we, like thousands of others out there, were both left awestruck. Not only by the writing, which is excellent for someone your age, but the story itself is mind-blowing. I honestly had to remind myself throughout that it *is* a true story from end to finish. I can't even begin to imagine what it was like actually living through all that… And then reliving it a second time when writing the book.'

'Yeah.' Farao winced despite himself. 'It was hands down the most difficult time of my life. There were a lot of lows. But writing about it actually was very therapeutic. It gave me a sense of closure.'

'Interesting.' Carrie cocked her head to one side. 'So would you say that you're over everything that happened to you, then? Is there hope for everyone else out there who's a little screwed up too?'

'Well,' Farao smiled, 'I wouldn't say I'm a hundred percent fine now, but I'm getting there. It's taken a lot of self-reflection and a lot of work to get to this point. It hasn't been easy, and I don't know if I'll ever be completely ok with everything that happened, but I definitely believe that I can get to a place where it's not painful to live with.'

'So,' Craig said, 'I guess we can remind our listeners, for anyone living under a rock who hasn't heard about or read the book, what those difficulties have been for you. You're one of four brothers, and you guys lost your parents pretty early on.'

'Yes, I was just a few months old when my father died, and just ten when my mother died.'

'I mean'—Craig shook his head in disbelief—'that's got to be a whole lot of baggage on its own already… But that's not even the whole story. You were raised by your brothers. I believe your elder brother'—Craig glanced down briefly at his notes—'Terran was your legal guardian. And at the end of last year, one day you fainted at school, which led your brothers to learn that not only did you have a life-threatening genetic condition, but that you had inherited that condition from the man who sexually assaulted your mother... What's more, they decided *not* to tell you what they discovered, but to take you on a decoy adventure to France to find your biological father?'

There was a moment of silence in the studio.

'Yep.' Farao gave Craig an awkward smile. 'Yeah, that's about it.'

'Jeez.' Carrie whistled. 'I mean... *wow.*'

'Yeah.' Farao nodded, grinning at the look of astonishment on the hosts' faces. 'I woke up in the hospital, a bit unsure about what had happened, and they all spring on me that we're going on a road trip. They made up some story, and thinking of it now I can't believe I fell for it... But anyway, before I knew what was going on, we were on the road.'

'Did you ever suspect that there was more to the trip than they let on?' Carrie asked.

'I did,' Farao answered after a pause, 'but I never really spent too much time wondering about it. I did think the whole thing was odd... But then again, I was getting free out-of-school time, and I was getting to hang out with my brothers, and I think back then that was all that mattered. I used to be really self-centred...' he added as an afterthought.

'And would you say you're less self-centred now?' Carrie smiled.

'I think I still am,' Farao said. 'But I'm much more aware of others now. I never used to think about anything beyond what was going on with me. And that's the main thing that writing the book did. It made me appreciate how much others have done for me throughout everything that happened. It made me consider what my brothers went through, for instance, which I didn't really think about at the time.'

'I think Terran's one of my favourite characters in your story,' Carrie said dreamily. 'Trying to keep everything and everyone together at all times, forgetting himself in the process… I personally can relate to that.'

'I suppose there's something for everyone to relate to in that story,' Craig said with a nod, 'and that's what's made it so popular.'

'Yeah…' Farao sighed. 'Terran's carried us all through this, even long before we knew about the illness. It can't have been easy for him. I realise that now.'

'There's one thing I'm curious about,' Craig said, leaning forward. 'You mention therapy quite a lot in the book, as something that helped you move forward through everything that happened. But I get the sense that there's still a bit of a taboo about therapy, especially if you're a bloke. How did you feel about sharing your experience with the world?'

Farao thought for a few seconds.

'You know,' he said slowly, 'before everything happened, I spent a lot of my time feeling ashamed for some reason or other. Ashamed of who I was. Ashamed of not belonging. I never felt like anyone really got me, or saw me for who I was. And all that made me angry. But I guess by never being open about the real me, I never gave anyone the chance to truly understand me. It was exhausting, having to pretend all the time, to hide myself behind the appearance of who I thought I should be. Just because I was worried people wouldn't like me or approve of me if they knew who I really was… But all this…' Farao shook his head. 'All this has made me realise that the more you worry about what people think, the fewer genuine connections you'll be able to build. Because you'll never give anyone a chance to know you. Changing that starts with not hiding anymore. No longer pretending. And me being honest about how much therapy helped me, about how talking about all of this, actually saying it all out loud, helped put my thoughts and feelings in order… That's me no longer pretending. And whoever doesn't agree with that… Well. I guess that's their problem, not mine.'

There was a moment of silence in the studio.

'Amen to that!' Craig finally exclaimed. 'Remind me how old you are again?'

'I'm eighteen.'

'You sound much more mature than your age,' Carrie said, sounding impressed.

'Well.' Farao shrugged. 'I wasn't always. But I've had to do a lot of growing up in the past few months. It's just a shame that it took all this pain and struggle to get to where I am now.'

'By the way,' Craig asked, 'did you ever find out who the donor was? You talk about him quite a bit in the book.'

Farao felt his face soften a little, as it often did when he wondered about the mystery man.

'I didn't... His main condition for the procedure was that he should keep his anonymity. I don't think I'll ever know why...' He paused. 'But I guess one of the reasons why I wanted to tell my story was that I'll be never able to thank him. I hope that maybe, one day, he'll come across the book, and understand how much his selflessness mean to me. He saved my life. More than just helping my body fight the illness, he gave me a second chance to live fully. I was a bit lost before... Actually, I was completely lost. He gave me a chance to find my way. And that's something I will never, ever forget. If you're listening to this this, sir, thank you. From the bottom of my heart. Thank you.'

There was an odd stillness in the studio, a weird sort of solemnity, as Farao's words sank in around them.

'Thank you, Farao,' Craig eventually said, his voice a little lower than it had been before, 'for joining us today. It's been a pleasure talking to you. For all of our listeners, we're giving away ten signed copies of *The Long Way Home*, so don't miss out on your chance to get your hands on one! How can people enter, Carrie?'

'All you have to do is answer this question: how many Dhawan brothers are there? Two, three, or four? And text your answer to seven-eight-nine-seven-eight-nine. Texts cost one pound fifty, plus your standard network charges. Or enter for free by posting your answer on our Facebook page. Winners will be selected at the top of the hour and receive a signed copy of Farao Dhawan's book, *The Long Way Home*! Coming up next, we have Colton Smiles' "Drowning". We'll be back after the break.'

Farao smiled to himself as the first notes of the song resonated in his headphones. The producer signalled from behind the glass panel, and both Craig and Carrie took off their own headsets. Farao copied them.

'Thanks, mate,' Craig said, shaking Farao's hand. 'It was nice to meet you! Can we have a quick selfie for social media?'

They posed together for a picture, the producer soon signalling that it was time for the hosts to get back into their seats.

'Good luck with everything,' Carrie said, walking back to her station, as the young assistant appeared to escort Farao back out of the studio.

The others were still waiting in the corridor, and the look on their faces told Farao they'd been listening to the interview. Orson just wrapped an arm around Farao's shoulders and ruffled his hair, something that, in a different life, Farao had found incredibly annoying. It didn't bother him so much anymore.

'Well done, little bro.'

'Thanks, Orson.'

They started towards the exit.

'Look at you, such a celebrity!' Orson continued. 'How long do you think it'll be till someone buys the rights to make a movie out of it? Then I can finally retire!'

'Yeah,' Kendrik scoffed, 'because you work *so hard* you really need a break. You forget that now we work together I can see that all you do at the shop is flirt with customers…'

'My dear brother,' Orson declared, leading the way across the car park, 'if I don't want my skills to atrophy, I have to keep practicing.

And you really could do with taking a leaf out of my book, if you want my opinion…'

'I don't, thanks.' Kendrik rolled his eyes. 'You keep doing you, and I'll keep doing me.'

'Yep,' Orson chuckled, winking at Farao. 'If you keep refusing my help, I guess you'll just have to keep doing yourself…'

'Oh, piss off…' Kendrik grumbled.

Orson opened the car door and stepped aside to let Farao in.

'Terran, back me up here,' Orson pleaded. 'Isn't everything better when you have an active sex life?'

'Don't drag me into this,' Terran called out, sliding in behind the wheel, Juliette taking her place in the passenger seat.

'You've got to admit, though,' Orson kept going, 'you're much happier since you're no longer celibate, am I right?'

'Orson…' Terran warned, turning the key in the ignition.

'See, Ken?' Orson tapped Kendrik on the arm. 'All that pent-up energy needs an outlet, otherwise you'll end up a bitter, grumpy fuck like our dear older brother was for a while.'

Farao caught Juliette's eyes in the rear-view mirror and they exchanged a smile.

'Ok, moving on.' Terran rolled his eyes and pulled out of the parking lot onto the busy street.

'He wasn't a bitter, grumpy fuck because he wasn't getting any,' Kendrik argued, 'he was a bitter, grumpy fuck because he didn't know how to let his hair down. There's a difference.'

'Oy.' Terran raised his voice, as Juliette stifled a giggle. 'I'm sitting *right here!*'

'True.' Orson nodded, ignoring Terran. 'Juliette definitely helped him loosen up.'

'Maybe all I need is a Juliette of my own…' Kendrik shrugged.

'Let's not get ahead of ourselves, shall we?' Orson raised his hands. 'Monogamy doesn't have to be the answer. No offence, Juliette,' he added as an afterthought, patting her on the shoulder.

'None taken.' She smiled at him.

'Guys...' Terran groaned. 'Will you just give it a rest for five minutes, *please?*' Then, after a moment, stopping the car at a red light, he leaned in towards Juliette and said quietly, 'Though, for what it's worth, my life *is* much happier with you in it.'

'Oh, I know.' Juliette threw him a playful grin. She leant over towards him, caressing his cheek, and gave him a kiss. 'And the feeling's very much mutual.'

'See,' Orson exclaimed. 'I rest my case!'

'Dude, if anything, this proves *my* point,' Kendrik groaned.

Terran sighed. 'Oh, will you two just *shut up.*'

Farao listened quietly, a smile playing on his lips. He watched Terran and Juliette in the front seats share half-amused, half-exasperated looks at the other two's pointless bickering. But Farao wasn't fooled—he knew they were as entertained as he was.

This, Farao thought. *This feels like home.* And it was the absolute best feeling in the world.

Chapter 75
Terran

Terran hopped into the car as Farao settled into the passenger seat, hugging his backpack and closing the door behind him. The Monday morning air around them was warm, full of the flowery smells of June.

'Got everything?' Terran asked as he started the engine, rolling his window halfway down.

'I think so.' Farao glanced into his bag and sighed. 'It's not like I need much anyway.'

As the end of the school term loomed nearer, Farao had surprised them all by insisting on revising for his A-levels and sitting his exams. For the first time in their life, it was Terran who had tried to convince Farao to delay it another year, and Farao who argued in favour of doing the work and getting it over with. They'd never seen Farao so intent on completing his school work before.

Terran set the car off onto the street, glancing at the time on the dashboard briefly, reassuring himself they weren't late. They drove for a few moments without talking, Farao fiddling with the radio dials, finally settling on one that was playing a slow ballad Terran didn't recognise. Farao started singing softly along.

'By the way, where were you yesterday afternoon?' Terran said as he peered ahead, slowing down before a roundabout. 'I thought you wanted to cram in some last minute revision.'

Farao exhaled, readjusting his bag on his lap. 'I went to see Mel.'

'Oh.' Terran glanced at him. 'One of the girls you were talking to?'

'That's the one.' Farao nodded.

'Wait, what happened to the other one? Sarah, was it?'

'Serena,' Farao sighed, and turned towards Terran. 'Well, you know how I was out Friday night?'

Terran nodded—he and Kendrik had wondered where Farao had gone that evening, when he'd left the house looking unusually sharp. Orson had clearly known all about it, but refused to spill the beans.

'Well... Serena and I went on a date.' Farao grimaced.

'Wait, Serena? Or Mel?' Terran frowned.

Farao smiled. 'Friday was Serena. She texted me last week checking in on how I was doing, and I asked if she wanted to meet for a coffee or something. And...' Farao shook his head. 'It turns out we have *nothing* in common. Longest two hours of my life.'

'Really?' Terran frowned.

'Yep.' Farao grinned. 'I spent so long thinking about her, wondering what it'd be like going out with her... I guess I'd forgotten how much of that was all in my head. Because we'd never really spoken to each other before that, you know?'

'Yeah, I guess.' Terran nodded.

'And the whole time I was with her I kept thinking, *why is this so hard?* I just couldn't find anything to say. And neither could she, it seemed like… So we sort of… I don't know… Left it there, I guess. It was so awkward, I think we were both a little relieved when the date ended.' Farao laughed.

Terran made a face. 'Doesn't sound good.'

'Nah, it wasn't.' Farao shook his head again. 'But it's ok. I guess if it hadn't happened I would always have been wondering whether or not it would have worked…'

Farao fell silent for a minute, gazing out of the window.

'You know the funniest thing?' Farao eventually said, his eyes still out on the London streets. 'When I got home after that, all I could think about was that I'd spent so much time with Mel and it'd never felt like effort. It was always so easy hanging out with her, like neither of us had to try so hard. At the time, it'd made me believe I was good with girls, I think.' Farao let out a loud breath and ran his fingers through his hair. 'It hadn't even occurred to me that it wasn't about me at all. It was about her, about Mel, and how good we were together.'

Terran signalled to turn left and waited for the car ahead of them to move.

'And?' he prompted.

'Well, I guess it took all this for me to realise it *was* Mel all along…' Farao smiled. 'So, the next day I tried apologising to her. Tried texting and calling her. She totally ignored me, which I can't really blame her for. Not after I turned her down at the hospital. She's got pride, Mel…' Farao paused and smiled to himself. 'But I thought if Juliette could forgive you after all the crap *you* pulled, maybe there was hope for me, too… So, yesterday, I showed up at her house. Completely uninvited. Thinking if she wasn't going to change her mind I might as well get closure on it, face to face.'

'Ballsy move.'

'Yeah... Ballsy... Desperate... Whatever you want to call it.' Farao laughed. 'She wouldn't even come to the door at first. I was sitting by her front door for an hour before she agreed to hear me out. And all that while her mum was bringing me tea and biscuits, it was actually pretty funny.'

They were almost at the school gates now, and Terran slowed down, not wanting to rush the end of Farao's story. At the very back of his thoughts, the distant memory of another car ride with Farao, at the beginning of the school year, back when they barely said ten words to each other without arguing, popped into his mind's eye. The recollection made him smile.

'Anyway, I told her I never meant to hurt her feelings... That I'd been an idiot, really... That I didn't see it before, and it'd taken me a long detour to get there and make me realise I missed her. Told her I wanted to be with her. Properly.'

Terran was impressed. 'How did that go down?'

'Well, not great at first, obviously. But she listened, at least. I had to do a fair bit of grovelling to convince her I was serious about it.' Farao gave him a satisfied smile. 'But she came round in the end. We're going out this weekend, when both of us are done with exams. Turns out honesty *is* the best policy after all.'

'Who would have thought...' Terran mused, watching as the crowd milled around outside the school building.

'I guess after everything that happened, admitting how wrong I'd been and asking for her forgiveness didn't seem so scary anymore.' Then he added, almost to himself, 'A lot of things aren't so scary anymore...'

Terran looked at Farao and nodded again. He parked the car and Farao got out.

'Are you ready?' he asked, gesturing to the gates.

'As ready as I'll ever be,' Farao said, and with a last wave at Terran, he made his way slowly through the gates and into the main building to face his exams.

Terran watched him go, noticing that many of the students were gaping at Farao as he passed, some of them clicking a picture of him from a distance. Farao paid them no attention. His book had gone viral so quickly, and weeks later, the story was still trending all over the internet. Kendrik, Orson and Terran had watched Farao handle it all expertly, amazed at the poise he showed. Terran had never felt more proud in his entire life.

How mad was it, Terran thought, that not so long ago they knew so little of each other, sharing barely more than living quarters? *And now...* Now everything had changed, and for the better. He smiled to himself as he turned on the ignition. For once, he knew without the shadow of a doubt that if his parents could see them now, they'd be proud, too.

Epilogue

The four men stood around the blazing funeral pyre before them. They were all wearing white, the colour of grief in this part of the world. To one side, the pandit dressed in saffron-coloured robes was muttering prayers. He was holding his arm high above him and swinging a long metal chain back and forth, at the end of which was attached a fuming *haandi*, a handmade earthen pot filled with burning charcoal and sandalwood incense.

'*Ram nam satya hai... Ram nam satya hai...*' the priest was intoning in rumbling murmurs.

They had lit the pyre on a stone platform by the river Ganges in Haridwar, India, where they were to scatter the departed's ashes. The air was filled with the smoke from the fire, mixed with the aromas of spiced street food and cow dung littering the alleyways for miles around them. The river was gushing past, unperturbed by the human activity buzzing on the solid ground of its banks. The crowd in the streets was going about its business, quite oblivious to the people bathing in the freezing cold holy waters and those who were holding their own funerals a short distance from each other.

The pandit finished his prayers and walked to each of the four men in white, placing a streak of red on their foreheads and resting a hand on the top of their heads, muttering a final mantra under his breath as he did so. He brought his hands together in prayer and inclined his head to them. A second later, he was gone, and the four men found themselves standing side by side by the burning pile of logs. They stood there for a long time in silence, until the flames had shortened and the logs on the pyre had blackened to coal.

Eventually, they moved as one towards the river, taking a seat on the stone edge of the platform, their feet dangling above the rushing water.

'He was always there for us,' Terran said, his gaze out on the opposite river bank.

The others nodded, and Terran turned to glance at the funeral pyre, on which Amit's body had been consumed by the flames. Twelve years had passed since the year that had changed their lives. The year that had seen Terran, Kendrik, Orson and Farao Dhawan go through the seven hells together and emerge back victorious, stronger than ever. The year that was to set the next decade as the happiest time of their lives. It hadn't always been easy, because life never was a series of smooth rides, but they had embraced it greedily, with a renewed appetite for adventure.

They had gone into business together, taking over the music shop where Orson had once been the star employee, a venture which Amit had heavily invested in, despite their protests. Orson and Farao ran music classes on the first floor, whilst Terran handled customers and Kendrik managed their marketing and their admin.

They had travelled the world together. They had laughed and cried together. They had watched each other grow.

They had taken turns sitting with Farao on the countless occasions he'd had to be checked up at the hospital, and waiting with him to hear the doctors say his condition was still, thankfully, under control.

They had been best men at Terran's wedding to Juliette, just after the happy couple had moved into a small terraced house a few streets away from their Battersea family home.

They had helped Kendrik move when he met Sofia, the woman he wanted to settle down with, leaving Orson and Farao to share their parents' house.

They had waited impatiently in yet another hospital corridor when Juliette went into labour, until they knew everything was fine. Both times.

They had celebrated the birth of Kendrik's three children with the same excitement.

Orson and Farao had played favourite uncles to their nieces and nephews on many an occasion, filling their parents' old house with screams of joy and laughter.

They had been there for each other, at every step of the way.

And they had made this journey together, after Amit had passed away, to fulfil his last wish of being cremated in India, where his own ancestors' ashes had been dispersed into the river Ganges.

'We should have brought the tequila,' Kendrik said.

'Ask, and it shall be granted…' Orson exclaimed with a grin, pulling a sealed bottle and four small plastic tumblers from his bag. 'Ta-dah!'

They all smiled.

'Got it at the airport,' Orson said, unscrewing the bottle and pouring the brown liquid in each of the tumblers.

They each took a glass and sat in companionable silence for a little while longer.

'It's been quite a ride, hasn't it?' Terran was the first one to speak.

'It really has.' Kendrik nodded.

Orson grinned a mischievous grin. 'It's not over yet!'

The other three exchanged a glance, because that very look on their brother's face never boded well.

'Please tell me you haven't planned anything crazy for the rest of our trip?' Kendrik sighed.

'Crazy?' Orson exclaimed in mock outrage. 'Me? I'm offended you would even suggest such a thing!'

'Yeah.' Farao smirked. 'Because you're usually the reasonable one in our clan.'

'Do what you want,' Terran chimed in, 'but if anything happens, *you're* the one who'll have to explain it to Juliette…'

'Come on, guys,' Orson cried out. 'When have I *ever* failed you? I'm not the type to lead you astray!'

'Really? What was Mexico, then?' Kendrik rolled his eyes, and Farao snorted.

'Mexico was different, Kendrik,' Orson said calmly, 'Mexico was Terran's bachelor party trip! It had to be legendary!'

'And Dubai?' Terran piped up.

'Dubai was a celebration of Kendrik finally leaving the nest, moving in with Sofia, an actual, real, flesh-and-blood woman. Surely that was worth a good party!'

'Yeah…' Kendrik mumbled, 'Obviously you weren't the one who had to go back and explain the fucking *tattoo*…'

'You lose the bet, you have to pay up, that was the deal!' Orson smiled at Kendrik's sullen expression. 'And she got over it in the end, didn't she? No harm done!'

'At least I settled down, unlike *you*…' Kendrik grumbled.

'My dear brother, for you it's settling down, for me it's locking myself up and throwing away the key. The logic of it just doesn't add up!'

'You could at least have tried not to rope Farao into your lifestyle,' Terran said calmly, though he knew well where the conversation was headed.

'Guys, I wasn't roped into *anything*, ok?' Farao lifted his hands up in defence. 'I'm happy the way things are.'

'What happened with Hannah? I thought that was going well?' Terran asked.

'Same as usual…' Farao sighed. 'She wanted kids.'

The others simply nodded. They knew of their brother's insistence that he would never pass on his medical affliction to another human being.

'Shame…' Kendrik said, giving Farao's shoulder a squeeze.

'It is what it is…' Farao sighed. 'It's fine.'

A young girl in rags walked up to them, holding an even younger boy by the hand. They had dirty faces, their bare feet dusty and calloused, their hair matted to their little heads. The little girl handed each of the brothers a small orange marigold, which they took. The young boy, who couldn't have been much more than three, gave them a toothy grin and held out a filthy palm.

'Nothing's ever free, is it…' Kendrik rolled his eyes as Orson placed five thousand rupees in the little boy's outstretched hand.

They watched the children's eyes open wide with wonder and surprise, before they turned around and ran off.

'Funny how things turn out,' Terran said, and they knew by the tremor in his voice that the two children reminded him of his own.

'A toast,' Farao said, lifting his glass into the air. 'To Amit, who did more for our family than anyone ever did.'

'To Amit,' the others said in unison, and they drank the contents of their tumblers in one go.

'And…' Orson filled their glasses again. 'To us. To this incredible ride called life. To everything we've been through, and everything that is yet to come. To us,' he said again, raising his tumbler. 'The Dhawan brothers.'

They all raised their glass and repeated solemnly:

'The Dhawan brothers.'

The End.

Acknowledgements

This book, like my first one, has been many years in the making. And, like my first one, it couldn't have seen the light of day without the support of some incredible human beings.

Thank you to my wonderful editor, Vicky, who was the first person to meet the brothers and whose support in making each draft more polished has been invaluable.

Thank you also to Emma and Ellie for doing such an incredible job on the final proofread.

Huge thanks to all of you in the Bookstagram community who have showered me with grace and kindness, especially when I struggled to keep in touch consistently.

A special thank you to Jess, Juliane, Lauren, and Tara for your friendship —I may not have met all of you in person yet, but your presence in my life has made being on this writing journey so much more enjoyable.

To my wonderful team of ARC readers: THANK YOU. The logistics of publishing a book can sometimes be daunting, but you all have made this part of the process so much smoother and kinder than it otherwise could have been.

To my soul sisters—Claire, Klaudia, and Thalia. Thank you. For being here, for being you, for everything.

Last but by no means least: to you, dear reader, thank you. From the bottom of my heart: thank you. Thank you for reading this book, thank you for choosing to spend your precious time supporting me and my work. I'm so incredibly grateful.

Lucie Ataya

A Note From The Author

This second edition of *The Dhawan Brothers* came rather unexpectedly when Amazon KDP suddenly terminated my account with no notice and little in way of an explanation.

However, what might have felt, once upon a time, like a blow to my confidence and my writing endeavours, turned out to be a real test of how far I've come.

Not so long ago, something like this would have felt stressful and frustrating. But I surprised myself with how grounded I managed to be throughout the entire incident. *Something good is coming out of this*, a voice within me kept saying. And so it has. Because the support I received throughout my battle to try to get out of Amazon KDP jail was more incredible and caring than I could have anticipated.

I feel so grateful to each and every one of you who reached out during that time. Your support and kindness have meant more than I think you realise.

I first self-published through Amazon KDP because it was the easiest and cheapest way to get my work out there. I am and always will be grateful to the platform for allowing me to get past that first hurdle of releasing my books into the world.

In many ways, I'm also grateful for the automated, robotic, unempathetic process Amazon KDP support put me through when I tried to understand the termination. It very quickly felt like begging an abusive ex-partner to take you back, after they dumped you for no reason. As someone who's been in that very position in the past—possibly more times than I'd care to admit—this didn't sit well with me. Gone is the time where I'd allow anyone to treat me with such disregard and unkindness. I'd choose to start over on my own every single time. This incident showed me how much I've grown. And that, I know, is priceless.

So here's to old chapters and new beginnings. Here's to community rallying together and supporting each other in the good and the not-so-good moments. Here's *The Dhawan Brothers'* second lease on life. Here's to finally choosing myself—every. Single. *Fucking*. Time.

Lucie x

Please leave a review!

Reviews greatly improve the chances of success of any book and are a great way for you to support Independently published authors.

It helps other readers find the book, and know what they can expect from it.

It really, *truly* makes a difference!

If you enjoyed reading *The Dhawan Brothers*

please, *please,* **please** take a moment to post a review on the site where you purchased the book and on Goodreads.

Lucie Ataya

About the Author

Lucie Ataya grew up in Tours, France where her passion for writing and her love for the English language were born.

She studied modern languages, took a random detour through Radford, Virginia, in the US and moved to England to complete a Masters' Degree in Sociology at the University of Bristol. She now lives in London, England, with her Cocker Spaniel Veer and her Burmese cat Leela.

Lucie has worn many hats in her life—amongst others: Yoga teacher, blogger, book editor, professional BETA reader, project manager, energy healing practitioner… Some labels have stuck, some haven't, but her love of writing and storytelling has been one of the very few things that has stood the test of time.

When she's not writing, working at her day job for a B-Corp in the Tech industry, or obsessively cramming for a new creative project, Lucie can be spotted walking with Veer, trialing independent coffee shops, or indulging in crafty projects.

Her first novel, *No Pain, No Game*, is a dystopian thriller, and was published in 2020.

Shortly after, in April 2021, seeing a need for more content to help independent authors on their journey, she released *Passing It Forward,* a free non-fiction digital guide aimed to help indie authors navigate the process of self-publishing and book promotion.

Find out more at https://www.lucieataya.com

Or on Instagram: @lucieataya

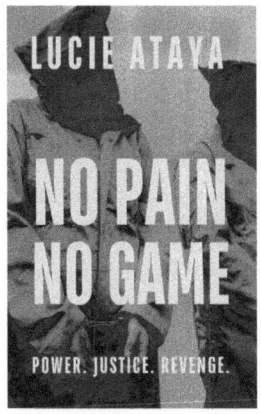

By The Same Author

What would it take for you to endorse human torture?

What if it were for the greater good?

...Are you sure?

In this alternate version of modern-day Britain, sky-high crime rates and a state of economic crisis mean people live in a climate of fear – while yearning for change, hope and justice.

To tackle the nation's prison overcrowding issue, Sean Cravanaugh, a fearsome television magnate, has devised a radical and controversial solution: a live televised show, pitching selected convicted criminals against one another in a series of dangerous and painful challenges, a fight for their lives and a rare chance at freedom.

In the world of 'No Pain, No Game', Sean Cravanaugh decides who lives or dies. With his razor-sharp instincts for deciphering and manipulating people, he takes us on a journey bound to make us question our own sense of morality.

No Pain, No Game follows the intertwined paths and struggles of those who find themselves, willingly or forcefully, entangled in the show. They lead us into a world of pain and trickery, where nothing and no one truly is the way they seem. Can they cope with the nation's anger and hatred, standing as they do in the eye of the storm?

Who will lose everything, and who will come out unscathed?

Visit Amazon now, or scan the code below to get your copy of *No Pain, No Game* today!

Turn over for an extract of Lucie Ataya's

No Pain, No Game

Published in 2020

Lucie Ataya

NO PAIN
NO GAME

Lucie Ataya

Prologue

The little girl pulled the curtain aside and watched through the living-room window as police cars rushed down the street, stopping abruptly in front of their house. The cars' lights sent red and blue rays flashing all around them, bursting through the darkness, illuminating the sleeping street, reminding her of a firework display she had once seen with her father.

Men and women in uniform poured out of the vehicles, rushing into the front garden, marching in her direction.

The little girl glanced back over her shoulder. Her father was slouched against the doorframe between the entrance hall and the living room, his head in his hands, sobbing. She went to him, her stuffed rabbit hanging from her clenched fist. She knelt down next to him, placing her hand on his shaking shoulder. She did not quite know what to say, so she said nothing. When he looked up at her, his eyes were full of tears. She rubbed his arm gently, cocking her head to one side. He brought one hand to her face and cupped her cheek, with such love and tenderness that she felt maybe everything would be alright after all. He had always protected her. For so long it had been just the two of them against the world, surely this time again he would make it all ok. She gave him a smile, and he looked at her sadly. He kissed the top of her head. It was a gesture he had made so many times before, except this time it felt a bit different. She did not know why.

Outside, the pack of strangers was growing louder and more impatient by the second. They stormed up the short walkway to the house and pounded persistently on the front door. Someone was shouting something, though the little girl could not understand exactly what they were saying. She looked at the door, and turned to her father again, unsure what to do. But her daddy was looking only at her, watching her face in silence, tears rolling down his cheeks. That was when she felt scared too, because the look on her father's face was not the look of one who would make everything ok. He looked afraid, scared like she had never seen him before. She gripped his arm tightly, wishing for some reassurance. She did not understand what was going on. Everything felt different and strange.

Before either of them could make another move, the front door burst open with an ear-shattering sound and troops of people carrying guns stormed in, shouting and screaming and stomping their feet. The girl recoiled, curling herself up into a ball against her trembling father, her fingers squeezing his limp hand.

The police were all over the house now, zooming in and out of every room, up and down the stairs, gathering eventually in the little kitchen, from where the little girl could hear them talking animatedly. She buried her face in her father's stained, wet shirt, hoping that when she emerged the strangers would have left and everything would have gone back to normal.

But that did not happen. Two strong arms grabbed hold of her and tried to pull her away from her father. She kicked and screamed and held on tight to her father's hand. He was squeezing her fingers in his palm now, but two men were on him, pinning him forcefully to the ground, pulling him away from her, forcing both his fists behind his back. The girl called out for him, terrified. Her father was shouting her name and all she wanted was to join him, to hide in his arms until all of this was over. The policemen surrounding her father were beating him with large black sticks, and the little girl screamed for them to stop, as loud as she could, louder than she had ever screamed in her life. A moment later her father stopped calling out her name. In fact, he had stopped moving altogether, and was lying still, facedown on the hardwood floor. The little girl struggled, craning her neck to get a glimpse of her father's face. His forehead and cheeks were bathed in red. He appeared to be asleep, just like her mummy was, on the kitchen floor. The little girl thought this an odd time for either of them to go to sleep, when so many people were in their home and she felt so alone and scared.

Two policemen dragged her father away, and she watched them disappear through the front door. She collapsed on the living room floor, her shaking hands clasped around her stuffed rabbit's ears. She felt suddenly very tired, exhausted by the effort of trying to understand all these strange things happening around her. The pain and terror were too much for her to comprehend, and though she willed herself to stay awake, she could feel her eyelids growing heavier and heavier.

The last thing she was somewhat aware of was that she could see people hunched around her mother's body. She could almost glimpse the dark, velvety, crimson liquid surrounding her mother's head like a halo on the white tiles of the kitchen floor.

And then, a moment later, she drifted into nothingness, and everything around her disappeared.

Lucie Ataya

Fifteen Years Later

Lucie Ataya

Chapter 1

Shauna Mullighan

With just a few minutes to go before the live broadcast, the news studio was buzzing with activity. Shauna was sitting at her desk, at the ready. From her vantage point, she observed the incessant ballet of the members of the crew, rushing around as they attended last minute items ahead of the night's programme. In her two decades in the news industry, Shauna's favourite moment had always been the countdown to the live evening broadcast, whether she had been assisting in the background early in her career, or later as she had moved to the other side of the camera.

There was something intense about the chaos that preceded the well-organised and polished show the public eventually saw. Looking at the evening news, the glossy well-lit studio and the presenters' flawless appearance, one could not have guessed the frenzy that had been going on until the very last moment to build such a perfect facade. Being part of this well-oiled act of deception always made Shauna feel like she was privy to a secret very few could fathom. It gave her goosebumps every time.

She glanced at the giant digital clock on the wall in front of her, behind the cameras. The countdown to the start of the programme showed they had a little over three minutes to go. At the far end of the desk, the evening's two guests had already been settled down, their faces matte with the excess makeup they all had to wear. Neither of them was talking.

Shauna looked down at her notes and reviewed her headlines. Or, she thought, 'headline', in the singular. The one and only topic on which the country had focused for a long time now was their sole discussion point for the evening. She sighed audibly, shaking her head, like she always did when she pondered how exactly they had all got in this situation.

It had been the longest way coming, but eventually they had all paid the price for years of bad decision making. She wished she could pin it all on the government, but she knew too well that it was not true. A decade ago, mounting tension between the nation and its mainland allies had forced the government to offer the country its very own referendum. The people had rejoiced at the opportunity, so loudly and so openly that the noise of their contentment had covered the lobbying and brainwashing orchestrated by radical parties and organisations to influence their votes.

Shauna often said that one had to call it what it was. It had been a real shambles, and their great country had become a laughing matter for all of their neighbours, friends and foes alike. Politicians kept changing sides, contradicting each other, their own parties and, more often than not, themselves. Personalities from all walks of life had an opinion. It had become impossible for anyone to make out the truth from lies, the results of legitimate surveys from the unfounded threats of another world war.

A year after the referendum's announcement, the people expressed themselves and, by doing so, had proven many a sociologist's point by showing that not only could the masses be manipulated into believing anything, but that whoever caught the public's attention could influence the most crucial of national events.

The country had voted. And their choice was to sever their ties with the international coalition their country had been a leader in for well over half a century.

It had all gone downhill from there, in Shauna's opinion. It had taken years for the new political leaders to negotiate the nation's exit strategy. These had been dark times of division, uncertainty and failure, but it was nothing compared to what history still had in store for them.

'Live in one minute,' the producer announced in Shauna's earpiece.

She jumped and straightened on her seat, adjusting the papers in front of her and settling her face in what had come to be her live-television facial expression.

'Five... Four... Three...' The producer chanted, 'Two.... One... And we're live!'

'Good Evening, I'm Shauna Mullighan and you're watching the evening news on LiveTV2. The plan to which the Prime Minister gave his official consent a few weeks ago, designed to tackle the long-standing issue of the country's off-the-charts criminal rates and prison overcrowding, is finally due to launch tomorrow. The proposal was the brainchild of former Minister for Internal Affairs Valery Swan and entertainment tycoon and Channel55 CEO Sean Cravanaugh, and it has divided opinions ever since the idea was first put on the table. In tonight's edition we will review what little we know of the new plan and the reasons why it has caused so much controversy.'

Shauna turned to one side, and the cameras shifted, widening their angle to include an impeccably dressed young man sitting further down the long desk.

'Matthew Dalston, you're our Senior Economics and Social Affairs analyst here at LiveTV2. Before we go into further details about this new plan, can you remind our viewers of the chain of events which brought this about?'

'Of course, Shauna,' Matthew smiled. 'One of the challenges our government faced after the breakup with its allies was the way in which the prison staff unions took advantage of the disruption to push for jobs and salary increases.'

The images on the screen behind them shifted to display silent footage recorded at the time.

'The government failed to peacefully resolve the situation,' Matthew Dalston continued, 'and within weeks, all prison staff across the country went on general strike. Prison inmates were left unattended for days on end until, one fine day, prisoners in the country's leading penitentiary establishment managed a mass escape. The first one of that scale in the history of our nation. Prisoners across the country followed suit and managed their own escape. By the time prison staff returned to their posts and police forces were deployed, the damage had already been done. Crime rates rocketed, setting the country on a path that was beyond repair.'

'Thank you, Matthew,' Shauna shifted back to face the main camera, 'and now let's look at the mysterious new plan aimed to solve the nation's troubles. Our correspondent James Carson is live from the capital. Over to you, James.'

Shauna kept looking straight at the camera. From the corner of her eye she saw Matthew Dalston quietly stand up and leave the studio. She waited for the image on the screen to split, allocating half of the space to her other colleague. James was standing rigidly on the spot, gripping a large and fluffy-headed microphone. A few seconds elapsed before he started speaking, as always with live connections. Shauna could never quite pinpoint why, but this handful of silent moments, where she had to stare fixedly at the camera, always made her want to giggle.

'Thank you, Shauna. I am standing here in front the Cradle Arena in the capital, which is where this new plan is due to be put into action tomorrow evening.'

The images on the screen shifted to show footage from their archives, illustrating James's commentary.

'Three years ago, the Prime Minister received the shocking results of a report by the NHRA, the National Human Rights Association, revealing that every single penitentiary establishment in the country was dangerously over-crowded. This meant the government had to release hundreds of convicts with minor offences into the streets each year for lack of space to keep them behind bars.'

The screen shifted to a colourful animated graph.

'We have also seen over the last few years a major rise in public discontentment,' James continued, 'causing the biggest exodus in the history of our country, with an immediate snowball effect on our economy.'

The graphs faded into footage of the Prime Minister, shown exiting his car and walking swiftly up the steps to the government's headquarters.

'Two years ago the Prime Minister put together a crisis cell and, of all suggestions on the table, the plan by Valery Swan and Sean Cravanaugh was designated to be put into action. Now,' James cleared his throat, 'this plan is controversial, to say the least, as it comes in the form of a competition, called 'No Pain, No Game', which is to be broadcasted live on television. Convicts serving a life sentence, or awaiting death penalty have been given the opportunity to sign up. The winner will see their sentence immediately waived and will be entitled to any cash made during the competition. The losers on the other hand, will be executed...'

The image refocused on James' somewhat incredulous expression.

'The exact rules of the game remain a mystery,' the camera spun around to reveal the crowd behind James. 'I'm standing here in front of the Cradle Arena where the opening ceremony will be aired live on Channel55 tomorrow evening. This is James Carson, live from the capital for LiveTV2. Back to you, Shauna.'

James' face disappeared as the camera zoned back in on Shauna, who had taken a seat with the night's guests.

'I am joined in the studio tonight by National Human Rights Association spokesperson Sarah Khan and Professor of Modern Economics Patrick Gregson. Sarah, you were involved in the original NHRA report commissioned by the Prime Minister, is that correct?'

Sarah Khan sat upright on her chair, trying her best to appear confident. To a trained eye like Shauna's, the young woman's nerves were obvious. She felt vaguely sympathetic towards her.

'That's right. I was the main project coordinator for the report,' Sarah Khan responded with defiance, betraying her apprehension at tackling the subject.

'Did you have any idea at the time that the report would lead to such a controversial solution?'

'Absolutely not,' Sarah said firmly, 'and I would by no means call this a *solution*,' she emphasised the last word derisively, her hands forming imaginary air quotes by the sides of her face. 'Suggestions in the report pointed towards the creation of more penitentiary establishments and increases in police forces on the streets. This lunatic idea of solving prison overcrowding through a televised game was most definitely *not* ours.'

'Of course, Sarah, and this is the position that the NHRA has been reaffirming ever since the proposal has been put forward. However, fresh controversy was sparked when Josh Carter, the Head of the NHRA, announced he will be a judge on the show.'

Shauna used the woman's first name deliberately, as if addressing a child, and she could see Sarah's face flicker with annoyance each time. The young woman sat a little straighter on her seat, a sure and probably unconscious sign, Shauna knew, that she was trying to make herself seem more assertive and in control than she actually felt.

'This is not an endorsement of the whole concept or premise of the plan. Mr Carter has been very clear since the announcement was made that he only agreed to be on the panel because he felt responsible for the ridiculous turn of events our report triggered.'

Shauna paused for a moment after Sarah finished talking, glancing knowingly at the camera, her eyebrows raised. This way of looking intently at the camera had become her trademark, as if she were exchanging some sort of in-joke with the audience. People loved that about her, or so their consumer polls said. She could not have made it plainer that she found Sarah's argument risible. Sarah's lips parted but Shauna knew better than to allow her to continue talking. She turned towards the second guest.

'Right,' she concluded with a tone that left no room for further discussion. 'Professor Gregson, you have been supportive of the 'No Pain, No Game' concept. I can't say that this has been a popular view amongst the people we have interviewed on our programme.'

Patrick Gregson was a well-kept man in his early forties, with an undeniable twinkle of charm in his manner that most likely fuelled the fantasies of more than one of his students.

'Certainly, Shauna,' he threw her a casual and irresistible smile. 'Something I often tell my students is that the measures taken to solve a problem have to be proportionate to the extent of the problem you are facing. With the degradation of the living conditions in our country and the major rise in criminal activity, we simply cannot get the nation back on track with flaky measures. Because the situation is so drastic, and none of the generic solutions worked, the government had to think out of the box. I agree with Miss Khan here, in that 'No Pain, No Game' is the most insane, loony idea our government has sponsored to tackle our horrendous criminal rates. Where I disagree, however, is that I believe only an insane solution can allow us to put an end to such an insane problem.'

'So you don't believe that the Prime Minister had a choice in the matter?' Shauna asked, ignoring Sarah's expression of incredulous outrage.

'Not anymore,' Patrick Gregson shook his head. 'Whether this new plan is the way forward, only time will tell, but at this stage it's worth a try.'

'Indeed. Looking at the panel of judges, alongside Josh Carter we'll have…' Shauna looked down at her notes, 'the founders of the plan, Valery Swan and Sean Cravanaugh, and pop star singer Camilla. Sarah, what do think of this panel?'

Sarah Khan appeared taken aback at being drawn back into the discussion and it took her a couple of seconds to regain her composure.

'Well,' she articulated slowly, 'I'm not sure how Camilla's nomination came about. This doesn't seem to be her natural area of expertise.'

'I can only agree', Patrick Gregson nodded. 'Camilla isn't someone people would have expected to take part in such a scheme. She's mostly known as a bubblegum pop star for teenage girls,' he chuckled, as though he thought it to be the most ludicrous profession in the world. 'I don't care one bit for her music, but my niece is one of her biggest fans! My guess, which is as good as any at this stage, is that Camilla is there to help bring a lighter touch to what could otherwise quickly become a very heavy and unglamorous subject matter.'

'Thank you both for joining us tonight,' Shauna turned back to stare directly at the camera. 'All will be revealed tomorrow. Stay tuned for more analysis on LiveTV2 as we will discuss the events in our evening edition. This was Shauna Mullighan, bringing you the latest news on LiveTV2. Goodnight.'

Chapter 2

Sean Cravanaugh

S ean Cravanaugh was standing in the middle of the stage, which he had requested to be positioned right at the centre of the Cradle. He was looking up around him, turning slowly to take in the entirety of the arena, imagining what it would look like filled with thousands of his fellow citizens screaming and clapping their excitement.

When he and Valery Swan had first put their idea forward to the Prime Minister, a very, very long silence had followed their presentation. Derren Clarke, who was serving his second term as the country's leader, was looking exhausted and desperate. On that very day, he explained to both of them, he had received a final warning from the United Nations that there would be no more external help and that he was now to be left to his own devices to either salvage the situation or to finish burning the country down to the ground completely.

'Prime Minister, I understand you may be sceptical, but we are confident this will not only solve prison-crowding issues and lower crime rates, but also improve public morale and work wonders for your re-election campaign.'

Derren Clarke looked at Sean warily and rubbed his eyes with his thumb and index finger, as if to force the words he was hearing to fully sink in.

'This is quite a drastic approach, to say the least,' he finally said.

'Absolutely,' Valery intervened, 'and we are conscious of that. I must, however, beg you to consider it seriously.'

Derren Clarke stared at them from behind his desk. The dark circles under his eyes made him seem much older than he was. He sighed before sitting back down in his chair and leaning in towards them, his hands clasped on the wooden desk in front of him.

'Ok,' he finally conceded, 'run me through it one more time.'

Sean worked hard to suppress a smile. Nothing better than a desperate man to sign off on the most desperate of measures.

'We will select a hundred life sentence or death penalty convicts for the show. Convicts who aren't selected for the competition will be either executed, if they are awaiting death-row, or transferred to Cartford Hill in the North of the country, where they will be, shall we say, left to their own devices.'

'What does this mean exactly?' the Prime Minister asked.

'Off the record, sir, they will be left to die. At some stage, Cartford Hill may very well suffer from a disastrous incident. After all, gas leaks or fire breakouts are fairly common occurrences these days…'

There had been silence once again in the Prime Minister's office, as the implications of Sean's words sank in.

'What would we tell the public?' Derren Clarke voice was almost a whisper.

'The official answer, sir. That whatever happened was an accident,' Valery answered. 'All prison staff in Cartford Hill and anyone involved in the plan will be signing iron-clad confidentiality agreements before any of it is put into action.'

The Prime Minister sat back into his chair, his right hand resting on his cheek. Sean knew he was waiting for his conscience to kick in, for his well ingrained morals to take over and tell him he was insane for even considering what was being put in front of him.

'And this… what did you call it…' Derren Clarke glanced back at the folder marked 'confidential' open on his desk, 'this 'No Pain, No Game' competition. Do we have legal grounds for it?'

'We'll be taking convicts through to a pre-selection process, during which they will be made to sign a waiver,' Sean said. 'A revised version of a power of attorney consent form, which gives the government full control over any decision made for them, as far as life or death decisions, without them being able to appeal. The show,' Sean continued, 'will take place in the Cradle Arena, one of the capital's most symbolic locations. Contestants will go through a series of challenges, and the winner of the show will see their sentence written off. All of the others will be executed.'

'It seems a little drastic,' Derren Clarke's forehead wore a deep frown, 'it wouldn't make us any different to the Nazis!'

Sean felt Valery's stare on his shoulder but did not look across at her. The last thing they wanted was for the Prime Minister to feel cornered.

'The Nazis were on a mission to eradicate anyone who did not correspond to the criterion of perfection they had set for their nation. This is not what we are suggesting. Convicts are *criminals*, they made a deliberate decision to enter a life outside of the rule of the law,' Sean leant forward, his voice as cold as ice. 'It's high time the nation stopped sympathising with the very individuals who are sucking the life out of our economy. And, may I remind you that the proposal also provisions for the state to receive a generous share of the profits to rebuild the country from its ashes.'

The Prime Minister stood up and took a few steps to the window. Sean smiled internally, because that was the moment he knew victory was theirs. Give anyone the choice between their own life and that of a stranger's and they will throw the stranger under the bus. Fear and pain, he had come to realise over the years, turned the most honest and decent citizen into a madman in a matter of seconds.

'I can't tell whether you're a genius or a lunatic,' the Prime Minister said, turning to look Sean straight in the eyes, 'all I know right now is I'm left with no other choice but to accept.'

~ ~ ~

Sean snapped out of the memory and readjusted the collar of his jacket. He could hear the murmurs of excited voices coming from outside the Cradle, where thousands had already gathered, setting up makeshift camping sites in a long and messy queue before the arena's entrance. Give them the entertainment and they will come, he always said. Whether you were presenting a singing contest, or a gladiator-style fight to the death, people would never fail to follow. Such was the desperate state of their nation, which had left its citizens craving distraction to the point of no return.

Sean had never been bothered by the so-called ethics, or lack thereof in this case, of the plan he had put together. Soon, he thought, soon the country would return to its former glory, rid of its vermin and welcoming its most valuable citizens back with open arms. Of course, he was a business man first and foremost, and he had ensured that whichever way this enterprise went, he would be a rich and happy man at the end of it.

Some called him cruel. Some called him insane. Some said he had no ethics. Most would neither care nor remember the names they had called him once the game started and they all became engrossed in its intricacies and the new purpose it gave their miserable lives.

449

All around him, members of staff were finalising the last details before the grand opening the following day. When the production team did a quick light check and the entire arena lit up in bright shades of white, red and blue, a deep and deafening wave of applause and cries resonated from outside the arena. Sean listened to the sweet sound of success with an appreciative smile.

'Ethics,' he whispered under his breath, rolling his eyes and shaking his head, 'my arse.'

Chapter 3

Sean Cravanaugh

S ean stood behind the large wooden panels which delimited the backstage area, peering through a small gap, watching the proceedings on the stage. The arena was full and the audience had been waiting impatiently, their excitement growing palpably with every passing moment. When the lights dimmed, a sure sign that the start of the show was imminent, the thousands of men and women in the public exploded into a chaos of applause and delighted screams. Sean could not have hoped for a better omen.

They had opened the arena doors five hours earlier and it had soon become apparent that the fifty-thousand seats in the Cradle would not contain the immensity of the crowd that had gathered to attend the show. They had to setup last minute giant screens all around the arena for the thousands of people who had not made it into the Cradle.

Similar screening areas had been improvised around the country, in parks, bars and restaurants. Cinemas across the nation were ready to broadcast the show live. Before it had even begun, 'No Pain, No Game' was snowballing into the most gripping and incredible adventure the country had embarked upon in a long, long time.

'Ladies and gentlemen,' the commentator's deep voice purred through the entire arena, 'Welcome to 'No Pain, No Game'! Please give a warm round of applause to your host, Tyler Benson!'

A roar erupted in the Cradle as the nation's favourite television show host jogged onto the main stage.

'Thank you! Thank you, everyone! How are you all today!' He said it more as an exclamation than an actual question, but the effect was immediate as the audience shouted their excitement even louder. 'Today, folks, we make history!'

The audience applauded loudly and reverberations of the crowd's cries outside of the arena gave anyone inside the Cradle the impression of being at the very centre of the universe.

'Please put your hands together to welcome on stage your 'No Pain, No Game' judges!'

The panel behind which Sean was standing with his fellow judges began lifting up. A cloud of smoke escaped around them, loud music blaring and bouncing off every single inch of the arena.

'Top of the charts superstar, Camilla!' Tyler exclaimed, as the audience exploded in hysterical screams.

Camilla waved at the crowd, a broad smile plastered on her beautiful face. Her blonde hair cascaded down her shoulders and her back, over a stunning red satin dress which floated down all the way to the floor.

'Former Minister for Internal Affairs, Mrs Valery Swan!' Tyler continued.

Applause continued as Valery nodded politely to the crowd, her hands raised in the air. With her modern navy-blue dress and her greying hair tied in a tight bun at the back of her head, she looked like someone's posh grand-mother.

'Head of the National Human Rights Association, Mr Josh Carter!'

Josh Carter briefly waved at the crowd, but seemed reluctant to put up too much of a show.

'Last but not least… Ladies and gentlemen… Please give the biggest round of applause for your 'No Pain, No Gain' head judge, Sean Cravanaugh!'

The crowd rose to their feet in one single wave, as if under the same spell. Such was Sean's appeal. His brutal honesty and refusal to indulge in sugarcoating in times when all the public could hear were political lies had won him the citizens' support. They all loved the audacity with which he spoke his mind and always managed to get his way. He was admired, adored and feared.

Sean walked slowly down to the centre of the stage, the smile on his face as polished and impeccable as the dark designer suit he was wearing. He lifted his right hand to salute the crowd, and led the judges to their table, facing the stage, where they each took a seat.

'Tonight,' Tyler continued, 'we kick-off 'No Pain, No Game', during which one hundred convicted criminals will compete in a series of tasks. Starting tomorrow evening, over the next ten weeks we will see how they fare, because only one of them can win the ultimate prize… Before we introduce you to the contestants, let's have a look at their journey through the early rounds of the competition so far.'

Tyler turned around towards a giant screen behind him as the lights went down, plunging the arena in semi-darkness. The commentator's rumbling disembodied voice filled the Cradle.

'Over the last ten years,' the deep voice said in the background of a dramatic mixture of video footage and music, 'our country has fallen into chaos.'

The screen showed sections of news reports on street violence and crime scenes.

'We are outnumbered by criminals. Honest citizens are fleeing what once was the most prosperous land on earth.'

The audience boo-ed their support.

'Our government is struggling to keep all of these criminals behind bars, leaving horrible crimes unpunished.'

The audience was on their feet, their anger almost palpable.

'Tonight, we are bringing you justice!'

For a few seconds, the voiceover was drowned in the fury that had washed over the entire arena.

'From thousands, there are now one hundred convicted felons waiting to take part in the most challenging competition of their existence, in a fight for their freedom... and their *life*! From tonight, ladies and gentlemen, they will have to pay!'

The entire arena was in a mad frenzy of applause, screaming and foot stomping. The video ended and the lights slowly turned back on in the arena, illuminating the audience. Tyler walked towards the centre of the stage.

'Ladies and gentlemen, please welcome onstage your 'No Pain, No Game' contestants!'

A ray of light shot down towards the left corner of the stage where one of the side panels had lifted up, a cloud of fresh smoke filling the open space. A gigantic metallic cage was slowly advancing on the stage until it stopped right in its centre. The cage was divided into sections, with fifty men and fifty women standing, spread across four levels, facing the judges, their hands and feet tied with metal chains to the bars in front of them. They were wearing bright orange long-sleeved baggy overalls, over cheap grey trainers. Cameras and spotlights zoned in on them and they all appeared to recoil as one.

For a split second the entire arena seemed to freeze as the many observed and judged the few, with the hard cold stares of traders at a slave market evaluating the merchandise on offer. And for that one second the world stood still, on the verge of tipping over with the resounding crash of values and dreams shattering on the ground. Then the moment was gone, and the crowd was shouting profanities towards the hundred stunned souls on the stage.

'Let's get acquainted with our contestants,' Tyler announced.

The lights went down until one single ray of light remained, directed straight onto a woman standing at the left end of the cage's bottom row. She jumped with surprise at being singled out, her hands tensing around the chains securing her to the metal rail. One of the giant screens showed her dirty, tired face, whilst on another screen new video footage started. The commentator's deep voice was heard again as the images came and went.

'Contestant number one is Sarah Greensby. She was arrested eight years ago for the brutal murder of her brother, Daniel Greensby, over an inheritance dispute. She pleaded guilty to the crime and was sentenced to life imprisonment.'

As the commentator spoke, the images on the screen showed pictures of Sarah Greensby's smiling brother and images of his body after the killing had taken place. It all lasted a mere fifteen seconds, during which Sarah Greensby's face turned different shades of green and grey on the giant screen. Loud applause erupted as the video concluded.

The ray of light moved onto the contestant next to Sarah Greensby. The man looked positively terrified as his face appeared on the giant screens.

'Contestant number two is Greg Krane, also known as 'The Interceptor'. He was arrested four years ago for the robbery of the Herbert National Bank's main branch and then charged with the robberies of thirteen other banking establishments.'

The light moved on to the next person in line.

'Contestant number three is Alessio Martellini, infamous head of the Martellini cartel…'

Lucie Ataya

To be continued...

Scan the code below to get your copy of *No Pain, No Game* on Amazon today and find out what happens next!

Lucie Ataya

Milton Keynes UK
Ingram Content Group UK Ltd.
UKHW040759281124
3208UKWH00023B/75